GODDESS OF BLOOD AND SHADOWS

A VAMPIRE ASSASSIN NOVEL

MICHELLE A. DARNELL

HIDDEN LAKE
PUBLISHING

HIDDEN LAKE PUBLISHING, LLC

Cover design by: Ravven at ravven.com

ISBN: 978-1-962809-08-5

First Edition: March 2024

This novel is dedicated to Whitney, Holly, Adam & Scott.
In reverse order, because once in awhile, Whitney
deserves to be listed first.

Contents

Chapter 1
Sujani

"My priest?"

Sujani wrenched himself from his trance, throwing himself to his knees at the side of the bed. He dipped his head until it rested against the duvet. "My goddess." After a long five nights since their arrival at Arthur's old estate, it was about time she finally awoke.

"Where are we?"

Her voice was so fragile. Curse him and his inability to complete the resurrection ritual. If he'd been stronger, more *worthy*...

The blankets rustled as she raised her hand. "Open your mind to me."

"Of course." It was always an honor to share thoughts with his goddess.

Keeping his head down as he shuffled forward, he relaxed as her fingers rested against his temple.

"Now, show me what has happened since last we met."

The last twelve hundred years of memories flew through Sujani's mind, almost faster than he could fathom. She examined every one thoroughly before moving on to the next.

His blood raced past his ears, drumming out any background noise as his heart thundered against his ribs like one of his conjured storms.

Far too soon, her radiant touch disappeared as she collapsed back against the pillows. "My priest." She sighed. "What have you done?"

He blinked as heat rose through his chest, daring to raise his eyes to hers. Pushing his voice past his suddenly dry throat, he asked, "What do you mean, my goddess? I have resurrected you and prepared the way for your return."

She closed her eyes, shaking her head. "Was this something I asked you to do?"

"No, of course not." But she'd been dead, and not in the position to ask for anything. "I thought—"

"I am aware of what you thought," she said. With a bitter sigh, she leaned further into her pillows.

Dizziness threatened to overwhelm him at the expression on her face. He braced his hands against the side of the bed. "My goddess, surely you wish to live?"

She frowned. "You have never understood. My time was over." Piercing him with her gaze, her eyes fileted his soul. "Your time should have been finished, too. Neither one of us was meant to be here now."

Sujani blinked, his mind fizzed into static as his world crumbled around him. His vision turned watery. "Are—are you saying I should have left you as you were?"

She drew her eyebrows together. "No. You should have sacrificed me to the Bone Shard Blade, as I commanded."

Wetness leaked from his eyes and poured down his cheeks. "No. I…I couldn't bear it." He dropped his forehead to the duvet, unable to face her gaze.

"My priest." The weight of her hand rested on the back of his head. "Perhaps it was unfair, what my brother and I asked of you."

Sujani swallowed. Yes, it had been unfair, more than he could tolerate. He couldn't imagine life without her glory. But everything would be okay now that they were back together, once she was back to full strength.

"Leave me. I wish to rest and recover."

Pushing to his knees, he bowed at the waist. "As you command, goddess. I live to serve and am here when you need me."

He bumped against the hard wood of the door frame. Reaching behind his back, he fumbled for the latch with clumsy fingers. They slipped, finally snagging the metal and turning it. The deadbolt released.

Sujani backed into the hallway and closed the door. With a bone-deep sigh, he leaned against the wall and brushed the back of his hand across his eyes. It wouldn't do for any of the mortal servants to see how distraught he was.

He took a deep breath to call for Charles but paused. He couldn't face the other man right now, being so raw and with his mind in such turmoil. Charles' mental powers were considerable, and only with full control of his emotions could Sujani hope to keep his thoughts private.

He needed to decide what his next step was going to be. No doubt, Damon was working to murder Maja at this very moment. Sujani would have to be at the top of his game to prevent that. Even if it went against Maja's wishes.

At least he had an advantage—he was in possession of the Bone Shard Blade. Without that, Damon had no chance of success.

Something the other vampire no doubt knew, as well. So, the first thing he needed to do while Maja recovered was to make sure the dagger was secure, somewhere Damon would never find it.

Pivoting on his heel, Sujani marched toward Baron Arthur's library, now his own. One of his grimoires should have a protective spell that would suffice.

Several hours later, Sujani slammed his latest grimoire closed. *Of course!* He would never have overlooked such an obvious solution if he hadn't been so distracted with Damon.

All he needed to do to protect Maja from Damon, and to ensure that Damon met his demise, was to borrow Maja's divine powers—temporarily, of course—to put the other vampire in his place.

Six feet under the ground. Permanently.

Heaving himself to his feet, he rolled his shoulders and tilted his neck to one side then the other. The tension in his muscles from remaining in one position for so long slowly released, one fiber at a time. The joint where his spine met his collar bone *popped*.

Ah. That felt much better.

Grabbing a glass vase from one of the shelves with one hand, he tucked the grimoire beneath the other arm and ducked into the hall.

Turning the latch to Maja's quarters slowly, he peeked inside. "My goddess?" he whispered.

Silence echoed back at him.

Good. She was asleep. That would make things easier.

Slinking into the room, he pulled the door closed.

Maja lay in the bed, the moonlight shining on her face through the open window.

Being careful to step quietly, he padded to the edge of her mattress as he scanned the room. He would need a way to keep her immobilized.

At least they were in The Drowned City, the original flash-point for the Cataclysm. Numerous ley lines ran amok through the area, deposited in the height of the upheaval. They would give him all the power he needed, as long as he didn't wake her prematurely.

Setting the vase carefully on the nightstand, he placed the grimoire on the foot of her bed and flipped it to the appropriate page. Dragging a fang across his wrist, he opened a thin cut over his vein and held his arm above her face.

Two drops splattered against her perfect mouth. Her tongue reflexively licked her lips.

She roused as a bond snapped between their hearts with the ferocity of one of his lightning bolts. It crackled and sparkled with a blue-white energy.

He smiled. Exactly as he'd hoped. Reaching for his Talent and the power of the nearest ley line, he pushed them down the newly created bond.

Sleep, my goddess.

The command bounced down the connection and settled in her chest.

Maja tossed and turned, fighting the compulsion.

Grabbing a circlet of hardened air, he slammed it over her first wrist, reinforcing the shackle with a ring of lightning that crackled in time to the pulsing of the bond that linked them.

Thrashing, she pulled to the side and kicked the blankets off the bed as her eyes flew open.

"My priest!" Her eyebrows drew together as her jaw fell. "What are you doing?"

"Don't worry, my goddess. I've figured out a way to make myself stronger so I can protect you against Damon until you've recovered." He smiled. "It only requires a small bit of your life force. The restraints are for your comfort. I'll remove them momentarily."

The lightning restraint sizzled as she pulled against it, his Talent fraying at the edges. The air and lightning fractured under the weight of her power. "Stop!"

With a blink, he slammed a second matching shackle around her remaining wrist, splaying her arms out on the bed. He shook his head. "I can't. If he learns you're weak, he'll ruin everything, and I won't be able to build you the kingdom you deserve."

Maja stopped thrashing, her mouth agape. "My priest. Free me this instant."

He shook his head, reaching into his pocket for the ceremonial dagger. "I will, my goddess. In just a few minutes."

His head echoed with a sharp *crack* and a flash of crimson eyes seared his brain.

Sujani stumbled back as Ahion's malevolent stare burrowed into his soul. His heart froze, blood turning to ice crystals in his veins.

But that was impossible. Maja's dark twin had been dead for over twelve hundred years, murdered by Damon. His chest constricted until it burned. Blinking in a futile attempt to clear his thoughts, he rubbed his clammy palms desperately over his torso.

The agony of Ahion's gaze shredded his mind, until there was no conscious thought except pain and the endless red pools of the god's eyes as he tumbled into their depths.

Something hard struck one of Sujani's shoulders, the physical sensation jarred him from Ahion's psychic grip as a mental shield of black glass slammed down over his thoughts.

The anguish dulled to a low-grade throb between his temples that was easy enough to ignore.

His lungs heaving, Sujani wrapped his leaden fingers around the residual filaments of his Talent and forced them over Maja's ankles. Another encircled her waist, fully securing her to the bed.

Releasing his grasp on his magic, Sujani stumbled backward, slamming into a wall of muscle.

His knees went weak. "Charles!" Grabbing the other man's biceps, Sujani heaved as he waited for the room to settle. His throat was raspy, as though he'd been screaming.

Charles gripped his arms in return, bending down to catch Sujani's eye. His wide eyes bulged from his unusually pallid face as they flicked between Sujani and Maja. "What's going on?" His voice trembled, like a bow strung too tightly.

Pushing himself up and taking a step back, Sujani brushed the palms of his hands off on his robes. "What do you mean?"

The corners of Charles' lips tightened. "I heard you shrieking from two floors away."

Sujani blinked. Even if he had been screaming, the sound wouldn't have carried that far.

Giving him a flat look, Charles tapped his temple twice.

Oh. Yes.

Warmth spread through his stomach. For once, he was grateful for Charles' telepathy.

"What's going on?" Charles glanced at Maja, who glared at them from the bed.

"I encountered an unexpected obstacle. Nothing more." Sujani studied Maja. Odd, that she would use her brother's image in a psychic attack, knowing that, as her priest, he'd be more responsive to her visage. He chewed the inside of his cheek. Perhaps, after twelve hundred years of non-existence, Maja's mind had not yet completely healed.

She tugged on the wrist restraints. The scent of blood and burnt flesh flooded the room as the edges cut through her skin. "You will release me, my priest. This instant."

He bit the corners of his lips to hold back a scowl. "Why won't you let me protect you?" Damon was dangerous, his goals diametrically opposed to theirs. She had to realize that. This was the best way.

Charles raised his eyebrow as he glanced between the two of them. "Um, Sujani, perhaps you should...?"

"Thank you," he said, swallowing past his sore throat. He shot Charles a pointed glare. "For your timely intervention."

Narrowing his eyes, Charles studied Sujani for several heartbeats. "I don't think I want to know what you're doing. No, I *know* I don't want to. But be careful." He nodded to Maja. "It's dangerous to anger the gods. Even weakened ones."

Sujani caught himself before the impulse to flash his fangs at the other man took over. "This is necessary to stop Damon."

"Mmm." Charles eyed him for a moment then shrugged. "You have more experience with him than me."

Sujani bit back a snort. Perhaps from a time standpoint, yes, but Damon *was* Charles' father, after all.

"If you feel this is the right way forward," Charles continued, "I'll support it, but if you don't have immediate need of me, I prefer to be elsewhere while you do...whatever this is."

Sujani raised his eyebrows. That was as close to mutiny as he'd ever heard Charles before.

Maja thrashed, kicking against the restraints around her ankles. She pressed her lips into a thin line as she caught Charles' gaze. "No! Don't leave me here! Make him let me go! Please!"

Her emotion-choked voice grated in Sujani's ears. He clenched his jaw as a bitter aftertaste burned at the back of his throat. Why was she being so stubborn? Maja had never refused to listen to him when he was mortal.

He studied her pinched expression, her wide eyes filled to the brim with unshed tears.

The corners of Charles' mouth hardened, the characteristic sparkle in his eyes went dull. Neither of them had looked at him in such a way before.

Had he crossed a line somewhere?

"My priest, this isn't you." Blood from the cuts on her wrists soaked into the bed linens as she pulled against his restraints. "Did you truly go to all that trouble to resurrect me, just to murder me by stealing my power for yourself?"

The lightning crackled and fizzled as his Talent warred with hers. His heartbeat thudded in his ears.

She flopped back into the bed, chest heaving.

He shored up her restraints. "Don't be ridiculous." She must be aware of his feelings for her. "I could never hurt you, my beloved." He hadn't been able to sacrifice her as a mortal, and he'd never do such a thing now. She'd hardly notice the small amount he'd borrow.

After being dead for over a thousand years, Maja clearly no longer knew Damon like he did, and Charles wasn't old enough to fully understand the implications of their failure. This was the only way forward. Besides, he'd only borrow Maja's power to defend them all against Damon until such time as the goddess was strong enough to protect herself.

It was logical, and once Charles was able to see past his emotions, he'd realize it, too.

Checking that the obsidian mental shield was secure, Sujani nodded. "You may go. I'll call if I need you."

With a quick bob of his chin and one last empathetic glance at Maja, Charles spun on his heel and, with his shoulders pushed back, marched out the door, yanking it closed behind him.

As the latch clicked into place, Sujani turned to Maja. Adjusting the restraint so he could slide her arm over so that it hung off the edge of the bed, he set the vase on the ground beneath it. "I'm really sorry to have to do this. But it's the only way I can be sure to hold Damon off until you've recovered. I promise, I'll only take what I need."

She jerked, trying to yank her wrist from his grasp. "Why are you doing this? Listen to me! Stop!" She blinked at him as a tear forced its way from the corner of her eye and tracked down her temple, losing itself in her hair. "This will be your downfall!"

His gut wrenched. Shaking his head, he looked away. If he let his feelings get in the way, she'd have him so twisted inside and out that Damon would storm roughshod over everything he had spent the last millennium working toward. And that wouldn't be acceptable at all.

His stomach hardened to match the painful tightness in his throat. That she would reject his motivations...reject *him*, after all he had done for her. All he was going to do.

With a mental flick of his Talent, he slapped a restraint over her mouth. "I'm sorry, my goddess. I can't have you distracting me."

Soon enough, she'd see that he'd been correct. Then things would be as they were meant to be between them.

Pulling a ceremonial dagger from his robes, he sliced the delicate skin at Maja's wrist.

His fangs throbbed as the first drops slipped from her fingers and splashed into the vase. The back of his throat burned, but he dared not drink from her directly. There was no telling what drinking divine blood would do to him.

He glanced at the grimoire, still laying open at the end of the bed. Fortunately, the book had plenty to say about how to distill and purify strong blood without losing its essence.

Hopefully, this would work.

The moon dropped two finger-widths in the sky as Maja's blood dripped one holy drop at a time into the jar. Finally, enough had gathered to fill a chalice as the wound on her wrist clotted.

Ignoring the pallor of her normally tanned skin, he swiped the vase off the floor.

Carrying the glass and its precious contents to the end of the bed, he glanced at the first step of the ritual.

Place the crystal vial containing blood to be distilled at the center of the arcane circle constructed as described on the previous page.

Sujani blinked and ground his teeth as he flipped a single leaf of parchment back. A detailed sketch with several symbols—some he was familiar with, and some he'd never seen before—drawn within it.

Very well. He was no artist, but he could replicate the drawing.

Chewing on the inside of his cheek, he glanced around the room. There were no inkwells or paints, so he would have to use blood. His eyes slid to the glass vase, cradling her blood.

The blood of a goddess, surely, would make for the strongest circle, and thus the best outcome. But hers was precious, and he'd need every drop she could spare.

Drawing his ceremonial dagger, he dragged it across his palm. The sharp pain as the blade sliced his skin teased a righteous smile onto his lips. This small sacrifice on his part would be returned to him in spades once Damon met Final Death.

Sujani's blood welled from his hand. Dipping the tip of his blade in the liquid, he knelt on the ground beside the open grimoire and began painstakingly copying the symbols.

The beam of moonlight had long slid off Maja's face by the time he finished connecting the last symbol to the first. With a groan, he pushed to his feet and leaned to one side. Something in his lower spine popped, releasing the pressure that had built there while he'd been on the ground.

The cut across his palm turned pink as he watched, then disappeared.

Place the crystal vial containing blood to be distilled at the center of the arcane circle.

He placed the glass vase as directed, frowning at the uncouth clank it made against the floor.

Surround the vial with the essence of Moonlight Orchid to sanctify the vessel.

His heart jolted. Moonlight orchid? He shook his head. That flower was out of season this time of year. He'd need a substitute.

Setting the grimoire down, he stepped into the bathroom adjacent to her suite. The overwhelming scent of orange, vanilla and cinnamon filled his nostrils.

He groaned. The mortals had gone a tad bit overboard.

From the corner of his vision, Maja jerked on the bed, pulling her arms against his restraints. Tear tracks sparkled down her cheeks. He flared his Talent, reinforcing the manacles of hardened air.

They held. For now.

He should have drained more of her blood, to keep her slightly weaker until he'd had time to distill and absorb her essence.

He snatched the closest perfume vial and squinted at the label. Midnight Orchid. Perfect.

Clenching the container to his chest, he grinned. That should be close enough. Aiming the spritzer at the glass vase sitting in the middle of the blood circle, he spritzed a fine layer of the oiled scent in each direction and found the next line in the grimoire.

Add one tear from a star celestial to the crystal vial to symbolize the celestial being's pure essence combining with the mixture.

He brushed a hand over his head, pulling the stray strands of hair from his face with a sigh. In his twelve hundred years of existence, he'd never heard of a star celestial. But it wasn't a star celestial whose essence he was seeking...

His gaze slipped to Maja.

She turned her face away as he approached, squeezing her eyes shut and sending a fresh course of tears down her cheeks. *<Don't you dare touch me!>*

Ignoring the viscous twist in his gut at his goddess' rejection, he gently brushed one finger down her jaw, careful to avoid the gag covering her mouth. Removing his hand and stepping back, he held his fingertip to the light. One dew-drop goddess tear sparkled.

With a flick, he sent the tear into the vase.

A pressure whooshed through the room, popping his ears and raising the hairs on his arms. Energy crackled along his nerve ends.

Excellent.

With a heavy sense of finality settling in his stomach like a hunk of lead, Sujani stepped up to the grimoire.

Repeat these words: Alagak dagotti esencia dragiti innem na elmentos: apuii, danum, angan, draga, larweg.

The unfamiliar language caught in his throat and tangled with his tongue, but as he repeated the incantation a second time, his skin jumped with the familiar pull of blood magic.

A purple-black mist formed in the vase, churning like miniature clouds riding at the head of a magical storm. Maja's blood quivered as large bubbles rose from it with a loud *pop* until the fluid was at a rolling heatless boil.

The magic crested in a wave that effervesced the very blood in his veins. He took a deep breath, his lungs expanding as the warmth spread through his weightless body. The bond between them stretched. "See, Maja?" He turned to her. "See what we can accomplish together?"

She lay flaccid against her pillows, her pallid cheeks sunken and stretched over her bones. Her empty stare and quiet sigh bored straight into his gut.

Shaking his head, he spun away. She'd see, then she'd understand and forgive him.

She always forgave him.

As the tail end of the magic faded, Sujani grasped the vase and studied the dark sludge that remained. The mixture wasn't particularly appetizing, and carried the faint scent of rotten eggs.

<*It is your own betrayal you smell, my priest.*> Maja's weakened voice echoed in his mind. With a muttered curse, he pulled his obsidian mental shield back up, blocking her.

Swallowing past the thickness in his chest, he brought the vase to his lips and poured the vile concoction down.

The world contracted then exploded outward with a viscous snap as the liquid hit his stomach and absorbed. Ribbons of fire and power raced through his veins, leaving golden trails in their paths. The constant burn of Hunger at the back of his throat disappeared. The reservoir at his core that housed his Talent swelled and expanded until surely his ribs must explode from containing the pressure. The intricacies of his abilities spread before him, as though clearly spelled out in an apprentice's textbook.

Throwing his head back with a gasp, he stared at the ceiling. Every living being and inanimate object was connected to him and to each other through the faintest of ethereal threads that if he blinked just right, he could catch their iridescence from the corner of his vision.

He reached out and plucked a strand, as though he were playing a lute.

In the courtyard outside, a freak gust of wind rose at the stimulus and toppled a tree.

This. This knowledge, this connection would be what allowed him to finally defeat Damon so he could clear the pathway for Maja to rule. He just needed a few nights to figure out the limits of his new power, and how to best utilize it.

Turning, he met her sad gaze. "Don't worry, my goddess. Everything will be over soon." Then all of this would be worth it.

Spinning on his heel, he yanked the door open. "Charles!"

The other man must have been lingering nearby, because moments later, footsteps rounded the corner. "Sujani?"

"Come here and drink." He opened a cut on his wrist and waved Charles forward. "I'm going to teach you how to throw lightning. Then, I have a message for you to take to Damon."

Chapter 2
Adina

Adina glared at the handful of tiny bones piled on the table in their room at the nameless backwater inn on the northern edge of Gorlinia. They were small, the largest no bigger than a finger bone. She bit her lip as she picked one up and held it to the lantern. "I don't know. It's not like there's some magical dust or potion you can sprinkle on these that will glow if they're dragon bones." Hopefully, Sujani didn't realize René had stolen them and assumed they'd been lost during their fight before he resurrected the goddess Maja.

René glanced at her from where he paced across the room and frowned. "Sujani said you're a mage. Can't you do some sort of blood magic thingie and figure it out so we can finally end Damon?"

Her stomach plummeted to the floor. "You want me to perform blood magic?" What a thing to ask, especially as he'd been a victim of it himself back in Brachia.

"Volunteering to be her blood sacrifice, are you?" The undercurrent of protectiveness hardened Erik's words as he glared at René.

Adina shook her head and sighed in exasperation. This was all useless, anyway. Sujani and Damon were so far above them in Talent and raw power, they didn't stand much of a chance. "Don't be an idiot, René. Even if I could do blood magic—which I can't—I'd have no idea what ritual to use." It wasn't like she could go to the nearest library and borrow a grimoire.

Hana's melodious voice rippled across the study as she intercepted René and, intertwining her fingers with his, brought his relentless pacing to a stop. "Good thing, too. Because you can't have him." Her eyes sparkled with mischief that contrasted the somber mood of the room. "He's mine."

Supposed dragon bones forgotten, René grabbed Hana's waist and pulled her to him with a growl in the back of his throat. With his eyes glued to her, he addressed the rest of them, "While you stick-in-the-muds are figuring out the bones, we'll be in my room."

Adina rolled her eyes more out of show than true annoyance. It made her heart sing to see Hana so happy, even if her taste in men was questionable. They were all likely to meet Final Death when Sujani and Maja came for them, anyway. Hana may as well wring whatever joy she could from their final days.

As the pair disappeared into the hallway, Adina caught Erik's attention. Gesturing to the bones, she shook her head. "I really have no idea what to do here. It's not like we can ask Sujani or Damon. Any bright ideas?"

"Only dim ones, sorry."

She tried to smile at his attempt to lighten the mood but couldn't force her muscles into compliance.

With a sigh, he picked up a bone and held it close. "It's too bad they don't have 'Dragon Bone' carved on the side. That would make it easy."

Adina raised her eyebrow and gave him a flat look. He wished...

He tossed the piece back into the pile, where it clacked into place with the others. "I'll tell you what." He rubbed his hand down her back. "Let's put them away and we'll work on it more tomorrow. There's not much we can do, anyway, until we locate a non-ruptured confluence of ley lines."

Adina sighed. He was right. The first time Damon and Sujani fought, they'd destroyed a bunch of ley lines and created a new volcano in Brachia. Damon hadn't bothered to confirm before he disappeared, but she suspected there had been even more of the mystical lines in the cave where they'd found the Bone Shard Blade. After all, what other force could literally topple a mountain?

As Holt had once said, Sujani was very good at dropping mounds of rubble on other people.

"Besides," Erik said, pulling her thoughts back to the present, "the sun will be up soon."

A quick glance outside revealed more of the never-ending drizzle that seemed the norm for northern Gorlinia. At least, since Sujani had raised Maja. Flooded streets, mudslides, perpetually soggy and chilled clothing... Just more things on the list that made her miss the Saldanian Desert.

She sighed and turned to the unrolled map sitting to the left of the bone pile. "There ought to be some sort of pattern or layout to the geography of an area that would point to the ley lines." She waved her hand over the parchment. "I mean, if they're powerful enough to create volcanos or level mountains, they ought to have some influence on the formation of those landmarks, right?"

"That makes sense," he said, sitting in a chair beside her. "But I don't think they're that easy to find. Maybe they move? Remember how surprised Damon looked when Sujani exposed them back in Brachia?"

She shook her head. "No...I was too busy trying to figure out how we were going to get out of there alive to care about Damon's emotional state." But that meant Sujani knew how to locate ley lines, so it was possible.

Erik chuckled. "Fair enough."

Heavy boots came to a stop outside the door. Adina caught his eye as the knob rattled and swept the pile of dragon bones off the table and into their pouch just as Damon stepped inside.

Erik leaped to his feet, the chair legs screeching across the floor. "What are you doing here?" He pulled his sword and pointed it at the intruder.

Adina's gut clenched as her free hand wrapped around her falchion's handle. The last thing they needed was Damon skulking about. She surreptitiously slid the sack of bones into her pocket as she stood. Reaching for her Talent, she blew a quick gust of air away from them, lest Damon attempt to catch them unaware with his stench, and thus take control of their bodies.

His platinum hair flashed red in the candlelight as his classic leather cloak trailed water across the floor. He caught each of their eyes as the corner of his mouth ticked upward at Adina's conjured breeze. "Hello, Adina. Erik."

Adina glanced around the room, peering into the shadows. After all, wherever Damon went, Septimus wouldn't be far behind. Her fingers tensed around her falchion's grip. She wasn't quite sure what to make of Septimus at the moment—half the time he opposed them, and the other times his help was invaluable. And while he didn't seem to be inclined to try to kill her anymore, they still had a long way to go before she'd allow herself to relax in his presence.

"Your father isn't here, Adina." Damon's smooth voice filled the room and raised the fine hairs on the back of her neck.

"What do you want?" Erik asked.

Damon shook his head and flapped the water from his cloak, intentionally spraying Erik. "I'd like the rains in Gorlinia to stop, boy. Along with the fires in Champeaux and the earthquakes in Brachia. Wouldn't you?"

Adina blinked, her mouth going dry. She caught Erik's gaze from the corner of her eye. They'd had no idea the extreme weather was anything other than a localized fluke.

Damon's eyes flashed red. "A localized fluke?" He pinned her with a glare. "Sujani raises a literal goddess, and you think this craziness is nothing but a *fluke*?" He slammed his palms against the tabletop. "You haven't lived through a Cataclysm before, but I have. Let me tell you, this was exactly how it started. The only way to stop it is to plunge the Bone Shard Blade into Maja's heart. But Sujani possesses the dagger, and, since he summoned her, he's unlikely to help us kill her."

Adina glanced at Erik and raised her eyebrow. "Oh? Help *us* kill her? Are we working together now?" As if they would *ever* team up with the likes of Damon.

Pushing himself off the table hard enough to scoot it toward them, Damon paced, unknowingly following the same path René had just minutes ago. His voice cracked with repressed emotion. "Vampires weren't the only change that came out of the Cataclysm, you know. It wiped out over ninety percent of the mortal population, either due to the natural disasters or the exposure to raw magic, and completely revised climates." He pierced Adina with a glare and flashed his fangs. "Did you know the Saldanian Desert used to be a rainforest? And this time, it'll be even worse, because Maja's brother, Ahion, isn't here to counterbalance her power."

Adina chewed on her lip. Damon was many things, but she'd never seen him scared or desperate before. The situation must be worse than they realized. "If Sujani knew what was going to happen, why did he raise her?"

Damon shook his head. "He always loved Maja too much. He became obsessed, even before the Cataclysm, when the world sat on the cusp as it does now. He cared more about being in her presence than the survival of that which she held most dear—the land and those upon it. Even with a direct order from her, he couldn't kill her, even to literally save the world."

Erik cleared his throat. "Sujani will never give up the Bone Shard Blade to us, and we don't have the ability to forge another."

Adina braced for Damon to detect the lie. They couldn't forge one *yet*.

He didn't react.

Thank goodness. Apparently, Damon wasn't paying much attention to their surface thoughts. Really, though, all they needed was a confluence of ley lines.

"Ley lines *and* dragon bones," Damon said.

Adina froze. Damn. He probably knew the ritual, too.

She glanced up, accidentally meeting his gaze.

"Only an idiot would assume I'm not listening," he said. "Also, princess, you may have a decent amount of magic in your blood, but all the dragon bones and ley lines in the world wouldn't allow you to forge a blade strong enough to kill a goddess on your own. Even if you drained every last drop of blood from your body. And of course I know the ritual. I was there, remember?"

Adina's chest constricted as she flung her hands wide, gesturing to the room. "So, help us! You don't like the weather? Worried about another Cataclysm? Then instead of standing there whining about it, *do* something!" Rage boiled up, turning her vision crimson. "You've done nothing but stand in our way at every possible turn. You delight in every misfortune we suffer. And you have the nerve—"

"No!" Damon cut her off, chopping through the air violently with one hand. "Not your misfortune. Sujani's. Everything I've done has been to prevent what happened on top of that mountain two days ago. I have fought tirelessly to prevent Sujani from resurrecting Maja." He stepped forward, slamming his balled fist against the wooden table.

"Bullspit!" He bared his fangs. "I even hauled him off your unconscious corpse before he could end you and complete the resurrection ritual." Tilting his head to the side, he exposed his neck, and the deep scar over his carotid. "And I got this as thanks because he used my blood, instead!"

Adina fought the urge to bite her cheek and spit the resulting blood at his feet. It was too bad Sujani hadn't drained Damon. Then at least then there would be one less First Vampire for them to contend with. She clenched her jaw and squeezed her falchion's grip.

"Your motives aside," Erik said, stepping between them, "why are you here? You didn't come just to rant and spout doom and gloom."

"No." Damon snarled, clenching his fists as he reined in his anger. "I came here to ask for your help to end Sujani and prevent a second Cataclysm." He spun away, disgust written across his features as he paced. "Seven was right, coming here was a bad idea."

Adina's gut hollowed. Another cataclysm? She glanced at Erik, who subtly shook his head.

Ignoring his suggestion, she pinned Damon with a stare. "How much time do we have?"

Damon blinked, his incredulous expression gone almost before she registered it. He studied her for a heartbeat. "The last time, it took thirty days."

She brushed a stray hair out of her face as her throat went dry. *By the gods...* They had a month, maybe less, to figure out how to kill a goddess and end Sujani.

"And that's a best-case scenario." Damon stepped forward. "Circumstances are a little different this time around." He stared at her then turned his attention to Erik. "All the more reason for us to work together. Between my knowledge and your—"

Shoving her alarm to the back of her mind, she spun to face Damon. "Why would we trust you after everything you've done? And what makes you think I'd ever willingly work with my father?"

Damon gaped at her as if a third eye had sprouted on her forehead. "What are you talking about? Seven has done nothing but protect you since Sujani forced him to create you."

Adina choked back a laugh as she grabbed the back of one of the table chairs to steady herself. Damon's definition of protection needed serious readjustment. "You mean like when he nearly beat me to death during the Assassin's Guild meeting in the Drowned City last month?"

"How else could he show them you didn't have value as a hostage, so no one would think Khalid's move was worth repeating?"

She blinked, a little steam dissipating from her sails. Oh. "How about the time he attacked me when I was on my way to Brachia to meet Sujani?"

Damon rolled his eyes. "Do I really have to spell that one out for you?"

Erik tilted his head to the side. "To keep her away from Sujani?"

Damon snapped his finger and pointed at Erik. "One point for the sidekick!"

Adina bared her fangs, but Erik put a calming hand on her shoulder before turning his attention to Damon. "We'll have to talk about it with the others. René and Madalina will be hard to convince."

The corner of Damon's mouth turned up in a sardonic smile. "Why do you think I approached you two first?"

They'd have to do it. Her distaste for him aside, he was their best shot. And if they didn't work with him, the entire world would suffer.

<I knew you'd be smart enough to see reason.> Damon's voice echoed through her mind.

She glared at him. *Get out of my thoughts!*

Erik stood beside her, glaring at Damon, oblivious.

<Listen, princess. I don't like the idea any more than you do, but I happen to like this world, and I intend to do everything in my power to prevent Sujani from destroying it. If you want to keep your unlives beyond the next month, you'd do well to convince the others to work with me.>

Ugh. She shook her head. Considering he'd forced René to kill his own father, and had mind controlled most of them at one point or another, that was easier said than done. A lead weight settled in her gut.

Damon spun and headed for the door. "I'll give you two nights to think about it. In the meantime, I suggest you re-evaluate your options and how much you want to live through this. When it comes to saving the world, I am literally your only option. Unless, of course, you want to meet Final Death, along with most of the mortal population." Opening the door, he stepped through and disappeared with a dramatic flip of his cloak.

The door latch clicked into place as Damon's footsteps retreated.

"By the seven gods," Adina murmured, when she was certain he was out of ear- and mind-shot.

Erik cleared his throat as he returned his sword to its scabbard. "I don't think a world under Damon's thumb would be any better than a world under Sujani and his goddess."

She met Erik's somber gaze. "I think you're right, but he has a point. We can't take Sujani and Maja on by ourselves. We need him." She swallowed. "It's too bad we can't forge another Bone Shard Blade, give it to Damon, and let him fight Sujani. Then we would just need a sure-fire way to guarantee we can end whichever of them survives." If Damon won, her father would probably teleport him somewhere safe until he healed, which meant they'd either need to kill Damon immediately after the fight or figure out a way to neutralize Septimus so he couldn't teleport. Or both. And there would still be Sujani's goddess to contend with. Adina put her face in her hands. "Ugh."

Damon was right. They needed him.

Erik gestured to the satchel in her pocket. "Maybe we have enough dragon bones to forge two blades? One we can give to Damon, and another in secret?"

She raised her eyebrow. "I know you have a decent mental shield from all your time with Charles, but I don't think the rest of us would have a rat's chance in the desert of keeping a secret like that from Damon, especially long-term." She opened her mouth to say something but paused. "That doesn't mean we can't use him to help us find ley lines, though."

Erik nodded. "And maybe some authenticated dragon bones?"

"It just may be crazy enough to work." An invisible weight lifted from her shoulders. She hated feeling like she was stumbling about with no clear path forward.

He took her hand and squeezed it. "Let's make it our new Plan A then, shall we?"

Now, they just had to convince everyone else to go along with it.

She raised her eyebrow. "I don't suppose you could teach the rest of us how to keep Damon or Charles from reading our minds?"

He shook his head. "No. Unfortunately, you really need a telepath to teach that, and to confirm if you're successful or not. I doubt Charles or Damon would be so accommodating."

She chewed the inside of one cheek as her gaze drifted to the window.

They'd all have to be even more careful with their thoughts going forward.

Chapter 3
Damon

Damon knelt at the large boulder in a cave outside of town. Water dribbled into his face. Brushing his fingers through his hair and squeezing as much liquid from it as possible, he flung the drops away. At least Adina was smart enough to be open to working with him to defeat Sujani. Some of Seven's pragmatism had rubbed off on her, after all.

Reaching into his pocket, he pulled out the gold ring he'd picked up from the jeweler on the way into town—the one he'd commissioned to be set with an ancient sapphire. The stone had been carved and polished well before the knowledge of faceting had been discovered—even before the Cataclysm.

Soul-stones were rare and hard to come by.

Fortunately for him, the mortal jeweler had no idea the value of the artifact in his possession and had been absolutely flummoxed when Damon had refused to let him facet it. Personally, Damon didn't care if the stone sparkled or not, just that it had the potential to house a soul.

Viktor's soul.

Assuming, of course, Damon could master the necromancy required to resurrect his former soul-slave.

Necromancy had always been Viktor's calling, not his.

Shaking the water from his bag, he removed the vials of vinegar, myrrh, and bloodbane, as well as the packages of oakum and alum. Setting the ring on the most level portion of the stone, he sighed.

"This had better work." Where was a quality necromancer when he needed one?

Mixing the alum with the vinegar turned the brown liquid turbid. He set the vial aside and worked on adding the bloodbane and oakum into the thick myrrh. Once the spices were combined, he arranged the gooey mixture into a circle, with a depression in the center. Gently, he laid the ring in the middle and poured the vinegar and alum solution over it.

"Te kworem il hanc le'vat," he muttered. "Il hanc Viktor Knoll."

The ground beneath him trembled, the faintest ripple of magic pulled through the earth to his call.

It was not enough.

Emptying the rest of the vinegar until the ring was completely covered, Damon leaned over the mixture and repeated his words, throwing the full force of his will behind them. "Te kworem il hanc le'vat. Il hanc Viktor Knoll!"

The magic of the earth shuddered and turned, a sleepy old man content to remain abed for eternity. Viktor's soul remained steadily out of reach.

He clenched his teeth. Curse the study of necromancy, and everyone who'd ever practiced it.

Taking a deep breath, he exhaled forcefully through his nose. Now what? As powerful in other schools of magic as he was, he had no gift for manipulating the undead, despite being one himself.

Sitting here stewing about it wouldn't change the facts of life. The schools of magic never mixed, with good reason—the consequences could be explosive and deadly. Even for him.

Glancing around the room, he rolled his shoulders. Pulling on two schools of magic at once, blood and necromancy, could well bind him into his own soul-slave ring. And if that happened, the last thing he needed were witnesses who might accidentally figure out how to use such a thing. Namely, Charles or Seven.

For the moment at least, he was alone. That may change at any time. It was now or never.

He clenched his teeth, pulled on the power of his blood and grabbed a fistful of that recalcitrant magic, hauling it to himself. It resisted, like those stretchable bands merchants used to tie tarps over their loads. He yanked harder. Something popped between his eyes and a thin trail of blood leaked from one nostril.

A drop landed on the ring with a splash.

The magic released as though those resistant straps had been severed by an invisible blade.

The magic flowed up Damon's arm so quickly it set his nerves on fire. Red light reflected off the stone walls as his Talent flared in response. He gasped as the wave of power ripped through him and leaped into the ring. The magical backlash flung Damon out of the cave and into the pouring rain. The air exploded from his lungs with a sharp twinge up his spine as he landed on his back in a puddle. Mud soaked into his shirt and hair, chilling him to the bone.

But at least he still had a spine. And a body. Now he just had to see if the spell worked.

He leaped to his feet and stormed inside, heedless of the muck dripping from his hair and down his cape.

The ring remained on the boulder where he'd left it, surrounded by a faint char mark. The concoction of spices and blood had been destroyed. The stone seemed to glow, lit faintly by an inner light.

One edge of his mouth curled up in a smile. *There you are.*

A sudden change in air pressure signified Seven's arrival.

Damon snatched the ring and slammed it deep into his pocket. He snarled as he spun on the other man, rage flaring anew. After all, a large chunk of Adina's trust issues with him were the other man's fault. "Few parents have worked so hard to make their children loathe them so much. Did it ever occur to you once in the last hundred years that having Adina hate you may not be the optimal situation?"

Seven's deep voice echoed from the shadows at the back. "Don't you dare judge my parenting skills unless you want to discuss your failure with Charles." He stepped into the light of Damon's lantern, arms crossed in a way that emphasized his bulging biceps and chest. Like the deepest shadows of the night, Seven seemed to suck all the light into himself. "Your son is the right hand of your sworn enemy," he continued. "Care to comment on that?"

Damon flashed his fangs at the other man as a twinge at Charles' betrayal stabbed through his gut. "And he will go down with Sujani."

Seven grunted, unimpressed, as he pointedly studied the dirt splattered all over Damon. "How did it go? I take it by your mood that we are not joining forces with Adina and her friends?"

Damon shrugged off his dripping cape and hung it over a rock near the fire to dry. "I gave them a few nights to think it over."

Smirking, Seven lounged against the wall. "It didn't go as smoothly as you'd hoped, huh? I told you so. What, did Erik throw you out into the mud?"

Damon clenched his jaw. If he didn't know better, he'd think Seven was intentionally sabotaging his efforts. "It would have gone better if you hadn't done such a thorough job of conditioning Adina to hate you."

"She doesn't hate me, she fears me."

Damon bit back a growl as he wracked his brain. "Same difference." He would need to come up with a backup plan in case Adina couldn't convince the others. "They know about the ritual to forge a new blade, somehow, but don't have any idea where to find ley lines or dragon bones."

Seven blinked. "Dragon bones?"

Damon rolled his eyes as he tugged off his mud-soaked boots. "Once upon a time, they were more than mere fairytales, you know." Until the Cataclysm wiped them out, along with so many other magical beings.

He shook his wet hair out of his eyes. "The problem is, I also have no idea where to find any." The Drowned City would be a possible candidate, as Ground Zero of the Cataclysm, but the chances of any of the bones they'd used in the ritual to create the original pair of Bone Shard Blades still being where he and Sujani had left them was slim after a thousand years.

Dragons had once lived all over the world, but the vast majority had preferred to make their homes in caves. Any such dens would have been long-since disturbed, their bones crumbled to dust, except in the most extreme locations. He really didn't want to go mountaineering in the infinitesimal hope of finding an undiscovered dragon skeleton before time ran out and Sujani and Maja destroyed the world.

Hopefully, Adina and the others would agree to go on that hunt for him.

In the meantime, he'd focus on locating another nexus of ley lines.

Damon paced across the cave, ignoring both the trail of wet footprints behind him and Seven's piercing stare. The second problem was he had no idea how to locate ley lines. Clearly, it could be done, as Sujani had demonstrated so spectacularly in Brachia. And whatever that pompous self-absorbed Surinian could do, Damon could do better.

If only he could figure out how.

Damon raised an eyebrow and glanced at the other vampire. "We need a lot more people looking for dragon bones and ley lines than just you and me. Even if we can convince your daughter and her friends to join us."

Seven grimaced. "I know. I'm not an idiot."

"We should put your Assassins Guild on the task."

Clearing his throat, Seven raised an eyebrow and asked, "You want me to send every assassin in the guild on a scavenger hunt for bones from a creature that hasn't existed in over a thousand years?"

Red tinted the edges of Damon's vision as a burning wave crested his gut. He hated when Seven was intentionally thick-headed. "Unless you have a better idea. Do you think they'd be more effectively used to find ley lines?" As if a bunch of thug-assassins would have the magical sensitivity to trace or detect such disturbances.

The other vampire exhaled forcefully. "You'll have to pay them. Assassins don't work for free, no matter how imbecilic the task."

Damon waved his hand. "Promise them whatever they want. My coffers back in Esnaria are plenty full." It wouldn't matter, anyway. If he succeeded and ended Sujani and Maja, the rest of the world would be his to rule as he pleased, and he wouldn't have to pay Seven's assassins. If he failed, he'd be dead, so it didn't matter.

"Ahem."

Damon and Seven whirled around, glaring at the figure darkening the entrance to their cave.

Charles stepped out of the rain, long rivulets of water running from his handlebar mustache.

Well, speak of the devil...

Damon threw up his shields just as Charles' insidious mental fingers wove around his mind. Pushing the annoying phantom tentacles away, he growled. "What do you want?" Just what they needed—Sujani's loyal minion poking around while he and Seven were trying to figure out how to bring Sujani down.

Charles shook out his cloak, spraying droplets around the room. "Don't be like that. You know why I'm here, what I want."

"No," Damon said. "I know what Sujani wants. I know nothing of why you're here." Or why Charles was so frustratingly loyal to Damon's arch nemesis.

Speaking of his arch nemesis, where had Seven gotten to? Damon tried to scour the shadows without being obvious.

Charles pinned Damon with a hard glare. "I'm here to deliver a message."

Damon held back an eye roll. "Of course you are."

"Sujani knows what you're up to and sends this warning: Don't try anything to hurt Maja, or he'll finish what he started in the cave of the Bone Shard Blade."

Damon snarled and lunged.

Lightning snapped from Charles' upraised hand as the scent of ozone permeated the room.

The energy slammed into Damon's chest, throwing him back with the stench of burnt skin. Heat raced across his nerves as he bit back a scream.

Lightning was Sujani's Talent, not Charles'.

"What manner of sorcery is this?" Damon rumbled. Even when he possessed someone, he couldn't transfer his Talent to them.

Such a skill could certainly be useful, were there anyone competent enough to risk sharing his abilities with.

Charles shook his head as the last of the energy dissipated. "So predictable, Father. Every time." He brushed his palms off on his pants.

"Sujani knows you well. Think hard about your next move. With Maja at his side, Sujani is invincible, a god by proxy."

A dagger of ice stabbed Damon between his shoulder blades, twisting viciously. He'd nearly been such, with Ahion as his ally.

Before Sujani betrayed them and made Ahion's sacrifice meaningless. Before the Cataclysm.

"You won't win." With a dramatic flare of his cloak, Charles turned and marched back out into the storm.

Damon stared into the pouring rain as his blood rushed past his ears. Charles was wrong. He could win if he moved quickly. Maja must still be weak. The disasters would likely continue to build until she reached full strength and pulled the world so far out of alignment that another Cataclysm erupted.

His son's shadow disappeared into darkness as Seven's voice ticked Damon's ear. "What's the point of telling you not to do something Sujani knows you'll do anyway?"

Indeed.

Sujani was up to something. Even if it was just flaunting his ability to transfer his Talent to Charles.

Damon glared at Seven, annoyance flaring through his muscles at the man's re-appearance. "Scared of Charles, now, are you? Jumping away every time he shows up?"

Seven rumbled deep in his throat. His knuckles popped as he clenched his fists. "Of course not. But my mental shields aren't strong enough to keep him out. Did you want him to know what we were talking about right before he appeared?" He crossed his arms. "Because I was under the assumption we wanted to keep those plans *private*."

Damon turned away, taking a few steps to put some distance between himself and Seven's hulking form. If Sujani intended to intimidate him into rolling over and showing his belly like a good mongrel by showing off this new ability, he was in for a world of disappointment.

"Seven, try not to be intentionally dense. It doesn't become you." Damon fingered the gold ring in his pocket, sliding it onto his middle finger and spinning it in a circle until the ancient sapphire faced upward.

He'd show Sujani what he could do, goddess or no goddess.

Pressing his thumb against a fang, he punctured the skin. As the blood welled up from the wound, he pressed it over the sapphire.

"Viktor! Get your measly spirit out here. I have a job for you."

Chapter 4
Adina

The following morning, Adina sat cross-legged on her bed as she ran her fingers through Madalina's long black hair. "So that's the plan," she said to everyone as René lounged in one of the chairs across the room fingering the satchel he'd pickpocketed from Sujani. "We need to confirm if those are dragon bones and if not, find some. Then, trick Damon into helping us locate a confluence of ley lines so we can perform the ritual and forge a new Bone Shard Blade." And somehow secretly create a second weapon so they could use the spare to kill Maja while Damon and Sujani fought each other. But with telepaths like Damon running around, she couldn't tell the others that part. She'd also have to be very careful not to think too much on it, either. Adina's gaze flitted from person to person as she panned across the room, meeting each of their eyes.

Near the door, Sigfried's prominent brow hung low in concentration, shielding his eyes from view. Hana leaned her head on René's shoulder, her unfocused gaze staring off into the distance. Erik winked when her eyes met his.

René furrowed his brow and stared at Adina. "Boy, you don't ask for much, do you?"

"René—" Madalina started.

He waved his hand in a chopping motion, cutting her off. "No, seriously. Listen to yourselves. Yes, you may be able to get Damon to help us find ley lines. But do you really trust him to help us and then leave us to go on our merry way? Remember," he waved his hand around before jabbing at his temple, "he possessed me and made me kill Marcos! He can take over any of our bodies and do whatever he wants with them." He crossed his arms and shook his head. "No. No way. I'm not going to work with that bread-bandit."

Frustration welled in Adina's gut. Not that she wasn't sympathetic to his feelings…Charles had briefly taken over her mind, too, back in The Drowned City and she wasn't eager to repeat the experience. But they didn't have many options. "Do you have any other suggestions? We can't just sit around and wait for another Cataclysm."

"What about Madalina?" René asked, jabbing a finger in her direction. "Can't she just have a vision that tells us where the dragon bones and ley lines are?"

Madalina shook her head. "It's raining outside. I can't see the stars. And you know they only talk to me when *they* want to, about what *they* want."

"Well, have you ever tried asking them?"

Madalina jerked back at the acid in his tone.

René opened his mouth, but Hana put her hand on René's bicep and whispered something to him too quietly for Adina to make out.

René paused, closed his mouth with a pop and studied Hana. "You know what? You may be on to something." A wide smile split his face as he turned to the group, anger disappearing as suddenly as it had flared. "Why don't we go see the Gaelle De Guignes?"

The what? Adina shook her head and blinked. She'd never heard of such a thing. "What's that?"

He gave her a sly smile. "Not a what, a who." Glancing around the room, he leaned forward and continued, "The Gaelle De Guignes is an oracle of sorts on the northern border of Champeaux. It lives somewhere in the middle of a swamp and is supposed to answer a pilgrim's questions and provide help."

"Supposed to?" Erik's too-loud voice cut in from where he leaned against the edge of the bed just out of her reach. "You've never been there before, I assume?"

René scoffed. "Of course not, don't be daft." At the blank expressions on everyone's faces, he sighed. "The Gaelle only appears to those it wishes to. We may get lucky and find it immediately, or we may tromp through the bogs for months and never run across it." He held up a finger. "But, if we do find it, it will answer our questions." He swallowed. "At least, according to rumor."

Adina shook her head. By the seven gods… "You want to go wander around Champeauxian bogs in search of an oracle who may or may not want to see us?" It was a plan with an infinitesimal chance of succeeding. The sad thing was, she was desperate enough to avoid Damon and her father that she was seriously considering it.

"Do you have any other suggestions?" he parroted back at her.

She thought about it for the space of several heartbeats. Traipsing through a bog didn't sound like her idea of a fun time, but would it be less frustrating or dangerous than working side-by-side with Damon?

Probably. And she wouldn't have to spend every waking moment guarding her thoughts or being around her father. But… She met Erik's gaze and took a deep breath. "Damon proposed we work together against Sujani and Maja."

Erik turned to her. "I thought we decided against that?"

She shook her head. "You decided. Think about it." She turned to the rest of them, every muscle in her body tense. "What chance do we have? Us! We stand no chance against Sujani, much less a *goddess*! We need to do everything we can to not mess this up. Even if that includes working with the lesser of two evils." Turning to René, she swallowed past her suddenly thick throat. "Trust me, I don't want to work with Damon any more than you do." Possibly less, given his alliance with her father. "But I don't think we have much choice."

"I choose the bog," Sigfried said.

Madalina nodded. "Damon can't be trusted." She turned her head to face Adina. "And I'd love to meet a for-real oracle."

Adina cleared her throat. As far as she was concerned, Madalina was as much of an oracle as anyone hanging out in a marsh. Maybe René had a point, and they should get her somewhere she could talk to the stars, just to see if they had any better ideas.

Except that it had poured in Gorlinia for two solid days and didn't show signs of letting up anytime soon. Especially if Damon was right, and this was related to Maja's resurrection.

Glancing at Erik and Hana, Adina received subtle nods from each. "Okay," she said. "Damon gave us one more night to 'think about' working with him. Personally, I vote we leave immediately to get as much of a head start as possible." She'd have to figure out a way to feed Damon any information they found, because no matter how the others felt, they'd need him before the end.

The others stood and headed toward the door.

Adina reached out and caught Erik's arm. "Wait."

He turned toward her with a raised eyebrow.

She nodded at his armor. "You may want to ask the innkeeper for an oiled bag or tarp to wrap your armor in."

Frowning, he glanced at himself before meeting her gaze. "Oh?"

She fought back a sigh remembering their journey through the Brachian bog during her stupid assignment to kill a blood mage. Men.

"It's pouring rain. All that water can't be good for your suit." He opened his mouth, but she cut him off. "We're not likely to come under attack. Any bandits or predators are likely to seek shelter in this deluge. We'll be the only ones crazy enough to be out in this rain at night." She winked. "Besides, you're plenty deadly with just your sword."

He studied her for a few heartbeats before nodding. "You're right, of course. Just like you always are." Heat sparked in his eyes as he raised her knuckles to his mouth and kissed them.

Heat flashed through her blood as the ethereal golden bond between them sparkled. With a mental groan, she pushed the feeling aside. There would be plenty of time for that later, when this was behind them.

Hopefully.

She forced a chuckle and gave him a gentle shove toward the door. "None of that, sir. We can't afford any further delays."

Flashing him a quick grin at his mock-crestfallen expression, she shook her head and turned back to the table. His footsteps retreated down the hallway. She glanced around the room. Nothing crucial stuck out as vital for the journey, and the lighter they traveled the faster they'd reach their destination. The parchment pages with the ritual to forge the Bone Shard Blade were folded securely in a pocket inside her robes, where they would hopefully be protected from the rain. Especially if Erik managed to secure more than one waterproof cloth.

Reaching for a spare piece of parchment and a quill, she scratched out a quick note to leave with the innkeeper.

Less than fifteen minutes later, they left the warmth of the inn behind and stepped out into the rain. The owner had been willing to part with enough oiled canvasses for each of them—for a hefty price, of course. In this weather, protection from the rain was becoming a hot commodity.

Even Sigfried, with his strong preference for traveling in his bear shape, remained human and tucked under an extra-large tarp.

The battering of rain drops drowned out any background noise.

A thick layer of mud covered the road and squelched with every step, sucking at Adina's boots. Her foot slipped, sliding several paces to the side. Flinging her arms out, she showered the others with rain drops as she fought to avoid toppling face-first into the muck. Erik grabbed her arm, steadying her, and she flashed him a grateful smile.

It was useful at times, having someone nearby whose Talent was perfect physical control of their body.

"Ugh." René flapped his arms like chicken wings, shaking rivulets of water onto the road. "This is miserable. I can't believe I agreed to this."

"Not just agreed to it," Madalina said. "You suggested it."

He shook his head in despair that may or may not have been feigned as a cool breeze swirled around them, blowing a curtain of water into their faces.

"Come on, René," Erik said, hoisting his pack higher on his shoulders and continuing down the road. "This is no worse than the bog back in Brachia. At least this time we won't have to deal with soaking clothes and a blood mage."

Adina shuddered at the memory of the gargoyle's claws shredding her stomach.

René harumphed. "Be careful what you say. You'll jinx us."

She couldn't agree more.

Hana wrapped her arm in René's, gently nudging him forward. "The sooner we get moving, the faster we'll get to Champeaux."

It was almost amusing, how instantaneously René's disgruntled expression disappeared once Hana touched him. Warmth crackled in Adina's chest at seeing Hana so happy. Hopefully, that would be a portent of things to come.

Before she knew it, the warm lights of the small village were behind them, replaced by tall pine trees, whose long needles seemed to collect the rain while they waited for the perfect moment to drop globes of water on the group as they passed beneath.

Oiled tarps aside, Adina's boots had been soaked and caked with mud from the get-go. It was too bad they couldn't come up with the funds to purchase horses to ride to avoid having wet feet. Bracing herself, she leaped over a large puddle that lay across the trail. Her heels caught the edge with a slap, splashing muddy water up the back of her legs.

Great. Just great.

At least she wasn't mortal—the chill wouldn't kill her. It would just make her robes uncomfortably clingy.

Using a small bit of Talent, she ripped the water from her pant legs and flung it to the ground, where it belonged.

The forest pushed down on her shoulders, an invisible weight as it loomed above. Fine hairs on the back of her neck prickled as her shoulders slowly rolled inward.

Sigfried pulled up short as he glanced around. "Does anyone else feel like we're being followed?"

Adina stopped and peered between the trees that lined the road, their trunks straight and close together like bars in a jail. That would explain her unease, but it was too soon for Damon to have received her note so it couldn't be him. She studied the woods, alert for any sound or hint of movement that wasn't obscured by the ever-present deluge of rain.

The sound of metal against wood met her ears as Erik slowly drew his sword and lifted it to an on-guard position. Behind her, René did the same. Madalina stepped closer to Sigfried, who nudged her into the middle of the group.

A heartbeat passed.

Two.

"Anyone hear anything?" René whispered.

Adina strained to catch the faintest sound in the forest surrounding them and shook her head. "No," she said. "Except for this stupid rain." But her instincts were on fire, awakened by Sigfried's putting a name to the feeling that had been building since they'd left the inn.

Erik sidled up beside her, still focused on their surroundings and tilted his head slightly. "What was that you said about no one attacking us?"

She clenched her jaw. No sane person would be out in this weather. She should've known better than to suggest such a thing when Sujani and his resurrected goddess were involved. Pulling her sword from its sheath, she glowered. "Find the threat now, say 'I told you so' later."

The corners of his lips hardened as he gave a small nod.

She'd never hear the end of this. She would never recommend he take off his armor again. The universe seemed to take delight in taking any advantage of the opportunities to throw problems their way every time he removed that blasted plate mail.

"Look!" Madalina's clear voice rang out. "The ghost girl!"

Adina whipped her head around, her gaze following Madalina's pointing finger.

A young girl in a cornflower blue dress floated between two nearby trees. Adina blinked. It looked to be the same ghost who had led them to the blood mage, Viktor Knoll's, house back in Brachia. Where the gargoyle had nearly ended her.

Adina's stomach did a barrel roll as her mouth went dry. She swallowed past her tight throat. "Is that—"

"It's her!" Madalina smiled and waved. "Hello, Joan!"

Erik and René's blades flashed in her peripheral vision as they turned to face the ghost.

Adina brandished her own sword. "If the blood mage's ghost is here, then Viktor is probably somewhere nearby, as well."

Erik shook his head and glanced at Adina. "I killed Viktor in Brachia when he was trying to kill René. Right before your father kidnapped you."

Great. Her stomach hardened. "Looks like death may not have been so permanent for him, after all."

René shuddered, the blood draining from his face. "And since Viktor is Damon's soul-slave, Damon is likely around, too."

Adina's stomach plummeted. Of *course*, Damon had been watching the inn. He probably expected them to try to run.

Joan drifted closer until Adina could distinguish each drop of rain that passed harmlessly through her. Sometimes, it must be nice to be incorporeal.

The ghost met her eyes. The forlorn expression on Joan's face twisted Adina's heart, and she nearly reached out to comfort the poor girl. She dropped the tip of her blade slightly.

"Why are you here?" Sigfried asked, his voice snapping Adina's thoughts back to the present threat.

"Where's your master," René asked, the tightness in his voice matched the subtle shake of his sword.

Joan fixed her gaze on Madalina, who remained safely huddled in the middle of their circle, as protected as she could be. Her mouth opened and closed as though talking, but no sound reached Adina's ears.

A large drip of water fell from above, splashing her on the crown of her head. The splat was loud enough, she winced. When she opened her eyes, Joan was gone.

She whirled to face Madalina. "Where did she go? What did she say?"

Madalina furrowed her brow and frowned as she glanced over her shoulder before meeting Adina's gaze. She leaned forward and dropped her voice. "She was here to warn us. Damon knows where we are, and Viktor's on our trail. We need to do something—magically—to throw them off or they'll catch us."

Adina chewed the inside of her cheek as she glanced around. What did that mean? How did one *magically* throw one of the most powerful vampires in the world off their tracks? She blinked and focused on the others, only to find them staring expectantly at her.

"What?" she asked as she waved in the general direction Joan had appeared in, showering them all with more water from her oiled tarp. "You guys think I know what the ghost meant?" She was no mage. Even if she were, no way was she a match for Damon or Sujani.

Madalina shrugged. "Well, Sujani did want to train you. You must have *some* magic in your blood."

She huffed. Sure—he trained her for all of maybe two weeks. "Not enough to be of any good here, even if I had any clue how to use it."

"You have the Talent to control water," Erik said. "Possibly air, as well?"

Well, he was right about that. "True. Maybe, if I get lucky, I might be able to hide our footprints, but that'll take a lot of energy. And it won't do anything to stop someone from pursuing us with magic."

"But it's a start," Hana said.

Adina signed. "Alright." Hopefully this wouldn't be a wasted expenditure of Talent. While blood wasn't going to be nearly as scarce as it was in the Saldanian Desert, they didn't have a ton of time to sidetrack and let Sigfried hunt for them.

"Everyone move off the path," she said, waving for them to stand behind her.

Reaching into her core for the residual energy that refilled every time she fed, she grabbed a handful of Talent and sent it toward the water that covered the ground. The liquid swirled back and forth, like the waves she'd once seen on a beach nearly half a century ago. Back and forth the water lapped, as far as she could see and feel, the repetitive movements smoothing out their footprints and slowly erasing the evidence of their passing.

Several minutes later, breathing hard at the expenditure of energy, she opened her eyes. The water ceased its movement.

The mud looked as though no one had traveled through it for days.

Pride welled up in her chest at how well it had worked.

"How far does the effect extend?" Erik asked.

She brushed her hands off on the front of her pants. "About a third of a league. If they don't come after us right away and give the rain a little more time, the effect will be gradual, and they might not even notice exactly where my Talent kicked in."

René whistled in admiration.

"Our scent is gone, too," Sigfried said.

"Good." That wasn't something she'd thought to aim for, but she'd take the win.

Hana cleared her throat. "It's very impressive, Adina, and I don't mean to minimize it, but we shouldn't stay here. At best, the ghost and the blood mage controlling her know where we are. At worst, they've reported that info to Damon."

Adina bit her lip as her stomach roiled. He must not have gotten her note. If he had, there was no way he'd waste time following them.

"She's right," Erik said. He glanced around. "Any thoughts on going off-trail? To make it any harder for them to follow us?"

Sigfried stepped forward. "I will lead us. Follow me." He turned and ducked between two trees, more nimble than a man of his size should be. Madalina followed. Globules of water fell from the branches every time he brushed past them, showering them with splatters and drowning out the sounds of any possible pursuit.

René flicked his sword to get most of the water off, shoved it into its scabbard, and held his arm out to Hana. "Shall we?"

Taking the offered arm, Hana met Adina's eyes with a brief smile, and headed into the woods.

Adina used the smallest bit of Talent to dry her sword before she tucked it back into its sheath at her waist. At least the oppressive feeling of being watched had disappeared. She rolled her shoulders, loosening the muscles.

Erik gestured ahead with the hand that wasn't holding his sword. "After you, m'lady. I'll bring up the rear."

They were halfway up a ridge, well under the protection of the trees, when Sigfried pulled them to a stop in front of some boulders. "This is a good place."

"A good place to what?" René asked as he came up behind him.

Madalina flashed her teeth at him. "Why, to wait and see who's following us, of course." She plopped down on one of the boulders, gesturing for him to do the same.

Adina joined them, sitting on the rock beside Madalina. She scoured the trail they'd been following, muscles tense for any sign of movement.

Swallowing, she wrapped her fingers around the hilt of her falchion. "Do we know for certain someone's coming now?"

Sigfried shook his head. "No. Just a feeling."

A large bunch of drips fell from the tree boughs and splatted them.

"Ugh." If only they could get rid of this incessant *rain*. She raised her arm above her head, palm toward the sky. Burning a small burst of Talent, she hardened the air above them so it formed a translucent umbrella like the flowery parasols the noble women of Champeaux carried to keep the sun off their oh-so-delicate skin. The rain hit the hardened air and tumbled to the ground around them.

"About blasted time," René muttered as he shrugged out of his tarp. Rivulets of water cascaded to the ground. "This thing is cramping my style. If we get caught in a fight, it'll seriously slow me down."

Madalina raised an eyebrow. "More so than being soaked to the bone?"

Adina rolled her eyes. Without his luxurious surroundings and full serving staff, there seemed no way to satisfy René. Whatever Hana saw in him was buried very deep.

Erik sat on Adina's other side with a relieved sigh.

"What's that?" Hana asked, pointing back toward the trail.

A dark shadow floated up the road, following their footsteps. It disappeared behind one black tree and emerged on the other side, just to vanish behind the next one like it was playing a ghastly game of hide-and-seek.

Adina's gut twisted. She hadn't even thought about her father being around, much less traipsing up the path in the rain after them. Damon must be holding something big over him, to get Septimus to agree to being out and about in this weather.

"It's the wraith!" René's loud voice made her jump.

She slammed a cylinder of hardened air around them with an audible thump, hoping to seal in any other unexpected noise. The last thing they needed was one of them announcing their presence when she'd worked so hard to erase all the traces of it.

The black shadow paused, turning toward them.

"By the gods, René," Adina hissed, flashing her fangs at him. "Keep your voice down!" At least it wasn't Septimus.

Her pounding heart rushed blood past her ears, drowning out the rain as they waited with bated breath to see what the wraith would do. The pitter-patter of rain beat against her air-umbrella, matching the cadence of her racing heart.

After several breaths, the shadow turned to the trail and resumed its course.

Madalina frowned, whispering, "You're right, though, René. It's definitely the wraith of Viktor Knoll, that blood mage from Brachia. The one Damon enslaved." She squinted, peering into the darkness. "I think it's best if we all be quiet and don't move so it won't find us."

Adina agreed. The last thing they needed was another gargoyle fight. She shuddered as the memory of the beast's claws shredding her stomach ripped through her.

"A little late for the quiet bit," Erik mumbled, slanting a glare at René.

"Sorry, I was surprised," René said. "Don't bite my head off."

Hana reached out and brushed her palm down Adina's wall of hardened air. "This is amazing," she whispered. She turned toward Adina. "Is it soundproof?"

Adina turned her attention to the road. "I don't know, but I certainly hope so." The wraith didn't move like Septimus at all, and their size was totally different. She should've known better than to assume it was her father without taking the time to verify. Jumping too quickly to conclusions like an untrained assassin would get her ended sooner rather than later, just like Septimus predicted.

And the last thing she wanted to do was prove that jerk right.

Madalina reached over and squeezed her knee, a supportive smile on her face. "It's okay, Adina. I would've thought it was Septimus, too."

The wraith's path continued, seemingly undeterred.

"If we let it get ahead of us, we may stumble upon it when we least expect," Erik said, keeping his voice low.

Adina ground her teeth. There were no good options.

"Well, the alternative is fighting it," René said with a scowl. "And I hope I don't have to remind you how well *that* went the last time, if it's still here?"

"Cut it out, boys," Madalina said with a stern glare. "You're not helping."

On her other side, Sigfried chuffed in agreement.

The water streaming over the wall of hardened air blurred Adina's view of the trail below. "Do you think this rain will continue all the way to the Gaelle De Guignes?" she asked, more to distract Erik and René before they got into an all-out fight than because she cared about the answer at the moment.

"I hope so," Erik said. "If what Damon said is true, and Champeaux is burning, they likely need all the rain they can get."

"What?" René exploded. "There are fires in Champeaux?"

"Keep your voice down, Frere René! Unless you want the wraith to find us?"

Looking appropriately chagrined, René leaned toward Adina and Erik. Dropping his voice, he whispered, "What is this about fires in my homeland? Tell me!"

Adina cleared her throat. "Damon says Sujani's goddess, Maja, is throwing the world's weather system out of balance by being resurrected. He blames her for the rains in Gorlinia. Apparently, there's also fires burning all across Champeaux and earthquakes in Brachia."

René's skin went pale. "Are there any fires near Duvale?"

When they met him with blank stares, he sighed and said, "A little town in the mountains, approximately twenty leagues south of Pierrevalle. It's where my castle is."

Adina shook her head. "I'm sorry. I don't know any more than that." She glanced at Madalina and Sigfried then back at him. "Maybe we can swing by on the way up to the bog? Is it very far out of the way?"

René opened his mouth and closed it again as the muscles in his face contorted.

"Tell the truth, Frere René," Madalina said, shaking her finger at him. "Remember, Sig and I know where it is, too."

René deflated like a popped balloon. He ground his teeth and stared at the mud in front of his toes. "No...it's nowhere near where we'll be. It's on the far side of the country." He swallowed. "Unless we take the Pass of Shadows around to the north, but that will add at least a week to our journey."

Would one week make or break them in the race to end Sujani, Damon and Maja? Probably, if Damon's quote of thirty days was at all accurate. It wasn't like they could do anything if there was a fire near René's estate...she couldn't control the element nearly well enough to have any hope of bringing a raging wildfire under control. Yet. "When do we need to make a decision?"

"In about three days. Pretty much as soon as we get to the Champeauxian border," he said. "The road will fork east and west."

She nodded, catching Hana's eye. "We have a few days, then. Let's see how much traveling off road and avoiding the wraith slows us down. We can re-evaluate once we get out of this blasted rain."

Chapter 5
Damon

"What?" Damon paced around the cave, his exclamation bouncing off the walls. "What do you mean, you lost them?"

The wraith formerly known as Viktor Knoll, the most skilled necromancer in all of Brachia and a passingly decent blood mage—for a mortal—hovered before him. If ghosts could cower, Viktor would be doing so.

Good.

He'd make Viktor pay for his failure. If Sujani and Maja won and a second Cataclysm erupted, Damon would lose everything, including his unlife.

It was a good thing Septimus had stepped out to attend to some Assassin Guild business. The last thing Damon needed was a witness to his minion's mistakes.

<I'm sorry, my lord.> Viktor's voice echoed through Damon's mind as clearly as if the wraith were speaking out loud. *<I tracked their footsteps in the mud, and Adina's magic blood. But both disappeared, and with the rain...>*

"You lost them in the rain?" He bared his fangs as his rage tinted his vision red. "You're incorporeal! A little water should mean nothing to your measly carcass!" Balling his hand that wore Viktor's sapphire ring into a fist, he swung at the wraith. The satisfying impact vibrated up his arm as Viktor slammed into the far wall with a thump.

Flexing and releasing his fingers while he shook them out, Damon sneered. At least, as the master of the ring that soul-bound Viktor, he could still physically affect him.

If only he had a more competent slave.

He reached into his pocket and crushed the note Adina had left him. It was too bad Baron Arthur had met his end back in The Drowned City. The baron had possessed a rare Talent for locating people. He would've been the perfect one to enslave and send after Adina's party. Heck, with Arthur's romantic feelings for Adina, it was quite possible no enslavement would've been necessary.

Damn Sujani and his twice-cursed goddess.

Damon exhaled and rolled his shoulders. Losing his temper now would get him nowhere. It was no use dwelling on the past and things he couldn't change.

"Tell me exactly what happened." Damon threw the full power of his Talent behind the command.

Viktor screeched, resisting. But no soul-slave could disobey a direct command from its master. *<I followed them as you instructed. Joan got to them first. She warned them—>*

"What?" Damon's vision narrowed until all he could see was Viktor's shadowy face, turned up from where he cowered on the floor. *Joan? What kind of name was that?*

The wraith raised its skeletal hands to him. *<About Sujani, only! I swear! She didn't say anything about you!>*

Damon towered over Viktor, his entire being focused on the wraith's thoughts. "Who is this Joan?"

Images of a young farmer's daughter flashed through Viktor's mind. From the days before, when Viktor was nothing but a talented healer. Before he'd studied blood magic and learned to control his necromancy.

Before he'd become useful.

He blinked, surprise momentarily washing away his rage. "You turned her into a ghost?"

<She rejected me. I had no choice.> The pitiful whine reminded Damon all-too-well of the petulant young man Viktor had been in his youth.

Damon's entire body shook with laughter. "I will admit, I didn't think you had it in you," he said once his amusement faded. "Condemning the woman you loved to an eternity of nothingness. You, Viktor, are a real piece of work."

The wraith deflated even more, if such a thing were possible.

Damon slapped his palms together, as if brushing off dirt. "Of course, you'll need to release her. I can't have a ghost about, mucking up my plans." More importantly, he couldn't have his slave owning a tool he had no power over. Such a thing would give Viktor a potential ally to work against Damon, without the constraint of the soul-slave bond.

Viktor stiffened, turning his face up to meet his gaze. *<No! You can't! I'll keep her under control, I swear!>*

Damon shook his head, clicking his tongue. "Now, you know I can't let that happen. One failure of a minion is more than enough. Two..." He sighed dramatically. "No, we can't have that." Spearing Viktor with his gaze, he threw the full force of his Talent behind his words. "Release her. Now!"

Viktor shrieked, his scream drove needles through Damon's ears and down his spine. Curling incorporeal fingers into talons, Viktor lunged.

Damon curled his hand with the ring into a fist and held it in front of him like a shield.

Viktor came to a stop, his arms thrown in front of his face, protectively.

"Release her!" Damon's command reverberated around the cave until the rain outside drowned out the echoes.

Viktor fell to his incorporeal knees. <*No!*> He tumbled backward until his shoulder blades pressed against the ground. His back arched as every muscle went taught.

A pale blue light coalesced in the air above him, like a large firefly. It hovered between them for the space of two heartbeats before it flashed, blindingly bright like one of Sujani's lightning bolts. Then, with a quiet sigh that sounded almost like a *thank you*, it disappeared.

<*No! Joan!*> Viktor rolled to his side, his desiccated body hidden underneath his black, ethereal robes. <*I'll kill you. If it's the last thing I do. I swear it.*>

Damon smirked as he twirled the sapphire ring around his finger. "You can certainly try." No soul-slave had ever shaken its master's yoke; that was the power of the spell and the likely reason all known copies of said rituals had long ago been destroyed.

Fortunately for him, the knowledge stored in his brain was not so easily eliminated.

And now, there was one less entity he had to worry about interfering in his plans.

"What was that?"

Damon flinched as Seven's voice echoed several inches from his ear. He bit back a snarl before plastering a wide smile on his face and turning to face his partner. "Seven. Perfect timing, as usual."

Seven gave him a flat stare before glancing at the wraith cowering on the floor at Damon's feet. Raising his eyebrow, he met Damon's gaze with a pointed question in his eyes.

Damon cleared his throat. "Nothing for you to be concerned about." He glanced over his shoulder at Viktor. Throwing more power behind the words, he said, "Now, get back out there and *find* them. When you do, follow them until you know where they're going. Then, report back."

With a jerky bow that had everything to do with the power of Damon's spell and nothing to do with Viktor's willingness to comply, the wraith faded from view.

Dusting his hands off on his pants, Damon turned his attention back to Seven. The large man looked none the worse for wear. A few drops of rain rolled off his oiled scalp and soaked into the vest he always wore that did more to emphasize his broad chest rather than offer protection or adornment. His pants fit snug at the waist and flared over his legs until they were tied tightly at his ankles, in the common fashion of men from the desert. In the rain, however, the style was laughable.

Damon almost hoped they were trapped in the deluge for a few minutes, just to see what Seven looked like soaking wet, so he could have that memory to hold gleefully close when he'd defeated Sujani and held the world trembling beneath his heel.

He shook his head. Work now, fantasize later. "What news of the guild?"

Seven cleared his throat. "They disperse, even as we speak. Though it would be easier if we had any more guidance on where to look."

Damon sighed. Seven was never happy, always demanding more than he had to give. Damon held back an eyeroll. If he had any idea where to find thousand-year-old dragon bones, he'd certainly not bother to bring the guild or anyone else into this. "I have given you everything I know. Time for the assassins to earn their pay."

"As minions in your scavenger hunt," Seven rumbled.

Heat flared in Damon's core. Why was the other vampire always trying to push his buttons? It served no purpose but to put them both on edge. "*Our* scavenger hunt," he said. "Or did you forget, our goals are the same?" For now, at least. He walked to the edge of the cave and braced his shoulder against the large boulder that rested there. "Now, the sun will be up soon. Help me put this where it belongs so we can get to sleep."

Seven grunted but came to stand behind Damon. Placing his hands against the rock above Damon's, they pushed. With a scrape of stone against stone, it rolled into place, sealing them in perfect blackness.

Damon settled his cape on the floor and laid upon it. Seven's heavy footsteps stomped to the far side of the room, where he settled in for the day with a thud.

Lying on the floor, Damon stared into the darkness. He was slipping. His soul-slave had managed to conceal a minion from him. Him! And all because he'd let himself become so focused on Sujani's actions, he'd missed the obvious betrayal right in front of his nose. Damon curled his hand into fists until his nails carved crescent-shaped holes in his palms as he ground his teeth. Viktor had a stronger will than he'd given the man credit for—a mistake he wouldn't repeat.

Now all he needed to do was wait for Viktor and the Assassin's Guild to do their respective jobs. But he could hardly sit in a cave with Seven for the days or weeks it took for them to do it while Sujani and Maja were loose in the world. And with Maja getting stronger every day...

He put his hands behind his head. Tomorrow night, he'd start his search for ley lines. Preferably somewhere drier, like Champeaux. Or maybe he'd go back to Esnaria. There was nothing quite as good at jogging his memories as a visit to the old homeland. Perhaps he'd find something of use in the bowels of the royal library. After all, the royal family of Esnaria had spent the last several centuries building the largest collection of magical reference books and grimoires in the realm. At his direction, of course.

Yes. Tomorrow, he would have Seven teleport him to Esnaria.

It was past time for him to check in on his kingdom anyway.

Chapter 6
Adina

Feeling five pounds lighter, Adina took off her oiled tarp and shook it out over the brown grass on the side of the path. A torrent of water droplets showered the dry grass. The parched soil soaked up the moisture almost faster than she could blink.

Three days after seeing the wraith, they finally crossed into Champeaux. And, as if the weather was aware of the precise location of the border, the pouring rain had ceased the minute they'd crossed.

Damon hadn't been kidding when he'd said Champeaux was burning. She kicked at the brown grass. If the rest of the country was like this, it was one giant tinder box ready to explode and carry them all one step closer to the impending Cataclysm. The faint hint of smoke tickled her nose.

She glanced over her shoulder. One hundred paces away, rain poured down, flooding the depressions in the trail and soaking everything else to the bone.

"It's so creepy," Erik said from beside her, his gaze following hers. "Definitely supernatural."

René snorted. "You mean divine."

Adina rolled her eyes and eyed her tarp. "I don't suppose it's worth carrying these heavy things around anymore. Maybe someone traveling in the other direction will find them useful." She went to toss hers by the side of the road.

Erik grabbed her arm. "Hang on to it. Just in case. You never know what the bog will be like. And they weren't cheap."

She clenched her jaw and sighed. He was probably right. She shrugged out of her backpack and tied the tarp to the outside instead. The others followed suit.

"Where to now?" Sigfried asked.

Adina glanced at the path. It forked, just like René said it would. She glanced at him and raised an eyebrow. "Well?" Despite having three days, they hadn't actually come to a decision, despite discussing it several times.

René sighed, his shoulders drooping.

Madalina put her arm on his shoulder and gave him a knowing smile.

"Do you trust your people?" Sigfried asked.

"Of course," René said, indignation written across his face. "They wouldn't be a part of my staff if I didn't."

"And are they smart?" Madalina asked.

He scoffed. "Yes. You know that. You live with me."

Picking up where they were going with this, Adina chimed in. "Do you trust them to do what needs to be done in the event the estate needs to be protected?"

He brushed his hair out of his face as he stared down the path leading to home. "I do, it's just... If it was your home, you'd go protect it without a second thought."

Adina opened her mouth to point out she had no home now, but paused. Would she put their quest aside for a week to go check on Baron Arthur's estate and his servants, if it was threatened?

Of course she would. The staff had served loyally for years, many for all their lives. That sort of devotion meant something, and she was honor-bound to repay that.

The gods knew the rest of the world didn't give a pint of rat's blood about her well-being like Arthur's staff did.

"Think of it this way," Erik said as he circled around into René's line of sight. "If we go to your manor, we may or may not be able to do anything. However, the more time Maja has to destroy the world, the more likely it won't be just your estate we lose, but the entire realm. If we hunt down this oracle instead, we stand a chance of defeating Maja before she triggers another Cataclysm."

"Hopefully including your estate," Hana added, for good measure.

"Wait a minute," Adina said. "René has a point. By serving him, his staff have put their lives in his hands. He is duty-bound to protect them if he can."

René froze, his jaw going slack as his arms hung limply at his sides. "Wait, what? You agree with me?"

She nodded. "I do. I would want to do the same for Arthur's staff if the situation were reversed." Crossing her arms, she glanced at Erik. "Loyalty matters and should be rewarded."

"Yeah! What she said," René added.

Erik spread his feet until they were shoulder-width apart and crossed his arms. "But if we delay and the Cataclysm erupts, then we'll lose not just your staff, René, but literally everyone will die. The entire world will end. A week could make or break everything."

Adina bit her lower lip and sighed. There were no good options. She met René's gaze and shook her head. This had to be his choice.

René scrunched his face as tight as he could and held it for a breath. "Fine! Blast it." He kicked a pebble down the path as hard as he could.

As the rock clattered to a stop at the edge of the path, he turned to them. "Let's go and get this done. The sooner we save the world, the faster I can get back to my estate and see to my affairs." He turned and stomped down the path on the right.

Adina smiled sympathetically. René had truly grown as a vampire since they'd first met. Last year, he would've never put the good of the world above himself. Her gaze flicked to the woman following along behind him.

Or maybe Hana had something to do with that.

"Come on, lazy pants!" René called over his shoulder at the rest of them. "If you stand there all day, I'm going to change my mind!"

With a chuckle and shake of his head, Erik headed off down the trail. "I suppose we better get on it then."

Sigfried shifted into a bear and knelt to allow Madalina to scramble onto his shoulders. With a grunt and a quick glance at them, he lumbered after René. Adina and Hana followed.

The road took them winding through the foothills and highlands along the base of the Frostback Mountains. To the south and east, rolling hills of vineyards and fields spread off to the horizon. At one time, they had likely been lush and green, teeming with all manner of birds and life. Now, under the haze of the waxing moon, the vegetation was shriveled and dying.

"It looks like autumn came early to these parts," Hana said when they stopped by the side of the road for a break.

René shook his head. "No. It's too early yet, the weather is too warm. This is a drought."

Adina took a deep breath. The smell of smoke had been steadily getting worse as the night creeped into morning. The ever-present haze seemed thicker to the west. If the fire was in that direction and it reached these fields, they'd light up faster than an oil-soaked torch.

Madalina stretched her arms wide as she yawned. "Hey, Frere René, any idea where we might find shelter for the day?"

Adina glanced at the sky. The moon still hovered a full two hands' width above the horizon. Plenty of time to find somewhere safe, as long as they weren't out in the middle of endless fields. She turned her attention to the foothills to their left. Surely there was a cave or other similar structure that would provide protection from the sun that they could stay in for the day?

René shook his head. "I don't know. I've never been on this road before."

Erik tucked his blood pouch, courtesy of Hana, into his pack and heaved himself to his feet. "If that's the case, then we'd best get moving. The more ground we cover, the more likely we are to find something suitable."

Adina stood, adjusting her sword at her waist. Her sore feet protested the too-short rest. Not for the first time, she wished for horses.

Madalina climbed back onto Sigfried's shoulders and ruffled the fur on the top of his head. "Don't worry. Sig here will smell out somewhere for us to stay. His nose is strongest in bear form."

Some of the tension between Adina's shoulder blades released. The others didn't seem nervous, so she'd put the heavy feeling in her stomach aside for now.

After all, there was no point in worrying over something that may not even be an issue.

Sigfried muscled his way past René to take the lead on the trail.

"Hey!" René pressed his lips together in a scowl as he scrambled after them. "What are you doing?"

"Don't be foolish," Madalina said with a wave of her hand. "You don't know the road, so there's no point in having you lead. Besides, if you're in front, all we'll smell is you, and that'll get us nowhere."

René slowed his pace for Adina and the others to catch up.

Erik slapped him on the shoulder in a friendly show of support.

Adina bit back a laugh as René stumbled forward and glared at them over his shoulder.

Erik blinked, a picture of innocence. Apparently after all this time, the men weren't above ribbing each other.

Half a league later, Sigfried pulled up short, blocking the trail.

"He smells smoke," Madalina said.

"That's nothing new," Adina replied. "I've been smelling the fires all night."

She shook her head. "No, not that kind of smoke. This comes with cooked meat and warm stew on a winter's night." She pointed over the next hill in front of them.

Adina frowned. Smoke was smoke, fire burned wood the same regardless of what it was used for. She shrugged...this was Madalina, after all. Personally, her first inclination was to steer clear, but with the warm connotations behind Madalina's choice of words, perhaps this was somewhere they could safely pass the day?

Stepping forward, she studied Sigfried's eyes. "Do you think this may be a good place to shelter?"

He grunted and shrugged. In a less serious situation, the human gesture in a bear would've been comical.

"Okay. I'll go check it out." She met each of their gazes as she drew her sword. "Stay here, I'll be right back." Pulling the shadows around herself, she stepped off the trail and into the brush. Away from the path, the undergrowth thinned, making it easier to approach. The moon hung only a finger's width lower in the sky as Adina settled at the edge of a glade that abutted the trail they'd been using.

A quaint cottage with whitewashed trim and shutters sat in the middle of the clearing. A water wheel clung desperately to its side, though the creek was bone dry. The gardens and flowerpots around the front door still boasted a few hardy flowers—Hana would know their types better than she. And Sigfried had been right. The aroma of cooked meat and stew permeated the air.

When she'd been human, it would've been enough to make her stomach growl in anticipation. As a vampire, however, it was just one more annoying scent that obfuscated any information she might have smelled about the owner of the house.

Despite the late hour, the insides flickered with the light from many candles. Whoever lived here was still awake, which probably meant they were no simple mortal peasant.

Double-checking her shadow cloak, Adina creeped from the edge of the woods across the clearing until she was underneath the front window.

Wood and pottery clacked on the other side, as though someone was cooking. Or brewing potions.

She bit the inside of her cheek and shifted her weight so she could stretch and peek through the corner of the glass.

A large wooden rocking chair sat in front of the hearth, which supported a merry fire, despite the heat and drought. A table large enough for a small family occupied the center of the room. Movement to her right drew Adina's attention. A woman with scraggly blonde hair and a blue apron tied around her waist limped slowly about the kitchen. Judging by the smell of sugar and lemon juice and the glass containers on the counter, she was canning some sort of round purple fruit. Her stooped posture and vacant expression hinted at a deep sadness that had Adina's gut twisting in empathy.

One of the good things about being a vampire was she would never have to deal with the infirmities that came with aging as a mortal.

She took a deep breath, parsing the scents for anything that smelled like Blood Magic...like the acrid scent that stuck to the back of her throat at Viktor Knoll's house. Or like Damon.

The overwhelming smell of food was hard to sort through, but she didn't detect any bitter or foul undertones.

Adina backed away from the house, letting her night vision return. She studied the rest of the clearing. Perhaps there was an outbuilding or other structure that would keep them out of the mortal's way and shelter them during the day.

A small outhouse near the north end of the clearing was the only other structure to be found. Adina wrinkled her nose as she backed away from it. Shaking her head, she sighed. There was nowhere here that would meet their needs. They'd have to move on and hope for the best further down the road.

She was halfway through the clearing, headed toward the trail when a voice called out behind her.

"Hello?"

Adina froze and glanced over her shoulder. She hadn't heard the mortal open the front door.

The mortal stood silhouetted with a hand to her forehead as though shading her eyes from the moon. "Who are you?" The woman was staring right at her.

Adina turned, checking her Talent to confirm she was still shrouded in darkness.

Her shadow cloak was fully intact.

The woman shouldn't have been able to see her, especially at night with the smoky haze half-obscuring the moon.

She made eye contact. There was no mistake—the mortal was staring right at her.

Her heart skipped a beat and her blood chilled. Curse the gods and her Talent for failing her. She stared for one heartbeat, then another.

With a sigh, Adina slipped her sword back into its sheath and dropped the shadows. There was no point if they weren't working, anyway. "My friends and I are passing through." She nodded to the road. "I only sought to confirm you weren't a threat to us. We will be on our way and won't bother you."

"Nonsense!" The mortal stepped off her porch and waved for her to come in. "The sun will be up soon. You should come inside before it's too late."

Adina shifted her weight side-to-side, instantly on high alert. There was no way a human could ascertain she was a vampire. Not at this distance, and in this lighting. "What did you say?"

"Trust me," the woman said. "No one wants to be on this road during the day. Plenty of unsavory characters about. Nasty weather makes some people desperate."

Adina forced her muscles to relax. "Thank you for the offer. But we can handle ourselves."

"I insist, please. I wouldn't be able to live with myself if I let unwary travelers march to their deaths."

"Our deaths?" Erik stepped into the clearing from the trail, just out of sight. The others were probably there, as well. "What do you mean?" he asked.

Adina raised her eyebrow at him.

He winked at her.

She rolled her eyes and shook her head. Men.

"Come inside, all of you," the mortal said, "and I'll explain."

A few minutes later, the six of them, including Sigfried back in his human form, were crowded around the table in the middle of the cabin as the mortal, Sophie, ladled heaping portions of stew into bowls set before them.

Adina nudged her bowl away. "Truly, this isn't necessary. We ate quite well not an hour ago," she lied.

"Nonsense," Sophie said. "Travelers always need a good meal. Especially nowadays."

"What did you mean," Erik asked, "about us going to our deaths?"

"There are a lot of bandits on the road, and soldiers looking for conscripts." Sophie eyed Erik's sword and armor as a spark of humor momentarily brightened her expression. "Though, I suspect the sight of a full-fledged knight will be a solid deterrent to many."

René huffed. "Indeed."

Madalina elbowed him. "Manners."

Sophie wedged herself in between Hana and Adina. Digging her spoon into the rich stew, she took a bite and waved her spoon at the rest of them. "Eat!" she said between bites.

Adina bounced her knee under the table as she met Erik's eyes with a small shrug. She took a deep breath and licked her lips. Here went nothing.

Sigfried took the dainty spoon in his oversized hand and studied it as though he'd never seen such a thing before, then cautiously dipped it into the bowl. Bringing it to his lips he chomped down and swallowed audibly.

Adina took a small bite. Flavor exploded in her mouth before she swallowed. It had been over a century since she'd eaten. Without being able to get any nourishment from it, there'd been no point. The food would now sit in her stomach like a rock until she could throw it back up later. But at least Sophie would continue to think they were human.

And it wasn't like the meal tasted bad. Quite the opposite, in fact. She swallowed another spoonful.

"This is incredibly good," Hana said. "I haven't tasted anything like this in…a long time."

Sophie beamed. "Of course you haven't! Food made with love always tastes the best."

"Will you share your recipe?" Hana asked.

Nodding, Sophie scraped her bowl, collecting the last remnants on her spoon. "Of course! I'm flattered you would ask."

"What are those things," Adina asked, pointing to the purple fruit crammed into the glass jars.

"Oh, just some plums I collected before the trees die from lack of water." The light extinguished from Sophie's eyes as she exhaled slowly. "A few more weeks, and I think the damage to the land will be permanent."

"It's too bad we can't move the rain up from Gorlinia," Adina said without thinking. "They could use a little bit of drought after the floods. A lot of their roads and cities have been washed out." Perhaps Sujani, with his ability to summon storms, could move the rain northward? She shook her head. No. He was too focused on his goddess, even if he cared one whit about the rest of the world.

One corner of Sophie's mouth curled down briefly. "Indeed. If only the weather worked that way." Polishing off the last of her bowl, she pushed away from the table. "But one cannot argue with mother nature, we are all subject to her whims." She stood, pushing her chair out behind her.

Sigfried frowned. "What is happening is not natural."

Sophie tripped on a loose board on her way to the sink. Her dishes clattered on the counter. "Oh?"

"Extreme weather that respects imaginary borders developed by humans is not natural." He glowered. "Someone is playing with forces they should not."

"Indeed," Sophie murmured. Setting her bowl in the sink, she brushed her hands off on her apron and turned toward them with an expression of forced cheerfulness plastered to her face. "Now, since you've been traveling all night, you'll want some place to stay for the day, I assume?"

Adina caught Erik's eyes, then René and the others. "Somewhere dark, if possible," she said, turning to Sophie. "Some of us find it hard to sleep with the sun shining." Technically, if the sun shone on them, they'd burn to a crisp, which would make it hard to sleep. So it wasn't *really* a lie.

Their host waved them to the back of the cottage. "How about the root cellar?"

Adina craned her neck to look where the woman indicated. In the shadows of the back corner, as far away from the entry as possible, a trap door beckoned.

Strolling over to it, Sophie twisted a latch and lifted. A ladder descending into darkness waited below. "I don't have any beds down there, and you'll be sharing the space with a few sacks of potatoes and flour, but it's dark." She pointed to the underside of the trap door and solemnly met their gazes. "And it latches from the inside. Just in case any of those brigands I was telling you about decides to try their luck."

Adina nodded. Indeed. For any woman living alone on a dangerous road, a secure panic room was a must.

"You should be safe here for the day, yes?"

"Yes," Madalina said, nodding her head emphatically.

René blinked, his mouth gaping at her quick acceptance. "Wait, what?"

"It's okay," Madalina said. "The stars are her friends. They say we'll be safe here."

Interesting. Adina glanced between Madalina and their host. Sophie's face was politely blank as she leaned against the counter, waiting for them to reach their decision.

The imminent press of the rising sun made the skin on Adina's back itch. They had lingered here so long, they didn't have much time left, unless they wanted to rely on Hana using her Talent to dig a shallow trench for them to sleep in, like she had the night Sujani had resurrected Maja.

Adina shuddered at the memory of the Bone Shard Blade slamming into her chest, draining not just her blood, but her very Talent and life energy. And the endless cold. No, thank you. That morning would give her nightmares for the rest of her unlife.

They crowded around the trap door. Cool musty air wafted up from below. As long as the door overhead stayed locked, they should be plenty safe from the sunlight down there.

Adina stepped forward and put her foot on the first rung of the ladder. Erik put his hand on her shoulder. "Let me go first?"

She raised her eyebrow at him. Switching to Hakki so their host wouldn't understand, she asked, "Do you think I can't handle myself?" First, he was hovering on the edge of the clearing, now he wouldn't let her go down a ladder? She needed to have a talk with him about his overprotectiveness.

Sophie watched, mute, waiting for her reaction.

They'd talk later, when prying eyes weren't around.

"Please, humor me?" Erik asked, also in Hakki.

Holding back a sigh and her eye roll, she stepped aside.

Sophie approached and handed him a lit candle, which he carried down the steps with him. A few breaths later, his voice floated up. "It's clear, come on down."

Adina scampered down the ladder, the others following behind. The root cellar was nearly a quarter the size of the cottage. Shelves clung to the walls, filled to the brim with more of those glass jars filled with various fruits, some of which Adina was familiar with and others, like the plums, she was not. Several burlap sacks filled to the brim were piled in a corner. Erik's candle cast flickering shadows around the room.

Yes, this would be acceptable for the day.

Sophie stood above them and pointed to a circular latch two hands wide in the center of the door. "To lock and unlock the door, just turn this handle like so." She turned it a quarter turn to the right, and four bars shot out, one in each direction that would hold the door down and prevent it from being pulled open. She turned it a quarter turn to the left, and the bars retracted.

"Interesting." René squinted at the contraption for several heartbeats before reaching up to spin the dial himself. "I've never seen such a contraption." He nodded to himself, a grin spreading across his face. "Whoever invented this is brilliant."

Sophie thrust her shoulders back and gave them a knowing grin as she curtseyed. "Thank you."

"You built this?" His slack jaw and wide eyes were comical.

Adina snorted. He'd walked right into that one. "There are no court engineers or metallurgists out here, René," she said.

Sophie nodded. "Quite so." She yawned and met each of their eyes. "Very well, then. Good morning, all. Sleep well."

As the door closed overhead, René latched it, then shook it hard for good measure. "I think we're safe enough. I didn't see any way to undo this from the outside."

Which was the point of a secure panic room, of course.

"It sure is nice of Sophie to let us stay here," Madalina said as she snuggled down against Sigfried in the back corner. "Quit worrying, everyone. We'll be safer tonight than we will be for many more nights to come." She closed her eyes.

Lead pooled in Adina's gut. "Do you know something you're not saying?"

Madalina gave her a sleepy half-smile but didn't bother to open her eyes. "Always, but most of it isn't relevant to our current situation. You're worrying too much. Go to sleep."

René grabbed one of the bags of flour and hauled it over until he was directly underneath the trap door. Placing the sack against the wall, he situated it like a pillow and lay on his back, staring up as Hana settled in beside him. Adina could practically see the gears in his mind working as he puzzled out Sophie's latching system, doubtless for use on his own estate.

Erik settled against the one corner that wasn't covered with shelves and patted the ground beside him. "Come join me?"

She sat next to him, shoulder-to-shoulder. Leaning to the side, she nudged him with her elbow. "So, want to tell me why you were waiting at the edge of the clearing instead of back where we agreed?"

He turned to face her, his blue eyes piercing her soul. "Do you think I'd let you go into danger without doing everything possible to ensure you were safe?"

She raised her eyebrow at him. In the firelight, with the way the stray lock of hair was curling on his forehead, it was impossible to be annoyed at him. She resisted the urge to flick the hair out of his face and forced a frown. "From my perspective, it seems like you may not trust me to handle myself."

"Is that what you think?"

"Keep it down over there," René muttered. "And, if you're not using it, give me the candle. The lighting over here stinks."

Adina pressed her lips together. Sometimes, René could be so self-centered. "Come get it yourself."

With an overly dramatic sigh, he pushed off the floor, snatched the candle from Erik's hand and settled back in his original spot.

Erik stroked his finger down Adina's jawbone, bringing her attention back to him. "Don't be upset. I nearly lost you twice the night we found the Bone Shard Blade."

Adina swallowed and licked her lips as she fought to not shift her weight uncomfortably. "And I had to watch you thrust your arm into the fire." Until his flesh had cracked and peeled. "You don't see me getting all overprotective."

He glanced at René before tilting his head until his lips brushed against her ear and whispered, "The next time, we may not be so lucky, and that thought terrifies me. It's not that I don't trust you. It's just..." He swallowed. "I don't want to lose you."

She snuggled in close to him and laid her head on his shoulder, straining to speak past thick vocal cords. "I don't want to lose you, either." She squeezed his forearm, now fully healed from the burn after several nights of successful hunts. Glancing up at him, she winked, overcome by a sudden surge of exhaustion that marked the ascension of the sun outside. "But try to rein in that overprotective streak a little bit, okay?"

His chest bounced once as he chuckled dryly. Leaning his head against hers, he whispered, "I'll try, but I make no promises."

The next evening, Adina opened her eyes to pitch blackness. The scent of sandalwood and earth surrounded her.

Right. They were in a root cellar, having eaten actual *food* last night, cooked by a mortal who'd mistaken them for human. At some point tonight, they'd have to throw it up and clear their stomachs before the food started to rot.

What a bizarre situation.

Erik shifted and pulled her closer.

She adjusted her head on his shoulder and took a deep breath.

More sandalwood filled her nose and she smiled. He smelled so good. "Are you awake?" she whispered.

He groaned and kissed her forehead. "Good evening. How do you feel?"

She opened her mouth to mention the cramp in her stomach from the food but paused. Her gut felt fine. In fact, she should be slightly Hungry from the effort her body expended to retain the dinner they'd eaten last night. But she didn't need to hunt at all, nor was her stomach uncomfortable. Something was going on.

"Oddly, fine," she said with a frown. "You?"

"The same." He swallowed audibly. "I don't think Sophie is who she seems to be."

Indeed. Her stomach churned as an acidic taste rose in the back of her throat. "Do you think she's a mage of some sort?" That would explain how she'd been able to spot Adina even though she'd been cloaked in shadows at the time.

"Almost certainly," Erik said. "The bigger question is, what does she get out of aiding us?"

"Maybe she somehow knows who we are or what we're doing, and wants to help us avert another Cataclysm?" Sophie hadn't been too thrilled about the weather, that's for sure. Perhaps she understood what was going on at a deeper level and had opted to stand against Sujani and Maja in her own way.

"Whatever the reason, we should be cautious," Erik said. "Even if Madalina considers her trustworthy."

Adina paused. She wasn't quite sure how much credence she gave to Madalina's stars. Especially when it came to their unlives.

And it was extremely disconcerting that she didn't need to expel the food she'd eaten last night.

A *snick* sounded, followed by a quick flare of light as René re-lit the candle. "What are you two lovebirds whispering about?"

Adina blinked her eyes against the sudden intrusion of light.

Erik cleared his throat. "We were noticing how we don't seem to be suffering from any ill effects from eating human food last night. And how we weren't Hungry. How are you feeling?"

René was silent for several heartbeats, the muscles of his face twisted in thought. "Huh." He pushed himself up until he was seated and turned to face them. "Well, that's weird. I feel totally fine." Throwing an uncertain glance up at the trap door, beyond which Sophie presumably waited, he continued, "The only time I ever ate food as a vampire, I barely went an hour before the urge to expel it became overwhelming. When I went to sleep last night, I remember thinking how well I was managing to keep it down. Now, I feel good. Better, even...I feel like I fed from two comely—"

Beside him, Hana stretched and rolled over.

"—two of Hana's blood bags," he amended with a quick glance in her direction.

Adina held back a snort. René was going to have to drastically alter his womanizing lifestyle if he hoped to remain with Hana. It made her feel warm and fuzzy inside to see their relationship blooming. "Yes, that's exactly how I feel, too."

"I told you, the stars are her friends," Madalina's voice pulled their attention to her and Sigfried in their corner. Madalina was sitting upright, looking for all the world like she'd been awake for hours.

"Did you know this was going to happen?" Adina asked. "That the food wouldn't hurt us?"

Madalina shook her head. "Not specifically. Just that she wouldn't harm us."

Hana pushed herself up. "I don't know about you, but I'd love to learn how to be able to make food like that."

Adina raised her eyebrow. "Do you think you could?" Even if Sophie agreed to apprentice Hana, the required magic may well be beyond her reach.

Hana chuckled, and with an exaggerated expression of mock offense that reminded Adina of René, placed a hand against her chest. "You doubt the Poison Master's skills?"

Adina bit her lip hard at the image of Hana as a gourmet chef. "Looking to branch out into another specialty, are you?"

Hana smiled back. "What is food, if not another type of poison to our kind?"

Well, when she put it that way... Adina shrugged. "I suppose. Maybe when all this is over?"

Hana nodded. "Frankly, as one of 'only three vampires with enough magic in their blood to resurrect a god'—"

Adina shivered as Hana parroted Damon's words from the night Sujani had resurrected Maja. The fine hairs on the back of her neck and arms lifted.

"—I'm surprised you don't want to learn."

Shaking her head emphatically, Adina frowned. "No. Not me. Potions and herbalism have always been your field." She wrapped her hand around her sword's grip to counter the sudden chill in her gut. "I prefer the simplicity of cold steel." At least a sword was straightforward in how it killed.

Hana flashed her a soft smile. "Sorry," she whispered.

Erik said, "We'd best be going. We need to find the Gaelle De Guignes, and that's not going to happen if we allow ourselves to be waylaid."

René met each of their gazes in turn. "Everyone ready?"

Adina nodded.

He climbed the ladder, grabbed the hatch with both hands and twisted. The four bars rotated, retracting into the locking mechanism. With a deep breath, he pushed the door open and stepped into the cottage.

"Good evening!" Sophie's voice floated downward. "You slept all day. I hope you're well-rested?"

René's footsteps thudded across the wooden floorboards above. "Cut the crap, lady. We know you know what we are. Why are you helping us?"

Erik slapped his hand over his face as Adina's stomach plummeted. This wasn't at all how she'd expected to confront their host. Curse René and his brashness.

Hana's face paled in disbelief. Half a heartbeat later, she scrambled up the ladder so quickly that, if Adina didn't know better, she'd think Hana had co-opted some of René's Talent for speed.

Adina grabbed Erik's arm and headed for the exit. "Come on, we better get up there."

"Please forgive him," Hana said, turning to Sophie. "His social skills leave a lot to be desired. What he *meant* to say," Hana's voice drifted down to them as Adina scrambled up, "was thank you for your hospitality and that we were wondering why you decided to help us."

Sophie leaned against the wall in the corner of the cabin that served as the kitchen, with her blue apron wrapped around a simple yellow dress that reminded Adina of a golden sunset. She looked exhausted.

Hana's glare had silenced René. The couple stood in almost the exact center of the room. René's slumped shoulders and frown was the most apologetic Adina had ever seen him. He turned to Hana. "A lot to be desired?"

She glared at him again, nodding pointedly to Sophie.

Behind Adina, Erik and the others climbed into the room.

René sighed. "Apologies, lady. Apparently, I spoke out of turn." He gave her a courtly bow and said through clenched teeth, "I appreciate the hospitality and would be forever grateful to learn why you decided to assist us last night."

Sophie's gaze danced over all of them before landing on René. "I helped you because for a talented group of vampires, it seemed to me like you could use all the help you could get."

Adina exhaled forcefully. Wasn't that the sad truth?

Behind her, Erik mumbled, "You have no idea."

"Despite Lord d'Bayeux's social faux paus," Hana said, "we are truly grateful to you. But we must be on our way."

Sophie nodded and glanced toward the door. "Best to get started early, then, to cover as much ground as possible." She gestured with her chin to a pile of wineskins sitting in the middle of the dinner table. "I made these for you today."

Adina stepped forward, searching Sophie's exposed skin for cuts or other wounds. She didn't smell any other mortals about, but six bags worth of blood was a lot for one human to lose at once. Sophie should be pale, well...*more* pale, than she already was. It was amazing she managed to remain on her feet.

Grabbing one of the bags from the counter, Adina released the cap and took a deep breath. It smelled like fresh blood. She took a drink. It effervesced in her mouth and down her throat like Hana's. Nodding to the others, she tied it to her waist. "Thank you. This is...very generous." Almost too much so, for someone they'd just met.

Hana stepped forward, her eyes wide and jaw slack. "I've never encountered another who can preserve life essence in bags like I can."

Sophie's eyes sparkled as a faint smile tugged at the corners of her mouth. "Take care of them. I have a feeling you'll need these before the end."

"Indeed." Erik buckled the blood bag to his belt and brushed his hands off on his pants. "Thank you again, lady. Your hospitality was very refreshing. I truly hope we meet again."

Sophie's eyes sparkled. "I have a feeling we will, knight. And I look forward to it."

Erik put his hand in the small of Adina's back and ushered her to the door. Sigfried and Madalina followed.

Adina paused at the edge of the deck and glanced across the clearing, peering into the shadows between the trees. "Do you think there's anything to what she said about bandits and worse on this road?"

Erik shrugged and jostled his sword. "Possibly. But we can handle a troop of bandits, especially if they're stupid enough to try to take on a group as heavily armed as we are."

Fair point. Still, something niggled in the back of her brain that she couldn't quite put her finger on. She scanned their surroundings for signs of reflecting eyes or worse, the shadow of the wraith moving between the trees. Nothing caught her attention.

"The smoke smell is stronger tonight," Madalina said.

"Yes, but that could mean anything," Erik said as he marched down the path from the cottage to the trail. "Most likely, it's just that the wind has changed."

Adina glanced up at the haze-covered moon. It didn't seem any hazier than it had been last night, despite the worsening smell. She was probably just being paranoid, and the last thing the group needed was her jumping at shadows.

Somewhere in the distance, an owl screeched in frustration.

Adina flinched, her hand itching to draw her blade.

The trees loomed tall overhead, pressing down from above as they rejoined the trail. The hairs on the back of her neck prickled as she peeked over her shoulder. The cottage sat quietly in the middle of the glade, its picturesque water wheel sitting motionless on its side. A series of candles inside cast a warm light through the windows as the clearing disappeared behind the trees and foliage. A stray breeze rustled the dying flowers on the porch.

"Does anyone feel like we're being followed?" Adina asked.

Sigfried shook his head. "I do not smell anyone."

Well, that was half a relief. "Would you be able to smell the wraith through this smoke if it was following us again?"

Sigfried stopped in the trail, his facial muscles contorted with thought. "No..." he said. "But I do not remember smelling the wraith before."

Erik studied her. "Do you want to stop and wait to see what comes?" His knuckles went white as he gripped his sword grip. "I trust your instincts. If you feel like something's here, you're probably right."

She studied the path behind them. As tempting as it was to not leave a potential enemy at their back, they had little time to waste waiting for pursuers that may just be figments of her imagination. She shook her head. "No, but let's not linger. Can we see if we can get to Pierrevalle quickly? Cover as much ground as possible?"

Sigfried adjusted his stance. A heartbeat later, his muscles and tendons snapped as his bones rearranged themselves. In the space of two breaths, a giant grizzly bear stood in his place. He knelt while Madalina scrambled onto his back.

Settling herself just above his shoulder hump, she glanced at them. "We're ready. Let's fly like the eagle."

Adina and Erik lengthened their strides as Sigfried lumbered down the path. Bears could cover a significant distance quickly, and his ground-eating pace had Adina and Erik jogging to keep up. The rhythmic clanking of Erik's armor settled Adina's nerves as she let her mind drift to other things.

Such as dragon bones and ley lines.

The moon had climbed to its pinnacle in the sky when Erik held up an arm to signal the others. "Hold up! I need to slow down, or we'll have to hunt before the sun rises."

Adina pulled up beside him, grateful for the momentary respite even though she didn't need to breathe. She winked at him. "You know, it'd be easier to run if you left your armor behind."

A warm glimmer sparked in his eye as he poked her in the shoulder. "No one would recognize me without my armor."

She opened her mouth to deny it but paused. Back in Brachia, right before Damon and Sujani destroyed the keep, the first time she'd seen him without his characteristic trappings, she hadn't recognized him. But that felt like ages ago.

She sat on a boulder and pulled off one shoe, shaking out a rock that had worked its way in. "Yep. Without that tell-tale clank every time you took a step, I'd have no clue."

He chuckled and a little of the pressure lifted from her shoulders. She'd happily live out her unlife striving to make him laugh like that every night. Its rich timbre was a caress. But first, they had to stop an evil goddess and save the world.

Lead settled in her gut, pulling her shoulders forward as the forest pushed down on them from above. She sighed. The reality was they were unlikely to succeed, so their remaining time together was limited.

They'd come to rest at the top of a small hill. A slight orange glow lit the horizon to the north. "What's that?" she asked, pointing. It looked almost like a sunrise, but it wasn't in the correct location, and it was far too early.

Her three companions turned to where she was pointing.

"That must be Pierrevalle," René said.

After a few heartbeats, Madalina added, "It's further away than it looks and will likely take us another night or two to reach."

Adina rolled her weight back on her heels. For being so far away, it was awfully bright. The capital of Champeaux must be huge.

Madalina, still seated astride the Great Gray Bear, tilted her head back to study the night sky. "There's a storm rolling in. It'll reach us before we reach the city, I think."

A storm? Adina squinted at the hazy but cloudless sky. Well, with Sujani and Maja about, anything was possible. Perhaps the storm would bring some much-needed rain to the countryside. It was good they had kept their oiled tarps instead of abandoning them at the border like she'd wanted.

"No," Madalina said, shaking her head as she studied Adina. "I don't think it's that kind of storm."

Adina sighed. Of course it wouldn't be anything so straightforward. Hitching her pack slightly higher on her shoulders, she glanced at Erik. "Well, in that case, I think we should try to cover some more ground before it hits. What do you think?"

He nodded, adjusting his armor. "I think I would be up for moving on. The sooner we find The Gaelle De Guignes, the more likely we can prevent another Cataclysm." His gaze strayed to Sigfried and Madalina. "Thank you for the breather. Let's continue to Pierrevalle."

Chapter 7
Sujani

Sujani stood outside the door to Maja's suite. It had been three nights since he'd figured out how to protect them both while she healed. Three nights!

She hadn't called for him, sought his counsel, or asked anything from him. Him! Her high priest!

A few of the mortals who served on the estate had entered and exited, seeing to her needs. They brought her food, arranged baths, everything she would need as she regained her strength.

But Maja hadn't summoned him.

His stomach churned. Surely, she wasn't upset with him. After all, she knew he always had her best interests in mind.

Being apart from her while she was so close was worse than any hell she could condemn him to. His heart ached, even as it lodged in his throat as he raised his hand to knock on the door. His knees went weak at the thought that the goddess might cast him from his position as her high priest.

He blinked and steadied himself against the door.

What if she replaced him with...one of the mortals?

Shaking his head, he inhaled deeply through his nose and out through his mouth. No. She would never do such a thing. He loved her and had literally dedicated the entirety of both his life and his unlife to her existence. She would not punish him so.

Taking another deep breath, he knocked on the door.

Silence.

His heart thudded against his ribs.

Surely Maja would not ignore him?

Knocking again, he asked, "My goddess?"

Still no response.

He glanced up and down the hallway. Fortunately, no one was around to witness him being left standing outside her door. Putting his hand on the latch, he said, "Maja? Are you okay?" Waiting only half a heartbeat, he turned the handle and pushed the door open.

An empty bed covered in a brocade duvet with matching curtains hanging above the bedposts stared back at him. The air-and-lightning manacles were nowhere to be seen. Maja was not in the chair by the hearth, nor by the window where she could gaze out over the city.

His manacles had failed... He shook his head as his gut hardened and turned to lead. He should've taken the time to hunt down the appropriate Moonlight Orchid essence for his binding spell, to make it as strong as possible. Out of season or not, a perfumery somewhere in the city should've been able to get him a sample for the right price. But Damon could've arrived at any moment.

Stepping inside the room, he pulled the door closed. He clenched his jaw as his heart jumped, threatening to beat its way out of his ribcage. Blood rushed through his ears.

This was Damon's doing. Somehow, some way, he'd kidnapped the goddess from her own chambers. He was the only one strong enough to have gotten through the blood wards.

And right underneath Sujani's very nose.

He squeezed his hands into fists until his fingernails carved crescent-shaped cuts in his palms. The scent of his own blood calmed his breathing and brought focus to his frantic thoughts.

He must not jump to conclusions. It was much more likely that Maja was bathing in the adjacent bathroom. After all, she wasn't a vampire like him, and could be active during the day. It was likely she was getting ready to retire for the night.

Which would explain why she hadn't responded to his knock—she hadn't heard it.

Stepping another foot into the room, he pitched his voice so it would carry into the bath suite. "My goddess?"

Still no answer.

He closed his eyes and listened.

No sound of splashing water or other noise indicated the bath was occupied. He would hate to walk in on her, but it would be worse still if she were in trouble.

Or kidnapped.

He steeled his spine against the butterflies in his gut. As her high priest, it was his duty to check on her, to confirm her wellbeing. If she was angry, he would promptly plead for forgiveness, at least knowing she was safe.

His footsteps echoed across the room. He stepped around the rug, encouraging the noise, to warn her he approached.

Pausing right outside the open archway, he cleared his throat. "My goddess?"

Still no response.

He stepped into the bathroom.

The space was empty. His blood turned to ice. The scented oil and shampoo he had delivered especially for her sat, unused, on the rim of the tub next to clean folded towels.

She hadn't bothered to use any of the luxuries he'd gone to such great lengths to procure for her.

Running his hands over his hair to smooth it away from his face, he turned in a circle, studying the suite.

Damon couldn't have taken her. His wards were still intact...unless the other vampire had figured out some devious way through the spells and wall of hardened air without destroying them.

By the mages...if Damon had figured out how to do such a thing, his power indeed eclipsed Sujani's. He needed access to more of Maja's blood, or his adversary would defeat him when next they met in battle.

Lifting his robes, he turned and fled out the door.

"Charles!"

He ran down the hall toward the suite Charles had claimed for himself, the one that still smelled faintly of Erik when the two of them had roomed together before Baron Arthur's passing.

Using his Talent to fling the door open as he approached, Sujani stuck his head inside. "Charles?"

No response.

This was becoming a disturbing trend.

He pinched his lips together and gnashed his teeth.

"Sujani, what's wrong?" Charles jogged up the hallway, pausing at whatever he saw in Sujani's face.

"It's Maja—she's disappeared! Damon must have taken her!" Sujani wiped a hand down his face, as though the gesture would help calm his pounding heart.

Charles put a hand on his shoulder. "Are you sure? Perhaps she's out in the garden admiring the stars?"

Sujani furrowed his brow. To his knowledge, Maja hadn't left her room since her awakening. She was too weak. He swallowed past the tightness in his throat. "Perhaps you're right." After all, as she recovered her strength, she would hardly want to stay locked in her suite.

Even though it was the safest place for her.

Charles squeezed his shoulder in sympathy. "Come on, my friend. Let's go find her. I'm certain she's fine. She is a goddess, after all."

He nodded. Charles had a point...despite her frailness, Maja was a powerful goddess. She could take care of herself, even with the likes of Damon.

And yet...

"My gut tells me something's wrong," he said as they speed walked through the hall. His chest burned, as though he couldn't get enough air into his lungs. "I've learned to trust my instincts."

"As you should. But before we lose ourselves to panic, let's do a thorough search." Charles closed his eyes, his face contorting in concentration. A handful of heartbeats later, he opened them and met Sujani's gaze. "The staff are looking for her, too. If she's on the estate, it should be merely a matter of moments before they find her."

Sujani flared his nostrils with each breath as his heartbeats piled up as he stared at Charles, waiting for some word.

The silence stretched and became heavy.

Charles' relaxed expression tightened until his lips pressed into a thin line as his gaze drifted off into the distance.

Sujani grabbed his arm. "What? What is it?"

Charles shook his head. "They cannot locate her. No one has seen her for the last two days. She's not in the gardens or the kitchens. The staff assumed she was resting in her suite and didn't want to be disturbed." He blinked, turning his attention back to Sujani. "You're certain no one got through your wards?"

Sujani scoffed. "Yes. They are impenetrable. Even for the likes of Damon." But the words fell flat. Like himself, Damon had always been a master innovator, pushing his abilities to the next level.

Or...

Sujani shuddered.

Or, Maja had left of her own accord.

Hardened air and a few blood magic wards would do little to keep her somewhere she didn't want to be.

But that was unfathomable. Of course she would want to be with him. He could provide for her, keep her safe, and help her consolidate her rule.

Charles stared at him, eyebrows raised, clearly expecting a response.

Sujani shook his head. "I'm sorry, what did you say?"

Charles cleared his throat. "I said, do you think Maja may have left on her own?"

"No, that's ridiculous. Everything she needs is here."

Biting the insides of his lips, Charles nodded as he studied the floor. "Very well, then. Suggestions?"

"Clearly, Damon has her. He's cunning and may have convinced her to leave the premises as bait to draw me out."

"Hmmm. Possibly." Charles stroked his handlebar mustache. "If Damon has any hope of thwarting our plans, he'll need the Bone Shard Blade."

"Indeed."

"And, if he can't steal yours..." Charles let his voice drift off and raised his eyebrow.

"He can't. It's safe, somewhere he'll never find it."

Charles nodded at the confirmation. "Then he'll have no choice but to forge his own, if such a thing can be done."

The tension in his chest released. "Yes. You're right, of course." This was another reason he kept Charles around. The man had a gift for cutting through to the heart of a problem. Sujani curled his index finger around his chin. "This isn't easily done, though...he'd need dragon bones and a large grouping of ley lines." As the words passed his lips, his stomach plunged to the ground.

His pouch of dragon bones...the one he'd worn every day of his unlife that had disappeared the night he'd resurrected Maja. He'd assumed them lost in the chaos, but what if...

Sujani snarled, turning away with a vicious Surinian curse. "He has the bones. I'm certain of it." Curse the ancestors. "Now all he needs is the ley lines."

And a god or goddess to bind them all together.

The floor dropped from beneath his feet, and he reached for the wall to steady himself.

Damon was more on top of the situation than he'd assumed. If he didn't figure out where Damon was holding Maja quickly, Damon would forge another blade and kill her, undoing everything he'd spent the last twelve hundred years planning for.

He couldn't let that happen—he wouldn't survive losing Maja again.

Turning his attention back to Charles, Sujani brushed his hands down his robes. "We need to make a list of all the possible places he might take her."

Charles frowned. "How many places can hold a goddess who doesn't want to be contained?"

"Not many, but Maja is nowhere near her full strength." And who knew what sort of blood magic Damon had at his command to aid him.

The hardened air ward vibrated.

Sujani's senses snapped to alert. Someone was trying to get into the estate.

Charles perked up at Sujani's shift in body language. "What's wrong?"

"Someone knocking at the front door." Well, technically, someone trying to sneak in the servant's entrance, but that was an inconsequential nuance. He waved Charles down the hall. "Come on. Let's go see who it is."

Perhaps Damon was coming back to try something else? But beyond kidnapping Maja, what else was there to do? It wasn't like this estate had a suitable location for forging a new Bone Shard Blade. Doing so in such close proximity to him was also the height of stupidity.

And as much as he may wish it, Damon wasn't stupid.

Sujani's shoes slapped across the cobbles as he and Charles crossed the courtyard to the servant's quarters.

The tiny houses were dark and claustrophobic. And they stank of mortal sweat and terror.

Perhaps he should've been more subtle in his actions when he'd first arrived. But the humans were insignificant, their lives passing in a blink. Tomorrow, no one would remember what he did today.

Pulling Charles against the wall, they scooched forward, hidden in shadows.

Just outside the fence line, a ghostly figure hovered several hand-widths off the paving stones.

Sujani blinked. A shadow wraith.

He hadn't seen one of their kind in...well, a millennium.

The specter lifted its skeletal hand. Nearly translucent rags, or flaps of skin, hung from the gaunt bones. Resting its hands against the shield of hardened air, it pushed.

The vibrations spread across the air like ripples in a pond. Almost like the wraith was trying to contact him.

Alright. He'd play.

Raising his eyebrow at Charles, he nodded for the other vampire to hang back. It was always prudent to keep an ace in the hole. He wasn't sure if Charles' mental powers would work on a wraith, but hopefully they wouldn't have to find out.

He stepped into the moonlight and up to the other side of the hardened air wall. "Yes?"

<You are Sujani?> The wraith's mental voice ran shivers up his spine like nails on slate.

Drawing himself up to his full height, he crossed his arms over his chest. "I am."

<I am Viktor Knoll.>

The blood mage who tried to kill Adina in Brachia. Sujani blinked as the corners of his lips hardened. He fought back the urge to bare his fangs and snarl.

Viktor nodded. *<Damon made me into a soul slave.>*

Sujani's stomach contracted, sending a bitter aftertaste into the back of his throat. "That magic was forgotten..."

<Not by those it should have been.>

Sujani blinked, being sure to keep the satisfaction that spread through his veins from his face. "For trying to kill my granddaughter and thwart my plans, you deserve your fate."

Viktor shrieked, the mental talons of his voice shredding Sujani's skull.

Half a heartbeat later, the sensation was muted as Charles slammed a metal barrier over his mind.

Viktor muttered a string of words, but through the mental shield, they were too muffled to make out.

Sujani raised two fingers and gestured to Charles.

The barrier lifted.

"Say that again," he said. "And if you scream at me one more time, we're done here."

<Damon betrayed me and cursed me to this fate. Then he forced me to banish my love, who I brought with me into death.>

Sujani froze, a primitive instinct long silent screamed in the back of his mind. Brought into death...

"Are you a necromancer?"

Viktor's ethereal robes drifted in a nonexistent breeze as he nodded, patiently waiting for Sujani to put the pieces together.

Sujani locked his knees before their sudden weakness betrayed him. A blood mage *and* a necromancer, at Damon's beck and call. No wonder he'd been able to kidnap and hold Maja so easily.

<As the enemy of my enemy, we could be allies, for we both want Damon dead.>

Raising an eyebrow, Sujani studied Viktor from his toes to the tip of his head. "You're his soul-slave. What makes you think I'll believe anything you have to say?"

<I'll give you this.> He reached into his pocket and held his fist between them.

Opening a small hole in the hardened air, Sujani reached through.

Viktor dropped a ring into the palm of his hand.

It was gold, set with a sapphire so ancient it had been carved before faceting had become popular. Sujani blinked as his throat choked closed. Rings capable of creating a soul slave were rare—almost as rare as those who at one time practiced the magic. He raised an eyebrow and studied Viktor. "You managed to steal your own soul-slave ring?" Damon wouldn't normally be so careless. But if that was the case, Viktor was no longer Damon's creature.

<*No. This is another.*>

Sujani chewed on the inside of his cheek as he studied the jewel. The possibilities of having his own soul-slave were intriguing. Perhaps, Maja... He'd have to consider that further. Sliding it into his pocket, he nodded. "You have my attention, and potentially, my assistance. What do you need?"

Viktor nodded. <*I will share information, but you will need to act on it.*>

Sujani nodded. "Agreed." After everything provided was suitably vetted, of course. He waved Charles forward. "And you will take us through your memories of the soul-binding spell, detail by detail."

As the other vampire stepped up beside him, Sujani tilted his head toward the wraith. Charles nodded.

He'd peek into Viktor's mind and make sure the wraith was telling them the truth.

Viktor glanced back and forth between the two men. <*Agreed.*>

Charles stared at Viktor. He flinched and scrunched his nose. After several heartbeats, Charles turned to Sujani, scratching the back of his head. "That's some ritual, Sujani. Are you sure you want me to share it with you?"

"Of course." *But not right this instant.*

Charles swallowed, stepping back with a nod.

Viktor drifted closer. <*Damon has the entire Assassin's Guild hunting for dragon bones while he seeks a confluence of ley lines. He's on his way to Esnaria now, to see what information his library contains on the matter.*>

Sujani inhaled slowly, in through his nose, out through his mouth.

Damon's stronghold, the capital of Esnaria, was a logical place to hold Maja until he'd gathered his resources and located his ley lines. But the rest...

"He already has dragon bones. What need does he have for more?"

The wraith shook its head. *<No, he does not.>*

Sujani glanced over his shoulder, catching Charles' eye in the shadows. If Damon didn't have them, then someone else had stolen them.

If the Assassin's Guild was working for Damon, then the alliance between his son and Damon was still alive and well. Therefore, if Septimus had the dragon bones, he would most likely have given them to Damon.

But there had been others in that cave... He narrowed his eyes. One of the young ones must have taken them, though if they knew the bones belonged to dragons, or what they needed to do to forge a Bone Shard Blade, he was at a loss.

Some tension between his shoulder blades released. If the children had his bones, then they were likely out of Damon's reach for now. As long as Damon didn't realize they had them, Maja was safe.

The chances of Damon managing to locate additional dragon bones this long after their extinction were miniscule. And the children would never locate one ley line, never mind enough to perform the ritual, even if they had the knowledge and skill to do so.

At least that bought him time. Time to find and rescue Maja.

Curse Damon.

"Where is he holding Maja?"

Viktor drifted closer. *<Who?>*

He held his hand up to indicate her height. "The sun goddess. Blonde, tan skin. Likely very weak." Especially if she was in Damon's clutches and he was doing mages-knew-what to keep her powerless until he could forge another Bone Shard Blade.

The wraith shook his head. *<I have seen no one by this description in his presence.>*

Sujani sighed, his shoulders drooping. That meant nothing except that the wraith wasn't as privy to Damon's secrets as he'd hoped. It seemed Damon was being smart and keeping Maja a secret, even from his servants.

Still...any inside information was better than none. Sujani eyed Viktor. Perhaps Damon's luck had finally run out.

The first thing he needed to do was eliminate Damon's resources—his allies and their workforce. "Can you take a message to Septimus? I'd like to make him and the Assassin's Guild an offer they can't refuse."

Viktor drifted closer. And, beneath his ghostly cowl, Sujani could've sworn he saw the faint shadow of a smile.

Chapter 8
Damon

Viktor hovered in the air in front of Damon in the hallway of the quaint roadside inn Damon had commandeered yesterday. If the mortal owners still lived, they'd certainly have been terrified at the sight of a wraith hovering in their main hall minutes after sunset. He wiped a speck of dry blood from the corner of his lips. Fortunately, that was no longer a concern.

<They are on the northeastern road through Champeaux. They head toward Pierrevalle.> The wraith's mental voice echoed through Damon's mind sending prickly shivers up his spine. *<The fires are to the east and north, moving fast. Unless the weather turns, they're heading right into them.>*

Dammit. Damon ran his fingers through his hair, ripping it away from his face. Wrath was a blasted bear, by the gods...surely between his animal instincts and little Madalina's precognitive powers, they'd be able to avoid the wildfires.

He studied Viktor. Clearly, the wraith didn't think so highly of the pair's abilities.

"What's in Pierrevalle?"

Viktor didn't answer, but the question had been rhetorical, anyway. Pierrevalle contained nothing except a bunch of poofed-up court-bred patsies who were so obsessed with their gold and appearance that they ceased to have any importance to the rest of the world. Especially now that Marcos was ended. There were no dragon bones or ley lines there.

Unless Adina and her friends knew differently, and he'd written Champeaux off too quickly.

Curse the mages.

He kicked the floor, his boot scuffing the old hardwood.

But he couldn't go to Champeaux now, when he was already halfway to Esnaria.

Damon spun on his heel and paced across the spacious room, lost in thought. Viktor hovered by the door, practically forgotten.

No. Esnaria was still the better bet, with his resources and connections there.

He needed an update from Adina as soon as possible. It was unfortunate Seven was too busy coordinating the Assassins Guild to babysit his daughter and her friends.

He tapped his fingers against the bar counter, his nails clicking across the wood that had been polished smooth by decades of spilled ales and dirty hands.

Viktor hovered into Damon's peripheral vision. *<Send me, master.>*

"What?" He did a double take. "Say that again?" Never once had Viktor volunteered to do anything for him. And, having had his precious Joan liberated less than a week hence, he was unlikely to start anytime soon. What was the old necromancer-turned-blood-mage up to?

<Send me, Master. I will watch them and make sure they're safe.>

Damon scoffed, waving the wraith away and turning to face the hearth. Viktor must think him stupid. "You're a wraith. What can you do if they get caught in a fire?"

<I am also a necromancer,> Viktor said, relentlessly floating back into Damon's line of sight. *<There is no shortage of dead I could make use of.>*

Damon paused. What would Sujani do when faced with an undead horde that wasn't bound by Charles' commands? After all, zombies obeyed only their creator.

And Damon controlled the creator.

He studied Viktor again. The wraith might be on to something.

But not right now. Later. The zombies could serve as a distraction, right before Damon plunged the Bone Shard Blade into Sujani's heart.

He sneered, followed with a bark of laughter.

Adina could wait for a while longer. Holding up a finger, he whirled on Viktor. "No. Not now. I need you to keep an eye on Sujani and Maja, so we'll know where he is when it's time to strike. If you can discover where some dragon bones or ley lines are in the interim, I'd consider that a stunning success and will reward you accordingly."

Viktor bowed and dissipated into thin air.

Damon rubbed the palms of his hands against his pants and settled his trademark cloak over his shoulders. The night was still young. If he set out now, chances were good he'd hit the Esnarian border well before sunrise. From there, it was just a two-day's jaunt to the capital, and he could start his search for the ley lines in earnest.

Perhaps, if he got lucky, Seven and the Assassins Guild would come through on the dragon bones before he arrived.

Two nights later, Damon marched up to the main gate into King's City, the Esnarian capital. It had been several years since he'd last visited, but not so long that the city guards had forgotten him. The head guard at the gate paled before bowing and waving him through.

Head held high and cloak flapping behind him, Damon marched up the streets of the market toward the castle. His castle, regardless of what the mortals living in the lower circles of the city believed.

This early in the morning, the only person moving in the market was the baker. The smell of warm bread wafted across the vendor stalls, almost drowning out the stench of manure, piss, and the general reek that went wherever large groups of mortals congregated.

His footsteps echoed off the cobbles and the surrounding walls. One thing he could say for sure about Esnaria—things were made to last. Every building, every road, was made of stone and brick. Sure, it made for loud streets during the day, but it had been over a millennium since he'd been out and about when the sun was up. It also made walking much less treacherous than when the dirt roads were rutted. A quick burst of pride spread through him.

This was his city. Had been his for a millennium, and, if he managed to dispense with Sujani and Maja, would be the seat of his empire for another thousand years to come. The castle, sitting proudly on top of the small hill in the middle of town, beckoned him home.

Eventually, with the vendor stalls behind him, Damon ascended the incline and stopped before the castle gates. The portcullis was down.

The portcullis was never to be closed, except in the event of a siege.

He spun around, evaluating his surroundings as his gut twisted.

There was no army, no sign of distress in the city. No extra guards patrolled the streets or, as far as he could see, the walls of the castle itself. No oppressive weight that would indicate a problem.

What was going on here?

He stepped up to the gate and peered into the darkness. Taking a deep breath and pitching his voice so it would ring off the walls, he called, "Hello?"

A shadow moved in the darkness. A stray flicker of light reflected off a silver helm. The guard stepped forward until he was just out of Damon's reach. He stood at attention, somehow managing to look down his nose even though Damon was two finger-widths taller than him. "The castle is closed. You may return after sunrise, like everyone else."

The faint irritation that burned in his stomach boiled over. Damon reached for his Talent and flung it at the stupid mortal who dared to refuse him access.

Him! The true ruler of Esnaria!

The moment his characteristic stench reached the guard's nose, the man froze.

A heady rush of power filled Damon.

It was good to be immortal, with power the humans could only imagine.

As soon as his Talent latched onto the man, Damon stared into his eyes and said, "Open this gate and let me through."

The full-bodied scent of the human's fear only elevated Damon's malicious enjoyment.

Moving clumsily, as though his actions were not his own, the guard stepped to the side and cranked a couple of levers. A heartbeat later, pulleys and chains in the darkness above groaned and the gate lifted.

Once the portcullis was high enough he wouldn't need to stoop to fit beneath it, Damon strode through. Turning, he faced the guardsman who had presumed to forbid him entrance.

"How dare you try to keep me from my own castle."

The man's eyes bulged as his nose flared. His throat convulsed as he swallowed.

"Let this be a lesson to the others," Damon hissed. Swinging his hand in a horizontal arc, he sliced the guard's throat with his nails. Licking the blood from his fingertips, he sneered at the man bleeding out at his feet. "It's too late for you, though."

With a sharp spin of his heels, he marched into the courtyard. Catching a passing stableboy by the arm, he pulled the youth up short. "Inform His Majesty that Damon has returned. I will be meeting with him tomorrow as the sun sets."

The youth stared at him with wide eyes for a breath before belatedly bowing. "Of course, m'lord. Shall I give His Majesty your surname?"

Damon's upper lip curled in a sneer, revealing his fangs. "Damon is all he needs to know."

The youth bowed and scurried off as fast as he could.

The pressure of the impending sunrise prickled the skin between his shoulder blades. He should still have plenty of time to get up to the suite he kept in the northern tower before falling dormant.

He strode through the foyer with its white marble floor and its columns and flying buttresses adorned with crimson and gold banners. Whoever thought it wise to put white marble in the entry to a castle was an idiot. But, keeping it clean was neither his problem nor concern.

His boots echoed off the floors as he strode through. Most of the servants scurried out of his way, either from past knowledge or good instincts. After his encounter with the guard at the gatehouse, he was in no mood for further mortal shenanigans tonight.

They'd probably discover the dead man right about the time he fell dormant. Which was fine with him. That was also something that would not be his problem.

It would be amusing to see how the castle reacted when he awoke tomorrow evening. When he received his explanation for why the mortal king had sealed his castle without permission.

Reaching the northern staircase, he took a deep breath and started climbing.

At some point over the last few years, someone had laid a crimson runner up this particular set of stairs. Its padding made climbing the stairs more comfortable, for certain, though without the echo of his impetuous footsteps, the stairwell seemed oddly empty.

His veins burned with the strain on his muscles as he ascended to the seventh floor. Dust littered every surface here. The only rooms on the top floor in this wing belonged to him. When he was away, it appeared the staff was lazy with the maintenance.

That would change tomorrow, too.

Stepping up to the one door at the top of the stairway, Damon rested his hand against the knob with a sigh. Tension released between his shoulder blades.

There was no place like home.

Now that he was back, no one, not Septimus, Sujani, nor even Viktor could bother him here unless specifically summoned.

With his first true smile since Sujani had resurrected Maja, he pulled the door open and stepped inside. The wards he'd painstakingly laid at the beginning of his rule snapped into place with a faint zing of energy that buzzed over his skin. They dulled his senses slightly, but ensured he was safe from all magical attacks.

The room was exactly as he'd left it. A down-filled bed with heavy brocade curtains filled one corner of the room opposite the cold hearth. Two windows faced south, but he'd had them filled in with stones from the nearby quarry centuries ago.

Moving toward the closest window, he inspected the mortar for cracks or other signs of weakness. Finding none, he moved to the second.

Satisfied that structural maintenance had not been neglected for his rooms as the cleaning had, he shucked off his cape and tossed it over the chair by the hearth. Turning to the door, he pulled it closed and grabbed the locking mechanism—a central dial that, when turned a quarter turn to the right, extended three beams to brace the side and top of the door against the frame. No one would be able to open the door without removing the entire wall, and he'd wake well before they managed that, if the mortals of the castle were stupid enough to try.

With one last smirk at the door, he pulled off his boots and crawled into bed to let the sun take him.

The following evening, Damon awoke to the sight of black brocade draped overhead. His vision and tactile senses were still muted courtesy of the wards, but nothing appeared out of place.

Not that he'd been worried. The royal family had been solidly under his heel for the last ten centuries, after all.

Rolling to the edge of the bed, he dangled his feet over and pulled on his boots. He strode to the door and turned the latch one quarter rotation to the left. The locking beams retracted with a loud clank. His wards collapsed and full awareness rushed through him with the tingling pain of a limb that had fallen asleep. Taking a deep breath and enjoying his renewed sensory acuity, he pushed the door open. Pausing, he glanced over his shoulder at the cape.

It still lay where he'd tossed it last night. He wasn't planning to leave the castle today, so there really was no need for it. But the king knew it was made of human skin, and its presence made the old royal extremely uneasy. With a quick grin, Damon snatched the cloak and fastened it around his shoulders.

Every little bit helped to remind King Reginald who was truly in charge. With one final glance around his suite, Damon pushed the door closed behind him. It slid into place with a soft click.

The king frequently held court in the evening, so Damon headed to the throne room, even though he was not in a mood for tittering nobles, bards and any other sort of entertainment the current royals favored.

Several minutes later, Damon stood in the entryway, staring at the vacant room. The dust-covered throne sat alone on its raised dais. No acrobats or jugglers danced around. No noble ladies batted their eyes at him from behind their fans.

Where was everyone? It seemed good old Reggie hadn't held court here for several weeks. For whatever reason, the king wasn't doing his job in Damon's absence.

His stomach twisted. This must have something to do with why the portcullis had been closed last night.

But if Reginald had known things were not as Damon expected, at a bare minimum he should have sent a servant to escort Damon to wherever the king awaited their meeting.

He'd have to put the man in his place.

Now he just needed someone to lead him to the king.

He peered in each direction down the hallway. There wasn't a single servant to be seen, which was odd, considering how busy the castle normally was.

Well, he definitely wasn't going to waste his night wandering until he happened to come upon the errant royal. And if the servants wouldn't come to him, he'd have to go to them. The kitchen—mortals always congregated around food, and a castle as big as this had many mouths to feed. He'd find someone down there who knew where the king was.

He bared his teeth and snarled in frustration. Otherwise, he'd slaughter the lot of them.

After far too much wasted time, he found his way down the appropriate staircase and was met with a blast of heat from the ovens. Several mortals bent over large bins of water, washing dishes. The last platters of leftovers sat on the central butcher block, left out for whomever wanted them.

His gut twisted. *Yuck.* Human food.

One of the washing girls noticed him as his feet hit the bottom step. She glanced up and performed a half curtsey before glancing over her shoulder. "Um, cook?"

A rotund little man with the stereotypical white hat and an apron that at one time probably matched the hat exited the pantry and regarded him from bottom to top. The man's face was vaguely familiar, so he must have been in the king's service for quite some time.

The cook's face paled. Blinking, he bowed so quickly he nearly fell forward. "M'lord. How may we help you?"

The corner of Damon's mouth turned up at the tremor in the man's voice. His fear was, of course, appropriate, especially given Damon's mood. "Where's the king?"

The cook's forehead wrinkled as he glanced around the kitchen in confusion.

Damon's temper flared. "I know he's not here, you idiot. Where is he?"

The man's throat contracted as he swallowed. He cast his eyes to the ground before Damon's feet. "Likely in his bedchambers, m'lord. Been there the last fortnight."

Damon frowned and did a quick mental tally. Had so much time passed already that the current king was ready to die?

Hmm. Well, that was inconvenient, but Damon certainly wasn't going to do anything to stop it. One didn't create vampires on a whim, and Reginald certainly didn't deserve the honor.

Damon stabbed the cook with his gaze and flashed his fangs. Letting his mask slip a little, he gave the mortals a glimpse of the monster that lived beneath his skin. "You will appoint someone to take me there."

The faces of the kitchen staff paled, and all looked away, trying to be as innocuous as possible.

The little round man swallowed again as he glanced around the room, noting their reactions. Brushing his flour-coated hands off on his apron, he stepped forward with an awkward bow. "It would be my pleasure, m'lord. Please, follow me."

The heat drained from Damon's blood as he followed the cook through the myriad of hallways and staircases up to the royal chambers. He shouldn't have intentionally terrorized the servants in his fit of temper. They weren't important enough to spend the effort on, and they'd have helped him regardless. Servants were trained to obey, after all.

His emotions were making him reckless. He was expending energy and effort on mortals who meant nothing.

He took a deep breath and released it as the tension drained from his shoulders. No...his true ire should be reserved for King Reginald.

To his credit, the cook was only slightly out of breath by the time they stopped in front of two large doors. Guards stood ready at either side. Fortunately for them, they weren't stupid enough to point their swords at Damon, though the glares they sent him were almost as bad.

His guide bowed to the guards. "M'lord Damon, here to see the king." His introduction complete, he bent forward again and scuttled out of the way.

The guards studied Damon as the cook's hurried footsteps faded down the hallway.

Heat bubbled up in Damon's chest and his fingers twitched with the urge to snap both the guards' necks. Clearly, he needed to come back to visit more often. People here were forgetting to fear him. But if he killed everyone who annoyed him tonight, very few would be left to run the government, and the seat of his future empire would fall into ruin. So instead of slicing their throats, Damon grabbed a thin tendril of his Talent and wafted it toward both men. "Announce me and let me pass."

Both men froze as his Talent grabbed hold of their minds. As one, they opened the doors before him. "Your Majesty," the one on the right said, "allow us to present Lord Damon."

Damon stepped into the room and was immediately overwhelmed with the stench of sickness and death. He scrunched his nose against the smell.

The mortal king, who had once sat so proudly on his throne, now lay in his bed a wrinkled, diminished old man, several decades older than Damon had expected. The parchment-thin skin around his face drooped to highlight every ridge and valley of his skull. Thin strands of white hair that had once been so black it almost looked blue spread across the pillow in a chaotic explosion. His sallow skin hinted at a long battle with death that would soon be coming to an end.

A servant rinsed a rag in water and placed it on the king's brow.

Damon had blinked and years had passed. He'd have to be more careful in the future.

Spearing the servants who attended their liege with his gaze, he spat, "Out. All of you."

A young man who was dressed far too well to be a servant leaped to his feet. "No! Go stuff yourself, you have no right to order us around."

Damon bared his fangs at the impertinent youth who couldn't have more than a quarter century behind him. His crimson tunic and gold sash were embroidered with the royal crest. The crown prince, then.

Reginald weakly raised his fingers and opened his mouth, but Damon was out of patience for the night. Grasping a generous handful of his Talent, he sent it toward the brash young man, making sure to catch all the servants with the rebound. "You will leave. Now!"

The mirror mounted to the wall across the way vibrated with the pitch of his voice.

The prince's eyes bulged, and he ground his jaw as, against his will, Damon's Talent forced him to march from the room. The servants meekly followed.

As the doors clicked shut, Damon grabbed a convenient sword and shoved it through the handles, effectively locking the doors until he removed the weapon. Dropping his hold on the prince and servants, he turned to the king.

"Finally. Alone at last."

King Reginald opened his mouth to say something but coughed instead. After several rasping breaths the attack abated. He grabbed the rag the servant had placed on his forehead and dabbed the blood at the corners of his mouth.

Damon held back an eye roll. Waiting for Reginald to say anything was going to take forever, and his time was short as it was. Extending a filament of Talent toward the king, he sat at his side. "No need to talk. Think loudly. I'll hear you."

<Have you come now, at the end of my days, just to taunt me?>

He scoffed. "Hardly. I'm here to raid your library." Technically, *his* library, but semantics. "I need everything your librarians can find on divine resurrection, the Cataclysm, ley lines, and forging divine weapons. And I need them tonight." The sooner he started researching, the better. "Or the world will suffer a second Cataclysm, the likes of which your son likely won't survive."

<My grandson, you mean.>

"What?"

<The boy you kicked out. My grandson. His father died several years ago in a hunting accident.>

Damon blinked. The youth had seemed too young to be Reggie's boy, but personally, Damon didn't care about Reggie's son's death or his grandson's age. He couldn't even remember the dead prince's name.

<You'll have to write the missive.> The king feebly waved his fingers against the comforter. *<I'll sign it on the condition that you leave my grandson out of your schemes.>*

Damon stood and went to the desk, pulling out a clean sheet of parchment and ink. "I have no interest in your heir, unless he can provide me information on resurrection, forging divine blades, ley lines or the Cataclysm." At least, not at the moment. Once he became king, however, that was a different story.

The spark of intelligence in Reginald's eyes told Damon he understood the same.

<Being born into this family is a curse.>

Damon tipped a small bit of sand over the parchment to absorb the excess ink then shook it to the ground. "Being born mortal is a curse."

Reginald coughed. *<Perhaps.>* He lifted his hand as Damon slid the parchment underneath it and placed the quill in his fingers. With a groan, he rolled to the side to peruse the decree. The scratch of his quill across the bottom was wobbly and uneven, but legible.

Reginald's signature was barely recognizable to what it had been half a century ago, but such was the curse of age. Damon ripped the paper away the instant the king's signature and seal was affixed.

<Now, I have very little time left. I would like to spend that which remains with my grandson. Send him back in.>

Damon's hackles raised at the order.

Reginald stared at him with an expression of infinite patience that didn't match the acidic tone of his thoughts. *<You have interfered and manipulated me long enough. Now, leave a dying man in peace and pray that you never find yourself in my situation.>*

Damon studied the king, his strong muscles atrophied away until he couldn't even sit up by himself. Pitiful. "My enemies would end me long before I turned out like you." Rolling the parchment into a scroll case, he saluted. "Reggie, good luck in the afterlife. I suggest you spend your remaining time praying to whatever gods you hold dear that I'm successful." And the knowledge that Damon was responsible for his grandson and kingdom's very survival was all the revenge he needed against the bitter old king.

Damon freed the sword barring the doors and threw them open. The servants, ever loyal, were waiting just down the hall. As was the young crown prince.

Walking past the guards as though they didn't exist, Damon left the doors swinging open behind him and headed down to the library. It was time to make the royal librarians earn their keep.

Later that morning, as the sun was about to rise, Damon climbed up the last flight of stairs to his rooms, a headache pounding away between his temples. Using his Talent to control the entire library staff to speed along their research had been incredibly draining, but a team of twenty researchers telepathically conveying what they read was much more efficient than letting them work at their own pace.

And the results had been worth it. He now had a couple possibilities for ley line confluences, as well as a legend or two about dragons he could forward on to Septimus for the Assassin's Guild to investigate. He would dig into the ley line possibilities tomorrow.

But if he was going to spend another day like today, the first thing he needed to do upon awakening was feed.

Finally reaching his door, he threw it open, stepped through and yanked it shut behind him. Spinning the circular latch to the right, the deadbolts swung into place and secured the door against intrusion for the day.

With a big sigh, he kicked off his boots, hefted his legs up onto the bed, and tumbled backward, closing his eyes. He didn't even bother to untie his cape from around his neck before the darkness took him.

His left foot was burning. It started slowly at first, like someone holding a match too close, but quickly spread until the searing pain ripped him from his slumber.

He ripped his eyes open, blinking against bright light that had no reason to be in his room that was both built to withstand and warded against the sun. Throwing his arm up over his eyes, he pulled his cape over his face just as the thick brocade drapes were ripped aside.

He hissed as sunlight spilled across his bed. His foot, which had been laying in a beam, burst into flames. Rolling away, he tangled his legs hopelessly in the comforter, landing on the floor face-first. His nose cracked, sending shooting pain across his face to rival the flames eating up his leg.

The cloth smothered the fire, leaving behind the diminishing pain as Damon instinctively directed life energy to heal the damage.

He'd drained his Talent reserves so much yesterday; it would be of little use to him today.

Blinking, he fought to clear his blurry vision as much as his sleep-fogged mind.

A silhouette moved in the light.

By Ahion! Maja had come for him.

His stomach hardened as his heart thudded against his chest so hard it hurt. Heat exploded beneath his skin.

He wouldn't go down without a fight.

Mustering what little Talent he had left, he hurled it at the figure.

There was nothing for his mental abilities to grab onto.

It was foolish of him to waste time trying to mind-control a deity. He shook his head, trying to force his thoughts into a coherent stream.

Something flickered in his peripheral vision, and he dropped prone as a blade swung through the air where his neck had been half a heartbeat before.

Since when did Maja use a sword?

Falling to the ground put him directly in a sunbeam. The skin on his face and arms sizzled. He screamed, rolling away. His lips and cheeks cracked and peeled at the movement.

Digging deep for the magic that lived in his blood, he shunted it to his palm, where it coalesced into a crimson fireball. Peering through burnt eyelashes, he searched the light for his assailant.

The quick patter of footsteps sounded to his left.

He hurled the globe of energy toward the noise. It burst against something hard—likely the stone wall—and exploded.

His assailant sprinted away from the detonation, tumbling into a somersault, and bouncing up right in front of him.

Damon blinked, willing his day-fogged brain and eyes to clear.

He was too exposed, his thoughts too muddled.

What he needed was a weapon, a way to fight back.

The *snick* of metal through the air hurled toward him. Throwing himself into a barrel roll, he leaped above the sword that parted the air where his ankles had been. Flaring his legs, Damon's right foot caught the other person across the face with a satisfying crack.

The silhouette rolled across the room.

Maja would have ended him by now. She wasn't one to toy with her opponents.

Which meant this was someone else. Someone who was stupid enough to attack him in his own stronghold.

Stupid. Or desperate.

Damon bared his fangs as he hurled another crimson ball of magical energy toward his foe, but it impacted the stone floor. He'd let himself become complacent, too weak to fight off an attack in his own home. "Who are you and what do you want?" he snarled.

That was a foolish thing to ask. Obviously, his assailant wanted to introduce him to Final Death. There was no other reason to knock holes in the wall and expose Damon to the sun in the middle of the day.

His wards should have prevented this whole thing.

His wards...

Damon shook his head in another attempt to clear the cobwebs. Had his spells been active last night?

He didn't remember.

His chest compressed as spots danced across his vision. A bitter, acidic taste burned at the back of his throat.

No. He couldn't panic and lose consciousness now, or he'd be true-dead.

Curses. He screamed and lunged for the bed, sitting squarely in the middle of a sun beam. Grabbing onto the closest post, he ripped it free of the frame and stumbled out of the light before his skin had a chance to do more than sizzle.

He'd regret that move later, no doubt. But at least now he had a weapon, and a chance of surviving. "Too cowardly to face me at night with honor?" His light-dazzled eyes scanned the blurry shadows of the room for movement as his heart caught in his throat. The weight of the oversized staff was reassuring in his hands as his chest heaved in and out at the exertion. "Let's see how you do now that I can defend myself, too."

A shadow skittered off to his right.

Damon swung the staff as fast as he could, for once in his unlife wishing for Marcos' Talent to slow his opponent's movements.

But he had killed Marcos, and there was no other vampire like him. More was the pity.

A sword came out of nowhere and bit into his side. Stabbing pain, as though he was being fileted, spread from his ribs out across his chest. His knees went weak at the sensation.

Dropping one hand from his improvised staff, he wrapped his arm around the blade, trapping it between his waist and his inner elbow. The weapon cut deep into his bicep and forearm. Jerking his torso, he ripped the sword from his opponent's grip.

Relaxing his hold, the sword dropped to the floor. He kicked it away with a viscous half-smile. Now he knew where his assailant was.

Swinging the staff over his head like a morningstar, he swung it around, ignoring the scream of pain as he stretched the severed muscles across his ribs. The club slammed into his opponent's gut. With a satisfying thump, the force of the blow sent the mortal stumbling across the room. He landed against the wall with a crack and a high-pitched groan.

Damon grinned. That groan hinted of youth. He'd bet a bucket of rat's blood his opponent was none other than the young crown prince himself. A burst of energy flooded through his trembling muscles, a second wind. "Foolish boy. Do you truly think you can take me on and survive?"

Steel scraped against stone as the prince used his sword to brace himself as he regained his feet. "It's worth the risk to free my family from you!"

Damon blinked. If he focused hard enough, he could distinguish the young prince, a lighter gray buried within the darker shadows of the wall by the hearth.

He strode forward. One final blow to the gut should disable the youth while he fed. For daring to attack him, the prince's lifeblood was forfeit.

Damon took a deep breath. The heady scent of the youth's fear brought a small measure of clarity to his mind.

The boy lunged, kicking Damon's staff so that it banged against his injured side.

Damon gasped, dropping the weapon. The wooden pole clattered to the floor with a thump. No matter. Now that they were both unarmed, he had the advantage.

Moving faster than he could track, the prince kicked again, catching Damon's ankles and knocking him onto his back.

He slammed into the floor, his head bouncing off the stone with a snap that echoed between his ears. His vision went white as the splitting headache radiated from his no-doubt cracked skull. The air exploded from his lungs.

The prince loomed above, arms extended as if to choke him.

Foolish mortal. Vampires didn't need to breathe.

Damon kicked him in the groin, lifting him over his head and throwing him into the center of the room. Scrambling after the boy, keeping his elbow tight against his injured rib, he pivoted his hip and slammed a left hook into the prince's side. A rib snapped beneath his fist and the royal gasped as he dashed away.

He grabbed the boy's hair and yanked, pulling his head up and exposing his neck. The arteries that pulsed just under his skin were tantalizing. Damon's peripheral vision blurred until all he could see was the faint pulse beneath the prince's skin. Their heartbeats synchronized as his vision tinted red.

The youth struggled, his fingers clawing across the stone floor, desperately trying to gain purchase.

Damon's fangs elongated and he pulled back his lips.

With a groan, the mortal spun, swinging his reclaimed sword in an arc toward Damon's neck.

The shriek of steel through the air hurled right for him. He released his grip on the prince's hair and raised his arm over his head.

The sword cut deep into his right forearm, lodging itself in the bone. With a scream, Damon wrapped his good hand around the blade and ripped it away from its bearer.

His own blood spouted from his hand as both edges of the blade sank deep.

The floor tilted sideways. If he didn't end this soon, he'd pass out from blood loss.

Damon shook his head. Enough of this. "You're a dead man," he growled, blinking.

A shadow on the ground in front of him crab walked backward.

Two unstable steps later, Damon stood above the prince, sword raised overhead. With a scream, he plunged it down into the boy's stomach.

The prince screamed.

A warmth spread through his body as he stood above his opponent, triumphant. Baring his teeth in a victorious grin, he ripped the blade from the mortal's gut before it could do too much damage.

The blood on the tip of the blade smelled divine. As his assailant writhed on the floor at his feet, he licked the blood from the blade.

The faintest hint of life effervesced in his mouth, bringing with it a small bit of clarity to his sluggish thoughts.

Reaching down, Damon grabbed the prince, tangling his fingers in his hair, and hauled him to his feet.

The front of the prince's pants turned wet, and the pungent stench of ammonia assaulted him.

Ugh! He wrinkled his nose in disgust.

He glared at the prince's pallid face. Round eyes that showed white all around stared back at him. "No...please," the mortal whispered.

Damon didn't deign to respond. The foolish boy had sealed his own fate when he decided to attack him.

Pulling the prince's neck to the side, Damon selected the largest blood vessel and bit down.

The warmth of life flooded through him, dulling each of his aches and pains as the youth's struggles grew weaker and weaker. The crack in his skull faded into nothing, taking the raging headache with it. The gaping wounds in his hands, arm and side stopped bleeding as the skin repaired itself. Finally, the blackened blisters on Damon's legs faded away, leaving healthy, pink skin.

As the corpse turned cold, Damon dropped it, leaving it where it landed. An acrid aftertaste stuck to the back of his throat.

With the influx of life energy came greater clarity. His wards were indeed not active, but they hadn't been destroyed. Some of the tension between his shoulder blades released. At least they could be reactivated. The two windows that he'd had bricked off so many centuries ago had been knocked open, allowing the sunlight to stream into his room.

His room. The one place in the entire world where he should've been assured of his own safety.

He glanced at the door, which remained latched shut.

So how did the prince get in?

It wasn't feasible to scale the exterior wall to knock the windows in, nor was there any debris scattered around the room to indicate such. And Damon wasn't about to stick his head out in the sun to confirm debris on the ground below, but its presence was a safe assumption.

The entry method must have been magical, then.

Damon swallowed. That would explain the aftertaste in the back of his throat.

He studied the prince's corpse as a glimmer of respect bloomed in his chest. Somewhere in the castle was a mage with enough power to deactivate Damon's wards and somehow teleport the prince directly into Damon's room. All while keeping the knowledge of their existence secret from him.

He'd never known anyone or any spell that could teleport. Except for Septimus with his control of shadows.

He blinked as his thoughts stuttered to a halt. And now that the prince was dead, it was going to be a thousand times harder to locate the mage responsible for this.

Curse the mages.

He paused. If Sujani could transfer his Talent to Charles, perhaps Septimus had done the same to this mage?

He shook his head. No, Septimus was too smart to betray him so obviously. Besides, from the smug expression on Charles' face, the amount of power needed to do such a thing was likely far outside Septimus' ability.

But if Sujani could transfer his Talents to others, as the only other First Vampire, Damon ought to be able to, as well.

He sighed. Well, that was two problems for later tonight.

His priority needed to be reactivating his wards and setting up some sort of protection from the sun before the energy from the battle wore off and he collapsed into dormancy.

Stumbling over to the darkest corner of the room, he sliced his left palm and, using his right finger, traced the rune there that activated the protection spell.

The runes in two other corners quickly followed.

Three of the four power points reset, he turned to the fourth point—in the corner flooded with sunlight.

He wouldn't be able to make it over there and remain long enough to redraw that rune until after sunset. Hopefully three grounding points would be sufficient. Normally a three-point ward spell was stable, just like a three-legged stool. But with an unknown mage around, it was impossible to know for certain.

He rechecked the latch on the door. It was turned as far to the right as it would go, the beams fully extended. A quick tug confirmed it remained as securely locked as it had appeared on first inspection. Despite the presence of the sun, it was safer inside his room than out and exposed to any castle resident who may wander by as he slept.

Using his improvised staff to reach into the sun-saturated area, he pulled the comforter from the bed. It was thick enough to provide shelter from the daylight. Especially if he stayed out of the direct path of the rays.

He glared at the twin beams of light on the far side of the room. Dust from their fight swirled through, glittering like millions of tiny pixies. Tracking the projected path of the sun, he set the down-filled blanket in the darkest corner, as far away from the thrice-cursed light as possible.

Grabbing the heavy chair by the hearth, he pushed it into the corner and tilted it on its side, where it could form an additional barrier.

Laying on the ground, he tugged his cape—which was miraculously undamaged—over his shoulders and pulled his knees against his chest until everything below his shoulders was protected. The large bedspread he yanked over that, covering his head, as well.

Heat from the sun's rays still warmed the blanket and for the first time in over a millennia, he didn't feel cold.

Taking a deep breath, he closed his eyes. He brushed his hair away from his face and swallowed past the sudden tightening of his throat.

Tomorrow, he'd inform Reginald of his heir's untimely death. Hopefully the king had a spare grandchild floating around...the last thing Damon needed right now was a power vacuum in Esnaria's line of succession.

But that was a potential problem for later tonight. Until it was a confirmed issue, there was no point in stressing over it.

As soon as he awoke, he'd have the royal librarians dig further into the ley line possibilities and find the mage that had assisted the prince, taking the time to kill him slowly.

Snuggling down into his protective blankets, Damon let the sun's warmth lull him into dormancy.

Chapter 9
Adina

As the sun ducked beneath the horizon, the weight of the day lifted. Adina opened her eyes. The cave they'd taken shelter in last night was pitch black, as it should be, but orange stars twinkled in and out of existence overhead. The ever-present smell of smoke that had followed them from the moment they crossed the border into Champeaux clogged her nose.

One of the orange lights fell from the sky above—a shooting star.

It landed on her pack, where it smoldered for a moment before bursting into a small flame.

By the gods!

Lunging to her feet, she scrambled over to it and slapped the flames out.

Lead pooled in her gut as she turned her attention to the ceiling above.

To the dirt that was held in place by the large root network from the ancient trees outside.

The roots were smoldering! During the day, it seemed the fires had caught up with them. If those supports gave way, they'd be buried where they slept.

Her heartbeat thrashed past her ears as invisible bands tightened around her ribs. Heat that had nothing to do with the flames outside burst through her torso.

"Everyone, get up! The ceiling's on fire!" She slung her bag over one shoulder and snapped her bedroll loud enough that it echoed through the small cave.

Sigfried's sleep-dulled voice mumbled, "Huh, what?"

Erik was at her side in a heartbeat. He put one hand on her shoulder and squeezed as he studied the roof above.

He pulled her to her feet. "Everyone, get up. We need to get out of here. Come help me."

Rustling sounded from a few feet away as the others roused themselves.

"It really does resemble orange stars," Madalina said, her voice low with awe.

Last night, Sigfried and Erik had rolled a large boulder over the cave's mouth before they'd all fallen dormant to guarantee protection from the sun. As one, they all braced against the boulder and pushed.

The stone was hot to the touch.

"Wait," Adina said, pulling back. "The fire must be right outside." Being immolated would end them as surely as being crushed. Her heart skipped a beat as the blood in her veins turned to ice.

They were trapped.

"Personally," Erik said, "I'd rather die on my feet, fighting, than slowly be crushed to death in a collapsed cavern."

Well, when he put it that way, she couldn't help but agree.

"If we get separated," René said, meeting each of their eyes, "we can meet up in Pierrevalle."

"Sounds good." She swallowed. Hopefully that wouldn't be an issue.

She shoved her shoulder against the boulder and nodded, though in the darkness it was unlikely he'd be able to see the gesture. The heat bled through her traveling robes. "On three, then?"

"On three," he said. "Take a deep breath. One…"

"Two," Sigfried said.

"Three!" Adina groaned as they pushed.

With the snap of a support root, the giant stone rolled away from the opening and down the short hill to the trail.

Clouds of smoke billowed in, riding a heat wave that seared Adina's skin. Ash caught in her hair and latched onto her eyebrows. The stench coated the back of her throat.

She threw her arm over her face as she choked. The roar of the flames and splintering of wood was deafening. The fire stirred the air and fanned it until it ripped at her clothes and snapped her hair around her face.

The roof cracked ominously overhead, showering them with sparks.

"Come on!" Sigfried grabbed Madalina's hand. Madalina snagged Adina's as she ran by, and Adina wrapped her fingers around Erik's.

The smoke was so thick she couldn't see Sigfried, no more than five paces ahead of her. The flames tinted the entire area orange and red, casting a surreal atmosphere over the entire area. Ash clogged her nose and caked her lips.

The heat seared her, raising blisters on her arms. Another blast of superheated air slammed into her face, drying her skin and pulling it tight until it felt like any movement would rip her apart like old parchment.

She squeezed her eyes closed against the discomfort, instincts demanding she preserve her vision at all costs. The hot air scalded her nose and lungs with each breath.

She fought back the choking sensation in her throat that threatened to overwhelm her senses. The last thing she could afford right now was panic.

Trees torched around them, bursting into flames overhead. High above, the trunks exploded, unable to contain the energy of the fire.

She was in hell, and they were all going to die.

Ahead of her, Sigfried stumbled backward as the fur on his buckskin vest exploded into flame. He tumbled to the ground. Madalina's shrill scream was lost in the roaring around them.

Oh, no.

Dropping her pack to the ground, Adina ripped out her oiled canvas and tossed it to Madalina who unrolled it and slammed it over him, smothering the fire.

When Sigfried lay still, Madalina lifted the tarp. With a grateful nod, she handed it to Adina as she turned to evaluate the blistering burns covering his torso.

Adina snapped the tarp once to clear it of as much debris as possible and shoved it into her bag, not even bothering to fold it.

Erik grabbed her upper arm and hauled her to her feet, adjusting the pack on her back. "Come on, we need to go! Otherwise, we'll all burn." His face was red and peeling. The hairs of his beard and eyebrows were curled from the heat and covered in ash and char.

Madalina grabbed Adina's hand again and pulled them forward.

Stumbling blindly behind Madalina and Sigfried, Adina stepped on a branch laying in their path. It exploded in a shower of sparks that showered her ankle and leg with embers. Reaching out with her Talent, she smothered them before they could catch and set her robes on fire.

Another blast of heat slammed into them.

Madalina shrieked as Sigfried abruptly dodged to the left. A tree several paces thick slammed into the ground where he'd been standing in a flurry of sparks.

Adina pressed her lips together, ignoring the stab of pain as her skin split. If she could tame the wind, the firestorm, they would stand a better chance of surviving. Pulling on more of her Talent, she willed the air to be still.

It took an unimaginable amount of strength to summon a storm, but surely it would require less to calm one.

The air seemed to pause; a pressure settled against her ear drums as though she'd fallen into water. With a heavy pulse that pressure exploded outward, the storm abated.

She smiled as a feeling of weightlessness spread through her limbs. The wild energy was held at bay by her will and Talent alone. The sheer amount of power made her giddy. This must be how Sujani felt every time he summoned lightning.

A heartbeat passed.

Two.

Her muscles trembled as her grip on her Talent faltered under the enormous strain.

With an audible snap, the wind and flames came rushing back, as though she were the center of a vortex. It slammed into them hard enough to throw everyone except Erik to the ground.

Adina slammed face-first into the dirt and ash that covered the forest floor. Dozens of sticks and rocks dug into her, sending spikes of pain along her burned skin. She blinked the grime from her eyes.

The wind ripped at the leafy canopy above them. With a creak and snap that she felt in her bones more than heard, a section of roots pulled clear from the ground as a tree pitched toward them.

Yanking on as much Talent as she could summon, Adina formed a wall of hardened air above them much as she had when Septimus had thrown Hana's poison at Erik back in Brachia.

The tree trunk slammed against the center of her shield and rolled to the side where it crashed to the ground. One of its branches punched through the dirt, opening a sinkhole.

The earth dropped out from beneath Erik's feet. His eyes went wide as he windmilled his arms to keep his balance.

Adina's stomach lunged into her throat. "Erik!" She reached for him, willing some of René's speed to her muscles.

Her fingers brushed his metal bracer as he plunged into darkness.

"No!" Her heart leaped into her throat as her body went cold. The phantom sensation of metal against her skin and the terror in his eyes as he disappeared ripped her guts to shreds. Her world snapped into pieces with a crack that reverberated through her skull.

It was her fault—she should've been faster. Should've reacted more quickly. René should've stepped in.

"Erik!" She lunged after him.

Madalina threw herself on top of Adina. "No! Wait, or you'll fall, too."

The firestorm raged about them, drowning out the rest of Madalina's words as it battered against her shield of hardened air.

Adina belly-crawled forward, Madalina clinging to her back. "Erik!" She peeked over the edge of the sinkhole into blackness.

Something moved below.

"Erik?"

He said something, but the wind and her rushing heartbeat made it impossible to hear.

Adina ducked instinctively as another tree snapped somewhere nearby.

Madalina tapped her on the shoulder and put her mouth near Adina's ear and yelled, "He says we should come down there! He thinks he found something."

Adina shook her head. If they followed, there may be no way to get back out. Rolling to the side, she slid out from underneath Madalina. Ripping open her pack, she pulled out a length of rope.

She glanced at the tree that had punched the hole through the ground. It looked sturdy, but the outside was charred and it smoked…there was no way to tell if it was stable, or to guarantee it wouldn't set the rope on fire.

Her eyes scoured the area for René, the urge to bite off his head for not speeding to prevent Erik from falling on the tip of her tongue.

Neither René nor Hana was anywhere to be seen. Lead settled in her gut as she clawed through her memories to identify the last time she'd seen them.

It was as they were leaving the cave. She'd just assumed they were behind Erik.

"Has anyone seen Hana and René?" she asked.

Madalina shook her head. "I thought they were behind you?"

"Me, too." *God's teeth.* She bit her lip. Hopefully, they were safe.

Madalina's lips pressed into a thin line as her gaze retraced their steps. "Frere René's smart. So is Hana. They'll be alright—we'll meet them in Pierrevalle." Her voice wobbled.

Adina chewed the inside of her cheek. She hoped Madalina was right.

Sigfried's voice rang out, making her jump. "Give it to me."

She turned her attention to him, one eyebrow raised. "What?"

He gestured for the rope. "Give me the rope. If you can keep this shield up so I do not burn, I will lower you down."

Adina glanced into the hole where Erik had fallen, back at Sigfried, then tossed him the other end of her rope with a nod. There was nothing she could do for Hana or René right now, but she could help Erik.

Sigfried caught the rough line, passed it behind his back and wrapped the end several times around his left wrist. With his right hand, he held the rope taught as he shifted his weight to his heels. "Okay. Ready."

Tossing the other end into the hole, Adina shimmied over the edge into darkness.

The cavern Erik had fallen into was almost peaceful. The shield of hardened air she held in place above the opening muted the wrath of the firestorm above. Hopefully, her Talent was strong enough to protect Sigfried and Madalina until they'd investigated whatever it was Erik had found. Maybe by then, the fire would pass them by and they could reunite with Hana and René, though she doubted it would be so easy.

Blackness loomed on either side of her, giving her no indication of how big this hole was.

A flaming branch twice as long as her arm sailed through the air, landing on the ground with an explosion of sparks.

"God's teeth!" Erik said from below.

Adina glanced up, where the silhouette of Madalina's head poked over the edge of the hole. She waved. "So you can see down there!"

The fire did little to illuminate the darkness, but it was a thoughtful gesture, nonetheless.

Scrambling the rest of the way down, she planted her feet on the stone and glanced up at the hole, a tiny pinpoint far above. "Erik?" She spun around, eyes searching the shadows. "Are you okay?"

"Just fine," he said, stepping into the light.

She scanned him from the tips of his toes to his head, looking for any sign of injuries.

Shaking her head and closing her eyes, her knees went weak.

He was alright.

The world pieced itself back together. With a deep breath, she flung herself into his arms. "How are you not dead?" She waved toward the ceiling. "That's an impossible fall."

He shrugged, rubbing her back in slow circles designed to comfort. "This was nothing. My Talent has protected me from worse."

Taking a deep breath to collect herself, she stepped away.

She shook her head. "A handy skill...you can survive collapsing castles *and* bottomless pits," she muttered. A pulling sensation uncurled in her gut as the smallest bit of envy reared its head.

Oblivious, he waved her closer to the fire. "Come here, look at this." He crouched down and ran his fingers across the rock floor. "It's smooth like glass."

Adina knelt beside him. He was right—the dark floor was polished until it glistened. She pressed her palm against it and refreshing coolness seeped into her skin. "Obsidian."

She stayed in place, savoring the stone's chill that sucked the heat from her burns. "The entire cavern is this way?" That would explain the darkness...the walls were so black, they absorbed all the light.

The heat from her skin flowed into the floor as though it were ice. She sighed as the tension drained from her muscles.

She could stay down here all night and let it cool her burns. "René and Hana are missing."

Erik's gaze drifted off into the distance for several heartbeats before he shook his head. "They were behind me when we left the cave. I don't know when we would've gotten separated." He swallowed. "Hopefully, they're alright."

Well, at least they had a prearranged rendezvous location.

Several heartbeats later, her Talent jerked as something crashed against her shields. They wobbled but held.

She thrust herself to her feet, cracking the burned skin on her elbows and knees in the process. The sharp pain that flared through her limbs was a just punishment for her actions. What had she been thinking? Wasting time down here laying on the ground while her friends waited above, sheltered from the fire only by a thin wall of hardened air.

Brushing her hands off on her pants, loosing a cloud of ash as she turned to Erik. "Madalina says you found something?"

"Indeed." He led her several paces away, to a large pile of logs and branches that stood at least the height of three men. The flames from the burning stick cast dancing shadows across the stack of wood.

Adina swallowed. *Thank you, Madelina.* Though the light wasn't bright, it was certainly better than nothing.

Reaching for one of the smaller twigs in the pile, she pulled on it. It didn't move. Also, its texture was wrong. "What is this?"

She peered at it, but without more light, it was impossible to ascertain any details.

As if he was reading her mind, Erik went to the burning limb Madalina had tossed them. He winced as he approached, close enough for the heat to blast his already-ravaged face, and nudged the wood with his toe, shoving it closer to the pile.

Adina ran her hand over the logs on the bottom of the stack. They looked like wood, but felt like rock, and were much heavier than she'd expected. She raised an eyebrow and turned to him.

"Petrified wood," he said, catching her gaze. "So old, it's been turned to stone. It must have happened when this cavern was sealed off." Laying his palm against one of the bottom support beams, he continued, "I bet this is older than the Cataclysm itself."

Older than the Cataclysm? Adina blinked. She couldn't imagine anything that ancient.

Except Damon and Sujani, of course.

Dragons had been rumored to exist before the Cataclysm. "Do you think...?"

Excitement sparkled in Erik's eyes as he met hers. "I don't know...let's go get a closer look."

For the first time in weeks, Adina's heart didn't feel like a lump of lead. Grabbing one of the branches overhead, she hoisted herself up. If this was indeed a dragon's nest, perhaps they'd be fortunate enough to find bones inside. Erik followed behind her.

In her excitement, she inhaled too quickly. Her torso convulsed in a coughing attack as her body worked to dislodge the ash caught in her throat and lungs. Erik's hand rested on her back, offering support.

Several heartbeats later as she caught her breath, she asked, "Do bones petrify?" Grabbing the next branch overhead, she pulled herself higher.

He chewed on the inside of his cheek for a heartbeat. "I've never seen any, but I don't see why not."

"Do you think we could use petrified bones to forge the Bone Shard Blade?"

Erik grunted as he heaved himself over a particularly large log. "No idea. Magical rituals are more your forte than mine."

Adina blinked as she crested the pile, her lips pressed into a thin line. Why did everyone seem to think she was some sort of master mage? "I'm no expert there, either, you know."

He shrugged, the sparkle in his eye a contrast to the anxiety that was making her twitchy and irritated. "We could always ask Sujani or Damon, if you prefer," he said. "Though, I think that would give away our secret plans..."

She fought back an eye roll. It wasn't fair to be angry at him when the proper source of her ire was Sujani. Her grandfather, who had literally stabbed her in the heart and tried to steal her Talent and unlife to raise some long-dead goddess. The older vampires could go rot for all she cared.

Reaching down, she grabbed Erik's hand and helped him over the final branch until he stood beside her. The burnt skin on her knuckles split, sending little daggers of pain shooting up her arm. She re-directed a small bit of life energy to heal her burns. Thanks to their magical dinner the other night with Sophie, she had a solid reserve as long as she didn't have to heal too many more times. The tension that had settled into her shoulders relaxed, taking the edge off her irritation.

Tangling her fingers with Erik's, she sighed. "I'm sorry. I shouldn't be taking my frustration out on you. It's just, this whole situation..."

He squeezed her hand gently. "Apology accepted. I'm more than a little annoyed at Sujani and Damon myself. My father is also due a karmic reckoning." He cleared his throat. "If I could end Sujani now and spare us this whole situation, I'd do it in a heartbeat."

She nudged him with her shoulder and frowned. "Don't try it...without a solid plan and the Bone Shard Blade, you'll only get yourself ended. And then I'd have to kill you for leaving me."

He chuckled, then turned his attention to the center of the pile of petrified wood, where a depression had been scraped out, just like a nest.

Adina peered into the shadows, but the meager light cast by the flames below was insufficient to breach the darkness. She glanced over her shoulder at the burning branch so far below. No way was she climbing down and hauling that thing all the way up here.

Reaching out with her Talent, and imagining a ladle for water, she scooped up a bit of the flames.

They fizzled and flickered into darkness.

Dammit. She'd failed to hold back the firestorm, and with catching Erik before he fell. No way was she going to fail a third time in a row.

Reaching out again, she wrapped the delicate fire in a protective shield of hardened air, leaving just enough of an open space at the bottom so the flames didn't suffocate. Perhaps the shield would prevent the tiny fire from dying.

The flame guttered, almost going out. She fed more Talent to it, until her ability was equally spread between maintaining the shield of hardened air above and nurturing the tiny fireball now floating toward her.

The back of her throat tingled. Perhaps she'd burned through more of the deep reserves of life energy than she'd previously thought. She swallowed as a butterfly flittered in her stomach. With the fire raging above, they'd be unlikely to be able to hunt anytime soon. She pushed the concern away—she'd deal with it later.

"Wow, you've got it," Erik whispered in awe.

"Shhh, don't distract me," she said, keeping her focus entirely on the blazing light that was no bigger than her fist.

Like a firefly, it coasted over their heads and alighted in the middle of the dip in the pile.

"Look!" Erik pointed. Scattered gray-white sticks and shell fragments littered the floor below them.

That took care of the answer as to whether this was a nest or not. Now they just had to determine if it had belonged to a dragon, or an extinct raptor of some sort.

Or something else entirely.

Erik was already scrambling down the side and into the bowl. Adina bit her lip, turning her full attention to keeping the fireball functional.

With their first solid lead on dragon bones, they may be one step closer to forging a second Bone Shard Blade. A lighthearted feeling spread through her chest.

The sounds of stone rubbing against stone came from below as he rifled through the nest's contents. "Any idea how to tell what might be a dragon bone and what isn't?"

She shook her head, only belatedly realizing that he couldn't see it. "No idea. I'd say take anything that looks like a possibility. Maybe Sigfried can help us identify them." He knew the most about wildlife of anyone she'd ever met.

She paused. The proper thing to do would be to go help Erik, but doing so risked breaking her concentration, and then the tiny fireball would disappear.

"Good idea." He paused. "I'm just going to bring everything. Better safe than sorry."

Something twisted in her gut. Too many possibilities were almost as bad as too few. "How much is there?" They could hardly carry an entire nest full of cast-offs with them through forest and bog as they hunted for the oracle.

"Quite a bit. I think it'll take me a few trips."

Adina squatted down to wait. Maybe they'd get lucky, and any dragon bones would have a magical feel to them, much like the Bone Shard Blade had. She shook her head as lead weights settled on her shoulders. She deflated. They wouldn't be so fortunate.

Adina's head was beginning to pound from the extended use of her Talent when, half an hour later, she hoisted herself back up the rope and over the edge. Rolling away from the opening, she took a deep breath and sighed.

Erik pulled himself over the ledge right behind her.

She pulled her pack off her shoulders and emptied the bits of bone across the forest floor in front of Sigfried. Erik added his load to the pile. Adina met Madalina's eyes for a brief heartbeat then turned to Sigfried. "Any idea if any of these might be dragon bones?"

Sigfried did a double take. "Dragon bones?"

Madalina stared at them with wide eyes before turning her attention to Adina. "What did you find down there?"

"A huge nest," she answered.

"Made of petrified wood," Erik added. "It's from before the Cataclysm, I think."

Sigfried grunted and squatted down to examine the findings as the firestorm battered Adina's shield of hardened air. The worst of the flames seemed to have passed but logs still smoldered and embers continued to rain down from the canopy overhead. All it would take would be one landing in the wrong place for the flames to reappear.

She fed more Talent into their shield just as a large branch peeled off its trunk and tumbled onto it from one of the trees above. It hit the hardened air in an explosion of embers. The reverberations echoed through her body as her Talent surged to compensate for the impact.

Ignoring the chaos surrounding them, Sigfried poked and prodded, picking up each bone or shard and turning them over in his hand before sorting them into two piles.

The headache had pounded Adina's brain into mush by the time he finally stood and turned to them. He pointed to the bigger pile on the left. "These are not dragon bones...they belong to other animals." Pointing to the other, much smaller pile, he continued, "I do not know what these are. They may be dragon, or they may be a different species that no longer exists."

He picked up a long one that resembled a larger version of the long, thin bones in a bat's wing and held it out to them. "This looks like a bird. It has lots of little holes in it, but it's too big."

Adina swallowed. Unless the wing didn't belong to a bird at all...

"The holes are supposed to make the bones lighter, but these are rock now, and too heavy." Frowning, he turned to Erik. "I do not think these will make a good dagger. They are too brittle."

Adina grabbed one of the 'not possible dragon bones' and flexed it. The bone snapped in half easily. With a sigh, she tossed the shards back into the pile as her shoulders dropped. It looked like Sigfried had a point. Weapons that would break at the first sign of stress were worthless. The last thing they needed was a dagger that shattered when she tried to force it through Sujani's breastbone.

Erik reached to his waist and untied the satchel of bones René had stolen from Sujani. "Here, how do those compare to these?"

Sigfried took one of the bones from the ouch and another from the "potential" stack and held them up.

Adina held her breath as he compared the two.

Just as the tension was so thick she could barely stand it, he tossed them back into their respective piles and pointed to the bones they'd discovered. "They might have been the same at one point, before those turned to stone. But since we do not know if any of these are dragon or not, it does not mean much."

She met Erik's gaze, her own disappointment mirrored clearly in the depths of his eyes.

"Well, maybe we should bring a couple of them with us to see the oracle, just in case?" she asked. Perhaps the oracle would have a suggestion on how to make them work for the ritual.

If they even *were* dragon bones in the first place. She sighed, scraping Sujani's bones back into the stolen satchel and handing it back to Erik.

Sigfried shrugged. "It could not hurt."

"Hey, guys, look!" Madalina pointed behind them.

Adina turned to follow her gaze. A wall of orange crested the hill less than a ten-minute walk behind them, borne by a sudden gust of wind. Her thin shield of hardened air would be scant protection against a firestorm. She flared her nostrils as her heart jumped, sending her pulse racing past her ears. "We need to get out of here. Now." Grabbing Erik's shoulder, she tugged him to his feet.

Erik snagged a few of the bigger specimens of unknown origin and shoved them into his pack. Glancing around the area, he turned his attention to the oncoming fire and paled. Squeezing her hand briefly, he nodded. "Let's go."

Sigfried raised his nose and sniffed. "This way. Come on." He took off at a lope away from the oncoming flames.

Adina and the others followed behind. Her feet pounded into the dirt with bruising force that matched her heartbeat, sending up clouds of ash and soot with each step. Within a few minutes, her focus narrowed entirely to keeping Sigfried's form in sight.

Heat blasted them. Flakes of ash and other debris slammed against her exposed skin, each small burn a contrast to the constant thump of her feet as the shock waves reverberated through her body.

Maintaining the shield of hardened air all this time had left her Talent pretty much exhausted, and her headache showed no signs of letting up any time soon. The back of her throat ached and burned with Hunger, but there would be nothing to hunt until they got far outside the burn area.

Several hours later, they reached a wide river. Sigfried ground to a halt on the banks and examined the length as the others lined up beside him. The water squelched up between Adina's feet, soaking her shoes and turning the ash that coated everything to mud.

The chill of the water was a small relief, at least.

The far side of the bank was untouched by fire, though the smoke still blanketed the entire area in fog. The trees stood like ghostly sentinels that wove in and out of the mist.

"What's over there?" Madalina asked.

Sigfried shook his head. "I do not know. All I can smell is smoke."

Adina glanced at the debris-choked water. Broken and burned logs floated by, as ash obscured whatever obstacles may lurk below.

With a grunt and the snapping of sinew and bone, Sigfried shifted into a bear. His fur was singed on the tips with large patches missing. Madalina climbed onto his shoulders before he plunged into the sludge.

Adina stepped back a pace as the ripples lapped the shoreline. She glanced at Erik. "I suppose finding a bridge is out of the question now, isn't it?"

He chuckled and gestured to his armor and gave her a rueful grin. "I assure you, I would've preferred that option." Taking a deep breath and stepping into the river, he waved to her. "I'll see you on the far side."

Adina watched as he sunk deeper and deeper with each step. Approximately one third of the way across, his head disappeared beneath the surface.

At least vampires didn't need to breathe.

Bracing herself, she put her arms over her head and dove in. The water felt like needles of ice that flayed her burnt skin. She gritted her teeth and kicked her feet behind her, using the last residual bits of Talent to propel her through the water and guide her around any unseen obstacles.

After what seemed like hours but was only a few minutes later, she clambered up the opposite bank. Sitting in the tall but dry grass several paces from where Madalina and Sigfried rested, she pulled off her shoes and squeezed the mud and water out of them. If she'd had any Talent remaining, she would have pulled the water from her hair and clothes just to stop the wet fabric from clinging to her painful skin.

Glancing across the river, she waited as her heart pounded through her ears.

A head of hair plastered to his skull broke the surface, less than thirty paces away.

Adina sighed, her shoulders dropping as Erik trudged up the riverbank.

Collapsing next to her with a metallic *clank*, he gave her a relieved grin before running his fingers through his hair. "Any chance of a speed-dry?" He pulled a few pieces of stringy plant bits from where they'd caught on his armor.

She shook her head as a heavy feeling settled in her chest. "Sorry. I would if I could, but I'm on empty." If only she'd been stronger, or hadn't wasted so much of her Talent foolishly trying to control the firestorm...

If only she could be *more*, they wouldn't have to go through all this.

"We cannot hunt here," Madalina said as she and Sigfried pushed to their feet. "Sig says there will be no animals within miles of the fire."

Adina groaned, her muscles trembling at the thought of resuming their trek through the forest without being able to feed.

Erik gestured to her belt. "What about Sophie's blood-bag?"

She froze, her jaw loose. "Oh, wow. I'd forgotten all about it!" This must be what Sophie meant when she said they'd need them. Releasing it from her belt, she poured some of the effervescent blood down her throat.

A burst of energy reinvigorated her muscles as the tingling bubbles flooded her veins. Her headache dulled and the pulsing ache of her burns quieted. Tilting her head back, she poured the rest of the blood down her throat.

A few heartbeats later, as the last of her skin healed and her Talent reserve refilled, she moved the empty bag to her belt. It was heavier than it should be—like it was still full.

Frowning, she pulled it up to her face. It bulged, as though overfilled. "Hey..."

Madalina leaned forward. Her eyes widened as her jaw dropped. "Never-ending blood-bags!" She took hers out and took several deep swallows before studying hers. She burst into a grin. "It's still full. We won't have to hunt anymore unless we want to!"

Adina studied hers. The magic involved in making such a thing... If only Hana was here to give her thoughts. Her stomach clenched at the thought of the other woman. Hopefully they'd find Hana and René in Pierrevalle. They could discuss these wondrous bags then.

"Sophie is quite the mage," Erik said, shaking his head as he heaved himself to his feet. "Come on. We'd best be moving on, or we'll still be sitting here when the Cataclysm hits." He reached down to help pull Adina to her feet.

With a quick smile, she pulled the water from all their clothing and threw it back into the river.

Minutes later, Sigfried had them following a game trail that meandered along the edge of the river. With no moon or stars visible, the only thing to navigate by were the distant orange patches visible in the blackness across the river.

If she never smelled the smoke of another forest fire again, it would be too soon.

"Sigfried," Erik called from the back of the line, "do you know where we're going, or how much longer until sunrise?"

Adina blinked. She hadn't thought of that. How much time had passed? With the rush through the fire and Erik falling into the obsidian cavern, the night was kind of a blur. They'd need another place to shelter from the day soon.

The bear grunted.

"He says we are going north, more or less, toward Pierrevalle," Madalina answered. "But he has no idea what time it is, or how much longer until dawn."

Adina sighed. Great, one more thing to worry about. She brushed a muddy and matted chunk of hair out of her face. The exhilaration of the blood-bag discovery was quickly wearing off. What she wouldn't give for a bath and her comfortable bed back at Arthur's estate in The Drowned City.

Her insides twisted with a sharp pain. That particular hole in her heart would probably never fully heal. Arthur was a great man and deserved to be remembered.

The best they could hope for out here for the day was a deep cave and the ability to somehow clean themselves up before they encountered some hapless mortals and scared the life out of them.

She followed behind the bear, wrapped in a blanket of misery and cursing Sujani for starting this mess.

Eventually the dry packed grass turned into hard dirt and rocks as the game trail turned away from the river and headed up into the foothills.

Their path wove higher, and soon they were above the tree line. Breaking through the smoke was like a cool fall breeze after a hot summer's day. Scattered boulders of granite dotted the mountainside, as though a giant had abandoned a game of marbles thousands of years ago.

Adina took a deep breath, as much to clear her nose and throat of the stink as anything else. The air smelled clean, with a slight hint of mint that came from somewhere up ahead. She glanced behind them. A blanket of impermeable darkness stretched as far as she could see, laying over the land like a fluffy down blanket. Overhead, the stars twinkled and the moon glowed, as though nothing untoward were happening below.

As if they hadn't nearly all been ended multiple times tonight.

She coughed as her lungs worked to expel the ash and other debris that had coated them over the past several nights.

"Hey, Sig," Erik called.

Several paces ahead, the bear and Madalina turned around. Sigfried tilted his head to the side, looking for all the world like an inquisitive owl.

"Any chance of staying up here somewhere for the day?"

Adina nodded. Her instincts whispered that they were safe above the smoke. Even if that wasn't quite true, as the fire could technically follow them anywhere.

Sigfried huffed and made some noise Madalina didn't bother to translate before turning around and continuing their steep ascent.

Adina's legs trembled as she fought to put one foot in front of the other. Her veins started to itch as the back of her throat started to burn. This steep grade wasn't doing anything to help her Hunger. "What made this trail? Mountain goats?"

Erik snickered as he followed behind her.

Madalina turned and glanced over her shoulder. "We should keep moving. Otherwise, we'll find ourselves without shelter for the night."

"It looks like the trail dips back down into the trees, then circles around the north side of the mountain," she said as Erik came to stand behind her.

He wrapped his arms around her waist and hugged her to him, stretching his chin to rest it on the top of her head. "Indeed. Perhaps we'll find something promising down there."

She hoped so.

With a huff and a shake of his large head, the Great Grey Bear clambered up the trail ahead of them. A cool breeze ruffled his fur and blew thick chunks of Adina's dirty and matted hair across her face. She tucked it behind her ear and swallowed.

"Come on," Madalina said, waving them forward.

Adina stepped onto the path after Sigfried and Madalina and accidentally caught Erik's eye. He gave her a quick smile. She glanced away before the heat could spread from her ears to her face.

She focused her attention on both the trail in front of her and to the north, Pierrevalle. They should be able to secure lodging and a bath there, at least. Especially if they could reunite with René and make use of his connections.

Chapter 10
Sujani

"What do you want, Sujani?" Seven's booming voice echoed throughout his study.

Sujani bit the corners of his lips as he fought to keep the frown from his face. Curse Seven and his theatrics. Plastering a smile on his face, he turned.

Seven stood several paces away, his large falchion hovering in the air a few inches from Sujani's neck.

Sujani raised his eyebrow and glanced pointedly between the blade and his son. *Really?* The King of Assassins was no idiot...no sword except the Bone Shard Blade could kill him.

The ever-present shadows that lingered in Seven's presence danced at the tension in his expression. Narrowing his eyes, he glared. "You have two minutes to convince me not to gut you and go back to my own business."

Sujani frowned as he parsed the tone of Seven's words. There was hatred and anger there, certainly, but also a thread of curiosity. They may have been estranged for the last century or so, but he still knew his son better than anyone else.

He shrugged, ignoring the blade at his throat. "Why come at all, then?"

Seven glowered. "Your wraith was very convincing. He promised the visit with you would be worth my time." Stepping forward, he glanced over Sujani's shoulder toward the door. Dropping his voice, he continued, "I don't know where you found that creature, but it makes a good messenger. It would make an even better spy or assassin."

A jolt of lightning sparked in Sujani's gut and he swallowed quickly to hide the victorious smile that threatened to explode across his face. "You want him? He's yours once Damon is ended."

Seven dropped his blade, sliding it into its scabbard. The tension in his shoulder blades released. "I ask again. What do you want?"

At last, Seven was ready to listen. Which was good, because with Maja gone, there was no time to waste. "I want you to recall the Assassins Guild from their dragon bone-finding mission and to break your alliance with Damon." Seven was a straightforward person. Hopefully he would respond better to a direct approach rather than beating around the bush.

Seven burst out laughing. "Oh, really? Why would I do that?"

Sujani bit back a sigh. "Are you truly happy having your highly trained assassins doing Damon's legwork? I thought the Guild was better than that."

The flash in Seven's eyes confirmed Sujani's suspicions—his barb had met its mark.

"I'm not asking you to move against him directly." Not yet. "Just pull them back and quit helping him."

Seven crossed his arms, the gesture highlighting his biceps and muscular chest. "What's in it for me if I do?"

Sujani shrugged half-heartedly, sliding his hands into his pockets as if this conversation was no more important than discussing the weather. "What do you want? Beyond the wraith, of course. Anything at all." He winked. "Remember, I have a goddess at my beck and call, so think big." At least he would, once he rescued Maja.

Seven was unlikely to discover the small lie. If Damon was keeping Maja's presence a secret from his soul-slave, he wouldn't reveal her presence to an uneasy ally such as the King of Assassins.

"Hmm." Seven stared at him, his gaze piercing Sujani's soul. Heartbeats passed as silence stretched between them. Finally, he took a deep breath. "I want to retire."

Sujani blinked, the only sign of surprise he'd let flash across his face. "Retire?" Surely, he couldn't be serious.

Spinning on his heel and pacing the room, Seven grimaced. "I'm tired of dealing with incessant whining." He waved one hand in the air with an almost Champeauxian flare. "Who should get the prime assignments, whose partner didn't hold up their half of the job, etc. After six hundred years, I'm sick of it."

Sujani opened his mouth, but Seven whirled away and continued, "I had hoped an heir would arise to take over, but there are only two vampires competent enough to not muck everything up. Adina has made it abundantly clear she has no interest in the guild, and the Poison Master has threatened to end anyone who *dares* to nominate her for the role." The ghost of a smile pulled at one corner of his lips as he glanced at Sujani. "And it's never a good idea to anger the Poison Master."

Sujani stroked his chin with a thumb and index finger as he nodded. Indeed. Even if Hana couldn't kill him outright with her poisons, she could make him quite uncomfortable if she put her mind to it.

Right now, that was one annoyance he didn't need. He had enough to deal with already, between reclaiming Maja and ending Damon.

Dragging his thoughts back to his goal, he cleared his throat. "Do you want to fully retire, or are you looking more for a personal assistant to handle the mundane tasks?"

"I want out." Seven slashed the air with one hand. "I'm done with backstabbing cantankerous assassins and mortal nobles who don't know how to keep their noses out of each other's business. There's a desert oasis somewhere out there with my name on it, and I'd like to spend the next century or two hunting it down. But without someone competent and strong enough to keep the guild in line, they'll degenerate into roving bands of thugs and tear the mortal cities apart."

If Sujani lived another millennium, he'd never have guessed Seven wanted to leave his title behind him. Even as a mortal, his entire identity had been wrapped up in assassinations.

Perhaps he didn't know his son quite as well as he thought.

"Why not just kill them all, then?" Surely, that was a viable solution.

Seven raised an eyebrow and glanced at him, shaking his head. "I tried that in The Drowned City. At least, with the most troublesome faction. It didn't go well."

That was an understatement. And, if Sujani understood correctly, whatever happened had driven Seven and his daughter even further apart. He hadn't been too concerned at the time because the estrangement had served his purpose.

Deep in his pocket, he fingered the soul-slave ring from Viktor. If he couldn't use it on Maja, Adina would be a reasonable alternative. "If I can convince Adina to assume control of the Assassin's Guild, would that be acceptable to get you to break with Damon?"

Seven snorted. "You stabbed her with the Bone Shard Blade and tried to sacrifice her to your goddess. She's not going to listen to you."

"Perhaps not," he said, with another casual shrug. "But she will listen to Maja. The goddess of light can be quite persuasive." Especially if she was under his control.

"If you say so."

Ignoring the doubtful tone in Seven's voice, Sujani pulled his hands out of his pockets and slapped them together as if they were dusty. "Excellent. Do you have a dagger?"

Seven didn't bother to dignify the question with a verbal response as he pulled a small blade from his waist and tossed it to Sujani.

Summoning the magic in his blood—augmented with what he'd borrowed from Maja, of course—until ribbons of energy crawled through his veins, Sujani braced himself. Just as the sensation became overwhelming, he drew the knife across his palm before he returned it to Seven. Glorious pain bloomed from the cut and spread up his arm.

Wiping Sujani's blood from the blade with his pants, Seven slashed his hand and grasped Sujani's in a bloody handshake.

"By my blood oath," Sujani said, "Adina will assume control of The Assassin's Guild. I will also turn over the control of the wraith, former necromancer Viktor Knoll, to my son, Septimus, the soon-to-be former King of the Assassins."

"And I swear to withdraw my support, and that of the Assassin's Guild, from Damon," Seven answered.

The magical bond snapped between them, an ethereal crimson ribbon spearing from his chest and Seven's, tying them together in an unbreakable agreement. The energy dissipated, leaving the fine hairs on the back of Sujani's neck tingling.

Brushing a hand over his smooth head, Seven stumbled backward as the magic released him. "By the gods."

Sujani smiled, the elation of his approaching victory warmed his frozen heart. "Not the gods. By the goddess."

Seven scoffed. "Your goddess, not mine."

Sujani tilted his head back and closed his eyes. Soon, Maja would be everyone's goddess. Once he recovered her from Damon's clutches and introduced her to the world. But, until that day...

Seven's heavy footsteps echoed off the stone. "I will go carry out my half of our bargain. Be sure you can fulfill yours, Father."

Sujani flashed his fangs as Seven jumped into the shadows and disappeared. He patted the ring in his pocket. "Oh, I will, my son. I will."

Chapter 11
Adina

Two nights later, Adina stood on the edge of an overlook above Pierrevalle. She brushed her dirty, matted hair out of her face as she stared at René's hometown.

Sigfried had managed to find them places to sleep each morning, as the Champeauxian highlands were apparently riddled with caves. It would be different in the bog, though. Hopefully René or Hana would have some ideas to solve that particular problem.

The lights of the city sparkled below, reminding her faintly of the fire they'd watched from the hills above the river...twinkling lights in the darkness. The entire city was surrounded by a thick wall, with what looked like gates facing the cardinal directions. The town served as the most southern trading center in Champeaux, and would be flooded with foreigners, so at least they didn't need to worry about looking more out of place than any other travelers.

Her gaze drifted to Sigfried, still in his bear shape.

Well, most of them, anyway.

"Should we wait for René and Hana up here or try to hunt them down in the city?" she asked, her attention turning to Madalina. René would likely head right to court, both to impress Hana with his connections and to seek out the luxurious lodging that would no doubt be found there. But she and the others would want to wash up somewhere else first, unless they wanted to attract the guards' attention and get chased out of the noble quarter before they could find their missing friends.

Madalina shook her head. "I don't think we'll find Frere René in court...they kicked him out after Marcos died."

Adina's heart skipped a beat. "What?" She flinched at the unexpected sharpness of her tone. He'd never mentioned being expelled.

But of course he wouldn't bring it up...he'd consider it shameful.

"But Marcos' death wasn't his fault," Erik said. "Surely they understood that?"

Madalina furrowed her brows at him and frowned. "Have you ever tried explaining blood magic and possession to mortals?"

Erik shook his head.

"They didn't believe him." She turned to the city below. "I've never been here before, so I don't know where a logical place would be to meet. Maybe there's a central market or area for notices?"

Or at least an inn where they could order a bath and sleep through the day, but Adina didn't say that out loud. Their finances were limited, and private baths could be very expensive.

"We might be better off bathing in the channel," Erik said, as he pointed to the river that abutted the east side of the city.

"Upstream of the city, of course," Adina said. No one ever wanted to bathe in or drink water downstream of a major settlement...it would be full of all sorts of undesirable things.

Erik smiled. "The river sounds great to me." He gestured to the Great Gray Bear. "Lead the way."

Less than an hour later, she pulled herself out of the cool stream and onto the bank. It had never felt so good to be clean. The last of the smoke stench finally left her nostrils, taking with it the urge to glance over her shoulder for approaching flames. Running her fingers through her hair, she plaited it in a long braid down her back.

Using a small filament of Talent, she pulled the water from her hair and clothing. The globe of water floated through the air until it hovered above Erik's head, where he still stood, waist-deep in the water. With a dramatic *pop*, it exploded, raining water and pulling several strands of hair into his face.

She laughed, feeling lighter than she had in days. Her limbs and body felt practically weightless, as if she could float over Pierrevalle's walls and into the city itself.

"Hey!" Erik's eyes sparkled as he slapped the water, splashing it in her general direction.

Madalina climbed up onto the bank beside Adina, gathered her hair into a ponytail and squeezed the water from it.

Adina whipped a small bit of Talent her way and pulled the rest of the water from Madalina's hair and clothing.

Madalina flashed her teeth in a bright grin. "Thanks."

The Great Grey Bear hoisted himself onto the bank. Snorting at the women, he braced himself.

"No, Sig, don't do that here!" Madalina said, holding her hands in front of her face as she turned away.

Adina pulled up a wall of hardened air just as he shook, spraying water in every direction in a twenty-pace radius. The drops lashed Adina's shield and rolled harmlessly to the ground.

Erik's warm chuckle heated something deep in Adina's core and she couldn't help the smile that spread across her face as he climbed up the embankment to join them.

Collapsing to the ground beside her with a metallic *clank*, he braced his forearms on his knees and glanced at her. "Well, that certainly does feel better."

Adina nodded at him as she pulled the water from his clothes, paying special attention to the leather straps that held his armor together. His hair looked so cute, the way the water made it curl into ringlets, so she left it wet. With a flick of her fingers, she sent his ball of water splashing into the middle of the river.

"Hey, you're not going to dry my hair, too?" he asked.

She winked at him, a playful smile teasing the edges of her lips. "I like the way it looks as it is."

Leaning toward her, he pushed his fingers through his hair then snapped it back and forth in an imitation of Sigfried shaking the water from his fur.

The tiny droplets splattered Adina before she could raise a shield. She laughed as she shoved him. "Cut that out!"

His eyes were molten as they met hers. "Make me."

Tiny currents of lightning ran up every nerve in her skin at the emotion behind those words.

Sigfried cleared his throat, the sound far too human coming from a bear.

Heat flooded Adina's face as she studied her feet. Now was hardly the time for biting. She glanced at Erik, who winked at her.

Later.

Like, maybe when they were in the city and had secured a few rooms at an inn.

"We should probably get going if we want to find something before the sun comes up," Madalina said, pushing herself to her feet.

Adina went to stand, only to find Erik before her, holding out a hand. His strong fingers closed around hers, helping her off the ground.

Brushing a few lingering pieces of dried grass from her clothes, she studied the wall. "So...what's our goal once we get inside?" René and Hana could literally be anywhere if they weren't welcome at court.

"Frere René wouldn't stay just anywhere," Madalina said, catching Adina's eye. "He'd stay on the edge of the noble quarter...as close to court as possible, but not so close that he'd be noticed by the mortals who expelled him."

Adina nodded. That definitely sounded like René.

Madalina turned her attention to her husband. "It's time to change. We will have a lot harder time sneaking a bear into the city than we will you."

Sigfried huffed, either in annoyance or laughter, it was hard to say. But a few snaps of bone and pops from his tendons, and he stood before them once again a vampire. Rolling his shoulders as he tilted his head from side to side, eliciting several cracks, he studied them. "Maybe find an inn for the day? Then look for René tomorrow?"

Madelina threaded her fingers through his as she stared up at him. "I think that would be a great idea." Swinging their interlocked hands forward and back between them like children bursting with energy, she led the rest of them toward the city walls.

The inside of Pierrevalle was much like the inside of any Hakkian city, with the exception that almost everything was made of stone and wood rather than adobe and carved sandstone. With only a few hours left until sunrise, the main streets were empty except for the occasional guard patrol.

Unfortunately, the lack of people didn't diminish the overwhelming smell of so much humanity crammed into a small space. The marketplace still contained the faint scents of warm bread and cooked meat, but outside the four square block area, the stench of rotting debris and excrement ruled the night.

Adina wrinkled her nose. She missed the clean breeze blowing across sand dunes beneath a clear night sky.

Erik pulled them to a stop at one intersection. "So...do we want a tavern, with its increased chance of learning something about the city that will help us locate René, or would we like a quiet inn with less chance of being disturbed during the day?"

Adina shrugged. "With enough coin, I would suspect either would be safe enough, as long as we aren't in a neighborhood where flashing said money would make us targets."

Erik nodded. "Good point. The noble quarter, it is." He glanced down both streets and chose the one that took them toward the castle, perched high on the hill overlooking the city.

Madalina made a show of patting her pockets. "If we're going to stay in the expensive inns, that'll run though our remaining gold very quickly."

Adina chewed on the inside of her cheek as she patted her purse, tied to her belt and hidden inside her robes. As much as she hated to admit it, Madalina had a point. She caught Erik's eye. "Maybe on the edge of the noble quarter, and instead of two rooms, just the one?"

He nodded, patting his sword. "Sounds prudent. Plus, it's easier to defend one location."

There was more to the world than battle strategy. And none of them would be doing any defending when they were asleep. "It's also cheaper," she said, wincing at the bite in her tone. It also meant she and Erik weren't going to get their night alone together to take a break from the stress of trying to save the world. She sighed.

The dirt-packed streets gave way to cobbles beneath their feet.

Madalina pulled them to a stop in front of a building with a sign above it with a large tree. "How about this one?"

Adina studied the facade. "The Grand Oak. Hmmm." It looked clean, and just nice enough to be acceptable for the neighborhood without being so ostentatious as to draw the wrong type of attention. Being on the far skirts of the noble quarter, the price was hopefully reasonable, as well. She scanned the upper floor. Small windows faced the street to the north, which would be good for avoiding direct sun exposure from the south. The windows were narrow, but they should make a good escape route, if needed. "I think it's worth a shot."

They stepped onto the porch and pushed through the main doors. The large entryway was empty except for one young mortal setting the fire in the hearth. She stood to face them, surprise flashing across her face. "Oh, good day, m'lords and ladies." She curtseyed, her simple linen frock was high quality, though the few stains and discrete patches did show signs of wear. "What can I do for you this fine morning?"

Erik cleared his throat and stepped forward. "I know the hour is unusual, but we've been traveling all night. Would it be possible to take a room for the day so we can refresh ourselves?"

Adina scanned the interior. The floor was clean, recently swept, and absent of any warped boards or holes that would indicate neglect. The faint tang of ale stained the air, but that was to be expected in a tavern. The bar was clean, and the glassware stacked neatly behind it. She nodded in approval. Clearly, the owner took great pride in their business. The rooms upstairs would likely be mostly pest-free, as well. If they were lucky, there might even be fresh straw in the mattresses.

The young girl studied them, her brow furrowed as she scanned each of them in turn. "Where are you from?"

Adina glanced at Erik, in his Gorlinian armor, and at her own desert robes. Even Sigfried looked like he belonged more in the mountains than in a large city. Of the four of them, Madalina was the only one who might pass for Champeauxian. "Our road has been long. We're in town to meet up with a friend, but I'm afraid we seem to have beaten him here." She pulled out her purse and shook it, allowing the coins inside to clank. "I assure you, we won't be any problem, and we'll be gone by nightfall."

The silence stretched as Adina fought not to shift her weight with impatience.

At last, the mortal asked, "Will you be needing any breakfast?"

Adina's stomach leaped as the thought of Sophie's meals popped unexpectedly into her mind. But she had no desire to eat normal food when it would only make her sick.

Erik shook his head. "No, we'll make do with what we have in our packs. Thank you."

She nodded and stepped forward for Adina to empty the purse contents into her hand. Sorting through the coins, she pulled out three copper pieces and handed them back, along with a room key that she'd extracted from the folds of her dress. "Upstairs, third door on the right." Her gaze flicked toward the stairway behind them that Adina hadn't noticed upon entering. "Please be careful to not wake our other patrons. It's quite early yet."

Adina and Erik nodded as she went back to lighting the logs in the hearth in preparation for the day.

The stairs were sturdy and barely squeaked at all as they ascended. The upstairs hall was narrow, with three rooms on each side. Sigfried had to turn sideways and hunch over to fit.

At least he wasn't in bear form.

Erik stopped at the far end of the hall facing the final room. Placing his hand on the latch, he pressed his ear to the door. After two breaths, he nodded to them and pushed it open. Once they'd all entered, he closed and bolted it.

A plain room spread before them, with a narrow mattress on each side covered with fresh linens and a sturdy stool near the window. Adina strode to the far side of the room and barred the shutters closed. She tilted her head to the side as she studied them.

The window faced south…the wrong way to avoid the sun. Crap. She glanced around the space for something to hang over the shutters to avoid any accidental sun exposure. The linens on the mattresses were too thin. Besides, who wanted to sleep on bare straw, anyway? She'd be pulling it out of her hair for a month. Her gaze landed on Sigfried.

"Sig, can I borrow your oiled tarp?"

His gaze flicked between her and the shutters. With a shrug, he untied the roll from Madalina's pack and handed the fabric over.

Nodding her thanks, she tucked the edge over the shutters and out the window, and again pinned the wooden slots closed, leaving the rest of the fabric to hang down inside. Grabbing the stool, she placed it below the window, where it could partially hold the tarp against the wall. Absent a strong wind, they should be well protected as long as no one disturbed it during the day.

Madalina dropped her backpack by one of the mattresses. "I think this'll do great. Tomorrow maybe we can split up and visit a tavern or two, maybe hunt down some of Frere René's old haunts and see if we can track him down."

"Sounds fair to me," Erik said, sitting on the other mattress and untying his boots. He paused and peered at Madalina. "Especially if you have a strong feeling that's what we should be doing?"

Adina turned her attention to Madalina. Had she Seen something? Adina's stomach fluttered as a light feeling spread through her body. Perhaps, at last, they'd have some sort of divine guidance.

Madalina's eyes were normal colored, not the creepy black they turned when she was in the throes of a vision.

Madalina blinked in surprise. "No, no feelings. The stars aren't talking to me right now...there's too much smoke in the air."

A jolt crashed through Adina's muscles. More smoke? She fought the urge to rip down her carefully constructed window drapes to throw them open and look outside, just to reassure herself there were no flames approaching.

But that was ridiculous. If the city were burning, the mortals would be making such a ruckus, there'd be no possible way they could miss it.

Adina sighed as she ran her fingers over her scalp, pulling her hair away from her face. She'd never be able to sleep in a room filled with smoke.

Erik settled on the mattress, staring up at the ceiling. After a few breaths, he turned his attention to her and patted the mattress in invitation.

She climbed in beside him, laying on her side and resting her head on his shoulder so she could still see Madalina. Taking a deep breath, she let the reassuring scent of sandalwood clear the smoke smell from her nostrils. "Any information on this oracle we're supposed to go hunt down? Or the bog it's in?"

Madalina pressed her lips together and shook her head. "No. I don't even think Frere René knows much about it. Maybe there will be a library we can look in while we're here?"

Erik turned his head to meet Madalina's gaze as he pulled Adina close. "I don't think Champeaux has centralized libraries like the Saldanians and Hakkians do. Here, each noble house keeps their own collection of books. You'd have to make friends with a family to be invited in, and even then, their collection will be vastly limited compared to what you saw in The Drowned City."

Sigfried grunted as he flopped onto the mattress beside Madalina and rolled over on his side, but he looked more relieved than disappointed. As Madalina tucked herself up against his stomach, he met Adina's and Erik's gazes. "Maybe we can ask some merchants. Or scholars. They know things about other places. Then we do not have to spend time digging through books."

"Not a fan of libraries?" Erik teased.

"No."

Sigfried's declaration rattled the wood, and someone pounded on the wall above Adina's head.

She put a finger to her lips. "Shhh." The last thing they needed was to be kicked out for being loud, just as the pressure from the imminent rising sun was causing her eyelids to droop.

Maybe she'd be able to get to sleep after all.

Erik yawned. "Okay. First thing tomorrow, taverns and merchants. Maybe we'll get lucky and get info on the oracle *and* find René and Hana." He wrapped his arm around Adina and pulled her close.

She had to admit, she was rather curious to meet The Gaelle De Guignes, and learn what it knew about dragon bones, ley lines, and stopping a mad goddess.

Chapter 12

Damon

Damon stormed through the halls of his castle. Some nights, ruling was not all it was cracked up to be. Especially on nights like tonight.

The king had died sometime during the day and, thanks to his grandson's stupidity, had left no remaining direct heirs. Damon did not have the time to rule his country himself, so now he had to choose a patsy to do it for him.

He brushed a hand through his hair as he descended the stairs from his suite. The problem wasn't the dead king so much as it was the lack of suitable minions to choose from. The court was full of certified ninnies who were so obsessed with their social status he couldn't trust one of them to not run the country into the ground while he was away.

It really was too bad Reggie's grandson, the crown prince, had decided to attack him. If he'd have left well enough alone, Damon would have happily left the boy as figurehead. Instead, he'd had to kill him to make a point, and thrown an unexpected wrench into his own plans.

The king's nephew was a potential option, but the child was all of four years old, which would require a regent for at least a decade and a half. Regents were almost more dangerous than a king—their small taste of power could lead them to kill or imprison their charge and grab the throne for themselves. He'd seen it happen over and over again.

Well, it wouldn't happen in his kingdom. Not now, not ever.

He reached the bottom of the stairs and, jabbing one finger onto his fang until it bled, he rubbed his blood over the sapphire ring. "Viktor!"

His voice echoed across the empty hall.

Black banners and flags hung from every terrace and wall. Most of the kingdom was gathered at the wake, including the servants, which explained the lack of mortals scrambling around.

At least he'd have the castle more or less to himself until daybreak. One good thing would come out of this, however temporary.

"Viktor!"

The wraith appeared, bowing low. "My lord?"

"I need an update. Give me some good news."

"Septimus and the Assassins Guild continue to hunt for dragon bones."

Damon rolled his eyes. "That's not good news. Good news would be if they'd *found* the blasted bones. Tell me about Sujani."

Viktor seemed to fold in on himself as he cringed. "I have not been able to ascertain much on Sujani."

"What!" Damon flinched as the glass in the nearest window shuddered. "What have you been doing all this time?" Something twisted in his gut, a long-ignored instinct screamed that his soul-slave was being less than honest. He speared his Talent for Viktor's mind, but the strand of power crumbled to dust as it reached the wraith. Apparently, his ability to read surface thoughts didn't extend to spirits.

How unfortunate.

But Viktor wouldn't be stupid enough to try to sabotage him. There were protections in the soul-slave spell against such a thing. If Viktor was actively stalling or not carrying out his orders, Damon would know, even without his telepathy.

He shook his head. There was no need to borrow trouble when he already had more than enough on his plate.

Viktor knelt before him, his hands folded in supplication. "The last time I saw him, he was at an estate in the noble quarter of The Drowned City, master. But there is a magical shield around the area that I cannot penetrate."

"A what?" Dammit. Leave it to Sujani to erect wards against the undead.

Sometimes, he wished his old nemesis was just a hair less intelligent.

"You can't get through at all?"

Viktor bowed so low his forehead nearly touched the floor. "I'm sorry, m'lord."

"Have you tried using a zombie?"

"Yes." The voice was nearly a whisper.

Curse Sujani to the depths. A ward strong enough to keep out a wraith and a zombie may also work against vampires and would require a prohibitively large amount of blood magic to dispel.

And only a fool wouldn't feel blood magic being used on his own wards.

That was a problem for another time. He could hardly leave off his work here to run back to The Drowned City. Especially when the librarians' research indicated there might be a confluence of ley lines along the northern border of Champeaux, in the exact opposite direction.

Whatever Sujani and Maja were doing would have to wait. He'd return to The Drowned City, new Bone Shard Blade in hand, slice through those wards and bury the dagger deep in Sujani's withered heart. Then he'd face whatever consequences with Maja. He would happily face Final Death, if his enemy was ended, too.

Chapter 13
Erik

Erik opened his eyes as the sun dipped beneath the horizon. Adina's hair spread across his shoulder and chest, filling his nose with the scent of jasmine and vanilla. The pressure of her head on his shoulder relaxed him, and he sighed as he pulled her closer.

The faint hint of ale and the sweat of many humans crowded into a small space drifted through the floorboards. Several boisterous laughs and slurred words that he didn't bother deciphering echoed from below.

Happy hour must be in full swing in the tavern. At least the ruckus would mask their exit.

Adina shifted beside him. "Erik? How did you sleep?"

The side of his mouth pulled up in a half smile. "Like a baby." He turned his head to face hers. "You?"

She pushed herself up until she was sitting. "Not bad for laying on a pile of hay in a foreign city."

Madalina opened her eyes and stretched.

"Well, shall we go find ourselves a tavern or two?"

"Sig and I can go to the Merchant's Hall. I'm pretty sure we passed it on the way in," Madalina said as she rolled out of bed. "The building was really big, so hopefully it won't give him claustrophobia."

Unlike a crowded tavern. That made sense.

"Where and when should we meet you?" Erik asked.

Madalina pursed her lips as her eyes clouded in thought.

"How about two hours before sunrise," Sigfried said, sitting up. "In the market."

"Sounds good." Erik bent over and laced up his boots while Adina freed Sigfried's cloak from the shutters and tossed it to him.

"What should we do with the room key?" Adina asked.

Erik eyed the stool. "Why not leave it here? Someone will be up to check on us eventually...they'll find it and that'll save us from having to hunt someone down to return it to."

"Okay." She shrugged on her pack as the others did the same. "Are we ready to go?"

Erik nodded. "Let's find René and Hana."

The noise was multiplied exponentially by the time they got downstairs. The press and flow of human bodies had Erik fighting not to roll his shoulders inward in an attempt to make himself smaller.

Fortunately, the stairs were only a few paces away from the main door, and it was only the space of a few heartbeats before they stood in the open air in the center of the street.

"If we were looking for René..." Adina said, letting her voice drift off.

"You'd want the taverns in the noble section," Madalina said. "Frere René wouldn't be caught dead in the poorer sections if he had any choice."

Erik nodded. Fair enough. The feeding options were likely to be more palatable, as well, if René and Hana had lost Sophie's blood bags. One never knew where the things that crawled the alleyways of the slums had been.

Adina wrapped her arm around his as Madalina and Sigfried headed back the way they'd come the prior night. "A romantic tavern crawl looking for René. Just what I was dreaming of."

He chuckled at the sarcasm in her tone as he patted her hand. "I promise I won't make it too miserable for you." He winked, the warmth in her eyes fanning heat through his chest.

She batted her eyelashes at him. "Such a gentleman."

"Come, my lady." He escorted her down the street, deeper into the noble quarter.

The moon had yet to rise over the horizon when he led her to a tavern a few mere blocks from the castle. Adina slid into the chair and shifted her weight as she dug the corset boning out of her side. She was resplendent in the burgundy and black velvet gown they'd pilfered from a clothing boutique down the road.

"Quit fiddling with it," Erik murmured as he took the seat opposite her, fighting the urge to adjust his newly acquired vest.

She scowled. "Why do people even wear things like this?"

"Hmmm, I couldn't imagine," he said as his eyes drifted downward. The dress in question accentuated every curve, from her breasts to her slim waist. Heat rushed from his heart through each limb. His fangs pulsed and threatened to lengthen to the point that they would protrude from between his lips.

Clearing his throat, he turned and studied the room. *Focus on something else, Erik. Anything but how good that dress looks on her or you'll end up embarrassing yourself.*

René would tease him mercilessly if he caught him in this state.

Erik caught the eye of a passing bar maid and gestured for two ales. They couldn't drink them but would look extremely out of place in a tavern without something in front of them. Moments later, two mugs full of the frothy concoction that seemed to be the night's specialty slammed down on their table as the bar maid passed by.

Adina reached over and slid one of the glasses to herself. Wrapping her hands around it, she furrowed her brow and stared into the liquid. "Do we have a plan beyond sitting here and waiting for René and Hana to find us?"

He shrugged, threading his fingers around the handle on his mug, spinning it in circles. "Short of going from table to table asking if anyone has seen Lord d'Bayeux, I have no idea."

Adina opened her mouth but froze as a mug crashed onto a table in the middle of the room. Liquid sloshed over its edges onto the floor as the noise drew everyone's attention and the tavern quieted.

A tall mortal dressed like a merchant in rich mauves and royal blues turned to the room, shaking the spilled ale from his hand. "Anyone here up for a drinking game?" He pulled out a leather satchel the size of his hand and emptied it onto the table. The firelight flickered off three colorful jewels, the smallest the size of his pinky fingernail, as they rolled to the center of the table. "Winner takes all!"

Adina's eyes sparkled as she smiled. "This is perfect!" Grabbing her mug with one hand and Erik's arm with the other, she hauled him from the table.

He snatched his ale and followed her. "What are you doing?"

"Follow my lead," she whispered.

As they approached the merchant's table, she set her mug down and tipped her head to the side. Reaching into her pocket, she pulled out the long silver chain Erik had given her back in The Drowned City, with the ring attached. Setting it on the counter, she met the merchant's eyes. "We're in."

Erik studied her, trying to figure out what she was up to, as his gut twisted at the thought that she'd so easily part with his old necklace.

She turned her head to face him and, out of view of the mortal, pressed her lips into a thin line and nodded to where the necklace sat on the table.

Grabbing a spare chair, he settled it next to her and reached into his pocket.

The garnet ring she'd given him back in The Drowned City cut into his palm as his fingers tightened around it, reluctant to give it up.

Her hand tightened on his bicep and released in encouragement.

Well, he trusted her. Here was his chance to prove it. Clearing his throat, he set the ring next to the necklace and met the merchant's gaze.

The garnet was almost twice the size of the mortal's gems. In the low light, it looked almost black.

The mortal picked up both pieces of jewelry, examining them closely. After several heartbeats, he nodded and added the two pieces to the pile of gems. "Anyone else?" he asked, spinning to address the entire room. "It doesn't look like either of these two can hold their liquor."

Erik leaned in close to Adina's ear. "What's the plan?" he asked in Hakki. Her ring was his most prized possession. "These games are usually scams. We won't win."

She gave him a sly smile as her eyes sparkled. "Trust me. Just remember to act surprised."

He sighed and pressed his lips together, holding back a sigh. He would trust her.

Worst case scenario, they could hunt the merchant down afterward and steal their things back. He clenched his hands against the smoothed edge of the table until his knuckles turned white and the wood creaked.

Three other nobles joined them, two men and one woman. Erik studied the three new arrivals. One of the men had the characteristic red nose and puffy eyes that came with habitually drinking too much ale.

He would be the one to watch out for, with his increased tolerance. The other two seemed as foolhardy as he felt himself.

A barmaid came by and topped off everyone's ales. The merchant raised his glass, met each of their eyes, and smiled. "Drink!" He tipped his head back and poured the liquid down his throat.

The nearest onlookers took up the chant as Adina and the others did the same.

"Drink! Drink! Drink!"

Erik's stomach turned. He and Adina would just end up in the back alley later, vomiting the ale back up. Not the most elegant or enjoyable way to spend his evening, but she clearly had a plan, so…

He tilted his head back and chugged the ale as quickly as he could. The cool liquid slid down his throat and curdled in his gut. But he could put up with the discomfort for the time being.

Two more rounds quickly followed. The red-nosed mortal belched loud enough to rattle Erik's eardrums. The merchant remained stone-cold sober.

Adina glanced at him and gave him a subtle wink. The gold tether between them vibrated.

Be ready.

He tensed, scooting forward until he was on the edge of his chair, ready to pop to his feet if needed as the barmaid refilled their mugs for a fourth time. His free hand drifted down to rest against his sword's hilt.

The spilled puddles and droplets of ale near all the participants pooled together and moved toward the center of the table, tracing paths toward the pile of jewelry stacked there.

Gasps and silence replaced the chants of "Drink, Drink!" as more and more of the onlookers noticed the liquid.

As the ale puddled in the center of the table, it formed a large, iridescent bubble, which floated into the air. Hovering just above eye level, it popped, splattering the contest participants with droplets.

The four mortals leaped back from the table with various curses, knocking their chairs aside and spilling their remaining beverages.

Erik mirrored their reactions. "God's Teeth!" Leaping to his feet, he knocked his chair out of the way, grabbed their ring and necklace, and pulled Adina away from the table.

He glanced between her and the bubbles of ale now floating up to the roof of the ceiling as though carried on an ethereal breeze. His eyes scanned the captivated and terrified expressions of everyone in the tavern and he bit back a smile.

Word of this unusual event would spread faster than the wildfires that devoured the countryside. If René or Hana were anywhere in the noble district, they'd hear about it within a few hours.

And would know exactly where to find them.

Leading Adina away from the press of people and to a wall on the far side of the room, he pulled her to him. "You're brilliant," he whispered in her ear.

She inhaled as his breath tickled her ear. Her back arched and she tilted her head back until it rested against the wall.

Heat flooded Erik's core, and his fangs throbbed. The sound of terrified patrons faded into the background as his gaze narrowed in on her mouth.

Leaning forward, he caught her lips with his. The scent of jasmine and vanilla surrounded him with every breath, every pulse of the artery at her neck.

She was brilliant, beautiful, and his.

With a groan, she threaded her fingers through his hair and pulled him closer.

He ran his fingers up and down her waist, the lace and bone texture of the Champeauxian corset was so different from the robes she usually wore. If he'd still been mortal, he'd have enjoyed peeling the dress off, layer by layer.

Her fingers wove through his hair, leaving tingling trails in their wake. Lost in the sensation, Erik broke the kiss, his lips trailing their way down her jaw to her neck.

She stiffened and pushed him away, snapping Erik back to reality.

Heat gleamed in her heavy-lidded gaze. "I think we may want to leave like the mortals and come back later?"

Blinking, he glanced around. Indeed, the tavern had nearly cleared out. The alarmed humans would spread the word of what had happened here. But it would doubtless be a while yet before René and Hana arrived. Taking a steadying breath, he shoved his desire aside, ignoring the ache in his fangs that begged for the blood that pulsed beneath her skin.

She traced the edge of her finger down his neck, along the ridge of an artery and gave him a mischievous half-grin. "Out back?"

God's Teeth... That look was nearly his undoing. He opened his mouth to say something, but his brain was too fogged with heat.

Grabbing his hand, she led him out the front doors and, after checking to make sure no one marked their exit, down a side alley.

One of the upsides of being in the noble district was their alleys were occasionally cleaned and didn't leave him feeling as though he'd walked through a sewer.

Under the cover of the shadows, Adina leaned against the tavern's wall and pulled him to her.

He lifted her up until the junction of her neck and shoulder was at eye level.

She wrapped her legs around his waist.

"I love this dress on you," he growled as he pressed a kiss to her collarbone. He traced a slow path up to her neck with his lips.

"Oh?" Her own voice was coarse with desire as she arched her neck to one side, giving him better access. She massaged his scalp with her fingers. "Two can play that game, you know," she whispered into his ear.

She kissed right below his ear and sucked his earlobe into her mouth, grazing it with her fangs.

Lightning zipped through him at the sensation, and with a deep groan, he plunged his fangs into her neck. A sharp sting cresting a wave of ecstasy plowed through him as she followed half a heartbeat later. As their hearts synchronized, he lost himself to her and the waves of ecstasy.

"Ahem."

A small rock rolled into Erik's foot. He ignored it.

"I said, ahem."

The familiar voice cut through the pleasure-fog in Erik's brain, as Adina pulled away. The connection between them shattered with a suddenness that left him reeling. Blinking his eyes, he grabbed the wall to steady himself.

Adina brushed the wrinkles from her gown and corset as Erik spun on the intruder. "What?"

René stood about ten paces away, arms crossed. The expression Erik had long ago learned to associate with courtiers, boredom with a hint of disgust, was plastered across his face. "I hope I'm not interrupting anything?"

Erik put his arm around Adina's waist and pulled her closer while he glared at René. "Clearly you were." And the bastard knew it. "Would it have been too much to ask to wait around front?"

René barked a laugh. "Please. I could smell your blood from half a block away. For all I knew, you were bleeding out in the back alley, dying."

Right. Rescue had likely been the last thing from René's mind.

Adina elbowed him in the waist, just enough to break his focus. She eyed René. "Is Hana with you?"

"She opted to wait out front."

Of course, she did. Erik ground his teeth so hard the tendons in his jaw popped.

"Well, at least Hana has some manners," Adina muttered. Pushing away from the wall, she pulled Erik toward the street. "Are you guys alright? What happened?"

Erik exhaled, mentally thanking Adina for the change in subject. Now was not the time to get into it with René, especially with his emotions running so high.

He caught Adina's eye and winked as they headed out of the alley.

Her cheeks turned red, and she glanced toward the ground, but she did pull him close with one arm for a quick side-hug before they stepped out onto the street.

Hana pushed away from the front wall of the tavern and gave them a slow smile. "Thank the gods." She grasped both of Adina's hands in her own. "I knew when I heard about ale that defied natural law, that must have been you sending us a message. I'm glad I was right." She embraced Adina. "I had no idea how we were going to find you in the city."

Eric snorted. Yeah...they hadn't exactly had time to work that out.

"What happened to you two?" Adina asked.

Hana ran a hand through her hair, pulling several loose strands away from her face. "I tripped. René stayed to help." She pulled out her blood-bag. "Did you guys know these things never run dry? Sophie's knowledge is leagues beyond my own. Even if I studied for decades, I'd never reach her skill level. These are amazing!"

Hana bit down on her smile as if she could hold her excitement in with just her teeth and tilted her head toward René. "We tried to drink them dry. The blood just kept coming."

"I've never felt so sloshy," René said as he frowned and rubbed his stomach. "I was uncomfortable for *nights*."

Erik smiled. "We'll never have to worry about feeding again."

Hana shook her head. "At least, not as long as you have that. I'm pretty sure I won't be able to replicate the process without Sophie's help, though. Nor will I be able to cook a breakfast we can all eat, but these are the next best thing."

"Where are Sig and Madalina?" René asked.

Adina cleared her throat. "They went to the Merchant's Guild, to see if they could learn anything about the trip to the bog to find The Gaelle De Guignes. We're supposed to meet them in the market." She glanced at the moon, judging its position relative to the horizon. "In a little over two hours."

Erik glanced over his shoulder, back toward the alley. Two hours was plenty of time, and he and Adina had had so little to themselves the past several months. They'd hardly been alone together since before Sujani had plunged that cursed dagger into her heart.

Since his world had ended in that same instant.

He caught her hand and threaded his fingers between hers, intending to lead her back toward the alley, but she turned to René.

"Do you have a place we can stay for the night?"

"Of course." He waved them down the street. "We should be able to stay in the Duke's country estate, it's just a half league outside the city to the north. With the fires, I'm sure it's been emptied, and the household staff will have pulled back into the city."

Erik swallowed his disappointment at the interruption. A country estate with their own private room would be much better than against a wall in an alley, even an exceptionally clean one.

He pulled them to a stop before they'd gone a half block. "We need to go back. We left my armor hidden in the other direction."

René frowned, glancing back in the direction Erik had indicated, and ahead, toward their destination. "I assumed you'd ditched the armor, permanently."

Erik scoffed. As if. Gesturing to his ridiculously tight vest and tunic, he said, "I'd have much preferred to keep it on, if only Champeauxian fashion allowed for it."

René shook his head as Erik and Adina turned around. "We'll wait here for you to catch up," he called after them.

As they walked out of hearing range, Adina nudged him with her shoulder. "I like you in that outfit, too."

He raised an eyebrow and studied her as the spark that had smoldered suddenly burst back into flames. "Oh?"

She traced the planes of his chest with one finger. "It shows off your muscles."

He pressed her hand flat against his pectoral. "You are driving me crazy."

Laughing she leaned her head against his shoulder and traced his bicep with the fingernails of her free hand.

He stumbled as realization hit him. "You're doing this on purpose."

"Of course. I wouldn't want you to get bored."

He glanced at the moon, high in the sky. God's Teeth... "With you? I don't think you'll ever need to worry about that." If he lived a thousand years, he'd never stop waking up in awe that he was lucky enough to be with her.

Her answering grin lit up the night as he reached under the porch of an unassuming bakery.

Pulling his armor from the shadows, he buckled it on as quickly as possible. When every piece was back in place and he felt more like himself, he took her hand, threading his fingers between hers. "Come on. Let's go fetch Sigfried and Madalina and get out of here."

"The merchants say there are no paths into the bog," Sigfried said as they settled into the luxurious furniture in the sitting room in the d'Bayeux country estate.

The entire manor was decorated in golds, oranges and greens that made Erik's eyes water. The color scheme at least partially explained René's penchant for wearing such garishly clashing outfits. But the chairs were comfortable, well-upholstered and didn't protest when he sat in them in full armor.

Adina perched on the arm rest beside him. "So, no one goes up there at all?"

Madalina shook her head. "Apparently not." She glanced at René. "There are no settlements up that direction, so the merchants have no reason to."

So much for gaining advanced intelligence on what they were getting into. Erik shifted his weight.

"Well, if we can't get any info on the area, it'll be just as hard for anyone following us," Adina said.

Erik paused. She had a point. "And with no people around, it'll be easier to detect if we're being followed."

Madalina turned to René. "But you *do* know where we're going? How to get there?"

He scoffed. "Of course, I do. Here, let me show you." Shoving himself to his feet, he crossed the room to the large bookshelf they'd all ignored upon arrival. He flipped through the scrolls at eye level, shoved a few books aside and pulled out a large sheet of folded parchment. Unfolding the paper, he spread it on the coffee table between them.

A map of Champeaux lay before him, containing more detail than any military map Erik had ever seen of the area. And considering the political tensions between Gorlinia and Champeaux over the last few decades, that was saying something. He scooted forward in his chair, devouring the information.

"We're here," René said, pointing at a black dot in the southern portion of the country. "We need to follow this road north." He moved his finger accordingly. "Then, when it forks here, we take the easterly route into the bog. This road isn't traveled much, like Madalina said, so it probably won't be in the best condition. Honestly, I wouldn't want to try it with a cart or wagon."

Well, that was good, because they didn't have either of those things. "Any chance of acquiring some horses for the journey?" Erik asked. Who knew how long they'd be tromping around in the marsh before they found The Gaelle De Guignes. The faster they could cover ground, the more likely they were to locate the oracle, get the information they needed, and return in time to prevent a second Cataclysm.

René met Erik's gaze. "Not unless you want to steal them from one of the farms on our way."

His neck and shoulders stiffened as he clenched his jaw. "You know I'd never—"

Adina put her hand on his arm and pulled until he met her gaze. "That's not what he meant." She turned her attention to René with a pointed glare. "He was merely pointing out that we don't have the funds to purchase horses. Not insinuating you'd steal them."

"Besides," Madalina said, "I don't think horses would do well in a bog, unless they can swim. Horses are heavy, and fragile."

Adina studied the map. "How many nights is it, do you think, traveling by foot?"

"To the edge of the bog?" René shrugged. "Between five and seven, I'd guess, depending on our pace."

Erik blinked. A week there and back cut them perilously close to Damon's estimate of thirty days.

And assuming they managed to avoid getting caught in another wildfire.

Erik asked, "Did the merchants say anything about fires up that way?"

Sigfried shook his head. "No." He glanced at Madalina. "But we did not specifically ask."

"It's okay," Erik said. "We'll just have to be careful, and more aware." They'd gotten lucky the last time. They may not survive a second round, even with Sophie's new-and-improved blood bags.

"Well." René rubbed his hands together. "I propose we retire for the day, and head out for the bog first thing tomorrow."

Erik glanced at Adina, who met his gaze with a heated one of her own. "Sounds good to me," he said. "Which room is ours?"

Chapter 14
Damon

The mortal librarian stood in front of his desk, waiting patiently for Damon to acknowledge his existence. The man had been motionless for several minutes, probably enjoying this rare breath of fresh air. Personally, he couldn't imagine the draw of living one's life buried in the dark and dusty stacks below the castle, but to each their own.

With a sigh, he crossed out the final name on his list of potential heirs. Setting his quill on the desk and folding his hands in front of himself, he turned his attention to the mortal in front of him.

"Yes? You have some news for me?"

The librarian bowed. "M'lord." He slid a paper onto Damon's desk. "Our research indicates a likely confluence of ley lines in this general vicinity."

Damon scoured the parchment with his eyes. "Where is this?"

The mortal cleared his throat. "It's a little-traveled marsh in the northeast portion of Champeaux. There's supposed to be an oracle in the vicinity called The Gaelle De Guignes." The man dared to meet Damon's gaze. "Our current theory is that the oracle operates there due to the power infusing the area from the ley lines."

Damon chewed the inside of his cheek. "I see." Intriguing. Personally, he'd always written oracles and prophets off as charlatans—scam artists who made their livings preying on the gullible and naive. "And what makes you think this..." He waved his hand in the air.

"Gaelle De Guignes," the librarian supplied.

He nodded. "...this Gaelle De Guignes is any different from the numerous other so-called oracles that have appeared and been debunked throughout the years?"

The mortal spread a few more papers across Damon's desk. "From what my staff can ascertain, every reported prediction The Gaelle De Guignes has made has come to pass." He chewed on the inside of his cheek. "Of course, there could be something that we missed, but it seemed like a valid lead worth passing on to you."

Damon exhaled as he studied the scratches across the papers. Fortunately, the librarian's handwriting was impeccable. He pulled one particularly interesting note closer for further study. This was definitely worth investigating. Assuming he could find someone to assign as regent until the former king's nephew was of age.

"Excellent work, thank you." Damon nodded. "You may go."

The man pressed his hands together and bowed before turning toward the door.

"Wait."

The mortal froze, hand halfway to the door. Turning around, he raised an eyebrow. "Yes, m'lord?"

Damon frowned. "You're an educated man. If you were to pick a regent for the next fifteen years, whom would you choose?"

The librarian opened his mouth, paused, and closed it again. "Why ask me this, m'lord? Surely you have advisors..."

Damon waved one hand dismissively. "Advisors who all suggested themselves, of course. I need an unbiased opinion who is more interested in the good of the kingdom than their own advancement."

The mortal blinked, eyes widening. "Then I am honored, m'lord." He thought for several moments.

Damon sent his Talent toward the man, skimming his thoughts as he considered each name and discarded it.

Finally, the librarian took a deep breath. "Consider Lord Redstone, m'lord. He has the charisma to lead, and the wisdom to see how the success of the nation will benefit him in the long term."

Damon scrubbed his tongue across the front of his teeth. The mortal had a valid point. A minor noble like Lord Redstone hadn't even made Damon's long list. An oversight that he should've known better than to make. This was what he got for letting his attention be pulled in too many directions. "Thank you," he said with a nod. "Now, you may go."

The mortal took a breath. "If I may ask a favor, m'lord?"

Damon raised his eyebrow. "A favor?"

"Please do not let it be known that I was the one who recommended Lord Redstone. It may make me a target for anyone you don't choose."

Damon studied the man. He was loyal, intelligent, and wise enough to understand how the world truly worked. It would be in his best interest to keep this one around as long as possible. He dipped his head once. "You have my word. None shall hear of our conversation from me."

The librarian's shoulders slumped as he exhaled. With a brief smile, he bobbed his head and disappeared through the door.

Damon took a deep breath. Well, he had a possible location he needed to investigate. Now, he just needed Seven to take him there. Immediately.

Fingering the soul-stone ring he wore, Damon jabbed the writing quill into the tip of his finger and squeezed until a bead of blood pooled on his skin. Covering the sapphire with his blood, he snarled, "Viktor!"

The wraith appeared in the middle of the room, hovering a mere pace off the floor. "What is it you want, my master?"

"Get me Seven. I need him here now."

Viktor disappeared with hardly a flicker.

Damon stacked all the papers the librarian had left on his desk into a tidy pile, which he shoved in the top desk drawer. It wouldn't do to have prying eyes read them when Seven arrived.

"Seven isn't coming."

Damon froze as his gaze shot to the doorway. "Sujani." His pulse thrashed in his ears as an invisible band tightened around his ribs. He grabbed his Talent with everything he had and threw a mental shield up between himself and the other vampire.

Though, if Sujani was accompanied by Maja, any precautions would be less than useless.

The ancient Surinian stepped through the door and into his study. His annoyingly stereotypical blue mage robes brushed against the stone floor. The fine hairs on Damon's arms lifted and prickled as Sujani drew on his Talent.

He couldn't let his rival throw a lightning bolt in here. The space was too small, too cramped.

Damon pulled on his Talent again and hurled a dagger composed solely of his mental strength at the other man. The black knife, outlined in red, sped through the air, toward Sujani's heart.

A teal ripple met the dagger, and the two exploded in a shock wave that vibrated Damon's furniture.

Sujani's hardened air shield.

"What are you doing in Esnaria?" Damon hissed. "This is my territory!" He tore his eyes from the blasted Surinian and studied the hallway behind him. Surely, Sujani would not *dare* violate their thousand-year-old agreement unless Maja was here to provide backup.

But the goddess didn't present herself.

Likely, Maja wouldn't make herself known unless Sujani needed her. So, it was in his best interests to not end Sujani immediately unless he wanted to find himself face-to-face with Maja.

Without Ahion by his side, he had no desire to face her. No chance against her or Sujani.

His gaze slipped to the doorway behind Sujani's shoulder. Perhaps she waited outside, just out of view?

Sujani followed Damon's gaze. The outer corner of one side of his mouth pulled up into a half-smile. "I've come to tell you, Seven is no longer yours. Maja and I have put him, and the Assassin Guild, to better use."

Damon bared his fangs. "You're lying!" He had to be...Seven hated Sujani almost as much as Damon did. He blinked as realization snapped through his body. "You had Charles do something to him." He ground his teeth together. The next time he saw Charles, the man was a dead vampire. It was time to end the threat his son presented once and for all.

Sujani smirked. "I didn't have to. All it took was a few words, whispered in the right ears, to turn him to my cause." He paused. "To *our* cause."

Damn Sujani to the depths. Below the desk, Damon clenched his hands so tight his fingernails cut crescent-shaped moons into his palms. "And what? You've come here to gloat?" He studied the old vampire. Sujani couldn't be here to kill him...he didn't even bring the Bone Shard Blade.

So...with no blade, what was Sujani up to? Gloating wasn't really his style.

Damon rallied his Talent and speared his mental fingers toward Sujani. The other vampire's mind shield felt foreign, impregnable. Damon ran his mental claws down it. The psychic sound of fingernails on slate screamed through his mind.

"I see you've had Charles augment your mind shield," Damon said, brushing his palms off on his pants. "Sharing Talents...most impressive. And foolhardy." And he'd end half the world without a second thought if he could figure out how the old dog had figured out that trick.

Sujani waved his hand and a breeze gusted through the study.

Damon fought the urge to stumble as his strength evaporated with the wind.

Footsteps, leather on stone, passed by outside his door. A mortal on a late-night errand.

Sujani stepped forward. "I have come to let you know Maja is nearly at her full strength. Make your peace with the world, Damon. You'll be joining Ahion soon."

Damon snarled and flung his Talent past Sujani and out the door.

The old Surinian flared his magic, as a dim blue-green aura surrounded him. "Ha! You missed!"

Damon tugged on his Talent. "You came to warn me about Maja and Seven? Did you seriously think I would believe you?"

The mortal whose mind he'd snagged in the hallway snuck up behind Sujani on near-silent feet.

Sujani splayed his arms to either side and gave Damon a mocking bow. "I do as she commands. Even you, my old nemesis, deserve that respect for your faithful service to her brother, Ahion."

Heat exploded through Damon's muscles as his red-tinted vision narrowed until all he could see was Sujani. "How *dare* you mention his name! You are not worthy!"

Sujani screamed, arching his back as a red-tipped sword point exploded from his ribs. He crumbled to his knees. The soldier who had come up behind him, met Damon's gaze.

<*Thank you. Now run!*> Damon released the mortal, who fortunately for him, was good at following directions.

Using Sujani's distraction, Damon speared his Talent for the old mage and shredded through his mental shields like paper.

Sneering at his opponent, Damon barked out a laugh. A flush of warmth exploded through Damon's body as Sujani's thoughts flooded his mind. He grabbed onto the desk, suddenly feeling so light he might defy gravity and fly.

"Your goddess has abandoned you!" He cackled. "It's about time Maja came to the right side."

The blood drained from Sujani's pain-contorted face.

Spreading his arms in ecstasy while he reveled in Sujani's ruin, Damon stared at the other vampire. "Now whose time has come, Surinian?"

Tingles of energy ran up the nerves on Damon's skin as Sujani rallied his power and Talent.

Damon lunged.

A thunderclap exploded in front of him, throwing him backward. With a flash of blindingly bright teal light and the stench of ozone, Sujani was gone.

Damon pushed himself to his feet as he rubbed his hands over his forearms, banishing the remaining tingles of Sujani's Talent.

Well, wasn't that interesting? Maja had abandoned Sujani.

He pulled his chair from behind the desk and flopped into it.

This was a twist. What did it mean, and, more importantly, how could he use it?

Despite what he'd hinted, Maja was not here, nor did he have any idea where she would be.

But, if he could forge a new Bone Shard Blade, and Sujani lacked the goddess' protection...

There might be hope for his survival, after all. Assuming, of course, the librarians were right about the ley line nexus. And that the Assassin's Guild had been able to locate some dragon bones.

He pressed his lips together in a tight grin. This might just work, assuming Sujani hadn't been lying about Seven.

Dammit. He'd gotten so distracted with the revelation of Maja leaving Sujani that he hadn't dug for the truth of Seven's betrayal.

Well, time enough to discover that when Viktor returned. Then he'd know one way or another.

Now, where would Maja have gone?

Damon brushed a hand through his hair, pulling the loose strands away from his face. It was not his place to hunt down the goddess. If she had other things to attend to that didn't hinder him, he'd let her be. Keeping his head down and his focus on forging a new Bone Shard Blade was the best path forward for now.

No doubt Maja would make herself known when it suited her, and not a moment before. There was little point in worrying about it now.

He snarled, baring his fangs at the spot where Sujani had stood. Why hadn't the old vampire left well enough alone? Maja's time had passed over a thousand years ago.

Love. What a senseless waste of energy. Worlds had been destroyed for less.

Pulling the map from the desk drawer one last time, he committed the librarian's notes to memory before shoving the pages into the very back, under his spare quills. If he ended up being gone for more than a few hours, hopefully the notes would be safe there.

He glared at the empty room.

Where was Viktor? Why wasn't he back yet?

Sighing, he chewed the inside of his cheek. Seven was probably being stubborn, intentionally making him wait in a feeble attempt at a power play. Viktor was probably too cowardly to return until Seven made an appearance, for fear of facing Damon's wrath.

Well, two could play that game.

If they were going to march through a bog, he'd need waterproof boots, and a different cape—one that wouldn't be damaged by exposure to water and mud. Now was the perfect time to go acquire them. Seven, when he deigned to arrive, would have to wait on him for a change.

Seven betraying him to Sujani…it was simply unfathomable.

Unpinning the cape's clasp at his throat, Damon removed the garment with a quick snap of his wrist as he marched out the door and up to his suite.

He made the trip up his tower to his room, changed out his attire, returned and slammed into his chair. The study was still empty. Grinding his teeth, he glanced out the single window. The moon had dropped two finger-widths in the sky and Seven still hadn't made an appearance.

His stomach quivered and he fought to not fiddle with the quill on his desk.

Perhaps Sujani hadn't been lying, and his most useful ally had abandoned him. The implications were staggering.

That Seven would have the nerve to betray him. Him! After Damon had worked so hard to save his precious daughter from Sujani—*twice!* And he'd nearly wound up the sacrifice to resurrect Maja as a result.

His upper lip pulled back in a snarl. If that was the case, Seven would regret the day Sujani first made him. He would see to it.

If he couldn't count on Seven's particular mode of transportation, he'd have to travel like a lowly mortal. *Ugh.* If the librarian's notes were accurate, even with the fastest horse it was a good week's journey to the bog. And the inconveniences of traveling...finding protection from the sun, a sufficient human population to assuage his Hunger, not to mention the discomfort of riding for such an extended amount of time.

He let his mind drift off, imagining all the punishments he'd bring down on Seven's head. And Adina's, too...guilt by association and all.

Eventually, the discomfort of the edges of the desk pushing into his forearms brought his thoughts back to the present. He glanced at the moon, another two finger-widths lower in the sky.

The night was aging as he sat here, doing nothing. The longer he waited, the more likely Sujani would reunite with Maja and come back to wipe him off the map.

And there was no way was he going to sit here and lose to Sujani through inaction. He was better than that.

He was better than all of them.

When it came to the final confrontation between him and Sujani, he'd be the last man standing. Even if it meant the destruction of vast swaths of his future empire.

With a growl, he shoved his chair back from the desk. The wooden legs screeched as they gouged scratches through the stone floor. Storming from the room, he slammed the door closed behind him.

He froze as his mind caught up with him about twenty paces down the hall. Before he left, he needed to designate someone to be in charge. *Curse the mages.* Spinning on his heel, he headed back toward his study. Grabbing the first mortal to cross his path, he fisted the man's shirt and pulled him to a halt. The rising stench of the servant's fear did little to improve Damon's mood. "Get Lord Redstone to my study. Now."

He dropped the trembling human and pushed him away. It would likely take several hours for the lord to be summoned. It was, after all, the middle of the night, and minor nobility didn't lodge as close to the castle as the higher nobles.

As tempting as it would be to write the decree quickly, then wake the royal secretary to meet Redstone to sign the paperwork, Damon really should be there to make sure the noble understood his expectations as Regent to the Throne. And who *truly* ruled Esnaria.

His skin itched and crawled to be on his way to The Gaelle De Guignes rather than sitting around letting Sujani get the lead on him. But it would do little good to kill Sujani, end Maja and conquer the world, only to return to find his home kingdom in shambles.

He sighed.

Some nights, being the ruler was almost more trouble than it was worth.

Almost.

Sitting back down in his chair, he pulled out a new sheet of paper and, dipping his quill in the inkwell, he began to draft the Decree of Succession.

Tomorrow evening, he'd have the stablemaster ready the swiftest horse, and be on his way as soon as the sun dropped below the horizon.

Tomorrow. Once Esnaria was set to rights.

Chapter 15
Adina

The marsh smelled like decay and rotten eggs, but as far as Adina was concerned, it was a welcome change from the smoke. A fine mist hung across the ground, creeping over the open pools of water and over the low-lying isthmuses that connected chunks of land.

She shifted her pack on her shoulders as the ground squelched beneath her oiled shoes. Grabbing the bootstrap, she yanked as she stepped, reclaiming her footwear from the endless mud. They'd been walking more or less northeast for the last six days. René had been right, the road into the bog was in terrible condition, making the going slow and arduous. He'd neglected to mention the muck that devoured everything except the skeletal cypress trees that poked out of the fog like old hag's teeth.

But she could deal with mud, especially if it didn't come with pouring rain like it had in Gorlinia.

Off to her left, a snake dropped from a tree branch into the water with a *plop* before it slithered away to the susurration of cicadas.

Ahead, René pulled to a halt. "I can't tell which way the road goes from here."

Adina paused, holding her breath. Her fingernails dug into her palms. If they were lost, then the whole last week of this misery was for nothing, and they had no hope of hunting down The Gaelle De Guignes and getting answers.

Sigfried stepped up beside him, staring into the grayness. "Perhaps this is where we start to look for the oracle?"

Adina glanced at Erik, meeting his gaze. The discomfort that fed the butterflies in her gut reflected in his eyes. "I don't know if wandering around a bog is necessarily the best option," she said. "We may well end up permanently lost and never find our way out." Her blood chilled. Then they'd never stop Sujani and Maja in time to prevent another Cataclysm.

"No, we won't," Madalina said, pointing at the stars. "See those three bright stars there, that form kind of a triangle?"

Adina frowned, studying the sky where Madalina was pointing. "Yes..."

"Those are the collar of Leo the Lion. They point south. If we get lost, we can just follow them."

Erik reached out and patted Madalina on her shoulder. "Our own little navigator, huh?"

"We can go back out the way we came by keeping the stars on our left. Then, we'll know we're heading west."

Adina shrugged. That seemed fair. She was happy enough—well, as much as she could be—following the others through the bog. Especially if it got them some answers on their potential dragon bones and the location of a nexus of ley lines.

René groaned as his foot slid on a slippery patch of mud and sunk into the water. "Ugh." Several water strider bugs skittered across the surface into the fog.

Hana grabbed his arm to steady him as he pulled himself free.

The sludge clung to his boot like glue, reluctant to give up its treasure.

Pulling on a bit of her Talent, Adina pushed the viscous liquid away.

Something about it made the fine hairs on the back of her neck stand on end. "I don't know that we want to disturb the water. Something about it feels wrong."

"How so?" Erik asked, his hand going reflexively to his sword hilt.

She shrugged. "I'm not sure…it's giving off the same energy I feel anytime I'm in Sujani or Damon's presence."

Erik's knuckles turned white as he squeezed the weapon's handle, but he didn't draw it. He peered at the area around them as though searching for something. "No. That doesn't sound strange, considering either one of them could be out there watching us right now. If it feels dangerous to you, we should proceed with caution."

Her stomach hardened as she glared at the skeletal trees surrounding them. The wraith could be out there, too. Or her father.

Sigfried cleared his throat. "We should go this way."

When Adina glanced at him, he was pointing north. She raised her eyebrow and tilted her head to one side.

"The air doesn't stink as much in this direction," he said at her quizzical expression.

Grabbing a bit of her Talent, Adina conjured a breeze from the direction he indicated.

Inhaling deeply, he met her eyes with a satisfying grunt. "I smell something up that way that doesn't belong in a bog."

Adina's stomach filled with butterflies. She scanned the surroundings for any movement. A frog croaked and jumped into the water with a *plop*, the sudden movement catching her attention.

René raised an eyebrow and tapped his formerly wet foot on the ground. Crossing his arms, he leaned on one hip. "Can you be more specific? What's out of place?"

Adina swallowed, silently wondering the same thing. Sig had the best nose of any vampire she'd ever met.

Sigfried shook his head. "It smells like dry wood with a hint of sage."

Hanna frowned. "Sage doesn't like to grow in soil that's always wet and requires full sun." She gestured at the mist crawling across the ground. "This is hardly the ideal environment for it."

Sigfried nodded. "As I said."

Adina bit the inside of her cheek. From blood mages to mischievous fae, there were few beneficial reasons sage and dry wood would be in the middle of a marsh. The last thing they needed right now was another complication.

She studied the shadows between the cypress trees surrounding them. Perhaps it was some plot of her father's. After all, he was working with Damon. The two of them could be out there, right now, just waiting for her and her friends to fall into their trap.

"Okay," she said, wrapping her fingers around her sword. "Let's go check it out, but we need to be careful."

Forming up behind Sigfried, they picked their way cautiously north.

A half-league or so later, René pulled to a halt. "Hey, guys. My foot feels funny." Pulling up his dripping pant leg and pulling off his boot, he pivoted to the side.

The portion of his skin that had been exposed to water had turned black.

Adina's heart skipped a beat. *By the gods!* She took a half-step back, away from the water's edge, just to be extra safe.

"God's teeth!" Erik muttered. "What manner of sorcery is this?"

Adina blinked. Indeed. There were more threats here than met the eye.

Bracing one hand on Hana's shoulder, René peeled off his boot and sock. Beneath, his skin was swollen and wrinkled, as though he'd soaked it in a tub of hot water for hours on end.

Which was ridiculous, because Adina had used her Talent to thoroughly dry it as soon as he'd been clear of the water.

Crouching to get a better look, Adina studied his foot. "How does it feel?"

"Tingly," he said, flinching. "Like something is stabbing the entire area with thousands of tiny needles."

Hana disengaged her shoulder from his grip and knelt beside Adina. Chewing her lower lip she lightly prodded his ankle. "Does that hurt?"

He shook his head. "I feel the pressure, but it just makes the needles worse."

"It's definitely swollen," Hana said. She raised an eyebrow and glanced up at him. "Are you allergic to anything?"

René scoffed. "Allergies?" Realizing she was serious, he scrunched his face in thought. "Not that I'm aware of. Maybe I'm allergic to cursed bog water?"

Ugh. Now was not the time to be making inappropriate jokes. Adina bit back the urge to snap at him. That wouldn't help the situation, either.

Hana took her fingernail and scratched at a bulge that looked like a thickened leaf on the side of his ankle. She worked her nail underneath it and gently pulled the thing off his skin. "Or leeches." She grimaced as she tossed it into the swamp. Glancing at Adina, she asked, "Any signs of magic?"

Licking her lips, Adina reached out with her Talent. She didn't exactly know what to look for, if magic would feel different to her than water or any of the other elements. Closing her eyes, she focused on his foot. The strands of her ability wove around the distorted flesh as though blown by the wind, but otherwise didn't react. After a few heartbeats, she sighed and dropped her shoulders. It would of course be too much to ask for the magic to feel tingly or whisper into her ear how to reverse it. "I don't think so, but I'm definitely not an expert." For that, they'd need Damon. She shuddered. Or Sujani.

René shook his head, as though he'd been reading her thoughts. "No. No way, no how." Pulling his foot from Hana's grip, he shoved it back in the sock and pulled his boot back on. "I'm sure it'll be just fine. I'll walk it off, and it'll go away eventually."

Adina frowned. Typical man. "You can't ignore every injury in hopes it will self-resolve. Especially if there's magic involved."

"We're immortal," he said with a huff. "We can recover from more than most."

René was being excessively pigheaded again. Adina met Hana's gaze, the solemnity in the other woman's gaze reflecting Adina's own thoughts.

With a sigh, Hana heaved herself to her feet. "You're being stubborn."

"I'm an adult," he said. "I have a right to decide how I treat my body."

Adina bit her lips to hold back a frown. Out here in the middle of nowhere was no place for bravado. She brushed her hands off on her pants as she stood. "You can do whatever you want, René. Just remember, out here, it's easy for small problems to turn into bigger ones."

"Let us know if anything changes," Hana added.

"Okay, fine. Yes, I will," he said as he met Hana's gaze. His voice softened as he stared into her eyes. "I promise."

She flashed him a quick smile before turning to the rest of the group. "Then, I suppose it's best if we continue?"

Adina couldn't agree more. The sooner they pressed forward, the faster they could get out of this cursed bog.

The next isthmus was particularly narrow. Small waves lapped at the tufts of grass. Adina spread her hands out to either side to avoid stepping in the water, like a gymnast on a balance beam, as she moved from clump to clump of turf. Behind her, Erik's armor clanked with each cautious step.

The cicadas went quiet. The silence smothered them like someone had thrown a weighted blanket over the marsh.

Ahead, Sigfried pulled to a stop and held up his hand. Everyone froze. Erik drew his blade with a soft *snick*.

Adina narrowed her eyes, peering into the mists ahead. A shallow hill rose from the water, blocking the view of anything behind it. She swallowed past the sudden dryness in her throat. The hairs on her arms stood on end, and she ran her hands over them to alleviate the itching.

Sigfried crouched on all fours, his bones and muscles shifting with quiet pops and groans. A few breaths later, the Great Gray Bear glanced over his shoulder at them.

Madalina whispered, "He says to stay here while he scouts ahead. What he smells is just over the crest."

Grabbing Erik's hand, Adina guided him to a larger patch of grass and plant matter that was wide enough to support them both. His steady presence at her side was more of a relief than she'd like to admit; the golden shimmering bond between them was so strong she could practically *see* it if she looked hard enough.

He gave her a half-grin and murmured into her ear, "Ready to meet this Gaelle De Guignes?"

She licked her lips. "As ready as ever."

He took her hand with his free one and squeezed.

She threw him what she hoped was a reassuring smile to hide the ice in her gut before drawing her own sword. "Do you think we're in for a fight?"

He shrugged. "Depends on who or what it is that Sig's tracking." He raised his eyebrow and turned to René. "Any thoughts?"

René shook his head, blinking. "What? What do you mean?" he asked, leaning forward, keeping his voice low.

Erik cleared his throat and whispered, "Any ideas what would smell like sage in the middle of this bog?"

"And dry wood," Adina added with a pointed glance at the wet marshland surrounding them.

René shrugged. "No idea. The legends don't associate any particular location in the bog or smells with The Gaelle De Guignes. It's like they're vague on purpose or something."

Hana frowned, her somber gaze encompassing each of them. "Or something."

Adina turned her attention back to the hill ahead of them, where Sigfried had disappeared. Coming here had been a bad idea. They should've worked harder to find another option.

But she could hardly let Sigfried face what lay ahead on his own.

Perhaps she should pull the shadows around herself and follow him?

She took a step forward and Erik grabbed her arm. "Where are you going?"

Adina opened her mouth then paused. Patience was a virtue, one she should seek to cultivate as an assassin. She sighed, deflating. "Nowhere...just wondering where Sigfried got himself to."

Madalina turned and waved them all forward. "Come on! Sig says it's safe."

Adina stepped forward, pulling her falchion from its sheath. Not because she didn't trust Sigfried—she trusted him with her unlife, as she did the others. But having a weapon ready against any unwelcome surprises was never a bad idea.

The grass grew longer the further they got from the waterline. By the time they reached the crest, the grasses were nearly to her waist. She crouched, using the long stalks as cover. The clear smell of burnt sage teased her senses and reminded her of the short time she'd spent training with Sujani.

Before he'd tried to make her his blood sacrifice.

She shook her head, shoving the memories of his betrayal to the back of her mind, where she locked them away. Now was hardly the time to lose her focus—it could get her or her friends ended.

A bundle of sage hung from scrubby tree branches. Stepping closer, she tilted her head and squinted. They resembled a crude representation of a person without a head—a triangular body with branches at each point extending out to form legs and arms.

The earthy, herbaceous scent tickled her nose, completely out of place in their current environment.

The fine hairs on the back of her neck prickled as a shiver ran down her spine.

These were magic.

Unfortunately, she wasn't experienced enough to identify what kind. It could be anything from blood magic to a simple herbalist charm.

Adina swallowed and circled around the closest figure, giving it plenty of space. As she crested the top of the hill, more sage, fashioned in a similar manner, hung sprinkled around the area in no discernable pattern. A fine mist spread across the ground, giving the whole area an ethereal feeling of anticipation.

A large grizzly bear approached them, eyeing the ornaments with a grunt.

"There's no one here," Madalina translated, her voice pitched low enough Adina had to strain to hear it.

Adina nodded at the eerie herb bundle. "This whole area is unnerving." Especially with the all-too-human figures strung throughout.

"I've never seen such a thing," Hana said, walking up to the closest one. She reached out with a finger to touch it.

Ice-cold dread flooded up through Adina. "No, don't!" She lunged forward as her voice echoed across the silent hill.

But the figure just swung harmlessly back and forth at Hana's nudge.

Adina glanced around the area. No signs of life moved beyond their group.

What she wouldn't give for the happy chirp of a cicada or croak of a frog right now.

She jumped as Erik put his hand on her shoulder. "Are you okay?"

Despite the comforting presence of his hand, she shook her head as her eyes skated over the edges of the too-silent clearing. "No. This whole area feels heavy, like it's waiting for something to happen." She swallowed as her voice cracked. "Don't you feel like we're being watched?"

Erik shook his head. "No, but I trust your instincts." Turning his attention to the others, he said, "We should stay together."

René and Hana stepped closer without argument. Madalina turned her attention to the sky and smiled.

Adina glanced up. The stars were faintly visible through the mist. A few isolated clouds blocked the moon as they drifted by on their celestial journey. Her stomach hollowed as she stared at the distant sparkling lights, a reminder of how isolated and insignificant they all were.

There would be no blood mage to save them if something went wrong out here.

Sigfried rumbled, pulling Madalina's attention his way.

After a heartbeat, she whispered, "Sig says if there's no one nearby, do we want to stay and see if someone comes, or press forward?"

Adina glanced around the hill. She had no desire to stay anywhere near these sage ornaments longer than they had to.

René cleared his throat. "I think it's safe to move on." He peered at one of the hanging bundles from the corner of his eye. "Clearly, this is not the oracle we seek."

Hana untied one of the hanging bushels the size of her forearm and tucked it in her pack.

"What are you doing?" Adina hissed.

Hana shrugged. "I'd like to study it. I've never seen sage used in this way, and I want to see if I can figure out what its purpose is."

Adina shuddered. This entire bog, and everything in it, felt cursed. "I don't know that removing that is the wisest move."

René stepped into her line of sight. "Why not? It's not like it's been magicked to kill us in our sleep or anything."

"That you know of," Erik said. "We didn't think there was a problem with the water, either."

Sigfried rumbled deep in his throat.

Hana glanced at the bear. "This may be the only solid ground for leagues. We'll eventually need to find shelter for the day." She paused. "I could make us a small cave. And here, at least, we know it won't fill up with water."

Adina glanced at the crescent moon, which was lower in the sky than the last time she'd thought about it. Based on what had happened to

René's foot, the last thing they needed was more exposure to the bog water. She eyed the bundles again. Yet...

"I don't know if I'd rather spend the day with the sage or the water."

Well, saying it out loud made it sound foolish. She was no child to jump at shadows.

A rabbit with gray and brown ticked fur hopped into the clearing and settled under one of the hanging figurines.

Adina froze. Speaking of things that were out of place...

Madalina tipped her head sideways. "Do bunnies like sage?"

Hana shrugged. "Maybe?" She walked over and, when the rabbit didn't hop away, unhooked the ornament above it and set it on the ground.

The animal took a few sniffs then disappeared into the grass.

With a shrug, Hana returned the figure to its branch.

"If we're going to stay here for the day," Erik said, glancing at Adina before meeting everyone else's eyes, "I'd like to take some time to clear the area, and make sure there aren't any unpleasant surprises waiting for us while we sleep."

Sigfried snorted in agreement and moved off into the brush, likely to do that very thing. Erik followed.

That was a good idea. Squeezing the handle of her sword, she moved to join them.

"Adina, will you watch my back while I get the cave built?" Hana asked.

Adina froze halfway through a step. "What?"

René put both fists on his hips. "Hey! Am I not sufficient protection?"

Hana gave René an apologetic smile. "I agree that there's some sort of power here, and I'd feel safer with two swords at my back, just in case I do something to disturb it."

René ground his teeth.

Hana smiled and batted her eyelashes at him.

He sighed, dropping his fists in exasperation. "Fine!" He pierced Adina with a glare. "But if we get attacked, I get first dibs."

Adina shrugged. "Fine with me." If they got in a fight, he could have as many of their attackers as he wanted. She eyed the sage bundles. Five, six, seven, eight...there were twelve in the immediate vicinity, not counting the one Hana had pilfered.

Putting her back to Hana and René, Adina scanned the edge of the clearing again.

Hana took a deep breath and the earth beneath their feet shifted.

Taking a few steps away to be out of the construction zone, Adina studied the hill. To her left was a large, crumbling log that had been bleached white with age. Likely the source of the dry wood Sigfried had smelled earlier.

Madalina perched on one of the smaller branches of said log and watched Hana work.

Several minutes later, Hana brushed her palms off on her pants. "There we go! Everything should be ready for the morning. And I'll be able to cover the opening easily enough once we're all inside."

René smiled, flashing his teeth at them. "Great. Now we can relax and wait for Sigfried and Erik to return." He strutted over to Madalina and leaned against the dried wood, trying to look like he wasn't favoring his foot. He leaned against the tree. Something cracked, like when she'd stepped on a scorpion once.

René jumped back, wiping his hand off on his pant leg. "Ew! Gross! Who put a bug there?"

"It's just a cicada skeleton," Madalina said. "If you didn't want to touch it, why did you put your hand there?"

René huffed. "Obviously, I didn't see it." Glaring at the crushed exoskeleton, he stormed around to the other side of Madalina, examined the log thoroughly, then slouched against it.

"Does his walk look worse to you?" Adina asked Hana under her breath.

Hana nodded. "Possibly. I'll ask him about it later when we're alone."

Adina ran her tongue across her teeth. Hopefully René's pride wouldn't get in the way of him letting Hana help him.

Hana rolled her eyes. "Men."

Adina sighed. "Right?" It wasn't going to be very amusing if it progressed enough that he couldn't walk himself out of the bog.

From across the clearing, René stepped through a particularly long patch of grass and into view. Flashing her an overly wide grin, he headed in her direction.

Adina froze as her gaze whipped around to her left, where René still lounged with Madalina. "Hey!" She drew her sword, pointing it at the newcomer. "Who are you?"

René lunged to his feet and was beside Hana in half a heartbeat, his blade also pointed at the other René. "You're not me! What's going on here?"

The second René halted approximately twenty paces away and met René's gaze. "You're looking for me, nobleman, are you not?"

Madalina burst into a big grin as she came to stand next to Adina. "The Gaelle De Guignes!"

The second René turned his attention to her, scanning her from the tip of her head to her toes before nodding in approval. "Well met, fellow Seer. For convenience, you can call me Gaelle." He turned his attention to Hana. "Why have you taken my totem?"

"Your what?" René asked.

Gaelle pointed at the nearest sage figure.

"I was hoping to study it," Hana said, removing the bundle from her bag. "I've never seen its like before. My apologies." She held it out.

Gaelle tilted his head, eyes going between the sage in Hana's hands and her face. His eyes sparkled. "Keep it. Let me know what you learn, Poison Master."

Hana blinked, the only sign of surprise that crossed her face.

Adina's brow hurt. Distinguishing between the two Renés was making her head pound.

The silence stretched for several heartbeats before Gaelle turned his attention back to her and Madalina. "Call your mates back. What I have to say to you should be said to all."

Adina shook her head. "What?" *Mates?*

Gaelle turned his gaze to her. "You are bonded, are you not?"

Adina opened her mouth to deny it, then snapped her jaw closed. Was *that* what this gold tie between them was?

Heat radiated from her chest, bubbling up until a smile burst across her face. Erik was hers.

One side of Gaelle's mouth pulled up into a grin as he winked.

Adina imagined herself grabbing that ethereal golden bond and *tugging*.

"Excellent," Gaelle said, nodding. "They'll be here in a few." He gestured to the rotting wood. "You may as well make yourselves comfortable."

At Gaelle's urging, Adina walked over to the log and sat on one of the branches along with everyone else. Her eyes danced back and forth between Gaelle and René, looking to pick out any possible difference so she could distinguish between the two, but the reproduction was perfect. Even down to his water-darkened boot.

Adina winced. Erik and Sigfried were not going to take the Gaelle's appearance well if he looked exactly like one of them... But, as an oracle, theoretically Gaelle should know that.

She peeked at Madalina, who sat on one of the smaller branches, leaning back against the log with one leg pulled up to her chest. She seemed totally relaxed, not at all worried about how her husband would react to find a second René in their midst.

Adina shifted her weight to balance more comfortably on her own branch. Perhaps she was borrowing trouble where none existed.

Gaelle turned, his gaze focused on the far side of the clearing. A heartbeat later, Erik and the Great Gray Bear stepped from the grass into view.

Both men froze. Erik's gaze flicked between both Renés before settling on Adina, the unvoiced question in his eyes.

Sigfried bared his teeth and growled.

"It's okay," Madalina called as she pointed to René on her left. "This one's real."

In spite of herself, Adina chuckled. "Erik, Sigfried, meet The Gaelle De Guignes." She gestured to the second René. "Gaelle, meet Erik and Sigfried."

Gaelle nodded as the two men cautiously circled the new addition and joined them against the log.

Erik leaned in to whisper in Adina's ear in Hakki, "What's going on here?"

"We seem to have found our oracle," she responded in the same language. "Though why he resembles René, I'm not quite certain."

"I can appear however I wish," Gaelle said. With a flash of silver light, he transformed into a mirror image of Madalina. A heartbeat later, a second flash of light revealed the same gray-brown ticked rabbit Hana had tried to give one of the sage figures to.

Adina's stomach jumped as tingles ran up her arms. "A shapeshifter?"

With a final silver flash, a duplicate of René again stood before them. He gave her a half-bow and gestured to the surrounding clearing. "Only thanks to the power that infuses the area."

Sigfried's muscles and bones shifted with several loud *pops* and *snaps* until he was once again in human form. He took up a position next to Madalina and crossed his arms. "You were not very hard to find."

Gaelle shrugged. "Why would I make it difficult? Your group is our best chance at avoiding a second Cataclysm." With a shudder, he continued, "Trust me. They're not pleasant."

"This power, is that what I've been feeling since we entered the swamp?" Adina asked.

Gaelle nodded. "You must have a significant amount of magic in your blood to feel it as strongly as you do."

Adina sighed. Lucky her.

"Speaking of..." Gaelle looked at René's foot. "You must have been exposed to someone with strong magic in their blood, as well, to react to the water the way you did."

René scoffed, glancing at his foot then not-so-subtly crossing it behind the other, out of view. "Really?"

"You're not bonded with anyone—" Gaelle glanced at Hana—"yet. So...have you shared minds with a mage?"

Adina choked. *Oh, no...*

René froze, the blood draining from his face. Several breaths later, he opened his mouth. "No..."

Gaelle gave him a flat look. "You'll need access to that mage again to clear the night-rot. Otherwise, it'll spread and consume you."

Giving up all pretense, René ripped off his boot and sock, studying his foot. Hana dropped down to her knee for a better look.

From Adina's angle, his foot looked about the same as it had before. She clenched her jaw and glared at Gaelle. How were they supposed to convince Damon to heal René?

Unless they had something he wanted in exchange. Something like dragon bones.

Gaelle's eyes flicked to hers once in acknowledgement before returning to René.

"It's spreading!" René's voice trembled as he scrubbed his ankle with his fingers. "It's further up my leg than before." He glanced at Gaelle, panic stringing his words together. "How do I get the mage to help me? He'd sooner watch me die than spit on me."

Galle shrugged. "How doesn't matter, as long as you can drink some of his blood."

René slid his hand through his hair, pulling it away from his face and stared at the ground. "Yeah, okay. I can do that. How long do I have?" His chest heaved in and out, his breathing becoming more rapid.

Gaelle shrugged. "Even the wisest cannot say. Days...weeks. No more than a month. Move quickly, Duke, if you wish to regain your duchy."

That caught René's attention. "Regain my duchy," he echoed. "You mean...there's a chance?"

The oracle smiled. "There is always a chance, as long as you don't give up."

René's eyes sparkled as he turned to Hana and gave her a quick grin.

"Where do we find ley lines and dragon bones?" Erik asked, stepping up to them.

Gaelle raised an eyebrow and nodded to Sigfried. "The dragon bones are closer than you may think. You must be guided by the gods themselves to have found the one tool strong enough—" He pointed to Erik's pack that held the petrified bones— "to forge the bones into a new blade."

Erik paused. "Wait...we need to use the petrified bones in the fold-forming of the new blades?"

Shaking his head, Gaelle smiled. "One does not fold-form dragon's bones. You flint knap them."

Adina furrowed her brow and shook her head. "Flint knap?"

"Strike the two as if they were flint and steel, breaking off shards until the remnant is shaped appropriately."

"God's teeth," Erik muttered.

Adina concurred. Maybe Maja, or Madalina's "stars" truly were watching over them. Hopefully somewhere around here there was enough petrified bone for two daggers. The weight that had been pressing down on her lifted as a lighthearted feeling flickered through her chest.

Perhaps they had a chance after all.

"And the ley lines?" Sigfried asked, speaking for the first time since he and Erik had returned.

"They're here, all around us," Adina said, splaying her hands wide. "I can practically *feel* them."

Gaelle nodded. "There are ley lines here, true." He pierced Adina with René's signature stare. "You will not draw on them for the forging. This convergence is mine and does not have sufficient power to accomplish what you seek."

Steeling her back and her jaw against the intensity of the glare as her own disappointment flared, Adina said, "Do you have a location you recommend that *would* support such a ritual?" It hardly seemed fair. They were supposed to be so close...

Gaelle studied them. "To recreate the beginning, you must return to the source."

"The source?" Adina held back a sigh. She grew tired of being talked in circles.

"The original center of the Cataclysm," Madalina said, peering at Gaelle.

Erik shook his head. "Which is where, exactly?"

"Perhaps if you used all the resources available to you, you'd know." Gaelle pressed his lips together in a tight grimace. Slowly shaking his head, he sighed.

Erik pressed his lips into a thin line and crossed his arms. "We don't exactly have a lot of time for word games."

Gaelle turned the full weight of his gaze onto Adina, making her skin crawl. "You were on the right path before. Trust yourselves and your blood will lead you to the origin point of the Cataclysm, where Maja and Ahion circle each other even now."

René held up a palm. "Wait...Maja we know about, but Ahion is dead. Damon killed him during the first Cataclysm."

Adina nodded. "Damon's entire existence revolves around that night."

Gaelle studied each of them as though they were children, too dense to comprehend a simple lesson. "A ritual designed to kill two gods, in failing to kill one, why would you assume the other was destroyed?"

Adina's knees went weak as she leaned back against the tree as the world abruptly tilted sideways. "You mean, Ahion's been alive this whole time?"

"That depends on your definition of alive. Was Maja? Neither one was able to interact with the world before now." Gaelle gestured to the south. "And once again, we have fires, rain, earthquakes, and all manner of natural disasters building to a second Cataclysm."

Adina shook her head, forcing her thoughts back to the present. "Do we have time to prevent it?" she asked, lifting her gaze to the oracle's.

"Who can predict the actions of gods? But you had best hurry. Even now, Sujani gathers their power against you."

Sigfried slung his pack over one shoulder. "Then we should leave now."

Gaelle shook his head. "No. The sun is too near the horizon. Sleep here for the day. My totems and the ley lines will keep you safe. Then, head south and east as quickly as you can."

Gaelle scanned each of them from top to bottom, threw a wink at René, and disappeared in a flash of silver light.

Adina took several steadying breaths as she reined in her thoughts. So that was an oracle. For some reason she couldn't quite put her finger on, she liked Gaelle. Glancing at Erik, then the others, she said, "If Ahion's alive, is that good or bad for us?"

Erik shrugged. "Uncertain. However, if Damon and Sujani are still at each other's throats, perhaps their gods will be also, and everyone will be distracted when we make our move?"

That may be a little too optimistic, but at least it was highly unlikely the two gods would team up against them.

"The stars say we should get in the cave now," Madalina said.

Adina turned to her, only to find Madalina's head tilted back as she studied the sky.

"Why do you say that?" René asked. "Dawn isn't for hours yet."

"True," she said, nodding. "But someone is coming...someone who's been following us since The Drowned City. We don't want him to discover we're here."

René froze, hand halfway to his blade. "Who is it?"

Adina pushed herself away from the log, toward where Hana had dug the cavern. "Personally, I don't want to wait to find out." She glanced intentionally around the clearing. "Especially if The Gaelle De Guignes didn't bother to stick around to greet them."

The faintest scent of carrion in the midsummer's heat reached her nose and she froze, ice filling her veins. "Damon."

Madalina went white as René seemed caught between charging off after Damon and ducking into Hana's cave.

Erik grabbed René's upper arm and hauled him toward the entrance. "Come on. Drink his blood later."

Two heartbeats later, they were all inside the cave as Hana resettled the dirt and grass over the entrance. She left one little spy hole so they could keep an eye on the clearing.

Adina pushed her eye to the opening.

"What do you see?" René asked.

"Shhh!" she said, putting her finger to her lips, even though in the pitch blackness there was no way he could see it.

Adina took a deep breath as a man-sized shadow stepped into the clearing.

Chapter 16

Damon

Chapter 16

Damon

Damon strolled up to one of the sage figures, snatching it off the tree. What an odd thing to do with herbs. Someone must truly have too much time on their hands. Turning the sage over, he peered around the clearing.

Eleven similarly shaped bundles hung from various branches throughout the area. He shook his head. As far as protective totems went, sage was pretty low on the power scale unless you were hoping for some extra luck.

The skin on the back of his neck tingled, and not just from the power that infused the vicinity.

The old librarian had been correct. More than one ley line ran through here, he was certain of it. He swallowed against the elation that warmed his chest. It was best to not get excited too quickly. After all, there had been no word from Seven, and he still didn't have any dragon bones.

He rolled his shoulders, stretching to rid himself of the tingles. Spinning to face the clearing, he took a deep breath. "I know you're here, oracle. I can feel you. Come out and let's talk like the immortal adults we are."

A heartbeat passed.

Two.

The grass to his right parted, and a figure emerged, dressed in black robes. A silver diadem crowned with a blue moonstone rested on his forehead, above a face with red eyes that had haunted Damon's nightmares for over a millennium.

Baring his fangs, he snarled at Ahion's visage. Damon's blood pounded through his ears as his vision narrowed until his entire focus was on the newcomer. A wound long since scarred over ripped open anew, nearly bringing him to his knees as the pain of loss a thousand years old tore through his chest. Pulling on his Talent, he hurled a handful of black and red-tinted daggers at the imposter. "How *dare* you wear his face?" His vision turned watery at the image of the one being he'd once served above all others, including himself.

Stepping to the side as the blades flew harmlessly past, the newcomer frowned. "You summoned me, vampire. I'm not one of your minions who can be called forth at your will. You'd do best to remember that."

Air hissed between Damon's fangs with each heaving breath. Gathering his Talent, he sent his mental fingers spearing toward the other's mind...

Only to be met with a flawless obsidian wall. There were no cracks or weaknesses he could exploit to gain entrance.

Regardless, this was not his god. The overwhelming ecstasy of being in the presence of such deific power was nonexistent. "Don't try your power plays on me, oracle. Despite your abilities, I can still kill you."

Ahion tilted his head sideways and stared at Damon.

Something the *real* god had never done.

Damon snarled. "If you can't get his body language right, then look like someone else." Anyone else.

Ahion chuckled. "Why would I, when it's so much fun getting under your skin?" He rubbed his hands together. "It's not so enjoyable being on the receiving end, is it?"

Damon lunged forward, reaching for Ahion's neck.

The oracle stepped back, holding up a finger. Wiggling it back and forth like a teacher chiding an errant pupil, he said, "Ah, ah, ah... Remember, if you kill me, you won't get answers to your questions. And you'll have sped all the way here for nothing."

Every muscle in Damon's body contracted as he fought the urge to rip out his throat for daring to impersonate Ahion. But the oracle had a point...he was here for answers, and if he gave in to his rage, he'd lose any advantage he had over Sujani. And Seven.

"I'm looking for a confluence of ley lines."

Ahion gave him a flat glare and raised both hands to gesture around the clearing. "And so you've found them, or were you not aware?"

Damon ground his teeth so hard his jaw popped. Later. He would kill this oracle later, slowly. "And dragon bones."

"The Cataclysm exterminated the dragons over a thousand years ago."

He took a step forward. "Yet some of their bones must remain, even now.

Amusement danced in the oracle's eyes. "Some, perhaps, are closer than you think."

Glancing around the area, Damon growled deep in his throat. "Are you going to answer my question, or not?" If he couldn't find dragon bones, he had no chance to forge a second bone shard blade to kill Sujani. And he could kiss his unlife and empire goodbye.

Ahion blinked at him. "I'm sorry...did you ask me a question?"

Damon grabbed his hair with both hands and pulled. *Ugh.* This was why he *hated* oracles so much. They were frustratingly pigheaded.

"Where can I find dragon bones?" The oracle's calm expression only served to fan the flames of his frustration.

"Why, in this very clearing, in fact."

"Ha, ha. Very funny."

"Another set of dragon bones lies attached to the hip of your rival." Ahon winked at him. "But surely you didn't need me to tell you about them."

No. He was already well aware of the fact that Sujani had the Bone Shard Blade, and that it was made of dragon bones, thank you very much. Exhaling forcefully through his nose, Damon paced around the oracle, keeping one eye on the man and using the other to scour the area for any possible hints of the existence of bones.

The imposter Ahion didn't even bother to turn with him.

After several tense minutes, Damon spun back to face the oracle. "You lie."

A sneer curled the oracle's upper lip as his nostrils flared. "I cannot lie! Be careful who you insult, vampire." Taking a deep breath, he continued, "You didn't really expect me to make it easy for you, did you?"

Damon lunged forward. Grabbing the imposter by his throat, he hoisted him from the ground.

"Death does not scare me." Ahion's wise eyes peered into his, the knowledge there driving an icy blade through Damon's heart. "I've seen what lies beyond, and it does not frighten me. But it *does* scare you, that your precious god won't be waiting for you when you finally arrive at death's door."

The fire that stoked his rage stuttered, ice replacing the heat that flowed through his veins. "You don't know what you're talking about. My god will be there to greet me with open arms. I was his most faithful servant, his high priest." Damon squeezed the oracle's throat a little harder. The hyoid bone shifted, pinching off the oracle's trachea.

A blinding silver flash of light burned Damon's retinas as his fingers closed around empty space, as though the oracle vaporized into nothing. He tensed, blinking as the lingering afterimage blinded him. Curling his fingers into claws, he braced for an attack. "Where are you? Do you resort to such cheap tricks now?"

After several heartbeats, his vision cleared. He stood alone in the middle of the clearing, calling to no one but himself.

Curse the mages.

He'd lost control again, and his one best shot at discovering the location of any dragon bones.

If the oracle had been telling the truth, then they were around here somewhere. Of course, a master liar could proclaim to never lie just as easily as a truthful man.

He shook his head. Following that circular logic was pointless—he'd only drive himself crazy.

Power called to power. Perhaps, before the Cataclysm, dragons had congregated here, drawn by the call of the ley lines. In which case, the entire swamp could be filled with their ancient bones.

He stared absentmindedly out into the mists, where the water lay beyond. His mind wandered to the last words the oracle had spoken to him before disappearing. About Ahion not waiting for him after Final Death.

Damon shook his head, forcing his thoughts away from the chilling prospect. It was ridiculous, of course. He'd been the god's high priest and had faithfully served up to and through the Cataclysm, even sacrificing that which he'd loved above all else—Ahion himself.

No. The oracle had merely been trying to get a rise out of him, much like it had by choosing to appear as his god. And, Oracle or not, there was no way anyone could know for sure what lay beyond.

It was time to put the oracle's words aside and find some dragon bones.

Of course, there was no way he would be the one tromping through the bog searching for them. Perhaps a seeking spell?

He glanced around the clearing again. With all this sage about, this may be the ideal place for a little bit of location blood magic.

Snatching three of the sage figures from where they hung, he placed them in a triangle at his feet. A large, half-rotten log on one side of the clearing provided three forearm-length branches that he placed on top of those, pointing into the center of the triangle.

Now, all he needed was the sacrifice.

A wild rabbit with gray and brown ticking on its fur hopped into view. Spearing his Talent in its direction, he grabbed the animal's primitive mind, freezing it in place.

He couldn't have asked for a more perfect offering.

Grabbing the bunny by the scruff of its neck, he carried it over to the pile of sage and sticks. Drawing a dagger from his waist, he slashed its throat.

As its lifeblood covered the sage, he recited the appropriate words, pushing the power running through his veins into the spell. "Per magikae et sanguini mai, ostenda mili ubi pounont ossa draconae."

The rabbit's blood glowed crimson as it soaked into the herb leaves.

He paused and clenched his fists until his nails cut into his palms as his breathing stuttered. That wasn't supposed to happen.

Rabbit's blood shouldn't have enough magic to react.

A heartbeat later, the air filled with the scent of burning sage as the power of the blood magic poured through his veins. For the first time since Esnaria's old king had died, he felt light enough to fly. Taking a deep breath, he luxuriated in the rich artistry of a well-cast spell, and the joy of being moments away from victory.

The three sticks, covered in blood and sage ashes, hovered in the air, spinning like the arrow on a compass that couldn't find true north. They wobbled and tottered.

Damon bit his lower lip. The spell could not fail, or he'd likely never find any dragon bones.

The oracle couldn't have lied to him about them being nearby. The Gaelle De Guignes was supposed to prophesy only the truth, according to the old librarian's notes.

The sticks snapped into alignment and sped through the air, embedding themselves in the side of an innocuous rise in the middle of the clearing.

Well, wasn't that interesting?

Dropping his grip on the spell, he allowed the mystical energy to fade away as he slunk to the hillock.

The elevated area was too small to be a full-blown dragon's nest, or to cover a full dragon's skeleton. But perhaps a leg or a rib some ancient predator had carried off and buried?

Yanking the three sticks from the ground, he dropped to his knees and, taking the stoutest one, scratched a furrow in the dirt. Over and over he dug, each pass making frustratingly little progress.

After several minutes, he rested his weight on his ankles and wiped the back of his palm across his forehead. For being in the middle of a swamp, this dirt was remarkably hard, like the mortar used to glue rocks and bricks together.

But if the spell said his dragon bones were here, then his dragon bones were here. Unlike the oracle, blood magic didn't lie.

"I know you're here," he muttered as he dug into the earth.

The stick snapped.

"Dammit."

Tossing the useless thing away, he stormed to a half-rotten log and pulling out his dagger, cut off the largest branch he could before going back and resuming his digging.

Several minutes later, he stumbled forward as the branch pushed through into an open space and plunged into the earth.

His heart drummed in his chest as heat and energy exploded through him. He was mere moments away from the dragon bones.

Six sets of eyes glared back at him.

Oh, no...

"What are *you lot* doing here?" he growled.

The brown-haired woman standing next to René flicked her wrist as the air vibrated with her Talent.

Damon sunk knee-deep into the dirt that had mere moments ago been harder than mortar. He jerked his head back, blinking.

Someone with elemental control over earth.

Wouldn't that be handy when it came time to forge a new Bone Shard Blade?

He wouldn't be able to free himself from the ground without this vampire's blessing.

Damon snapped his arm forward, faster than an asp, and snatched Adina's arm, jerking her to him and spinning her around so his chest pressed against her back.

Erik lunged forward.

"Stop!" Damon said, pressing his finger and thumb on either side of Adina's windpipe, the nails angled to pierce skin and the major arteries in her neck.

Hello, princess.

Adina inhaled as she stiffened.

Your note promised me pertinent updates. It seems you've managed to find dragon bones and haven't bothered to inform me?

A distinct image of her baring her fangs at him flashed through his mind. *<Even if I'd had a way to contact you, just because the dragon bones are nearby doesn't mean we have them.>*

Erik froze, his gaze locked on Adina's face for several heartbeats before he turned a death-glare on Damon as he drew his sword. "Release her, or I'll end you."

Heat rushed through his veins as he fought the urge to squeeze her throat until it snapped. *Liar. My blood magic says otherwise, princess.*

Damon scoffed. "I'll end her before you take another step. But by all means, try me."

Adina stiffened as his mental words sunk in. Her wide-eyed gaze locked with Erik's.

Her voice echoed through his mind. *<We'll tell you where the dragon bones are, if...>*

A lighthearted feeling spread through Damon's torso as he fought to keep the victorious grin from his face. *Yes?*

<If you let René drink some of your blood.>

He glanced at the others. Surely this must be a trick of some sort. *What? No.* The last thing he needed was to develop a blood-bond with Marcos' bastard.

She shifted, crossing her arms. *<Then no dragon bones for you.>*

The outer edges of his vision turned red. *So be it.* Waiting a heartbeat to make sure Erik wasn't going to do anything foolish, Damon sent his Talent toward the group. Those closest to the front, Erik, Madalina, and the brown-haired woman, wrinkled their noses in distaste.

An errant wind blew through the clearing, ripping his Talent away from him.

Snarling, he shook Adina, his nails breaking her skin where they touched. "None of that, now, princess."

The muscles bulged in Erik's neck as every muscle in his body tensed. The leather of his sword handle creaked in his white-knuckled grip.

A thick bead of blood welled on Adina's neck. Hunger welled up in Damon's veins. It had been over two nights since he'd properly fed, after all.

Keeping one eye on the five young vampires and wrapping his other arm securely around Adina's waist, he licked his tongue up her neck. She jerked in his grip as the heady flavor of her blood exploded in his mouth, and he ripped his head away, lest he give in to the urge to bury his fangs in her neck and drain her dry.

The rage on Erik's face was worth the effort.

"Now," he said, licking his lips slowly as he stared at Erik, he jammed his fingers deeper into Adina's neck. "Where are you hiding my dragon bones?"

Chapter 17
Erik

Erik's blood, already running cold, turned to ice. Of course, he'd heard Damon and the oracle's muffled conversation, and he'd wanted to throttle Gaelle for telling the other vampire there were dragon bones in the area.

Clearing his mind of everything except Adina, still in Damon's grasp, Erik met Damon's gaze. "What dragon bones?"

And why wasn't René using his speed to attack Damon? They could kill two birds with one stone—get Damon's blood and free Adina.

Damon's eyes sparkled as he met Erik's gaze with a cruel smile.

Oh. That was why. How many of their minds had Damon captured before Adina had cleared the air of his stench? He may be the only one who'd managed to avoid it.

He should've been smarter, managed to warn the others somehow.

"The dragon bones you have, idiot." Damon turned his attention to Hana. "Release me now, and give me the bones, or Adina dies."

"You wouldn't dare," Hana said. "Sujani and Septimus would kill you for it."

Damon speared her with his gaze. "You've clearly been out of touch for a while, so let me catch you up on current events. Sujani has raised his goddess, and therefore has no further need for Adina. And even if Seven was stupid enough to come after me for killing his precious daughter, he has no hope of overpowering me."

The truth behind Damon's words hammered into Erik's soul like an executioner's blade. His gut turned to lead, and an impossible weight pressed down on his shoulders. For all his physical prowess, Damon was right—he was way out of their league.

Being so helpless while Damon threatened Adina felt like someone was dragging razor blades through his veins. What was the point of being strong when that strength was useless?

He met her gaze. He didn't have to be a mind reader to understand the expression on her face.

Don't you dare *give them to him.*

The golden bond sparkled between them in his mind, as if to remind him how things had been before it existed. He couldn't lose her now, any more than he could in the cave with the Bone Shard Blade. At least, if the world ended in a second Cataclysm, they'd go together.

Pulling the small bag from his waist, he tossed it to Damon and nodded at Hana. "Let him go."

Hana glanced between Erik and Adina, clearly torn.

Damon caught the bag and opened it one-handed, examining the small bones inside. "Excellent. I knew you were the smartest of the bunch." He turned his attention to Hana. Gesturing to his legs, still buried knee-deep in the dirt, he said, "Now, if you don't mind, I have places to go, weapons to forge, and goddesses to kill."

"Let him go, Hana," Erik said, his gaze still burning holes through Damon's skull. After all, Damon was their best shot for killing Maja. And he couldn't lose Adina.

Damon smiled. "You're right, Erik. I'm your *only* chance to avert another Cataclysm. Chew on that for a night or two." He paused. "Unless you *want* most of the life on the planet to perish. It'll be really hard to hunt if everything's dead. Assuming you're fortunate enough to survive."

Erik glared at him, the muscles in his jaw popping with tension.

Hana sighed.

Abruptly, the dirt locking Damon's feet into place shifted, and he pulled each foot free as though stepping from a pile of sand.

Shoving Adina away from him, Damon smirked at Erik as he stepped forward to catch her.

"I don't want to catch any of you following me," Damon said. "Stay out of my way and perhaps I won't end you when I kill Maja and Sujani and assume control of all the realms."

Holding a gasping Adina against him, Erik flashed his fangs at Damon. "Get out of here, before I change my mind."

Damon snorted. "As if the Butcher of Mireen could do anything to me." With a laugh, he turned away and sauntered toward the grass. With a final, irreverent wave over his shoulder, Damon stepped into the grass.

Adina glanced over her shoulder at Damon. "Wait!"

Erik's vision tinted red at the bruised rasp of her voice.

Damon froze mid-step and turned, a sly grin tugging at one corner of his mouth. Raising an eyebrow, he asked, "Yes?"

"Where was the origin point of the Cataclysm?"

"What are you doing?" Hana hissed.

Erik blinked and jerked his head back, studying Adina. Indeed—Damon was hardly a trustworthy source of information.

"Gaelle told us to use all of our resources," Adina said, nodding at Damon. "He was there...of anyone, he should know."

Damon turned to face them and crossed his arms. "Indeed. I do. But why should I share with you?"

Adina lifted her chin. "Because we know where a strong enough confluence of ley lines is. Didn't you say back in Gorlinia you wanted to work together? This is your chance to stand behind your words."

He blinked at her as the silence stretched for several heartbeats.

Based on the twitches in Damon's facial muscles, if Erik had to guess, he'd say Adina and Damon were having a very tense mental conversation.

Damon signed and waved his hand over his shoulder. "Very well. It's buried beneath The Drowned City. The Colosseum."

"And that's where the ley lines are," she said.

Damon cursed under his breath and brushed his hand through his hair. "Stay out of my way, and don't follow me." Spinning on his heel, he strode out of the clearing and disappeared behind the tall grass.

Thank the gods. He was finally gone. The last of the tension drained from Erik's muscles.

Turning his attention to the woman in his arms, Erik ran his hand through her hair. "Are you alright? What were you guys talking about?"

She nodded. "My voice will be a little raspy for a while." Turning her face to him, she frowned and smacked him lightly on the chest, ignoring his other question. "Why did you give him our dragon bones?"

Erik blinked. "Why do you think? He would have ended you. He already knew we had them, thanks to Gaelle." A wave of red-hot anger rose in his gut, but he quashed it back down as he pulled her into a quick embrace. There was little he could do about what the oracle had said now, so there was no point in dwelling on it. Instead, he turned to the others. "Any idea how long they'll be frozen?"

Adina turned to Sigfried, Madalina and René. "I don't know. Probably until Damon decides he's got a good enough lead on us that we can't follow." She focused on Hana and gestured to the destroyed outer wall of their shelter. "Do you think you can fix this?"

Hana nodded and pulled out her magic blood bag, taking a deep drink. "Easily enough if you give me a few minutes. Keeping him out for as long as I managed was fairly draining."

"You did well," Erik said before focusing back on Adina. He ran his finger down the side of her neck, the fingernail marks from Damon already almost completely healed. "I'm sorry."

She scoffed. "For what? If you're apologizing for letting him go, I suppose I forgive you. If you're apologizing for what he did..." She shook her head and pressed her lips together. "That's not on you to apologize for."

He sighed. But it was. He should've been faster, or anticipated Damon's actions, somehow.

"Stop that!" Adina grabbed his jaw and turned his head to face her. "None of this is your fault, quit acting like you think it is. The important thing to focus on right now is our next step."

Erik slid his sword into its sheath and rested one hand on the hilt. "I suppose we'll have to either find another source of dragon bones, and somehow confirm their authenticity, or we can steal the ones we had back from Damon."

Hana frowned. "It's a tall order, but somehow I think we'll have more luck reclaiming them than finding new ones."

Adina nodded. "Agreed. Now all we have to do is figure out how to free the others from Damon's mind control."

Hana nodded as she circled the other three. "Any ideas what Damon's range is?"

"No clue," Adina said. "I know he can't snare us if we can't smell him, but as far as lingering effects..." She let her voice drift off with a shrug.

Erik chewed the inside of his cheek. Unfortunately, the person with the best idea of how long Damon's powers lasted was René, having been mind-possessed by Damon in Brachia. But René wasn't in any condition to impart the information.

Assuming he even would. He'd been reluctant to discuss anything about that situation with any of them, as far as Erik knew. He took a deep breath in and exhaled. "I suppose all we can do is wait." He raised an eyebrow at Hana. "And, perhaps, give them some of your magicked blood."

"It certainly can't hurt." She grabbed her blood bag and poured a few swallows into each of their mouths.

They waited for one breath, two...

Sigfried, Madalina and René remained motionless, frozen.

The eastern horizon turned the faintest hint of orange.

Sunrise.

"Shoot," Adina muttered. "Well, it was worth a shot, at least. Hopefully they'll recover by tomorrow evening."

Hana stomped her foot once and waved her fingers as though building a phantom sandcastle. The mound of dirt from the wall Damon had destroyed moved back into place, sealing them inside.

As the last of the starlight reflected in her eyes, Erik caught a flash of Hana's pursed lips and furrowed brows as she glanced at René.

With a groan, Erik sat on the ground, leaning against the rebuilt wall as Adina sat beside him.

Hopefully tomorrow, they'd all awake refreshed and ready to hunt down Damon in a race back to The Drowned City.

Erik opened his eyes as the pressure from the sun dissipated. He shifted his weight, smiling at the vanilla and jasmine scent of Adina's hair where her head rested on his right shoulder.

"Erik?" Her sleepy voice tickled the fine hairs near his ear, sending delightful shivers down his spine.

He wrapped his arm around her and pulled her close as the events of last night tumbled back into his mind. "Good evening."

"How are the others?" she asked.

"It's still early, they're likely not yet awake."

She squeezed his arm before she rolled forward and pushed to her feet. "Hana?"

A quiet groan sounded from a few feet away. "What?" Scuffling met his ears as the other woman shifted, likely rolling over or standing.

"Can you let us out? I want enough light to check on the others."

Erik mentally crossed his fingers. If the other three didn't recover, they'd have no choice but to carry them through the bog, and he wasn't quite sure how they'd manage Sigfried. The large man would need three or four people to carry him, alone.

The southern wall of their enclosure fell away as though Hana was merely pulling curtains aside. Starlight spilled into their cave.

Madalina's eyes flew open and she scrunched her nose. "Gaelle!"

Adina stepped back, glancing around the area of the courtyard she could see. "What? What's wrong?"

Alarm rushed through Erik, pushing aside the flood of relief at Madalina's awakening. Grabbing his sword, he drew it as he searched for what had upset her.

Stepping past them, she ran to a burnt pile of sage, putting her hand on the corpse of a small rabbit.

The same rabbit they'd seen last night.

Glancing over her shoulder, she looked back at them, the moonlight reflecting off the tears in her eyes. "Damon used him for blood magic. That's how he found our dragon bones."

Erik's stomach plunged to the ground. "I thought the oracle was immortal?"

Madalina shook her head. "He may not have aged, but he could be killed just like anyone else."

An overwhelming sense of loss had Erik staggering. He leaned against the cave wall to avoid falling to his knees. You'd think, being an oracle, Gaelle would have foreseen his own death and avoided Damon.

Adina came up beside him, putting her hand on his shoulder. "Of *course* Damon would sacrifice the oracle with no thought to the consequences. He's selfish and rotten to the core."

Erik was so focused on Madalina and the furry corpse in front of her, he almost missed Sigfried's grunt.

Adina whipped around. "Sigfried! You're okay!"

Sigfried nodded, his eyes locking on Madalina. "Damon's mind stinks like sewage." He shuddered. "It is not a pleasant place to be."

Adina raised an eyebrow. "Feeling sorry for him, are you?"

Sigfried furrowed his brow and shook his head. "No. He brought it upon himself."

Wincing in sympathy, Erik reached out and thumped Sigfried on the shoulder. "Welcome back to your own head." Having Charles for a father, he knew better than most how it felt to have someone invade his mind.

René blinked and shook his head with a loud exhale. "Ugh. Yuck!" He stared at Erik. "Why does that bucket of rat piss mind control me every single time we meet?"

That was a bit of an exaggeration, but Erik held back his eye roll. "You'd think by now, you'd know not to breathe in his presence."

"Not breathe?" René scoffed, dusting off his shoulders and sleeves. "Not breathing is as unnatural as mind control."

Hana gave René a quick hug and kissed his cheek. "I'm glad you're alright." She pulled back and sent him an exaggerated frown. "I'm very disappointed in you. You gave me quite the fright, sir."

Small crinkles appeared at the corner of René's eyes as he fought back a smile. Grabbing Hana around the waist, he pulled her close as heat sparkled in his eyes. "I look forward to taking a long, *long* time to make it up to you, lady."

Madalina approached, carrying the small furry corpse. "Hana, do you think you could...?" Her voice drifted off and she swallowed hard before continuing. "I'd like to bury Gaelle."

Hana turned her attention from René and her gaze softened. "Of course. Where?"

Madalina turned in a circle, eyes searching the clearing for the perfect spot. "How about underneath the log? He'll be protected there."

Giving René a quick squeeze on his arm, Hana turned and nodded. The two walked toward the log, heads together as they murmured.

Erik turned and met the others' eyes, one by one. "Damon has our dragon bones." And it was his fault. His stomach curled in on itself before he could shove the sensation aside. "Our best shot to get them back is before he reaches The Drowned City."

Adina nodded. "And we need some of his blood to cure René."

Erik sighed. Too bad they hadn't had a chance for René to attack Damon last night before Damon had grabbed his mind. That would've solved one of their problems, at least.

Though knowing Damon, he'd have killed René for daring to attempt it.

Erik pinched the bridge of his nose and closed his eyes. This just got worse and worse.

And Gaelle hadn't known how long they had until the night rot spread from René's foot. They could be mere nights away from his Final Death unless they could catch up with Damon and convince him to share his blood with René.

Ha! As if that would happen.

Several minutes later, Hana and Madalina rejoined the group. Madalina stopped beside Sigfried and gave him a hug, leaning her head against his massive chest. He used one arm to pull her against him in an embrace. "Are we ready to go?"

Adina met Erik's gaze and nodded, dropping her voice. "I don't think there's anything left for us here, and we need to get help for René fast." She glanced around the space. "Even the energy in this area feels diminished. I think Gaelle gave too much credit to the ley lines, and not enough to himself."

Sigfried frowned. "Perhaps. But it did not save him."

Erik took a deep breath and exhaled. No. Power and strength alone wouldn't save any of them.

Taking Adina's hand in his, he studied the sky, locating the triangle of three stars Madalina had pointed out last night. Keeping them on his left, he headed back the way they came.

At the bottom of the hill, they encountered several deep footprints.

"A horse," Sigfried said.

Erik frowned, his gaze retracing their steps to the top of the hill. "It must have been Damon's...at least we'll be able to follow him easily enough in the bog." But once the mud ran out, it would be significantly harder. And a horse would travel much faster than they could.

He glanced at Sigfried. "Will you be able to track him outside the marsh?"

Sigfried shrugged. "Maybe. If the smoke doesn't clog my nose."

Erik adjusted his pack on his shoulders and stared off into the mists. "Well, let's get on our way, and we'll hope for the best."

He crossed his fingers for no more smoke, no more fires, and a smooth journey to The Drowned City.

Somehow, he didn't think it'd be quite so easy.

Chapter 18
Sujani

Sujani stood at the top of the sheer cliff that overlooked the Colosseum, more than a thousand paces below. The dull ache in his chest intensified. The adjacent cathedral, once the crowning jewel of Maja and Ahion's reign, was now crumbled and decayed, barely one story tall. The white marble columns surrounding the courtyard lay in ruin, large sections were scattered around the area, poor monuments to their prior majesty.

So much time had passed, and the world had forgotten the most stunning being ever to grace the mortal plane. Soon, everyone would bow before Maja's glory again.

If she was anywhere, it would be here, at the heart of her former domain.

Pulling on his Talent to stir the atmospheric currents, he slid off the cliff onto a platform of hardened air. The support settled as Charles stepped up behind him.

With a gust that ruffled his mage robes, they descended to the base of the stairs leading to the main entry. This was Maja's home. The least he could do was offer her the respect of entering through the front door instead of sneaking through the side like a common thief.

The stiff air beneath their feet dissipated as they alighted. The formerly white marble steps were stained grayish brown, their intricate detailing long-since worn away.

His footsteps echoed as he approached the gaping entrance. The heaviness of age and forgotten memories weighed on him, pushing his shoulders down. A stray breeze blew across the foyer as the doorway swallowed him whole.

The fountain that occupied the entry was dry, its interior mosaic covered with dead leaves and other debris. Without the habitual burble of water, the silence echoed, smothering them.

Charles cleared his throat as he stepped forward, running his fingers over the lip of the cistern. "Where do you think we'll find Maja?"

She could be anywhere. The library straight ahead was a likely option, or perhaps the chapel. He'd often felt the goddess' presence most strongly in those two locations when he was mortal. Gesturing, he caught the other man's eye. "Let's check the sanctuary to the left."

Poking his head into the room, Sujani swallowed past his dry throat. The raised dais remained in exquisite condition at the head of the room, even though it was mostly made of wood that was now over a thousand years old. A glossy oak table stood atop the platform with the gods' emblem showing the sun and moon interposed over stars, just as he remembered it. Not a speck of dust marred the surfaces.

Waves of memories slammed into him as he froze in the doorway. His chest constricted. The countless decades he'd led the solstice and equinox ceremonies at her behest tugged at his heart, threatening to overwhelm him. He'd lost so much that final night...and was so close to regaining everything, assuming Maja had returned to her original temple.

He squeezed the doorframe until his knuckles turned white and the old wood creaked.

Charles shouldered past him into the room, breaking his trance. "It doesn't look like she's here."

Sujani scanned the area before ducking back out. He sighed and shook his head. Perhaps she'd be in the library.

Heartbeats later, he padded into the long hallway that had served as the repository for their holy order's knowledge. One of the cushioned chairs tucked into the second cubby had been dusted recently, and a cheery torch burned in the wall sconce to the left.

His heart leaped into his chest. He fought to rein in the smile that threatened to burst across his face. *She was here!*

Now he'd be able to secure her and ensure he had access to her power whenever he needed it.

Pulling out the soul-stone ring Viktor had given him, he slid it onto his middle finger. Pushing his thumb against a fang, he split the skin and dribbled a few drops of blood over the gem.

He'd have to wait until the very last instant to mutter the words that would trap her, but there was no harm in preparing what he could in advance.

"What are you doing?" Charles asked.

"Shh!" He slashed one arm through the air. The last thing he needed was to lose the element of surprise because of the other man's carelessness.

Stepping closer, Charles dropped his voice to a whisper. He pointed at Sujani's hand. "What is that?"

Holding his bloodied ring up to reflect the firelight, he smiled. "Something to facilitate the transfer of energy between us until Maja recovers." He'd release her as soon as they'd defeated Damon, of course. Then he'd put the ring away, never to be used again.

Charles eyed the gem. "Uh, huh. I don't know how comfortable I am with whatever this is. By the mages, she's a *goddess*."

Sujani bit the corners of his lips as he glared. The other man's disapproval was meaningless, and he shouldn't let it bother him so much. Maja would forgive him once all was said and done. She always did. Her opinion was the only one that mattered. "You enjoy being able to throw lightning, yes?"

Charles scowled. "Of course. Anything that helps overthrow Damon is good." He paused. "As long as I don't think too hard about where that power came from."

Sujani harrumphed as his chest tightened. "Would you prefer to wait here?"

Charles studied him for several heartbeats before crossing his arms. "Perhaps I would. I'll guard your back in case anyone tries to flank us." He leaned against the wall, crossed his arms and glared in a perfect imitation of Septimus.

Sujani clenched his jaw and nodded. So, this was how things were going to be. Very well, then. If the other vampire didn't have the stomach to stand at his side and do what needed to be done, it would be best to get him out from underfoot. "Stay here. I'll come for you when everything is finished." Having Charles present, with his mind control abilities to help restrain Maja, would have been ideal, but only if he could trust the other vampire to hold strong at crucial moments.

The coward.

The muscles in Charles' neck clenched as he swallowed. He glanced over Sujani's shoulder down the hall, and back. The corners of his lips hardened. With a tense head-bob, he sat on the corner of the lounge chair and braced his elbows on his knees. "I'll be here."

Putting the recalcitrant vampire from his thoughts, Sujani slipped down the hall to the double-door that would access the courtyard, and the two sacrificial altars from that fateful night when Maja had ordered him to murder her. The memories he'd worked so hard to put aside from that evening hovered at the edge of his awareness, like black storm clouds on the horizon. Taking a deep breath, he placed his palm against the doorframe. Bracing himself, he cracked it open.

The narrow view of the courtyard stretched across the stone floor, over the closer of the two altars, past the broken columns and into darkness. Even though the Cataclysm had shifted this area underground, starlight dusted the marble in a soft grayish white.

A warm glow cast a golden reflection over the stones to his left. The light was too steady to be a torch. He smiled. Maja was here.

He slowly pushed his head further out the door until he had a clear view.

She slouched against the base of one of the remaining columns, staring at the stars. A golden flush radiated from her that reminded him of the first kiss of sunrise. Her skin was sunken. It hung from her arms and cheekbones, a sheer contrast to the eternally young maiden she'd been before.

Something about the resurrection spell had gone terribly wrong. He clenched his fist as the metal of the ring dug into his finger. All the more reason for him to be expeditious about protecting her until she was able to recover.

At least her weakness would limit her ability to resist. He glanced down at the soul-stone. The blood still glistened in the light. Good—it hadn't congealed yet.

She turned at his footsteps, her honey-colored eyes flashed red in the starlight as she tensed. "My priest! What are you doing here?"

Yanking on the teal bond between them to hold her in place, he moved in front of her and brandished his ring. Pulling a ceremonial dagger from his belt, he slashed it across his palm. Flinging his hand toward her, he splattered his blood over her face.

She blinked, her mouth falling open as she stepped back. Their ethereal bond crackled.

Slapping his bloody hand against her cheek, he said, "Te kworem il hanc le'vat. Il hanc Maja!"

"My priest! No!" She slapped him away with quick, jerky movements. Stumbling backward, she tumbled to the ground.

No! If he lost skin contact now, the spell would be wasted.

Lunging forward to wrap his free hand in her hair, he let her pull him down on top of her. "Te kworem il hanc le'vat. Il hanc Maja!"

Blood-red eyes blasted into his thoughts, driving the words he chanted from his mind, sending fire down every nerve ending. "No!" Ahion's voice shattered Sujani's eardrums and rattled his teeth. The world went quiet except for the long-dead god's screaming.

"Te kworem il hanc le'vat. Il hanc Maja!" Sujani whispered the incantation, their pattern on his lips even though Ahion's visage pushed them from his consciousness. He pressed his palm to Maja's cheek as she writhed weakly beneath him. *Yes.* This would be over soon.

His hand burned like someone was holding a candle to it. The teal ribbon between them flickered, its edges fraying. Strand by strand, the bond snapped.

No! No, no, no!

His skin cracked, blistered, and turned black where it touched her, searing him from outside while Ahion fried his thoughts from within.

Sujani bit back a scream. "Te kworem il hanc le'vat. Il hanc Maja!"

It was no use. The spell was crumbling.

Pulling the last of his Talent, he wound it around the cord and willed it to hold together with every fiber of his being. If he failed now, defeat at

Damon's hands was all but assured. The muscles in his throat tightened. He loved his goddess—he couldn't let her suffer that fate.

"Te kworem il hanc le'vat. Il hanc Maja!"

He wasn't sure his mouth was working anymore. Squeezing his eyes closed, he mentally screamed the words at Ahion. *"Te kworem il hanc le'vat. Il hanc Maja!"*

What he wouldn't give for Charles to block out Maja's mental interference.

Sujani paused. He knew what the mind shield felt like. After bonding and sharing his Talent with Charles, that exchange should go both ways.

Reaching for the nearly forgotten dark purple bond that connected him to the other vampire, Sujani reached for his mental armor. The shield resisted, a brief image of Charles drawing away flashed through his mind.

"Te kworem il hanc le'vat. Il hanc Maja!"

With the last word, Sujani sent a bolt of lightning down the purple bond. Charles released his hold, allowing his Talent to pour readily down the thread. A barrier slammed over Sujani's mind. Ahion's eyes disappeared. Sujani exhaled as his abused nerves calmed.

His head clear, he turned his focus to the blood connection with Maja. Her essence flowed through him with the radiance of a summer sunrise, creeping up his arm, through his torso, down his other arm and into the ring.

"Te kworem il hanc le'vat. Il hanc Maja," he whispered as the blood between their skin crumbled to powder and the soul-slave jewel began to sparkle as though lit from within.

The warm feeling remained in his chest as the teal ribbon between them stretched.

Maja was so weak. She had very little left to give. He'd have to be careful to ration what he had in preparation for when he finally met Damon head-to-head.

Rolling off Maja, he pushed himself halfway to his feet. His old joints popped and cracked in protest, but it would be blasphemous to stand while Maja lay on the ground. Bending over, he scooped her up, one arm beneath her shoulders and the other behind her knees.

She was remarkably light, nothing but skin and bones. His eyes danced away from the sunken appearance of her eyes, the cracked and faded skin of her lips. Fortunately, the ritual had invigorated him, feeding vitality to his aching muscles and joints. "Don't worry, my goddess. Everything will turn out for the best," he whispered as he heaved himself to his feet one step at a time. "Once I've defeated Damon, you'll have time to recover and then together we'll rebuild the world." He stared at his ring, still shimmering with the unmistakable light of a bound soul. "Together. Forever."

In the meantime, he would let her rest in what had been her favorite place, a small courtyard to the side, where she could watch the stars. Spinning on his heels, he headed for the library.

Chapter 19
Adina

A little over a week later, they picked their way through the scorched remains of the forest along the Champeauxian border. With Damon's prediction of the imminent Cataclysm hanging over their heads, they'd elected to bypass Pierrevalle in favor of expediency. After all, it had already been over three weeks since Maja's resurrection.

They'd lost Damon's trail just north of Pierrevalle, and René's limp was getting more pronounced. He'd finally taken to using a walking stick, but this evening the branch was functioning more as a crutch and their pace had slowed to a crawl.

Ahead of Adina, René nudged another charred bough the size of his forearm out of the way. "This is creepy. I much prefer hiking through non-burned forests."

"As do we all," Erik said.

Adina shook her head, not deigning to respond.

René spun around, flaring his arms to the side, palms up. "Where are the birds? The sounds of the night foragers digging through the loam?"

"Either fled or dead," Madalina said from her perch above Sigfried's shoulders.

The bear huffed at them.

Madalina blinked. "Sophie's cabin?" Flashing them a wide smile that showed her teeth, she said, "Sig says Sophie's clearing should be just over the next rise. If we're lucky, we may have a good meal and a cellar to sleep in tonight." She chewed on her lower lip. "Assuming, of course, the fire didn't burn everything to the ground."

Adina shuddered as the smell of her burning skin and the accompanying pain flashed through her mind. Even they, with their resilience and ability to heal, had barely survived. A mortal like Sophie would have had no chance.

Adina mentally crossed her fingers the woman had defied the odds. Despite the forest being incinerated for the last several leagues, she'd liked Sophie, and sincerely hoped the woman hadn't lost everything to the fire. Perhaps, with her enigmatic magic, she had been able to save her home. And even though Gaelle had said René needed Damon's blood to fix his foot, there was a chance someone with Sophie's skills would have an alternative solution.

But, if the worst came to pass, the cellar should have survived, at least, and they could shelter there for the day.

Adina pulled out her magic blood bag and took a drink. The effervescent life energy exploded against her tongue and reinvigorated her muscles. Her next steps felt a little lighter.

She smiled. If she lived a thousand years, she'd never get tired of that zapping burst of energy that only Hana's Talent could supply. The bag was now and would always be her most treasured possession.

Sigfried crested the rise and froze.

"Oh, no," Madalina said.

Her heart in her throat, Adina jogged the last few paces to catch up. "What?"

The clearing before them was black, empty of every bit of color and life.

"Where's the house?" Erik asked, coming up beside her.

"Burned down," René said.

Adina shook her head as she strode into the clearing. "No, that's not right. Even if the fire destroyed everything, there should be remnants—glass from the windows, the foundation supports."

She dragged her feet, in case the debris had been buried beneath the ashes.

The others followed her lead.

"The door to the cellar should be about here," she said, measuring the distance between herself and the trail. "The front door was over there, by where you're standing, René, and the kitchen over here, just to Madalina's left."

Erik's wide eyes met hers. "There's nothing here."

Not even a burned-out trap door or open pit into the cellar.

Adina brushed the back of her hand against her forehead as lead congealed in her gut. The charred remnants of once-tall trees circled the clearing, jagged teeth boxing them in. This was beyond bizarre. "It's like the house was never here."

She turned to face Sigfried. "Are you certain this is the right clearing?" But she was grasping at straws. In her heart, she knew...Sig hadn't made a mistake.

The bear snorted at her, a mixture of offense and consternation flashing through his eyes.

Adina shook her head. "Sorry. I didn't mean to imply you weren't doing your job, it's just..." Her voice trailed off.

"This can't be," Hana said. She tore her gaze from the floor and met René's eyes. She counted off paces from where she stood and marched across the clearing. Stopping at one point, she jumped up and down a few times. "There was a well. Right here! Stones don't burn, and fires don't bury open holes."

Erik ran his hand through his hair, pulling it away from his face. "It's as if she never existed, like we all hallucinated it."

Hana held up her magic blood bag. "A pretty lucid hallucination."

Adina licked her lips. "Indeed."

René cleared his throat. "I think it's safe to say Sophie wasn't a normal mortal."

Hana rolled her eyes. "We already knew that, my love. But I agree...she was more than she let on."

Adina scanned the clearing. It was a mystery they'd probably never solve. And there was nothing for it right now. "We'll have to move on...we need to cover as much ground as we can before we take shelter for the night."

Hana sighed, her shoulders drooping. "I'd hoped to see her again. I suppose her absence here means she escaped the fires, at least, so perhaps there is hope in the future."

Sigfried huffed.

"There are no human remains in this clearing," Madalina said. She paused, tilting her head. "Sorry...there are no remains of any kind." She scratched behind Sigfried's ear.

"Well, that's good, at least," René said.

Indeed. Well, they had no reason to stick around. "Come on," Adina said, gesturing to the others. "This area is giving me goosebumps. Let's put some distance between us and it before the sun rises."

As the others formed up and headed down the trail, Adina glanced over her shoulder at the barren clearing, covered in char and ash. A heaviness settled in her chest, like when they'd discovered Gaelle's death, as though the world had lost something wondrous, never to be seen again.

"She gave us aid when we needed it," Erik said, keeping his voice low enough that it wouldn't carry to the others. "Perhaps she was waiting here, just for us."

Adina smiled at his attempt to make her feel better. That was unlikely, but she wouldn't be the one to disabuse him of the notion. Hopefully she'd gotten wind of the fires and fled. Perhaps their recollections were off, and if they'd been more thorough in their examinations, they'd have located the cellar and the well.

But a thorough search would take time, and put them further behind Damon, which they couldn't afford.

"I don't suppose there's a way to skirt around Gorlinia on our way back to the Saldanian Desert?" René asked.

Adina blinked and shook her head as she adjusted to the new topic of conversation. "Why?"

René shrugged. "I don't relish walking through mud and rain again."

"Unlike the bog, at least Gorlinian mud won't reek of sulfur and rotting things," Erik said.

Adina sighed. That was true, but with the torrential downpours, it would be cold and uncomfortable. And with René's crutch, it would be even more challenging.

At least they hadn't thrown away their oiled tarps.

"Well?" René pressed. "Is there?"

Erik shook his head. "Not that I'm aware of, unless you want to climb through the Spiked Range...and this time of year, those mountains will be snow-filled and likely impassable."

Adina raised her eyebrow. "So, our choices are deadly mountains or rainstorms?"

He nodded.

"I choose the rainstorms, thank you very much." Not that she was averse to the cold. Or heights. Not really…it was the snow and slippery ice.

Erik squeezed her hand and smiled. "Me, too."

René scoffed. "You're just saying that because you're a couple."

Hana frowned as she stepped up to his side, wrapping her hand around his arm. "I prefer rain to snow and ice, too."

He huffed. "Are all desert people afraid of a little cold water?"

Hana's lips tightened into a thin line. "Really? You want to go there?"

René blinked, his jaw slack at her expression. "No, no, of course not. It was a joke." He ran his fingers down her arm. "It was in poor taste. Please forgive me." Pulling her close, he nuzzled the junction where her neck met her shoulders. "Please?"

Hana chuckled, pushing him away. "Alright, alright, you scoundrel. But the rain it is."

He sighed, putting a hand to his chest in a dramatic fashion. "Very well. I know when I've met my match."

Hana nodded, light again sparkling in her eyes. "And don't you forget it, sir."

Chapter 20
Adina

Adina stood at the crest of yet another sand dune as she stared down at the main gate to The Drowned City. It was hard to believe they'd been here only a little over two months ago. Only two months since Arthur's murder, when her world fell apart and re-formed itself. Pausing, she braced for the sharp stab of pain, but only a dull throb and fond memories remained. Arthur's staff would likely think less of her for moving on so quickly, despite all that had happened since his passing. She reached behind and caught Erik's hand with her own. Threading her fingers between his, she gave him a quick squeeze.

"Does it feel like coming home?" he asked.

She shook her head. "No, not really." Without Arthur, there was nothing left here to make it her home. Besides, that life was in the past. She smiled as she studied the man beside her from the corner of her eye.

Her new life, here and now. "Anywhere with you is home."

He chuckled quietly, deep in his throat, and put his arm around her waist, pulling her close. Leaning his head on top of hers, he sighed. "Likewise, lady."

"Hey you guys!" René called from where he leaned against his crutch at the bottom of the dune. "How far is it?"

Adina shrugged and glanced at him. "Maybe half a league," she called.

Nothing they couldn't do tonight if they hurried. The moon was still high in the sky. And personally, she'd *kill* for a comfortable bed to sleep in.

She glanced at Erik again as heat stirred in her stomach. And their own private room.

Holes in the ground were fine, especially when there was nothing else available. But Arthur's estate—she supposed it was Hana's now—was much more comfortable.

"If we get there tonight," she said to Erik, "we can lay out a plan and start looking for the Colosseum first thing tomorrow."

"Sounds good to me," he said. "Can you think of any reason we can't approach from the main road?"

"Other than possibly tipping Damon or Sujani off that we're here?"

He sighed. "Point taken. Any recommendations?"

She shook her head. "Maybe one of the smaller gates? But that's what I'd expect us to do, so if I were looking for someone trying to sneak in, I'd concentrate my efforts there."

Maybe they could climb over the walls in between guard rotations?

She shook her head. That was hardly feasible.

"What do you think, general?"

He blinked and raised an eyebrow at her.

"What?" she asked. "You were a general, were you not?"

He nodded. "Yes, but..."

Her eyes sparkled. "So...show me your tactical prowess." She gestured at the city. "How would you sneak six people in after dark?"

He studied the walls for a few minutes, absentmindedly chewing on the inside of one cheek. "I'd send them inside in groups of two...two through the main gate, and two each through a sub-gate. A large group would be more noticeable than small groups." He paused. "I'd also do it at the time with the highest traffic flow...not in the dead of the night."

Adina snorted. "Yeah...good luck with that."

"Maybe we just need to enter either right before sunrise, when the mortals are waking up, or right after sunset, as they're returning home?" He raised an eyebrow at her. "Is that an accurate assessment of the highest traffic volume after dark?"

She nodded. "It is."

He brushed his palms together, clearing off imaginary dirt. "Well, then, that's how we do it. We'll duck in right before the sun comes up."

"You and I'll take the main gate...it's the furthest from the estate."

He nodded as they headed down the dune to rejoin the others.

"It's about time," René said.

Adina bit back an eyeroll. "And it'll be a little longer." She met Erik's gaze briefly before turning her attention back to the group. René—always in a hurry. "It will be best for us to enter right before sunrise. That's when the most mortals are coming or going. At least, when it's dark out. René and Hana, you enter through the east gate. Madalina and Sigfried, the west. We'll have to race to the estate, but if all goes according to plan, we'll have comfortable beds to sleep in tonight."

Assuming, of course, everything was in place as Hana had left it.

"We've got a little over a half league to the city, then a few hours to wait outside until there's enough traffic that we might slip in without Sujani or Damon's spies noticing us."

Sigfried nodded and took Madalina's hand. "We will see you there."

"Good luck," Erik said.

"Sure, make us walk the furthest," René said as he gestured to his crutch.

Hana put her hand on his shoulder, shaking him lightly. "I used to live in that area of town, and I know it best. Once we're inside, we'll have the shortest trip to get to the estate."

René shuffled his weight, looking slightly abashed. "Oh. Okay, then. That'll work."

Adina met Erik's eyes. And the two of them would have the longest distance between the gate and their goal. Of everyone, they'd be cutting it closest to sunrise.

Erik winked at her, as if saying, *we've got this.*

She certainly hoped so, and that Sujani didn't have any surprises for them.

"We'll see you in a few hours, then," René said.

Hana sent Adina a quick smile then the two were gone.

"Well," Erik said, mischief sparkling in his eyes, "Shall we?" He held out his arm.

With an answering smile that had her heart soaring so high she hardly noticed the drag of the soft sand they walked through, she put her hand on his elbow and let him escort her to the main gate.

The moon hung two finger-widths lower in the sky when they stopped approximately fifty paces from the entrance. It was still dark enough that standing off to the side of the road as they were, they remained out of the guards' view.

The eastern horizon blushed with the faintest hint of sunrise.

"Well, now we wait," he said, leaning against a palm tree. Pulling out his magic blood bag, he took a deep drink.

Adina shook her head. "I don't think so. Look!"

A merchant caravan rolled slowly down the street. Several camels and wagons loaded with goods trundled toward the gate. Several bundles of silk and other exotic fabrics overflowed one cart. The tantalizing scent of spices hinted at the contents of another.

"I can hide us in shadows and sneak us in with the last wagon."

Erik smiled. "I knew having you along was going to be good luck."

With a chuckle, Adina reached for her Talent and pulled the shadows around them.

As the last camel passed, Adina grabbed Erik's nearly invisible hand and tugged him into place between the final two animals. "Try not to clink your armor," she whispered.

He snorted. "I'll try."

Yeah...stealth was not his forte. Hopefully the mortals would assume the noise was coming from the wagons.

At least the camels didn't seem to mind their presence.

"Halt!" The city guard held up his palm. "What do you have to declare?"

One of the mortals at the lead of the column cleared his throat. "Cloth and textiles, bound for the market."

The guard eyed the row of wagons. "And where are you from?"

"The Burning City."

The city guard held out his palm and rubbed his fingers together. "Entry tax is ten gold pieces, two per wagon."

Adina blinked. Entry tax? Since when?

After several heartbeats, the merchant sighed, pulling out a small leather satchel and depositing it in the man's hand.

"Very good." The satchel disappeared beneath the guard's armor as he smirked. "Move along. Move along."

"I hate corrupt officers," Adina mumbled. This is what happened when a good leader like Arthur was murdered, and his post taken over by lesser mortals.

Beside her, Erik patted her shoulder. "Stop the Cataclysm first, then we can deal with them."

Adina nodded. He was right, of course. Priorities.

The caravan proceeded far too slowly through the main gate.

As they passed beneath the portcullis, Erik tripped, slamming his hand into the camel beside him. His armor clanked as the beast swung to the side, threatening to dislodge its burden across the road.

Adina raised her eyebrow and glanced at him. In all the time they'd known each other, he'd never once stumbled. His Talent should prevent such things.

"What was that?" One of the guards lifted his hat and peered into the darkness, looking right at them.

Adina's heart jumped, thudding against her ribs. Reaching for her Talent, she shored it up, burying them in as many shadows as she could manage.

Several heartbeats passed as the caravan continued to move forward.

The guard finally turned his attention to the next person in line as the tension between Adina's shoulder blades released.

That had been close.

"Sorry," Erik muttered.

Wordlessly, Adina squeezed his arm. No, stealth was not his forte.

Once inside, she steered Erik to the side and dropped their shadow cloak. "Alright, we need to hurry. It's that way," she said, pointing.

They set off at a brisk pace. Any faster and they'd be running, but that tended to catch people's eye.

And the last thing they needed was to draw attention.

The weight of the sun was dragging her eyelids closed as the horizon turned from pink to orange. "Come on, we're almost there," she said when Erik faltered.

Turning the corner, Arthur's old estate came into view.

Thank the gods.

It looked as though she'd never left. The gardens out front were well-maintained, the pale desert lilies in full bloom, with their petals turned to capture the sunlight. The white-washed walls practically glowed.

Her spirit lifted at the sight. She was home.

An empty maw opened in her gut at that thought. Arthur was gone—this would never truly be 'home' again. But for now, it could be a welcome and familiar shelter. Glancing at the vampire marching beside her, she bit back the dull ache that was Arthur's loss.

Time dulled all pain, it seemed.

She led Erik up to the front door. Reaching for the handle, she smacked her hand against an invisible wall.

"Ouch!"

Ripples of air bounced off, making her ears pop.

"What's this?" Erik asked, splaying both palms against the solid barrier between them and the door.

Adina swallowed past her suddenly dry throat. "It's a shield of hardened air. Sujani must be staying here." Of all the things for her to not consider in advance... The impending sunrise dulled her mind and made her feel as though she was fighting against a river of molasses to piece her thoughts together. "He probably noticed me running into it. If he doesn't know we're here now, he will when he checks the wards."

Erik glanced around. "There needs to be somewhere else we can stay."

"Hey, you guys!" René's voice echoed from half a block away, as he hobbled up to join them, Hana at his side.

Hana frowned. "What's wrong?"

Adina shook her head and pounded her fist against the wall of hardened air. If Sujani already knew they were here, one more knock wouldn't do anything. "Sujani's sealed the estate."

René peered at her. "And you didn't think of that until now?"

Adina furrowed her brow and jerked her head back. "No! Did *you?*"

"Of course not!" He waved his free hand in an abstract flourish. "Magic is not my forte."

She rolled her eyes. "It's Talent, not magic. They're two completely different things."

René yawned. "Whatever. If we can't stay here, where should we go?"

Adina met Hana's gaze. "Nowhere close. At least, if we want a secure location. There are no inns nearby." This was solidly a residential area.

Hana rubbed her eyes, looking for all the world like she was trying to hold them open. A prospect that was getting tougher and tougher as the eastern horizon brightened. "I can drop us into the street. The earth won't support the road if I dig a cave for us beneath it." She glanced at René. "It won't be comfortable, but we'll be safe for the day."

He nodded. "Then do it."

She shook her head. "We need to wait for the others."

Adina glanced down the street, where Sigfried and Madalina should be.

No movement came from that direction.

René yawned again. "Okay. Well, I don't think I'll be able to make it much longer before I go dormant. I always fall asleep early."

Adina glared at him. "Don't you dare! Not yet. Unless you want to sleep literally at Sujani's doorstep."

He blinked. "Oh. Right. I suppose that wouldn't be a very good idea. Where then?"

Adina shrugged. "As far away as we can get without drawing attention."

Erik nudged her. When she glanced at him, he nodded down the street. She followed his gaze.

Sigfried and Madalina were just a few blocks down.

"Come on." Adina grabbed René by the arm and strode toward them. After all, if they weren't staying there, they may as well meet Sig and Madalina halfway.

René stumbled, and Hana grabbed his other arm in support.

As they approached, Sigfried frowned. "What is wrong?"

Adina shook her head. "Sujani's got the entire estate sealed off. We can't get inside, so we need to get as far away as possible before sunrise."

Suddenly, René went limp. He collapsed to the ground on top of his crutch.

"Dammit," Hana mumbled. She met each of their eyes. "It looks like we're sleeping here." She raised her hands. "Everyone, take a deep breath."

Adina did just as the hard-packed dirt shifted like water and swallowed her whole.

The ground flowed upward, threatening to clog her throat and nose. She extended her Talent to redirect it around her, but it didn't respond as water should. The back of her throat burned as the pressure from the dirt overhead pushed against her ribs and shoulders.

Adina fought the urge to take a deep breath, or to open her mouth. Despite not responding like water, the dirt would probably flow right into her lungs if she gave it a chance. And while she didn't need to breathe, that would still be uncomfortable.

The earth pressed in from all directions, crushing the air from her lungs. Her heartbeat thudded in her ears as her chest started to burn. She thrashed against the earth's hold.

Erik squeezed her hand, the steady presence, always at her side.

The simple knowledge that he was there helped her rein in the panic.

At least they'd gotten warning. Poor Sigfried and Madalina. Hopefully Madalina had foreseen something and been able to give Sigfried the head's up.

She hadn't even gotten a chance to ask them why they were late.

Adina gave in to the weight of the sun pressing down on her. The sooner she went dormant, the sooner she wouldn't have to endure being buried alive.

The black wave of unconsciousness slammed into her, pulling her under. The last thing she felt was Erik's hand, squeezing hers.

The next morning, Adina opened her eyes, and immediately regretted it as granules of sand and dirt scratched them. The unbearable weight of hard-packed earth pressed down on her.

Right. They were buried beneath the street, courtesy of Hana.

She pursed her lips into a thin line and squeezed her eyes shut. *Don't panic, don't panic, don't panic.* Clenching her muscles, she fought to move an arm. Nothing budged—the earth held her tight.

Her lungs burned, her ribs spasmed, trying to expand to pull in the smallest bit of oxygen. Reaching out with her Talent, she sought any air to pull toward herself.

Nothing responded. She was buried in an endless vortex of hard-packed sand and grit.

What had she been thinking, agreeing to let Hana bury her?

This was worse than being held by Damon or Charles. At least then, she could open her eyes and breathe.

She'd take facing Sujani over this any day.

Clenching her jaw until the tendons creaked, she thrust herself forward and back. If only she could create a little pocket of space. Then she could summon air.

Her prison refused to budge, and the back of her throat started to itch with Hunger from her needless energy expenditure.

She collapsed, letting the earth take her weight. There was nothing to do except wait for Hana to awaken and free them. Bringing the memory of the night at the Gorlinian roadside inn with Erik to mind, she imagined taking a deep breath of the cool, rain-soaked air. Breathing in and out, in and out, until her heartbeat calmed.

A quick pressure squeezed her hand and released. Erik, finally awake.

She clasped his hand in return.

At least they were together.

A brief stab of jealousy surged through her chest for René. He'd fallen dormant before Hana had buried them, and he'd likely remain dormant until well after she'd raised them.

Lucky bastard.

Then, like a sand demon spitting out the final bits of undigested bone, the earth lurched, and she shot free with such force she flew up and across the street.

Rolling with her momentum, she came to a stop against the wall of a house. Coughing, she used her grimy hand to scrub the sand from her equally dirty face. Blinking, she stared at the ground until enough of the grit had cleared that she could see clearly.

"God's teeth, Hana." She wheezed. "You weren't kidding."

The other woman didn't respond.

Adina pushed herself up until she was sitting upright and tucked the stray strands of hair beneath her headcloth.

She glanced at Erik. Gunk and dust had dulled his normally shiny armor. Grains of sand poured down from his hair, making his skin look darker than it actually was.

Despite being filthy, he was still the most handsome man she'd ever met.

Rolling to her feet, she brushed what dirt she could off her robes. "Hana?"

"Sorry," the other woman said from where she crouched over René.

A twinge of alarm snapped through Adina, and her heart jumped back into her throat. "Is everything okay?"

Hana brushed the dirt away from his face. "Yes. He's just taking his sweet time to wake up.

Just like always. Her heartbeat settled as she rolled her shoulders and turned her attention to Madalina and Sigfried. Madalina's black hair was hopelessly tangled, much as it had been the first time Adina had met her. Her black dress was so dirty it appeared tan.

Sigfried, of course, looked the same, with his uncombed hair and shaggy vest and pants.

"We're going to need a bath and fresh clothing before we can go anywhere public or do anything," Erik said. "And my armor could use a good polishing if I don't want the joints to be permanently ruined."

Adina took a deep breath, luxuriating in the free flow of air into her lungs. "Right. The bath houses." She glanced at him. "They should still be open. We can stop at the blacksmith on the way."

Less than an hour later, Adina leaned back against the edge of the large pool in the women's bath, across from Hana and Madalina. The warm water soothed the tension from her muscles as the sand and dirt drifted down, swept through the filtration system and out to wherever the baths carried their waste.

It had taken more than a little convincing to lure the blacksmith away from his dinner for a late evening rush job, but with the last of their coin pooled together, he'd been swayed, so hopefully by the time they were finished here, Erik's armor would be all polished and like new.

If she closed her eyes, she could almost imagine there wasn't a looming Cataclysm or impending showdown between her grandfather, his resurrected goddess, Damon, and the rest of them.

Almost.

What would it be like, to not have the literal fate of the world hovering over them like an executioner's axe?

Boring. It would be boring.

But she'd take a century or two of no excitement after the events of the past year.

"Adina? Hana?" Madalina asked.

"Hmmm?" Adina kept her eyes closed, luxuriating in the feel of the warm water moving past her.

"Where do you think will be a good place to stay for the night? As interesting as sleeping under the street was, neither Sig nor I want to do it again." Water splashed as she moved. "No offense."

Hana's warm laugh echoed throughout the empty chamber. "None taken. I'm sorry I didn't have time to warn you and your husband how uncomfortable it would be. It was a last resort."

Adina peeked her eyes open and glanced at Hana and Madalina. "We have more warning for tonight. We'll have time to come up with something." The truth was, they'd been extremely lucky to have Hana with them. Not just last night, but the entire trip. The woman had single handedly dug them a shelter every night since their meeting with Gaelle.

"Speaking of time," Hana said as the water sloshed around her, "I think we need to get on with the evening. Before Sujani gets it into his head to hunt us down."

Adina lifted her head and met the other woman's gaze as she voiced the one thought she'd been trying to keep at arm's length all evening. "Frankly, I'm surprised he wasn't there when we first woke up. If he was home, there's no way he didn't feel us pounding on his barrier."

At least, *she* felt it when things banged against the air shields she created. As someone with infinite more experience, Sujani should be even more attuned.

Unless he was distracted with something else.

Lead settled in her gut and suddenly the water turned chilly.

She stood, letting the liquid sluice off her as she reached for one of the fluffy towels on the edge of the pool. "I think you're right. The sooner we get started, the better." She certainly wasn't going to be caught in a bath, no matter how great it felt, when Sujani came for them.

Less than an hour later, she stood at the edge of the same sewer drain she'd crawled down with Arthur and Erik not even two months ago.

Perhaps the visit to the pools had been a tad bit premature.

Hana frowned. "This is the only way to get down to the ruins?"

"The only way we know of," Adina said. "It's not as bad as it looks."

Lies, lies, lies.

But it wasn't like they had much choice, if they wanted to end Sujani and Maja, and prevent a second Cataclysm.

Sigfried grumbled.

Adina eyed him. It would be a tight fit, but he'd made it down before.

"I'll go first," Erik said, stepping into the sewer pipe. Arranging the torch he carried in one hand, he descended the rungs as his head disappeared into darkness.

Taking a deep breath, Adina followed.

Several minutes later, they all gathered around as Sigfried's feet hit the ground. Erik, Hana and Madalina carried torches, which sent flickering light dancing among the shadows.

Maybe it was just her imagination, but this didn't smell quite as bad as it had the last time she was here. Hopefully that was a good omen. She sighed. "Well? The sooner we start, the sooner we can locate whatever it was Gaelle thought was down here that we needed to find."

Erik led the way.

"Do you remember where we're going?" she whispered.

Her voice echoed down the tube which took them relentlessly downward.

"I think so," he said. "At least, I recognize this tunnel."

Ahead, something crashed, followed by a high-pitched squeak.

Adina shuddered. Ugh. Rats.

Soon the passage opened into the large cavern with the ruins. The ceiling was lost in darkness.

Madalina grabbed Adina's arm and pointed. "Look! There's the broken pyramid where we saw the oracle!"

Adina met Erik and René's eyes as they pulled to a halt. "Do we want to try to recreate that? In case it gives us something else useful?"

Erik studied the area. "Sure. It seems like a decent place to start, and we don't really have any other leads."

Madalina beamed. "Excellent! I quite enjoyed this oracle. I'd like to speak to it again." Taking Sigfried's hand, she pulled her reluctant husband through the pyramid's entry. The rest followed.

"Does everyone remember where they were?" she asked.

Adina, Erik, and René positioned themselves next to their respective blocks of stone, one on each side of the pyramid.

Hana leaned against the door frame, Sigfried right behind her.

Madalina bit the inside of her cheek. "Right." She marched to the center point, equidistant from them. "I was standing here." She turned in a circle, staring at the ground. "There! That round disc. Sig, will you grab it and bring it to me?"

He shuffled forward, grabbing the plaque she indicated and handed it to her before retreating to the safety of the doorway.

Madalina glanced at the rest of them. "What happened next?"

"Then," René said, slapping the stone with his hand, "we put our blood on these, and the oracle appeared."

It sounded simple enough. Adina pulled out her sword and slid her thumb along the edge blade as the sharp pain shot up her hand. As the blood welled from the cut, she pressed it down onto the center of her stone table.

Erik and René did the same.

Madalina grabbed the plaque and held it to her chest.

Adina held her breath for one heartbeat.

Two.

Come on. Come on!

René cleared his throat. "Madalina, I think you need to bleed on that disc thing, too."

"Oh, right." She bit her thumb with one of her fangs and held it over the plaque until a few drops landed on the metal.

Adina took a breath, bracing herself as she stared at where the ghostly oracle had appeared last time. Butterflies danced in her gut.

Several heartbeats passed. Somewhere off in the distance, a series of drops landed in a puddle, echoing around the ruins.

"Nothing's happening," René said.

Adina licked her lips. If this didn't work, they'd be back to wandering around blindly as they hunted for The Colosseum. That is, unless Sujani found them first.

Madalina shook the plaque. "Maybe it's broken?"

"Or it needs more blood," Erik said.

Adina swallowed as the butterflies settled. "Perhaps it was a one-time use?"

"Let me try one more time. It'll be harder without the stars, but maybe if I imagine the oracle really hard, it'll summon it," Madalina said, biting her thumb again. A few more drops splattered on the disc as she squeezed her eyes closed. "Oracle? Can you help us?"

Adina's ears popped as a flash of red light exploded through the doorway and bounced off the plaque in Madalina's hands.

The metal screeched and split in two.

Madalina's face went slack, crestfallen, as the sundered pieces fell to the ground.

Adina's gaze whipped to the entrance, where the red light had originated.

"Now, now," Damon said, stepping forward, brushing his hands off on his pants. "Imagine finding you lot here. Again. What are you up to now?"

Sigfried growled and tensed, ready to lunge at him.

Damon held up a hand. "Stop, Wrath, or I'll make you regret that I spared your unlife in the swamp." He stopped halfway between Madalina and Sigfried, far enough to the side that he could keep all of them in view. "We have a problem."

"Oh, *we* do, do we?" Erik said.

"Indeed." Damon flashed his fangs. "It seems Sujani has misplaced his goddess."

Adina blinked as her jaw went slack. She must be hearing things. "What? He lost Maja?" After all he went through to resurrect her, that seemed excessively careless of him. Or Damon wasn't being entirely honest.

Damon gave her a sly smile. "Apparently the goddess has abandoned him." *<It makes you wonder what he's done to anger her so, doesn't it?>*

Adina shook her head. "Get out of my mind." She squeezed her eyes closed and imagined herself forcefully shoving Damon away. She had no way to tell if she was successful or not.

But if Sujani had ticked off his goddess, it would serve him right to lose her.

With a quiet clank, Erik stepped toward her.

Damon froze him with a glare. "Standing between us won't keep me out, butcher."

Erik's lips tightened into a thin line as his hand twitched toward his sword.

"And don't even think about that. Attacking me will only get you and your friends ended." He cleared his throat, his leisurely gaze encompassing each of them. "I need your help to forge a new Bone Shard Blade."

The world tilted sideways. Adina had to brace herself against the stone table to avoid her knees giving out. "Say that again?"

"What?" René yelled.

Damon sighed and repeated slowly, as though speaking to someone who didn't speak Common, "I. Need. Your. Help—"

"He heard you the first time," Erik said, cutting him off with a slash of his hand. "What he means to ask is, why should we help you?"

Damon spun to face him directly. "Do you want to survive?" He gestured at Adina. "Do you two want the chance to live your unlives together?"

Adina licked her lips and swallowed. The butterflies were back. Of course she did, but at what cost?

She met Erik's gaze. This had been part of their original plan, weeks ago. Though they hadn't exactly shared with everyone.

Clearing her throat, she looked Damon in the eyes. Thrusting her jaw forward and bracing her hands on her hips, she studied him. "If we help you, you'll allow René to drink some of your blood, then let us go. Peacefully."

He tilted his head to the side like an owl. "Why is it so important to you that I bond with Marcos' son? Do you even understand what that entails?"

Adina's attention flashed to the invisible golden bond that tied her and Erik together and shuddered. Being tied like that to Damon seemed a fate worse than death. Except that René did face such a fate without it.

Damon did a double take. "Ah, I see. Night rot. Terrible luck, but I'm afraid I don't have any desire to tie my life to René's with anything as permanent as a blood binding." He sneered "Sorry to disappoint."

René opened his mouth, paused, and slammed it shut again.

Hana stepped forward. "You can't leave him to die!"

He speared her with a flat look. "Can't I? Watch me. I need all the blood I have if we want any chance of defeating Sujani and Maja, and saving the world."

Adina caught Hana's eye and shook her head. They'd find another way, even if it involved holding Damon down and staking him before they stabbed him with his own Bone Shard Blade.

Damon pulled a dagger from his waist, sliced it across his palm, and placed his bleeding hand over his tunic. "As for the rest of it, you have my word, and my blood oath."

The very air crackled with magic at the words. The sparks danced up her skin, raising the fine hairs on her arms and on the back of her neck.

She'd never heard of a blood oath before, but she wasn't going to argue with whatever magic had just happened. "Very well. We agree." She caught René's eye.

His jaw muscles twitched as he ground his teeth, fighting against the urge to flat-out refuse.

Which was understandable, really, considering their history.

"René, he's the only chance we have to defeat Sujani," Adina said. *Please, please agree.*

The corner of Damon's mouth twitched up in a smile at her thought.

"And he has our dragon bones," Erik added. "It's not like we'll be able to get more."

Silence stretched and became heavy. After several heartbeats, Damon put his bloody hand back over his heart. "I also swear to not possess your mind," he said, staring directly at René.

The zap of magic snapped through the air again.

René thrust his jaw forward. "And Hana's, too."

Damon jerked his head back and raised one eyebrow, glancing at Hana. He rolled his eyes. "Very well. Her, too."

René flexed his hands and released them. "Agh! Fine!" He threw his arms up and turned his back to them. "But only until we end Sujani and send Maja back where she belongs."

"A truce." Something sparkled in Damon's eyes that turned Adina's core to ice. "Until then."

Adina's instincts screamed. Damon would betray them the first chance he got. They'd have to make sure they were prepared, because what she'd said was true—Damon was their only chance to end Sujani. She turned to Sigfried, Madalina and Hana. "Agreed?"

Sigfried glowered and glanced at Erik, who nodded in encouragement.

With a sigh, Sigfried looked at Madalina. "What do you think?"

She shrugged. "I don't know. I can't talk to the stars down here. But I think Adina's right—he's our best chance."

Sigfried grunted. "Very well."

Hana nodded, as well, her focus entirely on René.

"Sigfried, you may as well give Damon the other dragon bones."

Damon's face went slack before his eyes went wide and he flared his nostrils. "Other bones?" He flashed his fangs and turned to Sigfried. "Holding out on me, are you? That's a dangerous game you're play-ing, Wrath." He strode purposefully toward Sigfried, muscles tensed as though ready to attack.

"Ah. You swore a truce. No harming us," Erik said.

Coming to a halt a few paces away, Damon glanced over his shoulder at Erik. "So I did." Holding out his hand, palm-up, he glared at Sigfried. "Bones. Now."

Sigfried huffed, and, taking his sweet time, produced the two petri-fied bones they'd found in the ancient dragon nest. His face contorted and his hands clenched as though fighting the urge to part from them. Adina opened her mouth to reassure him when suddenly he relaxed and dropped them into Damon's waiting palms.

Damon ran his hands up and down the bones, as though they were more precious than gold. His eyes were soft as he shook his head side to side. "Amazing. I never thought..." Abruptly, he shook himself and focused on them.

He gestured to the space inside the broken pyramid. "Very well. We have what we need, and the ideal space to do it. Let's forge a second Bone Shard Blade."

A painful zap shot through Adina's muscles. "Here and now?" Weren't there preparations to make or rituals to perform? She blinked, her heart beating double-time. If things went too quickly, they might not be able to anticipate Damon's inevitable betrayal. And that could lead to their Final Deaths.

He speared her with a flat glare. "Unless you have any thoughts on why we should wait and give our enemy more of an advantage?"

She swallowed. Well, no. And that was a good point. Did they truly have everything they needed?

"Between you and the earth-mover over there—" Damon gestured at Hana— "we should have enough of the elements covered. And with these bones, the last thing we need is a confluence of ley lines."

"Which, according to Gaelle, are in the Colosseum," Erik said.

"Which is somewhere down here," Damon added. "We should be close enough now that I'll be able to tap into their power from here."

Adina swallowed. And hopefully far enough away that Sujani wouldn't find them immediately.

Damon smirked at her. "Exactly, princess. You're learning quickly." Turning to the others, he gestured. "Earth-mover, you stand across from Adina. I'll stand in the middle. The rest of you, find cover somewhere out of the way. This will get...interesting."

"Blood magic?" René asked, his face pale.

"No!" Damon snarled. "This is divine magic, the likes of which you'll never see again."

Grabbing the two petrified dragon bones, he laid them parallel to each other on the unused altar. Returning to his spot equidistant between all three stone tables, he pulled the dagger from his waist. Kneeling, he traced several symbols in a circle large enough for him to stand in. Sliding the knife over his palm, he collected a pool of blood on the blade and began tracing the runes, leaving a thin black trail in each.

"Hey," Erik said. "That's the same sort of thing Sujani did to save Adina." He frowned and crossed his arms over his chest. "I thought you said this wasn't blood magic."

Adina's stomach did a flip-flop and her attention zeroed in on Erik. "What?"

He flicked his eyes to her before turning his focus back to Damon. "When you were dying from the gargoyle attack." He pointed. "That's exactly what Sujani did to set up his blood magic ritual."

Adina leaned forward, reluctant to leave her post in case it unintentionally messed something up.

Damon growled deep in his throat. "This is *not* the same. The syllabary is entirely different." He shook his head. "If you can't tell the difference, then stand back and shut up until I'm finished."

"But you promised no blood magic," René said from his spot near the door.

Damon paused, flashing his fangs. "All magic requires blood, you idiots. Even our Talents require that we burn the energy we absorb when we drink blood." Even in the dim light, his eyeroll was obvious. "Just because blood is a component of the spell doesn't mean it's automatically blood magic."

Oh, really? Adina squinted. If only she'd been conscious at Sujani's ritual... She'd kill to know the difference.

"Blood magic requires a sacrifice." Damon's words were getting more and more curt. "No sacrifices here." He paused, peering at Erik and raising an eyebrow. "Unless you're volunteering, of course?"

Erik shook his head. "Just do whatever you need to do and stay out of my head."

"Quit screaming your thoughts at me and I will. Honestly, of everyone, I expected more mental control from *you*, what with Charles being your father and all."

Adina could practically hear the tendons in Erik's jaw pop as he ground his teeth.

"If you want to make yourself useful," Damon added as he pulled the smaller bones from the satchel at his waist, "use those bones on the table to grind these into powder."

Adina glanced between the bones in his hand and the large ones on the altar. "Really?" She reached into her pack and pulled out the weathered piece of parchment they'd pulled from Sujani's journal nearly two months ago—the one with the instructions for the ritual. "There's nothing about doing that in here."

Damon dumped the bits of bone back into the satchel and tossed it to her. "You don't expect a bunch of tiny bones to forge themselves into one large dagger, do you? I don't have time to explain every little detail to you. Either do it or give them to someone who will."

Erik walked over and took the satchel. Marching up to the altar as if he was a doomed man approaching the executioner's block, he poured the bones out onto the surface. Grabbing the larger of the two petrified bones, he brought it down on the small bone and smashed it to smithereens.

"Smaller," Damon said. "It needs to be a powder."

Adina's stomach turned to ice. That wasn't what Gaelle had said.

With a deep breath, Erik met Adina's eyes and pounded the bones again.

And again.

And again.

Hopefully Damon knew what he was doing. The oracle had been very clear that they were to flint knap the bones, not grind them into dust.

Finally, Damon stood, all of the symbols inked in blood. Brushing his palms off on his pants, he leaned his head to one side and the other, eliciting a sharp crack each time. "Now. Scoop the powder back into the satchel and bring it here."

Erik did as instructed, dropping the bag of powdered bones into Damon's waiting hand.

Adina took a deep breath and held it. This was it—the moment of truth. She met Erik's gaze.

His lips were pressed into a thin line, with a stiffness in his shoulders that reflected the same tension that settled in her gut.

"Now, ladies." Damon glanced at Adina and Hana. "Ready your Talents."

With her pulse rushing past her ears, Adina glanced at the old parchment with Sujani's directions for the ritual. Freeing one of her swords at her waist, she sliced it across her palm and placed her bleeding hand palm-down against the altar. Here went nothing. Catching Hana's eye, she nodded.

Following her lead, Hana swallowed and did the same.

Damon sprinkled the bone powder over the blood runes, chanting words in a tongue Adina had never heard before.

His magic was like ribbons being pulled beneath her skin. She bit her lower lip to hold back a grimace as she locked her muscles against the sensation.

As he shook the last of the powder from the bag, he tossed the leather toward the door and out of the way. "Ladies, when the spell is at its climax, I will need you to channel air, water, fire and earth and direct it into the circle." He smirked. "If it helps, you can imagine you're trying to attack me with the elements. Understand?"

Throwing as many elements as she could simultaneously at Damon sounded like a wonderful plan. She'd consider it a personal victory if he walked away damaged.

He waited for them to both nod their agreement. "Excellent. Now, repeat after me: Per potesta Ahionis et Majae, tiba praecipio et renovas."

Adina and Hana repeated the words several times until Damon was satisfied with their pronunciation.

Dragging his dagger across his hand to re-open the wound that had already healed, Damon stepped into the circle of runes and held his palm face-down until one drop of his blood mixed with the powdered bone in all four cardinal directions. "Now, ladies, if you please."

Adina pulled on her Talent, gathering it to herself. She should've taken the chance to down a few swallows from her blood bag, but the last thing she needed to do was alert Damon to their existence. He'd likely steal one for himself.

Though he did enjoy hunting. Perhaps their blood bags were safe, after all. Either way, it was too late now.

Her mouth formed the words practically before she could think them. The energy crackled through the air, jolting the nerves in her skin and raising the hair on her arms. Her Talent wiggled beneath her skin, ready to pounce.

A quick glance at Hana's wide eyes confirmed she felt it, too.

With each repetition of the incantation, the power of the spell built, cresting in larger and larger waves, all crashing into Damon, standing in the middle of the rune circle.

Adina's blood rushed through her ears, drowning out the sound of their voices. Her heart slammed against her chest, matching the cadence she and Hana set.

Just when the power of the magic was about to swallow her whole, Damon screamed, "Now!"

Pulling all the water from the air she could, Adina hurled it, along with a wall of hardened air and the fire from Madalina's torch at Damon with all her might. A wave of dirt, courtesy of Hana, followed close behind.

The elements collided in a golden flash. The reverberating echo was enough to rattle Adina's ears and make white spots dance across her vision. She gasped as the entirety of her Talent tore away, like deep roots of a plant ripped from their soil.

Her hand flew up to her chest, as though she could plug the gaping hole the magic left behind. She bent over the altar as she fought to force air into her lungs.

As she blinked the afterimages from the magic away, she shook her head.

It was the magic—she must be seeing things.

Sophie stood just behind René.

"Sophie!" Madalina turned and gave the woman a beaming smile and a hug that nearly toppled the pair to the ground.

Madalina's voice sounded oddly tinny, as though she were underwater.

Sophie smiled at Madalina before turning her attention to Damon as the magic raged around them. Her eyes were sunken, so much more so than when they'd first met her. Paper-thin skin hung off her bones over atrophied muscles. She'd aged decades in just the last few weeks.

"We were so worried about you!" Madalina said. "With the fire and your house disappearing, we thought you were dead."

Damon locked eyes with Sophie and went pale, dropping to his knees and prostrating himself on the floor.

The magic floundered and died, rattling in Adina's skull like fingernails on slate before fading away to nothing.

"Bow, you fools!" Damon snarled, keeping his forehead to the dirt. His voice had an uncharacteristic tremble.

Every muscle in Adina's body trembled as ice flooded her veins. There was only one being in the world who could make Damon bend the knee.

She met Sophie's gaze. "Maja?"

The goddess she'd nearly died to resurrect, who had cooked them food and let them sleep in her cellar, smiled and nodded.

Sujani's goddess, who had abandoned Sujani in favor of helping them.

It was too much to take in. Bracing both hands against the altar, Adina shook her head, willing her brain to process this turn of events.

"Stand, priest," Maja said, holding out a trembling hand.

His skin whiter than the petals of desert jasmine, Damon pushed himself to his feet, where he stood unmoving as though waiting for the next hammer to drop.

Maja's gaze slid over the runes encircling him. She clicked her tongue. "The ritual you're attempting cannot be completed without my or my brother's guidance." She frowned as she chewed the inside of her cheek. "I'm surprised you don't remember that."

Damon's throat spasmed as he swallowed. Staring at the dirt at her feet, he whispered, "I did. But desperate times..."

She sighed. "Indeed. My brother will be quite disappointed by your actions."

Adina froze.

Damon did a double take as he jerked his head up to meet her eyes. "You mean, Ahion..." He ran one hand through his hair as he blinked rapidly.

She gave him a ghost of a smile. "He lives, though he is very weak."

Damon's eyes went wide, his jaw slackened as a radiant smile spread across his face. "But how?" His voice was barely a whisper as his eyes brimmed with tears.

Arching her eyebrow, she glanced around the room before turning her attention back to him, the darkness shining in her eyes had every instinct in Adina's body screaming for her to flee. "The ritual failed to kill both of us, so it killed neither. It was a very complicated solution to design. My high priest's betrayal ruined many things that night and cost many lives."

"May I—" Damon stammered, paused and swallowed. His voice was soft as he tried again, "May I see him?" The wistful tone and far away look in his eyes was such a contrast to the jaded psychopath Adina had come to know, it was as if the world had tilted on its side.

"Soon. He's attending to something else at the moment. And we haven't much time before my priest realizes I've gone." Maja glanced around the pyramid. "Bring me the petrified dragon bones. Hurry."

"What do you mean, realizes you're gone?" René asked. The sharpness of his tone cut through the tension with a *snap*.

Damon scrambled to the back altar, grabbed the bones, and carried them over. Kneeling, he presented them to her.

Maja met René's gaze. "He has a ring. A soul-stone, and has bound my brother and me."

Damon stumbled back, his eyes widening as he clamped his hand over his mouth. "He did *what*?" His eyes widened. Nostrils flaring, he clenched and unclenched his hands at his side. "He would dare enslave a god?"

Adina blinked. Not just one god, but *two*.

By the mages...

Madalina's quiet voice floated through the room. "Is that why you're looking so ill?"

Maja glanced at her. "He siphons our power for his own use."

Adina's knees went weak. She planted both hands on the altar to steady herself. If Sujani had drained Maja and Ahion's powers to make himself a god by proxy, they had no chance against him.

Damon heaved himself to his feet with a guttural roar. "I'll end him and everyone he holds dear for this!" His black cape snapped around his ankles as he marched toward the door.

Between one heartbeat and the next, Maja's face disappeared, replaced by a male. He was gaunt, with prominent cheek bones, and black hair that brushed the top of his ears. His blood-red eyes flashed with repressed anger. "No!" The word bounced off the pyramid's walls and rattled around in Adina's skull.

His voice wasn't nearly as soothing and motherly as Maja's.

Damon froze, his entire body trembling. "Ahion." The words were little more than a whisper.

"We need you here, priest. The betrayer's time will come."

The tendons in Damon's jaw snapped and cracked as he clenched his jaw. Every muscle in his body clenched as the tension thickened the room.

Ahion reached out, his hand resting on Damon's shoulder. "Your loyalty is admirable and will be rewarded. But you must control yourself."

Time stretched for several heartbeats as the weight of the god's command pressed on Adina's shoulders.

With a swallow, Damon crumbled to his knees as if in slow motion, his forehead finally touching the dirt at the god's feet. "As you command."

Another blink, and Maja's visage replaced Ahion's.

Taking one bone in each wavering hand, she held them aloft. "Now, my brother's priest, stand in the rune circle. Quickly."

Wordlessly, Damon pushed himself to his feet and stepped inside like a dog on a leash.

Adina glanced at Erik. She'd been a lot more comfortable in Sophie's presence before she realized the woman masquerading as a mortal was a goddess. Judging by the corded muscles in Erik's neck and the way his sword arm twitched toward his weapon, he felt the same.

Near the doorway, René and Hana clung to each other, looking ready to faint.

Something released in Adina's stomach. She shouldn't feel quite so embarrassed at failing to identify a goddess who clearly hadn't wanted to be recognized. They were so out of their league.

"Continue the chant," Maja said.

What chant?

Damon started, "Per potesta Ahionis et Majae…"

Adina's mind scrambled for the forgotten words and picked up halfway through the line. "…tiba praecipio et renovas."

The magic built again, but this time it felt more vivid, or more intense. It climaxed as more of a gradual lifting rather than a tidal wave that threatened to overwhelm them all.

"Now," Maja said, nodding to her.

Grabbing all the elements she could, Adina took a deep breath and hurled them at Damon. With the extra boost from Maja's power, she managed to include some shadow force, as well. Hana's earth joined them as the elements circled him like an iridescent bubble.

Maja brought the two bones together overhead with an ear-splitting crack followed by a blindingly bright golden light, the likes of which Adina hadn't seen since her last sunrise as a human.

An extra weight settled itself at her right hip as the magic waxed then ebbed away. She shifted her stance and glanced down to see a bone white dagger fixed to her belt. The weapon vibrated with the same energy as the original Bone Shard Blade they'd found in the cave, before Sujani had raised Maja. Adjusting her robes to obscure it from view, she glanced at Erik.

He met her gaze with a solemn expression of his own. With a quick glance at her waist, then to Damon, and back again, he nodded.

His message was clear. Keep the blade hidden.

Fortunately, Damon was somewhat distracted at the moment as he stared at Maja, a flaccid expression that, if Adina didn't know better, she'd call awe. He gripped what appeared to be a near replica of Adina's new Bone Shard Blade in his right hand.

"Thank you, Maja." Damon dropped to his knees again. "It is an honor to be your vessel. I don't deserve it."

"No, you don't, but you may serve us anyway," Maja said, her lips pressed into a thin line. "And for the last time, rise. Unlike my brother, I prefer my priests on their feet and useful. You're no good to me on your knees."

Red flooded Damon's cheeks and forehead as he stood.

René spoke for the first time since Sophie revealed she was Maja. "Us? Is that like the royal 'we'?"

Maja turned to him with a faint smile.

"No. My brother is not strong enough to exist on his own." She placed a hand over her heart. "We must return to my priest."

"He's calling for you?" Damon's voice cracked with suppressed emotion.

Adina almost felt sorry for him. Almost.

"He is," Maja said. "And we have given you the Bone Shard Blade, re-forged anew, so you can punish him."

Damon blinked. "I—I have your permission? To end Sujani?"

Maja's shoulders drooped, her arms hanging by her side. "Yes. Like us, his time has passed." She pierced Damon with a gaze. "As has yours. The Final Rest calls to us all."

Damon nodded, though with the shock, he may not even have realized he was doing so.

Adina licked her lips. If Sujani had a blade, and Damon had a blade, and the gods desired both priests ended, why did she have a blade, too?

Maja's focus turned to her, just for a heartbeat.

Every muscle in Adina's body contracted as the knowledge exploded in her brain.

She was to kill the gods once the priests were ended.

Dragging a hand down her face, she exhaled and choked. Maja and Ahion certainly didn't ask for much, did they?

<*We are truly sorry to put this on you.*> Maja's voice echoed in her mind. <*But we cannot kill ourselves. We will stay long enough to ensure the world is safe once more.*>

And to make sure Damon and Sujani no longer held sway.

Adina nodded. She could live with that. Her hand itched to draw the Bone Shard Blade at her hip but revealing it to Damon would ruin everything. So instead, she made sure it was solidly concealed in her robes. "Now we have the blade," she said, eyeing Damon and Maja. "What's the next step? Are we ready to go find the Colosseum?"

Maja nodded and raised her hand, pointing further into the ruins. "You will see it once you pass through the catacombs." She caught Damon's eye. "Tread softly. He has allies about."

"You're not coming with us?" Erik asked.

Flashing him a quick smile, she shook her head. "No. If we go with you, as weak as we are, all may be lost." She turned on her heel and marched for the door. "But we will be there before the end."

Adina swallowed. That sounded promising. She tilted her head to the side, cupping her elbow with one hand and tapping her lips with the other. What did that mean?

She shook her head. It was probably better that she didn't know.

"Well?" René asked, glancing around once Maja had disappeared. "What are we waiting for?"

"Do you trust Sophie?" Sigfried asked.

"Yes!" Damon snarled, lunging two steps toward him. "Don't *ever* insinuate she would lie!"

"Calm down, Damon!" Adina stepped to his side and put her hand against his chest. "You know he didn't mean it that way."

Damon's chest heaved in and out with the force of his breaths. After a few heartbeats, the wildness left his eyes. He ran a hand through his hair with a prolonged exhale.

Once his breathing had stabilized, she glared at him. "Besides, it's a fair question. She's Sujani's goddess, not yours. Who knows where her loyalties lie?"

"Ahion's purpose aligns with hers. Or did you miss that whole thing just now?" Damon shoved her away and strode out from the pyramid. "I'm going to end Sujani for this. Good riddance to you lot."

She sighed. Having confronted a goddess and learning that his god was alive, she'd have expected Damon to be a lot more subdued.

Oh, well. If wishes were roses, the desert would smell better than a perfumer's tent.

"Which allies do you think she was referring to?" Erik asked as he lengthened his stride to catch up to her as they hurried through the exit.

"I would imagine Charles. I have no idea who else it could be."

"Septimus," Damon snarled from several paces ahead. His voice oozed venom. "The traitor has switched sides, apparently. Along with the entire Assassin's Guild." Even from this far back, the tension in his muscles was obvious.

Adina's footsteps stuttered.

Her father could be here? With the entire Guild? Her stomach flip-flopped as it hardened. They were in so much trouble.

She shook her head. No. That wasn't feasible. The members were assassins, not mercenaries or private security.

She thought back to the impenetrable barrier of hardened air that encircled the estate last night.

Besides, Sujani and his magic were all the security he needed.

But Damon would have no reason to lie, at least, not about that. And the anger in his voice...

They passed several other large buildings that were at some point likely governmental or religious in nature, but with their crumbling facades it was impossible to ascertain their original function without more time.

Damon was practically running as he led them through the city.

"Wait up!" René said.

Looking over his shoulder, Damon snarled. "No. You keep up."

"You were here before the Cataclysm," Erik said, jogging briefly to get closer to Damon. "So was Sujani. How is it you don't know where the catacombs and the Colosseum are?"

"A lot of things change over the centuries," Damon snapped over his shoulder.

Erik raised his brow. "Surely your memory isn't so deficient."

Damon flashed his fangs and rolled his eyes. "Idiot. After the Cataclysm, magic went awry. How else do you think an entire ruined city ended up in an underground cavern?" He pointed at a passing building. "That was the performer's hall in what's now called the City of Bones. It belongs on the other side of the desert, and yet, here it is. Care to explain that, butcher?"

Shaking his head, Erik glanced around. "So, things got shuffled around?"

"Shuffled and forgotten. The Colosseum probably hails from somewhere in Champeaux, based on the name." He shrugged. "It doesn't really matter where it came from. What's important is that it's here, and apparently in the same location where the temple was when I was alive."

Adina licked her lips and swallowed. If they failed here, things might well shift like that again. The entire world would be turned upside down. Most living beings would perish in the aftermath.

No pressure.

The gods didn't ask for much.

"They only ask for what you're able to give," Damon said. He paused, a slight catch in his step. "Except, apparently, in Sujani's case. Maja made a critical character error when it came to him."

Sigfried grunted. "Gods do not make mistakes."

Damon cackled. "Keep right on thinking that." The hard edge to his words had Adina dropping a little further back.

The street came to an end against the cavern wall. A stone stairway spread before them, wide enough for ten men to walk abreast. It descended into the darkness.

René pushed forward for a better view. "The entrance to the catacombs?"

Damon didn't bother responding as he conjured a ball of crimson energy that hovered above his palm. The light flickered off the steps and cast shadows on the walls as he descended at full speed. Within a few breaths, his bone-white hair had disappeared below.

Erik squeezed Adina's upper arm. "Come on, let's go. Before we lose him."

"Hello, Damon." Septimus' booming voice echoed off the stone walls. "Leading the children to slaughter, are you?"

Damon snarled. "Come here, traitor, and you'll see exactly what I'm doing."

Adina glanced at Erik and picked up the pace until Damon came back into view, a circle of red surrounded by shadows.

Heavy footsteps circled Damon, but Septimus himself remained hidden.

Adina spread her arms. "Stay back," she whispered.

Everyone else stopped behind her.

"Should we try to go around?" Erik asked.

She shook her head. "I don't think so...we'll get caught in the crossfire." And she had no desire to get into a fight with her father. Besides, Damon may well end him if they just waited a few minutes.

"We can't very well stay here and do nothing," Erik said.

Adina froze as Khalid stepped from the shadows in front of them. "Yes, of course you can."

Chapter 21

Damon

Damon pulled on his Talent as Seven circled him, spinning his twin scimitars like he was warming up his wrists.

Most likely, Seven was just trying to look intimidating.

Damon bared his fangs. As if he could be intimidated by Sujani's get. Yanking on a filament of his Talent, he hurled a crimson-tinted ball of energy to test the waters.

Seven turned to the side as the magical force flew by. Twirling his swords, he bent his knees and held both weapons up, ready for the next attack.

Flaring his nostrils, Damon pushed a wall of magic in front of himself like a shield and stepped forward.

Taking his right blade, Seven spun it a few times over his head as he flashed his fangs.

Damon raised an eyebrow. "Are you done posturing yet?" It was past time to end this traitor. Ahion was waiting.

Seven growled in the back of his throat.

Bending his knees slightly for better balance, Damon turned sideways so his right side was facing the other vampire. He shouldn't let himself be distracted from their goddess-given task of ending Sujani. But this wouldn't take long, and he'd take great pleasure in putting Seven down like the traitorous dog he was. Extending his hand, he beckoned the other vampire to attack him.

Seven lunged, both swords aimed for an overhead strike, one right after the other.

Damon caught Seven's first arm with his wrist, deflecting the leading blade. Ducking to the side, he leaned backward as the second whooshed by. Continuing his momentum, he spun in a circle, his cape cracking like a whip behind him. As he completed his rotation, he ended up back-to-back with Seven.

He smirked. The exalted King of Assassins should've seen that move coming—Damon had picked it up from him, after all. Looping one arm around Seven's neck, he channeled his pent-up rage into his muscles and jerked forward.

With a strangled gasp, Seven jumped, rolling over Damon's back, his head, then tumbling to the ground. Contracting his impressive stomach muscles, he leaped to his feet, swinging his sword for Damon's neck.

Ducking the blade, Damon called to the magic in his blood. Raising a hand, he batted Seven's sword away. The sharp edge kissed his palm, sending a jolt of sweet pain up his arm to mingle with the magic.

Blood poured from the wound, merging with his hand until he held a scimitar nearly identical to Seven's. Sneering, Damon met the other man's gaze. "If you want to play with metal, let's play."

Not waiting for his opponent's response, Damon jabbed his blood-scimitar at Seven's navel.

The other vampire knocked the sword away.

They exchanged blow after blow, their blades casting sparks of burning metallic bits into the air as they clashed.

Damon clenched his jaw as he hacked away, smashing his weapon into Seven's over and over again. In brute strength, Seven had the advantage, but Damon had the benefit of experience and wisdom. And righteous anger. No way was he going to give ground to a traitor.

He let Seven push him around the hall in a wide circle, giving the assassin time to exhaust himself with each deflected attack. The fury burning in the pit of Damon's gut would easily outlast his opponent's. Biting the inside corners of his lips to keep from smiling, he slashed at the pulsing artery in Seven's inner thigh.

Seven's muscles trembled at the strain of his onslaught as Damon lunged again and again. The King of Assassin's moves were just a split-second too slow.

Damon smiled. *I've got you, now.*

With one final parry, Seven flung Damon's sword arm wide. Using the opening, he turned and retreated several steps, buying himself time. He bent down, fingers brushing the corner where the wall met the floor as though sweeping dirt from the ground.

Spinning to face Damon, he flung five obsidian daggers. "Have some shadow force!"

By the mages!

Damon pulled his Talent and thrust it in front of himself. The projectiles embedded in Damon's magical shield. Red light vibrated through the area as his spell absorbed the power of Seven's attack.

Barely.

Dismissing his barrier, its power expended, Damon lunged, aiming for the other man's throat. "I'll spill your lifeblood across the catacombs!"

Seven's deep laughter echoed against his eardrums. "You're welcome to try." Stepping forward as he parried Damon's latest lunge, Seven spun his scimitar around Damon's blood-blade, until he had Damon's arm pinned between his ribs and elbow.

Seven squeezed.

Something in Damon's elbow popped, sending a sharp stab of pain up into his shoulder.

He clenched his jaw at the sensation. If he let it distract him, he'd be a true-dead vampire. And there was no way he would give Seven the honor of being the one to end him. Especially not when Ahion was counting on him.

His vision tinted crimson. With a snarl, Damon leaned forward and bit the junction between Seven's shoulder blade and neck. Holding with all his might, he ripped backward, his fangs tearing muscle from bone.

Seven roared as his spine arched.

The pressure against Damon's elbow released and he leaped back, flexing and releasing his arm as his blood rushed to repair the injury.

A heartbeat later, he spun his blade in a mimic of the sword twirling Seven had done at the beginning of their fight. The joint was still sore, but it moved as it should. Nodding in approval, he returned his attention to his opponent.

Seven spun, glaring at him over his bleeding shoulder, his teeth bared in a snarl. "I'll end you!"

Damon flashed his fangs. The assassin was welcome to try. He flicked his wrist, sending a wave of magic toward Seven where it slammed into him, smashing him against the wall with a crack.

Take that, traitor!

The back of his throat started to burn.

Curse the mages. He was going through his supply of power too quickly. After Seven, Charles would likely appear as his next obstacle, and he'd need every drop of power he had for his inevitable showdown with Sujani. Damon froze, blinking. *That* was Sujani's game!

His rival didn't care about Seven, or anyone else he set in Damon's way, other than how much they could drain him before their inevitable showdown.

Damon swallowed past a dry throat. He was such an idiot—he should've seen that coming sooner rather than waste his skills. It was exactly the same thing he'd do, were he in Sujani's position.

He glared at his blood-scimitar. It looked like he was using the sword from now on, conserving his Talent for later. Or he could drain Seven. There would be a certain poetic justice in that.

Lunging forward, his blade whistled through the air, heading for the other vampire's knees.

Seven's muscles bunched as he leaped over the blade and disappeared in a puff of shadows.

Cheater.

Damon backed up two steps, eyes scanning in every direction. "Are you scared to face me head-on?" Spinning around, he braced for an attack at his back. Nothing came. Turning to face the darkest spot of the corridor ahead, he scowled. "I never figured you for a coward."

The cold press of Seven's scimitar jammed into his throat, cutting into the junction between his neck and his jaw. The sharp edge of his second blade settled at the base of Damon's skull.

Damon closed his eyes and braced for the inevitable slice that would separate his head from his shoulders. He'd ruined everything, just when his god needed him the most.

I'm sorry, Ahion. I've failed you.

A large grizzly bear roared from somewhere behind Seven.

Damon blinked.

Wrath!

He'd forgotten about the others.

A large grizzly paw flashed in Damon's peripheral vision as it ripped Seven's first sword away.

More than happy to take advantage of the opportunity, Damon threw himself down and forward, away from Seven's remaining scimitar.

He landed face-first on the ground with a *whoosh*, the impact driving the air from his lungs and bringing dancing white spots to the edges of his vision.

With a groan and a spasm, he rolled onto his back. Above, Wrath's claws slashed, opening Seven's bicep to the bone.

Damon bared his fangs as the heat of elation raced through him, echoing the beat of his racing heart. That was one sword arm out of commission.

With a snarl, Seven rammed his remaining scimitar into Wrath's gut, twisting viciously. The grizzly's roar echoed down the hall.

"Sigfried!" Madalina's cry was lost in the cacophony of battle.

The grizzly collapsed, rolling away as his blood spurted across the floor. His bones popped and shifted until the bear disappeared, leaving a bloody Wrath behind.

Seven must have caught the main artery into his heart to drop him that quickly.

Would Holt care that his son had met Final Death? Damon frowned. He had no idea. If Holt did, it would only swing the man against Seven and onto Damon's side. But once Sujani was dead, the world would be his, and it wouldn't matter—Holt and the rest of them could go bite themselves.

Pushing to his feet as quietly as possible, he lunged at Seven, driving his sword into the large man's back. It slid in between his ribs and with a satisfying *pop*, pierced his heart.

Seven disappeared in a flurry of black mist.

Such a wound wouldn't keep the other vampire down for long, but it would buy Damon a few minutes to recover. His gaze fixed on the artery in Wrath's neck, its pulse rapidly becoming weaker and weaker. The burning flared from Damon's throat throughout his veins.

The wild man was dead already. Surely no one would begrudge him the last few swallows of life before they faced Sujani?

Wrath's clumsy fingers fumbled with a wine skin at his belt.

Damon shook his head as he surged forward. The things people do in a panic. No amount of water or wine would save him now.

Finally wrenching it free, Wrath brought the wine skin to his mouth and began to chug its contents. A drizzle of blood trickled from the corner of his lips.

Damon's steps stuttered to a stop.

What was this? Useful blood in a bag?

Such a thing was impossible.

Snatching the wondrous item from Wrath's weakened grip, Damon sniffed it.

The tantalizing taste of copper teased his nose.

Furrowing his brows and giving Wrath one final frown, Damon raised the wine skin to his lips and tilted his head back.

Blood overflowing with life energy exploded in his mouth and ripped down his throat, instantly assuaging the burning and washing away every ache and pain. Damon's eyes crossed as his vision blurred with ecstasy. Golden ribbons of effervescent energy raced down each of his arteries.

In his twelve hundred years of existence, he'd never tasted blood like this. Swallow after swallow passed his lips, settling into his gut. Damon stared at Wrath as though seeing him for the first time.

He held up the bag. "Where did you get this, boy?"

Wrath groaned as he curled up, protecting his stomach.

"Give it back!" Madalina stepped into Damon's view as she reached for the wine skin.

Damon held it above his head, well out of her reach. He snorted. "No. Not until you tell me where you found it."

She jumped, scrambling for his arm. "He's dying! He needs it more than you do right now."

Damon frowned. "No. Answer the question, or we'll watch him die together."

"He saved your unlife just now." Her glare cut through his soul.

Damon's stomach muscles hardened as he swallowed.

No. That was *not* guilt he was feeling. Not at all.

He turned his attention from her up to the blood bag, breaking their connection. The annoying ache in his stomach disappeared as he poured its contents down his throat. Miraculously, the wine skin still felt like it was completely full. Which was ridiculous, of course, except that he'd just downed what felt like two or three bags' worth.

With a smile, Damon batted Madalina away and tied the blood bag to his belt. It would come in handy for when he fought Sujani. Madalina and Wrath forgotten, Damon glanced at the shadows once more.

There was no sign of Septimus.

Rolling his shoulders to keep them from stiffening, he studied his blood-scimitar. The blade shone crimson in the torchlight. It would be even stronger with the potent, condensed blood in Wrath's wineskin.

Taking another deep swallow, he added another layer of blood to enhance the blade.

Now he was ready to take on Sujani. With one final glance at the others, he turned and stalked down the hallway.

Chapter 22
Adina

Drawing her falchion, Adina spun to face Khalid. Her muscles went slack. It wasn't possible. "I saw you die!"

He sneered at her, drawing his double scimitars. "Viktor raised me." He smirked. "I've been waiting for a rematch."

By the gods. A raised fighter with Khalid's skill was the last thing they needed right now.

Erik drew his greatsword. As though they'd planned it, they simultaneously moved to flank the newcomer.

Twirling his two swords to limber up his wrists, Khalid flashed his fangs in a wide grin.

Adina raised her blade in a two-handed grip. She lunged with a high attack aimed at his neck, where the faint scar remained from when Septimus had beheaded him in The Drowned City.

Khalid stepped to his left, moving to keep both her and Erik in view as he parried and riposted, his scimitar aimed for her stomach.

Erik stabbed low, twice. Each time, Khalid batted his blade aside with his offhand weapon.

Adina tapped Khalid's sword with hers, trying to draw his attention so Erik could sweep in for the kill.

Khalid crossed blades with her as he lunged, sweeping his second scimitar behind him to block Erik's strike.

She took a step back, dancing out of the way as she parried his attack.

Khalid reversed direction and she blocked again. With a sneer, he jumped forward, dropping his blade beneath hers at the last minute in a feint.

She arched her body, pulling her stomach in tightly, as the scimitar whistled through the air, close enough to cut through her outer robe.

Adina exhaled and shook a stray strand of hair out of her face. The muscles in her arms burned. That had been too close.

Khalid smirked.

They had to finish him quickly, or he'd wear them down until he could cut them apart, piece by piece.

Erik leaped, circling the sword in the other vampire's off-hand with his to trap it and rip it from his grip.

Khalid was too dexterous—he followed the motion and with a flick of speed from his wrist, freed his blade. Parrying Adina's next attack, he swung overhead, aiming for Erik's neck.

Adina's heart caught in her throat. *No!*

Erik raised his sword and the two slammed together, sending sparks flying.

Khalid swung at his throat again and again, as though attempting to chop firewood.

Adina leaped for Khalid with an overhead attack of her own.

He spun at the last minute, slamming his sword into hers and swatting it aside.

They exchanged rapid blows, one after the other, neither able to get in between the others' guard.

Between her and Erik, they slowly but methodically pushed Khalid back, until he pressed against the wall.

Erik swung his sword high. Khalid met him, their blades clashing with a jarring *clang* which echoed across the corridor and sent vibrations down Adina's spine.

She shook her head and blinked. It was a miracle their swords didn't shatter.

Baring his teeth as he clenched his jaw, Erik grunted as he strained to shove Khalid's scimitar aside.

Now was her chance. Adina leaped forward, aiming for Khalid's gut.

Khalid dropped his off-hand blade and ducked, letting Erik's greatsword fly harmlessly overhead as he blocked her attack with his offhand weapon.

She met his parry and flicked her wrist, bringing the tip of her falchion circling below his blade and around the hilt. Lunging, she stabbed the tip of her blade forward.

Stepping to the side, Khalid shifted his weight. The edge of her weapon kissed the skin at his waist, but the damage was only superficial.

Khalid laughed as she pulled back, her falchion covered in a thin coat of red.

By the gods. Could zombies even feel pain? They were outmatched.

Taking advantage of their opponent's distraction, Erik swung low, aiming for his knees.

With an impressive show of dexterity, Khalid jumped, doing a double backflip over both of their weapons and landed behind them.

"Ha!" he said, flashing his fangs.

Where was René? Or Sigfried? If they stayed at this for much longer, they'd tire and then Khalid, with his seemingly boundless energy, would prevail.

Adina glanced at Erik and nodded. As one, they lunged, both aiming for Khalid's heart.

Batting their swords away as though they were children, Khalid parried and riposted each attack as he slowly walked backward.

Erik froze mid-step, his back arching as though someone had stabbed him in the back. His mouth opened in a silent scream. A fine sheen of red erupted over his face.

Adina's stomach tightened as her blood turned to ice. "Erik!"

The air around her froze, ice crystals forming on her sword.

He fell to his knees.

Behind him, the wraith, Viktor Knoll, hovered, his hand where Erik's heart would have been.

Khalid sneered then barked a laugh.

<Finish her!> The wraith pointed at Adina as its voice echoed in her mind.

Adina flinched, slamming her palms over her ears, but it did nothing to block the wraith's voice from rattling around in her brain.

Khalid brought one blade to his forehead and jerked it downward in a salute. "As you wish, my master."

A stab of ice slammed through Adina's core. If Viktor was controlling Khalid directly, he'd likely be just as hard to kill now as the gargoyle was the first time they crossed blades with one of Viktor's creatures.

The memory of the gargoyle's claws shredding her gut wrenched the air from her lungs. Her knees buckled. She flared her nostrils as she fought to control her breathing. If she lost her composure now, she'd meet Final Death.

Khalid stepped forward, one scimitar slicing diagonally past her head while the second one hummed through the air at gut level.

Adina held her falchion high, redirecting his head shot and spun toward him until she was inside his guard. "Erik!" she yelled.

Please, get up!

Grabbing Khalid's arm, she used her momentum to spin him around until he faced the wall.

Khalid turned with her movement, using it to speed another slice at her head.

She bent backward as the tip of the blade flew past, less than a finger's width from her nose.

Ice settled in her veins. She'd only be able to dodge his swords for so long before her luck ran out. Especially with Erik out of the fight.

With a lilting string of Champeauxian curses, a flurry of colors flew by as René lunged for the wraith almost faster than she could follow.

Raising his eyebrow, Khalid's eyes flicked toward René.

With a scream, Adina pommeled Khalid in the face. His cheek bone collapsed with a satisfying crunch.

Khalid stumbled backward, blinking as a drop of blood welled at the outer corner of his eye. His chest heaved as his upper lip curled, revealing elongated fangs. "Wench! You'll pay for that!"

Adina risked a glance at Erik as he toppled to the ground, one hand holding him up as the other clasped his chest above his heart.

Khalid ran for her, spinning as his blades whirled like a dervish.

Adina ducked as she lifted one arm, capturing his leading wrist and trapping it in her armpit. With a twist of her free hand, she ripped the scimitar from his fingers. Half a heartbeat later, its grip slid into her hand.

She spun away, holding the falchion low and his stolen scimitar high in a guard position. A burst of energy zapped through her muscles at her small victory, rejuvenating her. Smirking at Khalid, she tilted her head. "Getting tired?"

"I'm just getting started." Khalid snarled and lunged at her and stabbed, aiming for her heart.

Adina parried and riposted with a slice at his neck.

Khalid stepped to his left at the last minute as the force of her lunge left her side exposed. He hissed in satisfaction as his blade kissed her side.

Aaah!

Burning pain exploded across her ribs, radiating up her arm and down her leg. Tucking her elbow against the wound, she screamed and hacked at him with her free sword.

Drops of blood slid from her wound, splattering on the floor.

Khalid blocked and scrambled back until he reached the staircase. With a backflip, he landed on the third step.

No! She couldn't let him get away. If he escaped, he'd only stab them in the back later when they least expected it.

Running to catch him, they traded two more blows before Khalid caught her scimitar with his. Spinning it around with quick flicks of his wrist, she lost her grip on the weapon, and it spun off to the side. She didn't dare take her attention from him to see where it landed.

Adina dropped to the ground as his blade cut through the air with a hiss overhead and swung for his knees.

He jumped over her remaining sword and lunged forward. Adina twisted her wrist, whipping her falchion around his arm. With a viscous twist, she snapped his wrist.

Khalid screamed as he dropped his remaining scimitar.

Snatching it from midair, she straddled him, the falchion to his throat and the scimitar against the back of his neck. With a grunt, she sliced.

For the second time, Khalid's head separated from his body. It tumbled down the stairs. His blood mingled with hers on the floor.

"And stay dead!" Inhaling air as quickly as she could to regain her breath, she leaned against the edge of the staircase and tilted her head to examine the wound in her side. Ripping her endless blood bag from her belt, she took several deep swallows. The burning eased as the cut stitched itself closed.

Her knees buckled. She slid down the wall until she sat on the stairs, the coolness of the stone seeping into her skin. She clutched the blood bag to her chest as her body worked to heal itself.

Chapter 23
Erik

The ice that burned Erik's heart was sucking the life out of him, drop by excruciating drop. It hurt worse, was deeper than any pain he'd ever experienced—including the fire in the Shadow Mountains during their gauntlet to claim the Bone Shard Blade.

He'd be damned if he stayed here and died on his knees. Heaving himself to his feet, he shook his head and shoved the burning sensation to the back of his mind. His Talent was *supposed* to give him perfect physical control of his body.

He glanced at Adina as Khalid's head rolled across the floor and settled against the far wall. She slumped, pulling her blood-covered hand away from her ribs to fumble with the blood bag tied to her belt.

She was wounded!

Clenching his teeth with a groan, he fought to move toward her but another wave of burning ice exploded throughout his body as the wraith shoved its hand back into his heart. Every muscle in his body spasmed, threatening to knock him to the ground. Each nerve in his skin burned as though on fire. His peripheral vision went black until he could only focus directly ahead.

"Erik! Catch!" Madalina's high-pitched voice cut through the sound of his blood pumping furiously past his ears. She crouched near where Sigfried lay on the ground in a puddle of blood. Alarm slashed through

Erik's gut, but the reaction faded as Madalina's cool-headed gaze met his. She held one of Hana's endless blood bags to Sigfried's lips.

Her torch flew toward him, trailing an arc of smoke behind it.

Extending his hand, he caught it right before it would have slammed into him. Spinning about, he slashed at the wraith.

After all, it had worked before, the first time he and René had fought Viktor in the keep back in Brachia. Perhaps the wraith would disappear if he threatened it with fire again?

René leaped forward, slicing at the specter with his sword. "Die, Viktor! Blood mage scum!"

Erik passed the torch through the wraith's back, at the level of his lower ribs.

The wraith's psychic scream ripped through his mind like fingernails that sought purchase in his brain so they could pull it in half.

God's Teeth!

Madalina screamed, slamming both hands against her ears.

René lunged forward, slicing back and forth so quickly Erik's eyes couldn't follow the movement.

The wraith recoiled, as though stealing some of Erik's life had turned it the tiniest fraction corporeal again.

<Do it!>

The wraith's voice echoed through his head, though as the wraith was facing René, it clearly wasn't speaking to Erik.

René froze, tilting his head to the side. He scrunched his eyebrows together as he scratched his temple with a finger. "Do what?"

<Kill me! I do not wish to be a soul-slave to the vampire.>

"Kill you how?" Erik asked as he drew his blade and sliced through the wraith's side. "This is hardly a death-wound for the likes of you."

Viktor spun toward Damon, who was rapidly walking away, and flung his hand out as though casting a fishing line across a lake.

Damon arched his back in a silent scream as his skin turned red and reflected the light of the torches. His blood pooled into a ball, as though drawn by the magnet of Viktor's power, until the globe hovered between them.

Damon stretched out his arm and contracted his fingers into a fist. "Viktor, you traitor!" <I'll make you wish you'd never been born!>

Damon's mental words echoed through Erik's mind.

The orb of blood wobbled, pulled between the two, then slowly gathering speed, flew back to Damon.

<No!>

A blinding teal flash of light illuminated the hallway, bleaching Erik's retinas with the jagged after-image of lightning.

Damon flew across the hall to slam into the rock wall. Black smoke rose from his cloak.

"That's enough of that." Charles stepped into the light.

The blood that had been headed for Damon snapped as he lost his grip. It reversed course and slammed into the wraith. The ethereal being turned solid. Viktor turned to René, his palms splayed wide. Tilting his head back, he closed his eyes and smiled.

<End me. Send me back, so I can rejoin my beloved in death.>

René blinked, giving the wraith an incredulous look. "What? Who?"

Erik was done waiting for René to make his move before Viktor changed his mind or Charles interfered. Taking a deep breath, he plunged his sword through the blood mage's ribs into his heart.

Viktor arched his back as every muscle in his body contorted.

René's rapier sliced halfway through his neck with a thin spray of blood.

Viktor collapsed to his knees.

Bracing his foot against Viktor's back, Erik ripped his sword free, being sure to twist it on its way out to do as much damage to the old blood mage's heart as possible.

With a final gasp and a faint smile, Viktor toppled to the ground.

René met Erik's eyes as he flicked the blood from his blade. "Well. I don't know about you, but I'm rather tired of killing this guy."

Erik pressed his lips into a fine line. "Indeed." Though, with a blood mage such as Damon around with the apparent ability to resurrect him, were they safe assuming *anyone* was ever truly dead? A heavy weight pressed down on his shoulders, accompanied by a hollowed-out feeling in his gut.

Apparently, the only way to make sure Viktor stayed dead was to end Damon. Erik added one more item to his mental list of reasons Damon needed to die.

Viktor's body crumbled into black dust that scattered as though blown away by an ethereal breeze.

The lingering ache in his heart released as though it had never been, leaving behind the burning at the back of his throat indicating he was low on blood. Bracing his sword tip on the floor, Erik scanned the carnage.

Damon and Charles circled each other further down the hall. Adina leaned against the wall, guzzling blood as quickly as she could, her swords dripping red. Madalina and Sigfried crouched against the other wall. It looked as though Sig had been seriously wounded. Thank heavens for Hana's endless blood-bags.

Speaking of...

He pulled his wine skin off his belt and took three deep swallows. The life energy effervesced, rejuvenating his sore muscles and restoring his energy.

Tipping his head side to side as he stretched, he wandered over to Adina. "Are you alright?"

She nodded and met his gaze. "Yes." Glancing down at Khalid's head, she kicked at it. "Hopefully this time, he stays dead."

Erik chuckled once. "Somehow, I think he will."

Adina raised her eyebrow. "Oh?"

He leaned in conspiratorially and whispered, "René and I just killed the wraith. Again."

She blinked. "Again? You mean, the wraith from Brachia? Viktor Knoll?"

Erik swallowed. "The same. This time, he wanted to die…" He shook his head. "He even stole some of Damon's blood to make himself corporeal enough so we could do it."

"Really?" She glanced at René. "Are you sure you two aren't hallucinating?"

René put his hand over his heart and bowed with a flourish. The bow was only slightly marred by the fact that he was essentially balancing on his good foot. "I swear it's the truth."

She glanced at Erik, studied whatever she saw in his face and shrugged.

Yeah, he wouldn't believe it either, if he hadn't seen it himself. "I guess being Damon's soul-slave is a fate worse than death."

"Well, yeah." She nudged Khalid's body with the point of her sword. "Hopefully once this is said and done, everyone who is dead stays that way."

He couldn't agree more.

Something slammed into the side of the tunnel further down, drawing Erik's attention.

Charles leaned against the wall, shaking his head like he was dazed. Several paces away, Damon flicked his wrist and gestured, as though he were summoning magic.

The putrid stench of Damon pulling on his Talent filled the corridor.

Erik glanced at Adina, ready for her to summon a breeze to blow the stench away from them.

She caught his eye and shook her head.

Right. Damon was their ally now, technically.

Erik turned back to the fight, his gut twisting itself inside out at the thought of supporting Damon over his own father.

But Charles had sided with Sujani, who had tried to sacrifice Adina to resurrect Maja. Erik rolled his shoulders and clenched his jaw.

His father had made his choice and would suffer the consequences.

Just as they likely would at the end, for supporting Damon. Even if Damon was victorious, Erik was under no illusion the ancient vampire would just let them go, despite his blood oath.

Further down the tunnel, Charles raised one hand over his head. A gust of wind barreled through the corridor seconds before a bright flash and explosion that rattled the very stones beneath their feet.

Erik yanked on his Talent and leaned forward as the blast wave washed over them. Everyone else was knocked prone.

He blinked, trying to clear the grit from his face and the afterimages from his vision. The air was choked with dust, and he couldn't make out what had happened to Damon or Charles. Red light flashed through the debris.

Damon was still alive, at least.

Reaching down, Erik snagged Adina's hand and helped her up. "Are you okay?"

Coughing, she nodded and glanced over her shoulder at the stairs leading back the way they'd come. Hana cleared the last two steps with a leap, landing next to René who pushed himself to his feet. He limped forward, favoring the foot he'd injured in the marsh.

Brushing a few rocky bits of debris from his hair, Hana asked, "Are you hurt?"

René cleared his throat and brushed the rest of the dirt off his shoulders. "No. Of course not. I'm fine."

Hana nodded to his foot. "How's it doing?"

His smile wavered for a heartbeat before he plastered it back on his face. "It's alright. No worse than before." His voice faltered.

"Let me see."

René opened his mouth but closed it at the unforgiving expression on Hana's face. With a sigh, he pulled his shirt up.

The swollen blackness was halfway up his ribs.

Erik chewed the inside of his cheek and shifted his weight from side to side. They couldn't afford to wait much longer. René may not be his favorite person in the world, but in his heart, the vampire was a good man, and didn't deserve to die this way. Somehow, they had to get René some of Damon's blood and trust Gaelle's word that would fix the problem. He had a feeling when the rot reached his heart, René would meet Final Death.

Not to mention, they'd need all the help they could get when it came to ending Sujani. René was definitely worth his weight as a swordsman.

Hana blanched. "That's almost twice as high as it was yesterday," she whispered, biting her lip as she turned to Adina.

Adina glanced at Erik before she shrugged. "Maybe it gets worse in Damon's proximity?"

Erik ran his hand through his hair. That made sense. The night rot had been almost stable for most of their journey from Champeaux. For it to only worsen tonight...Damon would have to be the trigger.

Rather poetic justice that he was also the cure.

Erik met Hana's eyes. From the hardness there, and the way she glared into the dust cloud in Damon's direction, her thoughts likely ran parallel to his. She slid one of René's swords out of his scabbard.

René froze, an incredulous frown on his face. "What are you doing?"

"Stay here," she said. Clenching her jaw, she held the sword at her side and marched into the dust cloud.

René stared after her with wide eyes.

"Hana, wait!" Adina jogged after her.

Erik glanced between Adina and René before turning to follow, his sword ready.

The haze was so dense, he could hardly see two steps in front of him. Somewhere ahead, cloth scuffled against stone. Someone grunted.

A breeze with the faint scent of vanilla sprung from behind him, blowing the dust and dirt further down the corridor. He blinked.

Damon lay in the corner, where the lightning bolt had thrown him. Hana stood above him and slammed René's rapier into his heart.

"Hana, no!" Adina called.

Damon froze, every muscle in his body going limp.

Hana ignored them, only waiting long enough to confirm Damon was immobilized before grabbing him by the collar and hauling him toward René. As she passed Erik, she raised an eyebrow. "A little help, please?"

Erik glanced down the corridor. Charles was nowhere in sight.

If Damon was correct, and Septimus was now working with Sujani, maybe Septimus had used his ability to jump between shadows to tele-port him away.

Taking one of Damon's shoulders, he took half of the man's weight. "He'll kill you for staking him, as soon as you remove that sword," he muttered.

Hana grunted. "He can try."

Erik studied Hana, a new respect for the woman settling in his gut. "Remind me not to ever piss you off."

Adina came up beside him. "Erik, don't make the Poison Master angry...she knows ways to kill a person you can't even imagine."

"And don't you forget it," Hana added.

As they reached René, who by some miracle had decided to stay put as instructed, Hana nodded at Erik. They dropped Damon at René's feet.

"Drink," Hana said.

René stared at Damon, who was by all appearances sleeping peacefully. Putting his weight on his bad foot, René reared back and kicked the other vampire in the gut. "This is what you get for possessing me and making me kill Marcos!" He kicked him again. "And for making me susceptible to this swamp rot." Shifting his aim a little higher, he pulled his boot back again.

Adina leaped forward. "That's enough!"

"Yes," Hana said. "Stop. Drink, and be done with it."

Erik bent over and picked Damon up, positioning him so René could grab him and bite his neck.

René lunged forward, sinking his teeth into the skin at the junction of where Damon's neck met his shoulder.

"Hey, where did this come from?" Hana grabbed a blood bag off his belt that was identical to the one at Erik's hip.

He glanced down to confirm his was still securely tied in place. Adina's was where it belonged, too.

"It's Sigfried's," Madalina said from where she still sat with her husband, several paces away. Her voice shook with an uncharacteristic hardness that tore Erik's attention away from René.

The tenseness in her muscles and rage in her gaze as she glared at Damon had Erik taking a step back. The hairs on the back of his neck tingled. Her eyes were fully black. His instincts screamed at him to flee at the predator before him.

An angry Madalina had power of her own. He'd never bothered to ask her how long she'd been a vampire...but with power like that, he'd bet his sword she had several centuries on all of them.

"Damon stole it while Sig was trying to drink to avoid bleeding out," she said, rising to her feet. "Stab him with the Bone Shard Blade now and be done with it." She took a step toward Damon.

Adina shifted, her hand going toward her waist.

"No, wait!" Against his better judgment, Erik stepped between Madalina and Damon. "I know it's tempting. The world will be a better place without him in it, but he's our best chance at defeating Sujani." Even with Maja on their side...for some reason, it didn't sound like Sophie could move against her priest on her own. "If we kill him now, we may well lose, and not only will we die, but we'll doom the world to a second Cataclysm."

He waited several heartbeats for Madalina to react to his words.

"Madalina?" Adina stepped up beside him. "Erik has a point. And besides, Sigfried is okay. See?"

Madalina blinked, turning her attention back to Sigfried.

He grunted, reaching for her hand. "I am alright. You saved me." His voice was thick, more gravelly than usual.

She blinked her eyes, shaking her head as though clearing it. She knelt beside him again, weaving her fingers between his. With her free hand, she traced his jaw line. "Very well." Her voice sounded like it was coming from very far away. "But if he tries to hurt Sig again, you won't be able to talk me out of it, Erik."

He swallowed as something released in his chest. He took a deep breath as his shoulders relaxed. "Fair enough." Crisis averted, for now. He glanced at Damon and flashed his fangs. Hopefully the old vampire would be less stupid, at least until they didn't need him anymore.

With a final swallow, René dropped Damon like a rag doll and licked his lips, removing the last traces of blood. Gingerly putting weight on his bad foot, he smiled then executed a complicated box step that could've come straight from a court waltz. "I can feel it clearing up." He lifted his shirt—the blackness was gone. "Ha!" He pointed his sword at the unconscious Damon. "Take that, scum!"

Hana wrapped her arm around his. He pulled her into an embrace and kissed her.

Erik cleared his throat. *God's Teeth, get a room.* "Did anyone see where Charles got to?" He glanced at Adina, who had been ahead of him when Charles disappeared.

She shook her head. "No...but the divot the lightning bolt left in the ground is impressive." Glancing around the hallway, she dropped her voice. "Can Charles throw lightning?"

Erik frowned, unease turning his stomach into lead. "No, of course not. His Talent is mind control."

Adina deflated. "That's what I was afraid of. Sujani's the only person I know who can manifest lightning...but I swear to the gods I saw Charles raise his hand and summon it."

"Can our Talents be transferred between people?" René asked, breaking Hana's kiss.

Erik shrugged. "I don't know." Turning to the oldest among them, he looked at Madalina. "Have you heard of this?"

Madalina shrugged. "No, but Sujani's quite a bit older than the rest of us. If anyone could figure out how to do it, I'd place my bet on him."

Erik held back a shudder as he studied Damon. If Sujani could channel his Talent through another, could Damon, as well? He shuddered. What a terrible thought.

Hana stepped up beside René, putting her hand on his shoulder. "How are you feeling?"

He grunted. "Like everything is back to normal." Standing on his good foot, he pulled off his shoe and sock.

The last bit of blackened swelling faded before their eyes.

Hana's shoulders dropped as she exhaled. "Excellent." She faced René head-on, a mock frown on her face and shook her finger under his nose. "No more stepping in strange swamp water, sir. I'll not have it."

René smiled as heat sparkled in his eyes. "You have my word, lady. I look forward to taking a long, long time making it up to you."

She put her hands on her hips and nodded smartly. "You'd better. And don't you forget it."

Hana tossed the blood bag she'd reclaimed from Damon to Sigfried. Madalina caught it and handed it to her husband as he sat up with a wince. Pulling the cork from the bag, he took several deep drinks.

Adina leaned down and grabbed the handle of René's sword where it stuck out of Damon's chest. "Everyone ready to move forward?"

René positioned himself in front of Hana. He met Erik's gaze. "Just in case he's angry," he mouthed.

Erik took a deep breath. If Damon was angry, then this was all for naught.

Adina ripped the blade from Damon's chest and tossed it to René. Wiping it clean on Damon's leg, he shoved it into his sheath.

Damon rolled to his side and gasped. "By Ahion! I'll kill you, if it's the last thing I do!"

They took a step back. Erik and René raised their swords.

Damon glanced at them. He jerked his head back as his eyes danced across each of them. "What are you all doing here? Where's Charles?"

Erik took a deep breath and emptied his mind of thoughts.

"We think Seven transported him away," Adina said, drawing Damon's attention.

"And what am I doing here? The hole from the lighting is way over there." He pointed back down the hall.

"You're welcome," Hana said from behind René.

"What?" Damon furrowed his brow at her. "Whatever." He heaved himself to his feet. "Come on. If Charles and Seven are here, the catacombs must be close."

Catching Adina's glance, Erik shoved his sword into its sheath and followed Damon down the tunnel.

The indentation where the lightning struck was deeper than he'd expected. Khalid's head would probably fit easily.

God's teeth. Sujani's power was unfathomable.

The tunnel ended at another staircase, though this one was natural rather than built. The steps were uneven and worn in the middle as though it had endured thousands of years of foot traffic.

Erik pulled on his Talent to keep himself steady. The others either ran their fingers along the wall for balance or spread their arms to either side like wings.

With each downward step, the dank stench of stagnant liquid overpowered his nose. Somewhere in the distance water dripped onto stone,

one droplet at a time. The sound bounced down the hall. If he stayed down here for long, the echo would drive him insane—a type of sonic torture.

As the stairs bottomed out, René pulled his hand back from the wall. "I just touched something round."

Erik waved his torch toward him. A horizontal row of skulls grinned back at him. Below the skulls were rows of other bones…femurs, arm bones, ribs, as though the mason had used the dead instead of bricks.

The fine hairs on the back of his neck prickled, as if a cold mist leeched from each and every eye socket and nostril.

"Ugh, yuck!" René shook his hand, as though he could fling the tactile sensation away. Wiping his fingers on his tunic, he shuddered. "This entire place is macabre."

"What did you expect?" Erik asked. "Catacombs are literally underground mass graves." The skin between his shoulder blades itched, as though the gazes of hundreds of dead men burned into his back.

Sujani wasn't here. There was no reason to linger.

René huffed and pushed ahead, following Damon's lead. His shoulders curled forward, and he adjusted his trajectory so he was in the middle of the hall—as far from the bones as possible.

Erik took a step to follow.

Adina leaned forward, studying the skulls. "They have symbols carved into them. René, come back."

Erik studied Adina. She didn't seem to notice the odd feeling he and René clearly had. Perhaps being an assassin for the last century had dulled her to unquiet spirits.

René glanced over his shoulder, his face pallid. "Why?"

She furrowed her brow and frowned. "Because you know more languages than the rest of us, and I don't recognize these."

With an overly dramatic sigh, he pivoted on his heel and stomped back to them. "Fine. What?" He stuck out his lip and huffed, glaring first at her, then at the skulls.

Ignoring the presence of the bones as much as he could, Erik moved the torch closer. From the right angle, the shadows highlighted engravings on each skull's forehead, right behind where their third eye would be. If one subscribed to that superstition, of course.

René squinted. "I hardly see anything."

Hana put her hand on his shoulder and gently pushed him forward. "You'll see better if you're closer."

He gave her a shocked, deeply pained frown before turning his focus to the wall.

Several heartbeats passed before he stepped back, shaking his head. "I recognize them, but I'm not certain where from. Sorry."

Madalina pointed at one. "This design was in Sophie's house. It was on her dishes."

Erik raised an eyebrow. "Truly?"

She nodded, pressing her lips into a thin line. "And this one, the moon and the sun, was on that plaque we used to summon that oracle the first time, in the broken pyramid." She glanced down the hall, in the direction Damon had disappeared. "I bet these are all symbols related to Maja, Ahion or the stars."

"It's still creepy," René said, running both hands up and down his arms as though trying to warm himself.

"Perhaps," she said. "But maybe if you try to focus more on the reverence whoever built this clearly had for the gods, and less on the death, you'll feel better?"

René turned away, shaking his head. "Whatever you say. Let's get out of here."

Madalina, Sigfried and Hana followed.

Erik took a step but paused when Adina didn't follow.

Instead, she ran her finger over the etchings in the closest skull. "Humans do tend to spend more energy on their religious sites and rituals than they do their own homes. I suppose this is more of the same."

"Possibly," Erik said. As a mortal and a knight of the Bone Shard Blade, that had certainly been true for him. His order had been focused on their religious mandate to the exclusion of everything else. "Let's catch up to Damon, shall we? Otherwise, we may miss all the action."

And with the final, secret Bone Shard Blade wrapped in her robes, that was the last thing they wanted to risk.

He breathed a sigh of relief when she finally allowed him to tug her away, down the hall.

The catacombs went for what felt like leagues. The tunnel forked several times, but Damon always stayed to the left, gradually increasing his pace. As though he'd been here before and knew where he was going.

The muscles in Erik's stomach and back tightened. "Hey, Damon," he called. "Don't you think we may want to slow down a little, so we don't rush into a trap?"

"What do you think that was back there, with Charles, Septimus, and everyone else?"

Erik rolled his eyes. "The first volley, maybe. You seriously don't think Sujani has more up his sleeve?"

Damon ripped his Bone Shard Blade from his waist, gripping the handle with enough force that his knuckles whitened. With a quick glare over his shoulder, he lengthened his stride even more.

"Let him go," Adina said, her voice loud enough Damon would no doubt hear. "If he wants to spring all the traps by himself, let him."

Erik opened his mouth. As tempting as that was, they needed Damon alive and well enough to fight Sujani. He glanced at the hardened corners of her mouth and her narrowed eyes as she glared at Damon's disappearing back and shut his mouth. Sometimes silence was the better part of valor.

The hallway contracted as though it was funneling them like livestock being herded into a crowding pen.

René moved so close to Erik he practically stepped on his heels.

"I don't like this," René said. "It's a perfect place for an ambush, with no maneuverability."

Indeed. Erik couldn't help but agree.

Ahead, a light appeared. Damon's silhouette flashed against it then he was gone.

"I think that's the exit," Adina said, grabbing his shoulder and pointing.

Hefting his sword as his stomach did a somersault, Erik swallowed. "Come on." At least Damon had flushed out any potential traps between them and the way out.

The exit from the catacombs was so narrow Erik practically had to walk sideways to avoid scraping the bones with his armor. Hopefully they wouldn't need to leave in a hurry.

The skulls gave way to a rectangular opening. The light on the other side was so bright compared to the relative darkness it was nearly blinding. He set his torch in a sconce at head level and stepped through the doorway.

Chapter 24
Erik

With a burst of warm light, the darkness of the catacombs fell away as though they'd never been. He stood on a balcony-type formation overlooking a rock courtyard with several tall pillars arranged in a circle. At one point, the pillars had supported a roof, or at least a horizontal beam that connected them all and provided support. The pillars on one side of the circle had been nearly smashed to their bases, as if by some giant's foot.

A sense of reverence washed over him, like when he'd first come into the presence of the Bone Shard Blade.

"This place is holy," Madalina said, coming up behind him.

Sigfried glanced at the courtyard so far below and groaned.

The hairs on the back of Erik's neck rose as he peered at Madalina from the corner of his eyes. "Oh? Why do you say that?" Something in the back of his mind whispered that she was right, though he couldn't see any physical indications that was the case.

"I feel it, too," Adina said. "Something happened here, a long time ago."

"The Cataclysm," Damon choked out. "This is where Sujani betrayed the world."

Erik turned to face him, where he stood frozen at the top of a steep staircase that wound its way down the cliff to the courtyard below. So many emotions flashed across Damon's face.

With a deep breath, he squeezed the Bone Shard Blade until the leather on the dagger's handle creaked. His lips peeled back in an angry grimace. "Sujani has no right being here, not after he desecrated the temple." His voice trembled.

"But Maja says he does," Madalina said, her attention fixed on the relics below.

Damon spun on her, his fangs bared as he hissed. "No!" He bent his knees as though he was going to pounce on her.

Sigfried stepped in front of Madalina. "You cannot argue with the gods." He crossed his arms and stared down at Damon. "You will not win."

Damon sneered. "Do you really think you can take me, Wrath?"

Adina cleared her throat and glared. "Are we just going to stand up here and delay the inevitable until we're certain Sujani is aware of our presence, or shall we make our way down there like we came here to do?"

Damon scowled before turning his attention to Sigfried and Madalina as the silence stretched like an overextended rubber band.

"Fine! But stay out of my way when we find Sujani." Turning around and snapping his cloak out dramatically, he began picking his way down the stairs.

"With pleasure," Adina mumbled as she moved to follow.

The stairs were narrow and steep. By Erik's best guess, they must be at least half a league below the city at this point. Possibly somewhere beneath the market, unless his sense of direction was completely turned around.

The cavern was as bright as day, but for the life of him, he couldn't identify the light source.

Taking another deep step, he grabbed the wall to provide a bit of balance. "Is everyone doing okay back there?"

"Yes," Adina said.

Sigfried grunted.

Oh, right. Sigfried was afraid of heights. Erik winced. This was probably just as bad for him as the hike up the Shadow Mountains when they were looking for the Bone Shard Blade.

"We will be fine," Madalina said. "Just like last time."

"Keep going," Adina said when he would have stopped. "You'll only make it worse."

Erik sighed. She was probably right, so he stepped down to the next level. What he wouldn't give for wings right now...

"Everyone hold on to something," Hana said from above.

Erik grabbed ahold of his Talent to steady himself as Adina sat right on the stairs.

Sigfried was already plastered against the cliff, his face pale and his eyes squeezed shut.

The cliff shuddered as the stone beneath their feet shifted.

The steps leveled, then as if the rocks were a plant growing at the height of spring, a banister grew with one support beam coming out of each step. The beams sprouted at the top until a handrail that resembled ivy stood between them and the sheer drop.

"Whew!" Hana wiped a bead of sweat from her brow and pulled out her never-ending blood bag to take a drink. "Hopefully that helps?"

Erik's jaw went slack as his eyes tracked the stairwell as it switchbacked down the cliff. Hana was a power to be reckoned with. No wonder René had been so immediately drawn to her.

Madalina's relieved voice floated down to him. "Much! This is really impressive. Thank you."

"We don't leave anyone behind, do we?" Hana said as she hooked her arm in René's.

He patted her hand. "Of course not, my lady."

Putting his hand on the banister, Erik continued down the stairs. They were much easier to navigate now that they were all one height. Damon was so far ahead he was little more than a black ant against the light gray of the cliffs.

Erik waved everyone forward, overcome by a sudden sense of urgency. They needed to get down there *now*. "Come on. We need to move faster, or we'll be too late."

Adina shook her head. "I have a bad feeling about this." Gesturing down to the courtyard below, she continued in Hakkian and dropped her voice to a whisper. "I expected Sujani to try something by now. We're completely exposed and totally vulnerable here. A bolt of lightning and we'd all fall to our ends."

Below, Damon lunged off the bottom stairs and stormed into the temple. "Sujani!"

His voice echoed off the stone.

Erik sighed. So much for any remaining element of surprise.

"I assume this is the Colosseum, then?" Adina asked, raising an eyebrow.

Erik followed Damon's movements around the columns, his stomach tight. Surely Sujani was waiting down there somewhere, ready to ambush them.

The air crackled with energy that made the hair on the back of Erik's neck stand on end. He glanced at Adina.

Her eyes went round as she looked at him. "Your hair's sticking up."

He reached up to pat his head. The metal in his wrist brace shocked his head and he jumped. "Ow!"

Sujani.

Adina grabbed his arm. "He's here. We need to get off these cliffs."

Erik couldn't agree more. "Come on." Turning, he jogged down the stairs, pulling on just enough of his Talent to make sure he didn't stumble head-first down the trail.

Nimble footsteps came up behind him until they were so close, they might trip each other and both tumble to their end. "René, back off!"

"Then move, you slow oaf!"

Erik furrowed his brow as he pushed himself against the rock face. If René was so anxious to meet Sujani in battle, he wouldn't stand in the way.

A discordant blur of colorful silk sped past in a blur. "Last one down's a rotten ninny!"

Holding back an eyeroll he caught Hana's gaze. She shook her head with a sigh.

Several steps above, Sigfried grunted.

Hopefully René's energy would be channeled to better use down below.

A bolt of lightning split the sky, momentarily blinding Erik. The thunder rattled his eardrums.

The stench of ozone rose to purge his nose of the last of the dankness of the catacombs.

Chunks of rocks tumbled down from the cliffs above. Erik grabbed Adina and pressed her against the cliff, shielding her with his own body as they tumbled by.

The scent of jasmine and vanilla surrounded him.

"Thanks for the gesture," she said, raising an eyebrow at him. "But you're not going to be much good to me if you get bashed in the head with a rock, either."

He smiled, a warm feeling spreading through his gut to push aside the cold lump that was building there the closer they got to the bottom of the stairs. Running a finger down her jaw, he winked. "Good to know you don't think I'd look better with a little off the top."

She scoffed and gently shoved him away. "I definitely prefer your head attached to your neck, yes. Come on." Grabbing his hand, she continued down the steps. "We need to get down there before René does anything stupid."

Or before Sujani decided to hurl another lightning bolt at them.

Erik glanced down into the courtyard. Damon was nowhere to be found. As a matter of fact, neither was René. He swallowed past a suddenly dry throat as he redoubled his speed.

The muscles between his shoulder blades relaxed as he finally set foot onto solid ground. He sighed, rolling his shoulders and tilting his head to either side until his neck popped. He'd had enough of climbing narrow trails attached to cliffs to last him the rest of his unlife.

Drawing his sword, he stepped out of the way as the others joined him. Adina followed his lead and drew her blades, as well.

Hana and Madalina's gazes roamed over the area, no doubt searching for René or anyone else who might be down here.

Sigfried's skin was pallid, and his nostrils flared as his ribs heaved in and out. Erik's insides clenched in sympathy. Sigfried's gaze drifted to Erik's and, noticing his attention, he shifted into his bear form.

Erik frowned. There was no need to be ashamed of conquering one's fear, much less to hide the physical effects. He squeezed his lips into a thin line. But now was not the time to have that conversation, so he filed it away for a later date.

"Did anyone actually see which way Damon went?"

Madalina shook her head. "No, but I bet he went in there." She pointed to a small opening on the side that he hadn't noticed.

"Alright." He squeezed the handle on his sword, checking his grip. "Everyone ready?"

Adina nodded. "Yes, let's get inside and out of the open."

He led them up the stone stairs. The white marble columns had a carved floral and vine pattern that looked at one time to have been filled with gold filigree. Now, however, only flakes remained.

"This place feels heavy," Sigfried said.

Adina nodded.

It was hard to disagree with the pressure on his shoulders, like the building was weighing them, judging. He half expected to be surrounded by flying buttresses, rosette stained-glass windows, and the smell of incense as priests chanted in the background.

"Well, three gods did used to live here," Madalina said as she nodded toward the entrance.

Above the door was the same symbol they'd seen in the ruined city above with the sun, moon, and stars. The hair on the back of Erik's neck prickled.

Taking a deep breath, he cleared the memory of incense from his nose. The ancient pantheon who'd resided here were much less predictable than the gods worshipped by mortals today.

He glanced at Madalina. "And you're sure Damon and René went this way?"

She shrugged. "Wouldn't you?"

He glanced at the door. It was the logical point of entry...once the rest of the group joined and they had backup. Not that Damon considered them competent support, but René should've been smarter.

Erik chewed the inside of his cheek as he studied the entrance, his honor warring with his desire for self-preservation.

"Come on," Adina said. "Let's get this over with." Taking a deep breath, she strode through the door.

The inside of the temple showed the same lavish origins as the pillars outside. Exquisite carvings flowed around the walls, as ethereal as the wind. A white fountain with gray marbling through it was dry but hinted at the former majesty of its construction.

Doors split off in all directions, one to his left, right and the third straight ahead.

"Well," Erik said. "Shall we go deeper into the temple?" He stepped toward the door on the opposite side of the room.

"Wait." Adina grabbed his shoulder. "Let's check the other two rooms first. Just so we don't leave an enemy at our back."

He glanced to each side. "Fair enough." He caught Sigfried's eye. "You take the one on the right, we take the left?"

The bear dipped his head with a snort.

Madalina put her hand on his neck and smiled. "Sounds good to us."

Sigfried led Madalina and Hana to the right as Erik and Adina crept to the edge of the left doorway.

This room had a lush red carpet that covered most of the floor. The borders were a highly polished blue-gray marble in a tone he'd never seen before. At the front was a dais raised approximately half a step with a shiny wooden table and a statuette that resembled a cross between a stylized sun and moon.

"The worship room?" Adina asked.

"Perhaps." And with its spotless and unworn look, it could have been used as recently as today. "Do you think Sujani...?" He let his voice drift off.

"I don't know. Maybe?"

Sujani didn't seem to be one who would stoop to restoring ancient temples, but with the drastic personality change that had come over Damon in Maja's presence, perhaps Sujani had experienced something similar?

A rustling of cloth on stone caught Erik's attention, and he snapped his gaze to his left.

René placed his palm against one wall as though he was trying to push it aside. "No matter how fast I go, I end up back here," he said without glancing at them.

Adina strode to his side. "What do you mean?"

René didn't respond, he just kept staring at the wall. "How is this possible?" He spoke quietly, as if he were speaking to himself.

Chills ran up Erik's spine. "René, what are you doing?"

At his voice, René finally turned his head to face them. His gaze remained far away, as though he couldn't be bothered to focus on them. "Can you feel it? The ripple in time?" He squinted, tilting his head to the side, as though he were staring at something only he could see.

He seemed awfully calm.

Erik leaned forward, studying his pupils. Maybe he'd drunk some bad blood?

Adina shook her head. "Ripples? In time? Are you sure you haven't been spending too long talking to Madalina?"

René shook his head and turned back to the wall. "There's got to be some sort of mechanism somewhere. If we break it, we can all escape."

Erik clenched his jaw. It was like René wasn't fully connected to this reality. Every instinct was screaming for him to grab Adina and head for the door, but he wasn't going to leave without figuring out what was wrong with René. "Escape what?"

René pointed to the statuette on the wooden table on the far end of the room. "Can you reach it?"

Erik glanced at their surroundings. There were no obvious traps or obstacles. "Of course."

Pushing away from the wall, he strode up the red carpet toward the dais. The thick padding sunk beneath his feet. Whoever had constructed the temple had spent more on carpet padding than most royalty.

No matter the society, mortals spent more time and energy on their holy places than anywhere else.

His legs strained with each step.

Walking on this carpet reminded him of hiking up and down the sand dunes in the Saldanian Desert. The muscles in his thighs and calves burned with the strain.

This was like walking through molasses. Pulling on his Talent, he pushed forward.

The final step to the dais was like watching himself walk in slow motion. Something popped in his nose at the strain and a trickle of blood slid down to his lip.

With a heave, he brought his hand up and brushed it away.

As his heel landed on the dais, he blinked—and was back against the wall with René and Adina.

Adina stared at him, jaw loose and eyes wide. "What happened?"

He ran a hand through his hair. On this side of the room, movement was normal. "I don't know." Glancing at the table, he shook his head. "I don't know anything about ripples in time, but it's like walking through a wall of hardened air. I stepped on the platform, and then *whoosh*, ended up back here."

She furrowed her brow. "Your nose is bleeding."

Absent-mindedly, he brushed the blood away again. His muscles felt so light now, movement was quick and easy.

"From back here, it looked like everything was going just fine, you were walking then suddenly you were here. Like Septimus had transported you or something."

He tore his attention from the other side of the room and met her gaze. "No...it doesn't feel anything like shadow-jumping."

She licked her lips. "I'm going to try." Grabbing her swords, she marched up to the platform. As soon as she stepped onto it, she appeared back beside him.

Her ribs heaved in and out as though she'd just run a marathon. Dragging the back of her hand across her forehead, she turned her head to look at him. "It feels like a wall of air to you, too?"

When he nodded, she turned her attention behind him. "René?" When he didn't respond, she waved her hand in front of his face. "René? What did it feel like to you?"

René blinked, turning his unfocused gaze toward her. "Time slows down, no matter how fast I move."

Erik stepped in front of René, staring at his face. His words belied frustration and fear, but his tone and body language were calm and relaxed. Something odd was going on with him—perhaps he'd tried to reach the dais so hard he'd popped a blood vessel in his brain?

"Interesting," Adina said as she stroked her chin with her pointer finger as she studied René. "The more I tried to use my Talent to get through the hardened air, the more resistance I encountered."

God's Teeth. "Me, too," Erik said. Which meant mortals might be able to approach without difficulty. A protective mechanism, of sorts, perhaps.

René turned back to studying the wall.

"I assume it must have been the same with him, too," she said, staring at the dais with a distant expression. "What is the temple trying to keep from us?"

"Maybe the gods don't want us on their altar?"

She chewed the inside of her cheek. "Maybe. But I didn't get the impression Maja would mind."

"Perhaps it's not her. It may be Ahion or 'the stars' as Madalina calls them." They hadn't met the famed stars yet, and who knew what their priorities were.

Adina put her hands to her temple. "This is giving me a headache."

"Aha!" René leaped back with a smile.

Erik flinched at the sudden noise, his hand gripped his sword.

René glanced at them, his eyes clear. "I've finally got it!"

A hidden panel in the wall no larger than his head popped open.

Inside was a contraption the size of Erik's fist that consisted of several metallic spheres that spun around each other like pendulums hanging from well-oiled gears. He stepped closer, studying the strange device over René's shoulder. "What on earth is that?"

"It's a chronometer, of course," René said, turning his attention briefly to Erik. "Can't you feel it?"

"Feel what?" The hard edge to Adina's tone echoed the cold lead pooling in Erik's gut.

René snapped his fingers in time to what could be his heartbeat. "The pulses it sends out. Each pulse flows through the room and slows as it approaches the dais."

Erik glanced between the so-called chronometer and the statuette on the table at the far end of the room. "Can you stop it?"

"And, if you stop it," Adina added, "can you restart it again?"

Erik raised his eyebrow and glanced at her. "Restart it?"

She shrugged. "If we bring it with us, it may come in handy in a fight against Sujani."

Or Damon.

"Fair point." He turned to René. "Well? Can you disable it? At least, temporarily?"

Reaching into his pocket, he pulled out a few thin pieces of metal and waved them at Erik. "What do you think I'm trying to do?"

Erik rolled his eyes and bit back his response. There was little point in aggravating the other man further. He glanced over his shoulder at the statuette on the table. It would likely fetch a decent price at any market if René could get his hands on it.

Several minutes passed and Erik glanced out the door to check on Sigfried, Madalina and Hana. They weren't in the main room, and he didn't see any sign of them through the door across the way. In the distance, something roared. "I'll be right back," he said. "I'm going to go check the other room to make sure the others are okay."

René wiggled one of his little metal probes and the chronometer clicked.

As Erik was about to step out of the room, he suddenly found himself right back by René's side where he started. "Hey!"

"Sorry," René mumbled as he continued fiddling with the device.

Adina met Erik's gaze behind René's back. "René, stop for a moment. Erik, try to leave the room again."

Butterflies leaped into his stomach. "Very well." Taking a deep breath, he approached the door. Bracing his hands on the frame, he stepped through.

Only to find himself back in the exact same spot he'd started—next to Adina and René.

The walls pressed in on him as though he'd been thrown in a dungeon to be forgotten for the rest of his unlife. He flared his nostrils, forcing himself to take deep, controlled breaths in and out.

In and out.

After his racing heart calmed down, he glanced at René. "Alright," he said. "What's going on?" This was no longer intriguing or funny. "Are you doing something to make it not let us out?"

René shrugged, not pulling his attention from the chronometer. "I have no idea. For some unfathomable reason, my tutors neglected to teach me anything about chronomancy or time loops." He huffed. "Hmmm...I wonder why?"

Erik opened his mouth to say something, but Adina put a hand on his shoulder. "It's okay. If we quit distracting him, we'll disable the device sooner and then we can go check on the others."

René suddenly tensed. "Hold on! I think I've got it!" He twisted his little metal probes and the machine shrieked like its gears needed oil before it clicked and came to a stop. "Woo-hoo!" He pumped a fist into the air. "Take that, chronomancer!"

Flashing them a wide grin that showed off his fangs, he dashed to the dais. Leaping onto the platform with both feet, he jumped up and down like a child. "See this! I'm on your stupid altar!" he screamed at the room. "Touching your stupid things! What are you going to do about it now?" Reaching out, he grabbed the statuette.

Erik glanced at Adina.

"Try it now," she said. "Before he does something we'll all regret."

Bracing himself against the lead in his gut, Erik stepped toward the door. If they couldn't get out, now, he didn't know what he'd do.

Snatching the chronometer from its cubby, Adina followed close behind him.

Erik paused at the door, reaching for his Talent to forcibly calm his racing heart as he stepped through.

Into the hallway.

His muscles relaxed as his knees went weak. They were out.

René had done it.

Adina came up beside him and flashed him a relieved grin. Glancing over his shoulder, she said, "Come on, René. Put the holy relic down and let's go before anything else happens."

"Spoilsport," René muttered. But he set the statue on the table with at least a modicum of reverence and followed them out the door.

"The others are in that room," Adina said, pointing across the way.

Or at least they were before they got stuck in a time distortion field.

"Hana's in there?" René's attention zeroed in on the other room. "Let's go!"

Erik and Madalina followed him as he marched across the marble floor, their footsteps echoed off the walls.

"Hana? Madalina?" René stuck his head through the door. "What are you guys up to?"

Erik blinked.

René was gone.

God's Teeth. Not again.

"We need to put a leash on that man," Adina mumbled.

René had disappeared far too quickly. "I think we're in for another time distortion," Erik muttered. Or something even worse.

"Fabulous." Adina glanced left and right. "Well, I suppose we have little choice but to go rescue them."

He sighed. "Indeed."

Shoulder to shoulder, they marched across the room to the door.

Chapter 25
Erik

As they reached the door, Adina grabbed his hand. "Wait, stop. I'm going to stick my head in. If I squeeze your hand, pull me back out."

"Sounds good." And if she disappeared like René, then he'd go right in after her, even if it meant dooming himself.

She gave him a quick smile, took a deep breath then stepped forward. Her muscles tensed, but she didn't squeeze his hand.

"What do you see?" he asked.

She didn't respond, only kept staring straight ahead.

Erik followed her gaze but saw nothing out of the ordinary. Just some off-white walls and another room with a red carpet in the middle. From where he stood, he also couldn't see Hana, Madalina or Sigfried.

"Adina?" He squeezed her hand.

No reaction.

He chewed the inside of his cheek as ice formed in his stomach. If she didn't either come out or react in the next few heartbeats, he'd pull her out.

One heartbeat.

Two.

Three.

"Come on, Adina. What do you see?" He shook her hand and pulled gently.

Her arm muscles relaxed and fell limp.

Tugging harder, he braced one foot against the door frame.

He may as well have been trying to move a marble statue.

His blood chilled as his heart thumped once against his ribs. That was the final straw. He wasn't going to stand out here and do nothing like some coward.

Throwing his shoulders back and bracing himself, he stepped into the room.

A strong breeze buffeted him, snapping his hair across his forehead. The back wall had disappeared, and they looked out over a courtyard with twin tables that could only be sacrificial altars. A short priest in a white robe with his salt-and-pepper hair pulled back in a long thin braid stood on one side, and a tall man in a black robe with bone-white hair stood on the other.

Sujani and Damon. As mortals.

A pile of sheets lay on each altar.

"What manner of magic is this?" Erik asked.

Adina stood next to him, her eyes wide as she stared at the scene ahead.

"I think this is the first time they tried to sacrifice the gods," Madalina said.

Her words pulled Erik's attention away from the diorama in front of them to where the others stood off to his right.

Adina tilted her head to the side as she studied the scene. "What makes you say that? Are you so certain we're not watching present-day events through one of the portal-things that Sujani likes to create?"

René shook his head. "No. It doesn't feel right. And all the details are wrong. We're watching the past, somehow."

Erik raised an eyebrow. "Details? How so?"

"Each column is finished with gold filigree. And even you can't deny both Damon and Sujani smell human."

Erik took a deep breath. René was right...there was no sign of Damon's characteristic stench, or Sujani's ozone. The time shifts in this temple were unfathomable. He gripped his sword and glanced down at Adina's hip, where the third Bone Shard Blade lay hidden.

Perhaps they could end this now, go stab Maja with their blade before Sujani could blow the entire ritual. They could avoid the entire Cataclysm, and save thousands, if not millions, of lives.

They could change the course of history.

Even if that meant he didn't meet Adina, never got to meet any of them. He glanced at each vampire beside him, marking their faces.

Goodbye, my friends.

He turned to Adina, his heart swelling as his throat tightened. Something snapped in his chest with a loss he couldn't comprehend. Swallowing past the thickness, he leaned in until his mouth was near her ear. "We should use the blade, and stab Maja when Sujani fails," he whispered in Hakki. "We can avert the entire Cataclysm."

Darkness sputtered in her eyes as she met his gaze.

She realized exactly what he was asking her to do, what he was asking her to give up.

Grabbing his tabard, she pulled his lips to hers and wrapped her arms around his neck.

Groaning as heat swelled through his chest, he pulled her close, his entire being focused on the feel of her lips against his and the smell of her skin.

"Hey! Get a room!" René slugged him in the shoulder.

Erik ignored him.

All too soon, she pulled away. "I love you." Reaching her hand into her robes as though she was grasping the Bone Shard Blade's handle, she marched toward Damon and Sujani.

The breeze picked up, buffeting them as though it was trying to push them back against the wall.

Reaching for his Talent, Erik steadied himself.

Adina bent into the wind and pushed forward.

In front of them, the scene seemed to speed up, going faster and faster as she approached.

Damon and Sujani circled their respective altars, their lips moving as they muttered words that the wind ripped away before their sound could reach his ears.

Six acolytes stood at even spacing in a circle around the two tables. One held a globe of water before him, another a fire ball the size of his fist, and so through all the elements, including a burst of light so bright it rivaled the sun, and a twisting cloud of darkness that reminded Erik of the shadows that enveloped Septimus every time he teleported.

Damon and Sujani stood face-to-face between the altars, each holding a bowl full of white powder that could only be crushed dragon bones. Drawing a ceremonial dagger across their palms, both priests held their fists above the bones as several drops fell into the powder.

They circled ever faster and chanted as Adina fought the wind for each step to reach them.

He'd call out to her to use her Talent to mitigate the gale, but Adina was smart. She likely already was.

"René!" Erik said. "Can you slow the time?"

René furrowed his brow and shook his head as though Erik had spoken an incomprehensible language. "What?"

He pointed at the chronometer. "Can you do something with that to slow down the ritual until Adina gets there?"

René started, as though he was just noticing Adina. "What's she doing?"

Shaking his head, Erik gestured for René to pay attention to him. "Never mind that. Can you do it?"

René shrugged. "Last time I checked, I'm no god." He smirked. "Unless you ask Hana, of course."

With a sigh, Erik rolled his eyes as a wave of heat rose from his chest. Now was *not* the time for inappropriate jokes.

Madalina tugged on René's sleeve. "René, use your Talent!"

He scoffed. "What do you mean?"

She pointed at the priests holding the bowls of bone powder and blood over their heads. "It's how you get fast. You warp time with your Talent. You're a chronomancer." She paused, peering at him. "Can you *unwarp* it?"

God's teeth! Erik stumbled against the door frame. Madalina was right—the truth of her words echoed in his bones.

René opened his mouth then closed it. He opened it again before shaking his head and running a hand through his hair. "Leaping hop-toads!"

He glanced at Erik, his eyes wide and his face muscles lax. "No. I can't. Marcos is the one who could make everyone go slow. I can only speed things up."

Erik grabbed René's other arm and pointed at Damon and Sujani. "It's just a matter of perspective! You may not be able to slow them down, but you *can* speed Adina up."

René's face turned ashen, and he flinched. "I've never tried my Talent on anyone other than myself."

Erik glanced at the two priests just as a ray of sunlight and a bolt of black lightning struck the uplifted bowls. "What's the worst that could happen?"

René blinked and stared at him like he was an idiot. "I fail."

"Right! And we're no worse off than we are now. I promise, we won't judge you for failing." He narrowed his eyes and crossed his arms over his chest. "But we will if you don't try."

Huffing, René pushed his sleeves up his arms. "Okay, fine. Here goes nothing." His jaw moved side to side. He scrunched his nose as he stared at Adina's retreating form.

The air around them seemed to wobble, like someone had dropped a tray of gelatin. Adina lurched forward a few steps before slowing back down.

Sujani and Damon lifted their daggers above their respective altars.

A blood vessel pulsed at René's temple as every muscle in his body tensed.

Suddenly, he collapsed, stumbling against Hana. "I'm sorry," he said, panting. "I can't do it. I *feel* what I need to do, I just don't have the strength." Reaching down to his waist, he pulled out his blood bag and took a deep swig. "Maybe if I go myself?"

Erik glanced at the tableau before them. "That would be better than nothing." He waved René forward. "Go, go, go!"

René passed Adina and slowed, until he was only a few steps ahead of her, moving just as slowly.

Erik lurched forward, his heart in his throat. "No!" They'd be too late.

"This has already happened." Sophie's voice echoed throughout the chamber.

Erik spun toward the sound.

Madalina gazed back at them, her eyes solid black, still speaking with Sophie's voice. "You cannot interfere. Nor do you have the power to overcome the time's rift created by the Cataclysm."

Erik's knees went weak. "A time rift?" What in the name of the gods was a time rift?

"Time works differently here," Hana said, stepping into his view.

Madalina nodded and turned to Erik. "Your intentions and sacrifice are noted. But this is not your time, knight."

He shook his head. "What do you mean?" Something in his chest relaxed at being given permission to fail. If a goddess said he couldn't prevent the Cataclysm, he was free to live his unlife with Adina, unburdened by the guilt of the death of millions. "How are we supposed to get to where we need to be?"

The twin Bone Shard Blades slashed through the air toward the figures laying on the altars as René blurred out of existence.

Her eyes still black, Madalina turned her attention to Adina and René as they raced in slow motion toward the divine sacrifices. "You have the chronomancer. Use him." She turned her piercing gaze back to him. "But he's untested, so be careful or he'll break. You'll need René before the end." Madalina turned toward the priests as the daggers plunged into the figures. "Brace yourselves."

Erik pulled on his Talent as a shock wave of light and shadow slammed into them.

Madalina's high-pitched shriek cut off as she slammed into the wall. René and Adina flew backward through the air, tumbling end over end until they came to a rest several paces away.

A blast of superheated air followed, baking his skin as though he were a mortal who'd spent a few too many afternoons in the sun. He opened his jaw, feeling the tight, dry skin of his face and lips stretch in protest of the movement. At least nothing split or cracked.

The floor beneath him rumbled as Sujani drove his blade into his own chest.

The earth heaved with enough force Erik could practically see the waves ripple outward from the altars. Wave after wave slammed into them, and only by keeping a firm grip on his Talent was Erik able to keep his footing. Sigfried, Hana and Madalina tumbled to the ground.

He caught a brief glimpse of Madalina's eyes—now back to her normal color.

A few chunks of marble the size of his fist fell from the ceiling. Erik threw his arm overhead to protect himself as his stomach hardened. His blood chilled. "Adina!"

Racing toward her as quickly as the roiling earth would allow, he fell to his knees at her side. "Are you alright?"

Scrambling for enough stability to push herself onto all fours, she nodded. "Yeah, I think so." She nodded toward Damon and Sujani. "It looks like we get to die in the Cataclysm."

Erik shook his head. "No!" Maja clearly didn't intend for them to meet Final Death, or she wouldn't have bothered to help, to warn them about René. "I think we can get out of here. We just need to get to the door!"

He glanced over his shoulder. That was easier said than done. "Come on!" Pulling on more of his Talent, he hauled her and René to their feet. "Hold on to me."

Adina wrapped her arm around his waist as Erik hauled René's arm over his shoulder and neck.

Keeping his lower back loose so it could bend and flex, like he would if he were on a ship, he slowly guided them to the exit. "There! Go!" He shoved René through the door, then Adina. Waiting one heartbeat to make sure they landed safely, he turned to Madalina and Hana. Grabbing both women by an arm he pulled them out, too.

"Alright, Sigfried," he said to the large bear, who struggled to get his feet underneath him. "I'm going to need your help for this."

All they really needed was for the earth to quit shaking for three heartbeats so Sig could catch his bearings and walk out the door.

Something exploded behind him with a deafening crack. The smell of ozone reached his nose.

He was getting very, very tired of lightning.

The earth split, finally giving up after the relentless shaking. Water surged from below.

Ice crystalized in his veins as a wave swallowed the sacrificial altars and barreled down on them.

Grabbing the Great Gray Bear by his ears, Erik tugged Sigfried toward the door. "Come on!"

They moved one step. Two.

"I can't swim," he said, groaning as he heaved the giant furry body toward the door. "Help me out here, won't you?"

He glanced over his shoulder. They weren't going to make it.

Sigfried's claws scrambled on the floor, snagging the red carpet. With a lunge they hurled through the door as the water slammed into the wall behind them.

He tumbled into the inner courtyard head-first, coming to rest against the edge of the central fountain.

"Erik!" Adina raced toward him. Reaching out her arm, she grasped his hand and pulled him to his feet. "You made it! We were starting to get worried." She nodded over her shoulder, and Erik followed her gaze.

Madalina embraced Sigfried, burying her face in his shaggy fur.

Adina ran her fingers through his hair, pulling it out of his face. "Are you okay?"

Erik blinked. There was no water here. No sign of any earthquake or crumbling buildings. In fact, other than them, the whole area was deathly silent.

As if a tidal wave hadn't just slammed into the opposite side of the wall.

Adina was still waiting for his answer. "Yes, I'm okay," he said. Tearing his eyes from the open door—beyond which everything looked completely normal, he ran a finger down her jaw line. "Sigfried is very large, and very heavy."

She bit back a chuckle. "Indeed." Throwing her arms around his neck in a hug, she pulled herself closer to his ear. "We failed. Now what?"

He shook his head. Apparently, she hadn't heard. "Maja spoke to us through Madalina. She said there was nothing we could do to stop what we saw...it was some sort of time echo caused by the original Cataclysm."

She sighed as her shoulders relaxed. "So, nothing we did could have stopped it?"

He shook his head. "No, but apparently René can control time, and will need to for us to beat Sujani."

Adina blinked at him, her expression blank as if he'd told her the sky was purple. "What?"

"Just don't tell René that," he whispered. "Wouldn't want to inflate his ego further."

Adina brushed her palms off on her pants and shook her head. "I'm sorry I suggested we check out the two rooms. It seems we've done nothing but waste time and get ourselves into trouble."

"No, that's not it at all. Because of you, we now know a few things about how time works in this temple." He smiled. "And we got to witness the Cataclysm. How many living people can say that?"

She raised an eyebrow. "None?"

Well, true…technically, they were all dead. "You know what I mean."

Light sparkled in her eyes as one corner of her lips creeped up into a smile. She took his hand in hers. "Hey, everyone. Are we ready to go and see if we can catch up to Damon?"

Erik's gaze drifted to the final door, the one at the far end of the entry hall. Who knew how far ahead of them Damon was, how much or how little time had passed since they'd entered the temple?

The Great Gray Bear rolled his shoulders, popping their joints as he shook his head side to side.

Madalina smiled at them. "Sig says let's go find some ancient vampire priests."

Erik grinned. At least their morale was still high. "Come on. Before Damon beats us to the punch and we miss all the action."

Chapter 26
Adina

After their misadventures with the first two doors, walking through the third was almost anticlimactic. A hallway stretched before them with enclaves between the pillars holding everything from bookshelves filled with ancient scrolls to reading nooks. A torch burned on every other pillar.

"Clearly someone has been here awhile." Erik's words bounced off the marble walls.

She nodded. "Sujani's probably been here on and off since he raised Maja." More than long enough to set traps or ambushes for unwelcome visitors.

Hopefully Damon had come this way already and cleared any of those out. She'd had enough surprises since finding the Bone Shard Blade in the Shadow Mountains.

They proceeded down the hallway. No spinning axe blades swung from the ceiling to slice them in half, no poisoned darts shot from holes hidden in the walls. This was, for all intents and purposes, a larger version of Sujani's study.

She stumbled to a stop.

Perhaps this *was* his original study, if he'd been high priest here before the Cataclysm.

What she wouldn't give for a month or two to study the knowledge in this room.

Erik paused. "Adina? Why did you stop?"

She shook her head and threw one last glance at the scrolls lining the walls. "No reason."

Madalina gestured to the walls. "She's looking at all the pretties, of course."

Adina smiled. Indeed.

The hall ended in a balcony that overlooked an open-air courtyard that was surrounded by walls on all four sides.

"Did anyone notice something like this when we were coming down the cliffs?" Erik asked.

The Great Gray Bear snorted.

"I didn't either," Madalina said.

Adina met Erik's gaze and shook her head.

"Clearly, we were at the wrong angle," René said. "It's hard to argue the existence of something right in front of our eyes."

Well, he had a point. Unless Sujani had recently developed a Talent for illusions.

"Hey, I think this might be the original site where the sacrifices were performed," Erik said.

Adina glanced at him and raised an eyebrow. "Oh?"

"The angle's wrong, but the layout is the same as what we just saw in the other room."

She studied the courtyard. Those two lumps of rock *could* have been altars at one time. Especially if she factored the rapid series of natural disasters that came with the Cataclysm and twelve hundred years of erosion. Crossing her arms, she nodded. "You may be right. What next?"

He studied the courtyard. Nothing moved. "I'm not sure, but I suppose we should get down there."

René put his hand on the banister and bent his knees. Flashing them a wide grin, he vaulted over.

"Well, that's one way to do it," Adina muttered. Shoving her sword into its sheath, she followed.

Bending her knees to absorb the impact, she spun in a circle, her eyes straining to capture every detail at once.

Across the courtyard to her left, the silhouette of Sujani's head appeared through a window that hadn't been visible from above.

She glanced at René. His gaze was fixed to their right as Damon strode into the courtyard, his cape flapping in the cool air.

"Sujani!" His voice echoed off the rock and marble. "Here I am. Let's settle this once and for all."

Adina caught René's eye before she glanced up. "Get down here," she hissed to the rest of them.

Erik and Sigfried landed next to her in the next heartbeat.

Madalina leaned over the balcony. "Hana and I should stay up here."

Adina nodded. Neither of them were trained in combat.

"Stay out of my way," Damon growled at them as he stomped past.

"Our pleasure," Erik said.

Adina crossed her arms and glanced at Erik. "Do you think we'll be safe out of the way over here?"

He shrugged. "Here's as safe as anywhere, I suppose."

Energy cackled through the air with the now-familiar sensation of Sujani readying a lightning bolt. The ancient vampire stepped into the clearing and raised his hand over his head, clenching it into a fist.

Damon rolled into a somersault just as the *crack* split the courtyard, popping back up to his feet. "Is that all you've got?" Pulling back his hand like he was going to throw a ball of some sort, he hurled a set of magical black-and-crimson daggers.

They bounced off Sujani's shield of hardened air with a teal flash of light.

The ripples from the impact vibrated through Adina's bones like beats on a kettledrum.

Damon pulled his Bone Shard Blade from his belt and sliced at the shield of hardened air.

The magic holding the air together crumbled like dirt before the blade.

Adina blinked as her jaw went slack. "The Bone Shard Blades can absorb magic."

That possibility hadn't even occurred to her.

René cursed under his breath.

Erik drew his sword and held it ready. "Good to know."

Sujani pulled the other Bone Shard Blade from his robes and lunged at Damon.

Lips pressed into a thin line, Adina stared at Damon and Sujani. Reaching into her robes, she pulled out the Bone Shard Blade Maja had given them in secret. Her arm muscles vibrated with the power emanating from the weapon.

René's eyes went wide. "Is that...?"

She nodded. "Sophie forged it at the same time she made Damon's and told me to keep it secret." She licked her lips as her stomach turned to lead. "It's for killing her, at the end." She swallowed past the sudden tightness in her throat.

Erik frowned as he kept his focus on Damon and Sujani. "Somehow, I don't think this will be that easy."

Damon blocked Sujani's attack and swung his Bone Shard Blade in a vicious arc toward the other mage's neck.

Belying his age, Sujani bent backward as the dagger sailed by above his nose. Bringing his heel up, he kicked Damon in the groin.

Baring his teeth with a grunt, Damon snarled as he hurled a ball of red magic at Sujani.

Septimus *poofed* in behind Sujani, and both disappeared in a cloud of shadows, re-appearing on the roof of the structure, two stories up. Sujani raised his hand, beckoning to something behind them.

A creature with ebony skin so shiny it almost looked wet jogged into the corridor. Its hide stretched over bulging muscles, each ripple of movement exaggerated the sway of the spines that rose from its back. Thin membranous wings whipped into place above its back. Cruel talons gouged the rock as green saliva drooled from its fangs.

Erik gulped. "A gargoyle!"

Adina blinked as she shook her head. This one looked even more grotesque than the smaller one Viktor Knoll had thrown at them.

Sigfried speared the monster with his gaze and growled, scratching his claws against the stone ground.

The meaning was unmistakable—the gargoyle was his.

"Me, too!" René whipped out his rapier and gestured to Sigfried. "After you, my good bear."

The Great Gray Bear roared as he charged and lunged at the gargoyle. René blurred as he ran to flank it.

The gargoyle reared, snapping at them with its fangs.

Sigfried feinted left but lunged right, his claws laying the skin open to the ribs beneath its left arm.

Damon twirled his hands as though he was unwrapping a spool of yarn and threw a ball of crimson energy at the gargoyle before turning his attention back to Sujani. "Get down here, you coward! Or are you afraid to face me mage-to-mage?"

The ball of mage-fire slammed into the monster, covering it in flame. A sudden breeze that seemed to come from all directions at once slammed into the gargoyle as though it was boxing the creature's ears.

The mystical flames stuttered out.

Sigfried lunged, swiping at the joint where the gargoyle's wing met its shoulder.

In an incredible display of acrobatics, the creature contorted itself, arching its back beneath Sigfried's swing. With a backflip, it soared into the air. Once it was just outside of the bear's reach, it turned to Damon. Lightning flashed in its eyes as it dove straight for him.

Erik drew his blade and raced for the gargoyle, throwing himself at it. His shoulder thudded into the gargoyle's already-injured ribs as he tackled it away from Damon.

Its claws scraped against his armor, gouging deep dents in the metal.

Adina's heart jumped into her throat. "Erik!" The memory of those same claws slashing her open had her stomach spasming as her knees locked in place.

Her ribs tightened as her lungs heaved, fighting to pull in enough air.

She should draw her blade and get over there to help before it was too late. Biting her lips, she glared at her feet as they stumbled, unwilling to step forward. The last time they'd fought a gargoyle, it had nearly ended her. If she didn't act quickly, Erik would die.

She glanced at Sujani, where he stood on the temple's roof, arms raised as he traded magical attacks with Damon.

Sujani was unlikely to use his blood magic to save her from the creature now—with Maja arisen, he had no further need of her.

The gargoyle flung Erik off its shoulder, trapping him beneath its foot. Its claws punched holes in his breastplate.

Erik groaned.

Adina squeezed her falchion's grip as the echoes of pain from its claws jolted through her stomach. She would not stand here and watch her grandfather's monster kill the man she loved.

Glancing up at Sujani, she caught Septimus' gaze. He glared at her as the corners of his mouth turned down.

Her knuckles turned white as the leather on her sword's handle creaked. He was right to be disappointed. What in the blazes was she doing? She was the daughter of the King of Assassins. And she would not stand by while her friends fought and died.

Holding her sword in front of her, she screamed and charged the gargoyle with all the speed she could summon. Slamming into its torso, she held her arm to the side, swinging in to stab the blade into its mouth as Damon had with the sand demon.

With the screech of metal against stone, her blade scraped across its cheek, harmlessly redirected.

The gargoyle spasmed, throwing her off.

She scrambled backward, windmilling her free arm to keep her balance.

The creature stepped off Erik as it circled her.

He rolled to the side with a groan.

"Are you okay?" Adina called, keeping her gaze on the gargoyle.

"Yes," he said. "Give me a minute."

She bit the inside of her cheek. Never, in all the time she'd known him, had he admitted to being incapacitated. Her throat tightened as her gaze skimmed over his armor. Curse the mages—with his armor in the way, she couldn't see anything. "How badly are you hurt?"

The gargoyle lunged at her, its fangs gleaming in the moonlight as they flung drops of spit through the air.

A giant furry body brushed past her, hurling her out of the way as it slammed into the gargoyle. Sigfried roared as he slashed at the creature's head and neck.

Adina tumbled to the ground, barely managing to keep her grip on her falchion.

The gargoyle spun around, slamming its tail into Sigfried, and throwing him into one of the temple pillars.

"Sig!" Madalina's voice echoed over the stone.

The bear groaned and rolled onto his back. His skin bubbled and his joints contorted until the bear disappeared and Sigfried the man lay in his place. Closing his eyes with a loud exhale, his head lolled to one side.

Adina's heart skipped a beat. *Oh, no.* Sigfried had been their best shot at damaging the gargoyle.

Back on his feet, Erik rushed past her and slammed his sword against the monster as if he were trying to chop wood.

A colorful blur raced around him to flank the creature. René paused long enough to jab his rapier into one of the scrapes along its flank.

The gargoyle reared, batting his blade away before he could stab too deeply.

The sword flew end over end until it slid to a stop at Adina's feet.

Erik swung his blade again as he stepped backward. It bounced off the gargoyle's neck with a metallic *clank*.

The gargoyle marched toward him, heedless of his ineffective strikes.

Erik's back pressed against the temple wall.

With a cruel smile, the gargoyle opened its maw for the kill.

"René, slow it down!" Adina leaped in front of the monster, jamming her spare dagger up between its teeth and ramming the pommel underneath the gargoyle's tongue.

It roared but abruptly froze as the dagger's point dug into the roof of its mouth. Glaring at her, it raised its upper lip in a growl and bared its fangs. With a quick jerk of its head, it slammed its jaw closed.

Her dagger snapped in half.

Lead congealed in her gut. *By the gods!*

So much for that.

Adina leaped to the side, running around behind it. Hopefully the thing followed her, giving Erik and Sigfried the chance to recover.

Spitting the mutilated blade aside, the gargoyle spun and swung its tail at her.

She tightened her core muscles and leaped as high as she could. Her heels brushed the ridges of its spiky spine as they *whooshed* by. Not daring to look behind her, she sprinted across the clearing.

The gargoyle's footsteps pounded after her, closer and closer.

She could feel the heat of its breath against the back of her neck. *Come on, René.*

Ripping her headcloth free, she pivoted on her right heel and covered the monster's face with the fabric as she stepped aside.

The gargoyle stumbled with a grunt and tripped, sliding chin-first across the rock and into the opposite wall. Its tail caught her ankles on its way past, ripping her legs out from beneath her.

She slammed into the ground with an impact that drove the air from her lungs. Her skull bounced off the stone and sent a blinding white flash across her vision. The falchion clattered out of her grip.

Ow.

The gargoyle leaped to its feet, shaking its head free of the scarf. Glaring at her with baleful eyes, it snarled.

Adina blinked as her vision cleared.

Across the courtyard, Erik hauled Sigfried to his feet. Ice stabbed through her heart—they were too far away to help her before the gargoyle squished her like a bug.

She opened her mouth to call for help, but the words froze in her throat.

Adina scuttled backward as the creature approached. Each step deliberate and precise, it was confident in its final victory. Its maw spread wide in a gruesome smile.

A light flashed in her peripheral vision and Adina turned.

A glass vial sailed through the air from Hana and Madalina's balcony toward Sujani.

Unhinging its jaw, the gargoyle lunged toward Adina.

The projectile slammed into the side of Sujani's head and exploded. He cried out as he and Septimus disappeared again in a mist of shadows.

The flicker of darkness faded from the gargoyle's eyes as the glossy sheen of its skin faded.

Adina squeezed her eyes shut as the dead creature crashed into her.

She took a deep breath. Two.

Her heart thumped against her ribs.

She was alive.

Ha!

She was alive!

Opening her eyes, she shrieked.

The gargoyle's fangs were open, the upper fangs pressed against her left cheekbone, and the lower fangs scraped her right.

By the gods...

"Adina! Are you alright?" Erik's feet vibrated the stone as he raced toward her.

The gargoyle had turned to stone mid-attack.

Adina blinked and stared at the statue like an idiot as flecks of grit tumbled onto her face.

The statue shifted and she scrunched her face closed, waiting for it to re-animate and snap its jaws shut on her head.

"Yes!" René's exultant cry echoed off the ruins. He pumped his fist into the air as he jogged into her view. "You're welcome! I slowed it down in the nick of time. Woo! I am the master of time!" He bent forward and flexed his arms like a gladiator.

Somewhere beside her, Erik groaned.

The statue levitated, hovering several hand-widths above her and flying to the side. Erik stood in its place, slapping his palms together to clear them from debris. He held out a hand.

Grabbing it, she let him pull her onto her feet.

"Are you okay?" His eyes roamed across her body, searching for injuries.

She patted herself down, feeling for any damage. One rib ached, either bruised or cracked. Everything else seemed to be intact. Even the Bone Shard Blade, hidden at her waist.

She'd survived. They both had.

Tears welled in her eyes as her knees buckled. She clutched his arms as the world stabilized beneath her feet. "I'm okay. Thank you."

Grabbing her in a bear hug, he buried his nose in her neck. "Don't ever scare me like that again."

She barked a laugh and shook her head. Wrapping her arms around his neck, she held onto him until she was certain her legs wouldn't collapse. "No promises, but I'll try, if you'll do the same."

Sujani and Septimus re-appeared in the middle of the courtyard, between the fallen gargoyle and Damon. The entire left side of Sujani's face was red and blistered. Some of the skin at his neck had melted away, exposing bright white tendons and red muscle.

Sujani threw a smirk their way before turning to Damon. Raising his arms above his head, he pulled air toward him. Smashing it into a compact ball as if it were snow, he hurled it at Damon.

A red-black shield appeared in front of Damon, fire licking at its sides. The globe of air slammed into the dark barrier. Flames exploded in a blast of orange light. The heat blew back against her skin, the fine hairs on her arms curling as though burnt. Half a heartbeat later, the nerves along her exposed skin burned as though on fire.

"God's teeth!" Erik muttered.

Across the clearing, Sigfried—still human—charged at Sujani. His hands transformed into a halfway state that gave him bear claws instead of fingernails. He reached for Sujani's throat.

"Come on! We need to get over there!" René pointed his sword toward Sujani and sped off, leaving them in a trail of dust.

Sujani flicked his wrist as though stirring a pot. A wall of air encircled Sigfried forming a bubble with him trapped inside.

Sigfried's momentum carried him past Sujani and Septimus and into the stone body of the gargoyle.

The bubble of air exploded, throwing Sigfried into René and over the fallen statue. Both men disappeared from sight.

Adina bent down to retrieve her falchion and glanced at Erik. Raising her eyebrow, she tilted her head toward Sujani.

He tightened his grip on his sword and nodded.

She sprinted to the left while he ran to the right as they circled in a pincer formation with Sujani and Septimus in the middle.

Sujani barked something in a language Adina didn't understand.

Septimus lifted his upper lip and bared his fangs. Holding both hands out to his side, one palm facing her while the other faced Erik, he summoned shadows. With an explosive pop Adina felt more than heard, two ebony hands taller than her sped toward them. Septimus' shadows roiled as they wove between the specter's fingers.

Adina pulled back her falchion and reached for her Talent. Her rudimentary control over shadows stood no chance against a master like Septimus, but perhaps her water ability would be able to ward off the worst of the attack.

A wave of dirt swallowed the shadow-hand and pulled it beneath the stone.

Adina stumbled backward and, with the immediate challenge eliminated, glanced at Erik just in time to see an identical wave of earth swallow the shadow hand racing for him.

She raised her eyes to Hana, still standing on the balcony.

The other woman gave her a triumphant grin, complete with fangs.

Adina raised her falchion in a salute before turning her attention back to Septimus.

Pulling on her Talent, she drew water from the air around them. The liquid gathered much more easily than it had in the Saldanian Desert...being so deep underground had its benefits, after all.

Ten paces to her left, the shadow hand burst up from below and showered her with sharpened bits of gravel. Adina curled the water around herself, deflecting the worst bits.

Holding her hands in front of her, she shifted the water globe as she stared at Septimus, waiting for his next move.

He curled his fist and made a punching motion, like he was boxing with an imaginary opponent.

The shadow hand mimicked the gesture and flew toward her.

Adina spread her water into a wall and froze it into dozens of sharp icicles. With a kick, she sent them hurling at the shadow hand.

Their tips barely touched the shadows before the fist batted them away. They clattered to the ground and shattered with a peal that rang like holiday bells.

Crap. She didn't stand a chance unless she started playing dirty.

Re-gathering the water and ice, she threw it directly at Septimus. The water stretched until it resembled a long pole, sharpened at the front like a javelin.

Septimus drew his scimitar and blocked, knocking the spear harmlessly to the side.

Adina flicked her wrist, her Talent pushing the water until it covered Septimus' and Sujani's feet. Pulling her elbows to her sides with a viscous yank, she froze the water to ice.

Septimus nearly lost his balance, and he windmilled his arms once as his abdomen contracted. His calf and thigh muscles bulged as he fought to break free.

Yes!

Adina ground her teeth as she contracted every muscle in her body as she fought to hold the ice in place.

Come on, come on, come on!

Erik's broadsword swung through the air, whistling as it shot for Septimus' neck.

Her father glared at her as he *poofed* away. Erik's blade sailed harmlessly past.

The ice that had been around Septimus' feet collapsed with the force of the pressure she was holding against it, and large cracks appeared around Sujani's shoes.

Black and red energy exploded in front of Sujani as Adina looked away.

Sujani wasn't her problem right now—Damon could handle him.

Her eyes danced around the courtyard, searching out every shadow. "Where's Septimus?" She spun, putting her back against Erik's as she held her falchion at the ready.

His hair and clothing rustled. "I don't know. Hana! Madalina! Did you see where he went?"

"No!" Madalina's voice rang out across the courtyard.

A lightning bolt slammed into the ground somewhere to Adina's left.

The black shadow hand grabbed Adina and Erik, squeezing them together as it lifted them off the ground.

Erik's armor dug painfully into her back as her damaged rib screamed.

The shadows drew back then threw them across the courtyard toward the dead gargoyle. Adina cried out as the wind ripped her voice from her throat.

Sigfried climbed over the ridge of spines along its back. Adina and Erik barreled into him and all three landed in a pile on the far side of the statue.

A heartbeat later, Sigfried groaned from beneath them. "Get off me," he muttered as he tried to stand.

René lay off to the side, propping himself up on one arm as he reached for the rapier laying on the ground a few paces away.

Erik rolled off the pile with a grunt. As Adina followed suit, he brushed off his chest plate and saluted Sigfried. "Thanks for breaking our fall."

Sigfried snorted and rolled his eyes.

Adina raised her eyebrow as she studied him. "Are you alright?"

Sigfried nodded, rolling one shoulder. "I will be. You aren't as heavy as the gargoyle."

She bit the inner corners of her lips and nodded. "Fair enough." Glancing over the dead gargoyle at Damon and Sujani, she whispered, "What do you think we should do now?"

Erik shrugged. "Well, your father threw us all the way over here. I think it's safe to say he wants us out of the way."

She snorted. "We must have been annoying him." They certainly hadn't been able to hurt Septimus, despite her best attempts. Raising the tip of her falchion, she glanced at them. "I don't know about you, but I'm not inclined to stand on the sidelines and watch."

Erik grinned. "Nor I."

Sigfried lifted his hands, brandishing his claws.

René flashed his fangs at them. "Let's go annoy them a bit more, shall we?"

They scrambled over the fallen gargoyle and sprinted toward Septimus and Sujani, shoulder-to-shoulder.

Septimus raised his arms as shadows coalesced overhead. "You fools! I'll end you for your stupidity!" He pulled back.

Something small and brown shot between Septimus' feet and scrambled up his leg, moving almost as fast as René. It unhinged its jaw and bit Septimus in the neck.

Dropping his control on the shadows, Septimus lurched forward.

The furry mammal clung to Septimus' back as he writhed, bones shifting as it became human.

Sigfried held out his arms, arresting Adina and Erik's charge. "Father!"

Adina stumbled as her muscles locked. She hadn't seen Holt since Brachia, right before Sujani had topped the keep.

Holt bore down, digging his knee into Septimus' spine as he pushed the King of Assassins into the ground. "What are you doing, Seven? Are you allied with Sujani now?"

"Stay out of this, Battle Weasel." Rage distorted Septimus' face as he jerked away, rolling over and successfully dislodging Holt's grip.

Holt grunted as he rolled to his feet. "I'll stay out of it as soon as you do." He pushed his sleeves up above his biceps. "In the meantime, pick on someone your own power-size."

As if to emphasize his words, a lightning bolt thundered overhead.

Septimus barked a laugh. "And I suppose you think that would be you?" Pulling on his Talent, he hurled shadow daggers at Holt.

The other man rolled to the side and drew a knife from his belt. "Leave the kids alone." He waved toward Sujani and Damon. "And leave them to their own devices, too. Aren't you tired of being their lapdog?"

Septimus clenched his hands as his eyes widened until the whites were visible all around. He bared his fangs and snarled. "My motives are none of your concern." Drawing his scimitar, he lunged.

A ball of black-red energy shot by, a narrow miss, and slammed into one of the crumbling altars.

Adina leaned toward Erik, René and Sigfried. "Come on, we can't stay here."

A lightning bolt caught Damon in the torso and flung him backward. He splatted against the wall and the smell of charbroiled flesh clogged Adina's nose.

Sujani threw his head back and cackled. "You see, Damon! With the power of my goddess at my side, not even you can hope to defeat me."

It was true. With blood leaking from his nose and ears, slumped down against the wall, Damon looked significantly worse for wear, while Sujani barely had a scratch.

Sujani lunged forward and buried the Bone Shard Blade to its hilt in Damon's chest.

Damon screamed as though he was being dismembered.

A wave of warmth radiated from Adina's body, accompanied by a lighthearted sensation. Damon was about to meet Final Death. Served him right.

Her heart skipped a beat, the heat turning to ice in her blood with her next breath. Damon couldn't die yet—they needed Sujani more gravely injured to have half a chance at ending him with their Bone Shard Blade.

Adina glanced around the courtyard. Sophie was nowhere to be seen, but that didn't necessarily mean she wasn't nearby. She nodded toward Sujani. "Come on! We need to keep Sujani busy so one of us can help Damon."

She shook her head, blinking. "I never thought I'd say that."

Erik gave her a sympathetic smile. "We stick to the plan, then."

Sigfried raised an eyebrow. "The plan?"

Adina nodded. "Let Damon and Sujani kill each other, then sort the rest out." And murder Maja. A heavy weight settled on her shoulders.

Sig huffed. "This is a good plan. Okay. Let's go harass Sujani."

"René, can you slow him down?" Erik asked.

"I can sure try. I should also be able to get the Bone Shard Blade free from Damon. Keep Sujani busy, and I'll sneak up and stab him in the back." He spread his feet shoulder-width apart, bending slightly at the knees. Shoving his rapier into its sheath, he nodded. "Go."

Adina clenched her teeth, the weight of the Bone Shard Blade heavy at her waist. She owed her grandfather a Bone Shard Blade to the heart—it didn't matter which of them did the actual stabbing.

They took off sprinting again, being sure to give Holt and Septimus a wide berth.

As they circled, Adina shoved her falchion into its sheath and pulled on her Talent. Summoning the water that remained in a puddle at Sujani's feet, she froze it, trapping his legs.

Erik swung with his greatsword.

Sujani raised his hand, countering the attack with a wall of hardened air.

Erik's blade bounced off with a loud *clank* as if he'd hit a metallic shield.

From the corner of her eye, a green blur sped past. René landed on his knees at Damon's side. Grabbing the hilt with both hands, he ripped the Bone Shard Blade from the other vampire's chest with a victorious yell.

The weapon crumbled to powder in his hands.

Sigfried swung for Sujani with both arms, claws extended.

Bending backward out of reach, Sujani punched, sending a ball of teal energy toward Sigfried. The energy blasted into Sigfried's chest, throwing him off-balance. His tunic smoldered with an odd gray-white smoke.

Adina's heartbeat skipped a beat. *Sigfried!*

She yanked on her Talent, conjuring a sharp icicle which she hurled at Sujani's back.

He twisted, his joints much more flexible than his physical appearance would suggest. Her icicle flew past, shattering uselessly on the ground.

She caught Erik's gaze. They needed to attack all at once, or Sujani would hold them off indefinitely.

Erik smiled, as though he could read her mind. Raising his sword he gave her a micro-nod.

Adina glanced at René, catching his eye. She yanked all the water from their surroundings she could and slammed it at Sujani just as Erik stepped forward and lunged with his blade.

René made a scooping gesture with his hands toward Sujani, as though he were piling dirt in the older vampire's direction.

Sujani made a ripping motion with both hands and a globe of hardened air surrounded him. Sigfried's claws slammed into hardened air and stuck, as though he'd slapped glue. Erik's blade froze in midair.

Adina dropped her water as it splashed uselessly against Sujani's defenses. Her heart thudded in her throat, a lead weight pressing her to the ground. They didn't stand a chance of overwhelming him, even with René working to slow him down. She clenched her teeth to hold back a sob.

The gods asked the impossible.

Erik yanked on his sword, his jaw clenched as he groaned.

The weapon refused to budge, hovering trapped in the thickened air.

Sigfried bared his teeth as he bit back a scream. His claws retracted as his hands resumed their human shape. The skin turned white as the hardened air pushed the blood from them. The joints contracted and warped.

Adina flinched in sympathy.

"Stop!" Madalina called from the balcony. "You're hurting him!"

Sujani glared at Adina. His words were so slow, she barely processed them. "Let me go, and I'll release them."

She blinked. *What?*

Sujani glanced pointedly at his feet.

Oh, right. The ice.

She released her hold on his feet. The ice turned clear and collapsed into a puddle in the space of a heartbeat.

Sigfried groaned as the air contracted, squeezing one final time before the pressure disappeared. He stumbled several steps backward, clenching and unclenching his hands.

Erik's blade clattered to the ground. He stooped as though to retrieve his sword, but ducked Sujani's slowed retaliatory strike and grabbed his arm.

Surprise flashed across Sujani's face.

Adina lunged in and snatched his other arm, pulling it out and away from his body. Grabbing the Bone Shard Blade from her belt, she rammed it into his side.

Her aim was off—it was too low to hit his heart.

René leaped from behind, ramming his rapier between Sujani's shoulder blades.

The old mage arched his back and screamed. "Enough!"

A wall of hardened air slammed against Adina and shoved her away with enough force to send her flying for twenty paces.

She rolled and popped onto her feet.

Erik, Sigfried and René pushed themselves up from where they'd landed, each too far away.

René's rapier was still lodged in Sujani's back.

Air hardened around Adina as Sujani stormed over to her, holding her in place. "For centuries, I've planned this, waited for the right time, for the right mortal—you—to be born. And now, as my plans come to fruition, you *dare* oppose me?"

Adina struggled, wrenching her weight from side to side to break his hold. She grabbed as much of her Talent as she could and battered his hardened air with her own.

Across the way, René, Erik and Sigfried all struggled against invisible bonds.

Sujani pulled a gemstone set in a gold band from his pocket—a sapphire, carved rather than faceted. Lightning crackled around the gem.

"And now, you die. And rest assured, you will forever suffer as my soul-slave."

Adina froze, her muscles turning to ice.

"NO!" The deep feminine voice reverberated through the courtyard, bouncing off the ground and temple walls.

The sapphire in Sujani's ring exploded as the area went dark, as if a giant had blown out a torch.

Or perhaps a goddess.

Millions of pinpoint lights twinkled in the sky above.

Which was ridiculous because they were leagues underground.

But the stars sparkled above, regardless.

Sujani froze, glancing over one shoulder and then the other. "What in the name of the ancestors is going on here?"

Adina struggled, but the wall of hardened air held her tight.

Madalina rose from the balcony on a bubble of starlight and floated down until she landed in their midst. Her dark hair floated in an invisible breeze, accentuating eyes that were fully black. The white light of the stars bounced off her alabaster skin, giving her an ethereal glow.

"WE ARE NOT HAPPY WITH YOUR ACTIONS, PRIESTS."

The hardened air holding Adina in place evaporated. She dropped to her knees.

Madalina's voice reverberated with power, a mix of hers, Sophie's, and Ahion's.

<Ahion!> Damon's mental voice sounded weak and thready as it slammed into her mind.

Something clicked in Adina's chest.

Oh, gods.

She bent, touching her forehead to the ground as her muscles trembled.

A movement caught her attention from the corner of her eye—Damon throwing himself prostrate on the ground. His white hair sparkled under the stars.

In front of her, Sujani slammed to his knees, as well. "My goddess…" He bowed. Splashing some of his blood on the jewel in his palm, he slid it onto his finger. "Come. Stand beside me as I set these unworthy scum at your feet."

"WE HAVE COME TO REPAIR THAT WHICH YOU DE-STROYED." Madalina glared at Sujani as she glided over to Damon. Rolling him onto his back, she studied the wound in his chest as it poured his blood over the courtyard.

Damon placed his hand over his sternum, his facial muscles contorted in a pained expression. His voice cracked as he whispered, "Ahion. I am so sorry I've failed you." His eyes sparkled with unshed tears.

Madalina shook her head. "WE ARE NOT PLEASED WITH YOUR ACTIONS, BUT FOR YOUR DEVOTION, WE FORGIVE YOU."

Damon's body deflated with a strangled sob. "Thank you, my god." He swallowed. "Will you be there to greet me, at the Night Gate?"

Madalina nodded. "REST, MY PRIEST. I WILL MEET YOU THERE SOON."

Damon nodded, closing his eyes. He grimaced, his face contorting for two heartbeats before he relaxed with a sigh.

Madalina exhaled as Damon's body crumbled to dust. As a gentle breeze carried the last of the ashes away, she rose and returned to Sujani.

Tears of blood and water rained down his cheeks. "Maja, I am so sorry for my failings. I acted out of love." His voice cracked.

Madalina took his face in her hands, wiping the tears from his face. "AND FROM ANGER, AND FEAR."

Putting both hands over his face, he bent forward with a cry.

Madalina rested her hand on his back. "YOUR TIME HAS ENDED, TOO, MY PRIEST. IT IS TIME TO JOIN US AT THE NIGHT GATE."

Sujani dropped his hands and stared up at Madalina. Shaking his head, he said, "But I resurrected you, brought you back into this world. We can rule, forever..."

Madalina shook her head. "OUR TIME WAS DONE TWELVE HUNDRED YEARS AGO. NOW IT IS THE TIME OF THE NEW GODS, THE NEXT GENERATION." The corners of her lips turned down as her forehead furrowed. "AT ONE POINT, YOU KNEW THAT, PRIEST."

His jaw trembled. "I am afraid..."

Madalina shook her head and held out her hand. "DON'T BE. WE DO NOT FORGIVE YOU FOR WHAT YOU DID, BUT WE WILL WALK WITH YOU TO THE GATE AND BEYOND."

Sujani fell to the side. No trace of the Bone Shard Blade Adina had jabbed between his ribs remained. He stared at Madalina, his expression a mix of adoration and despair.

"REST NOW," she said, brushing a strand of hair from his face.

Sujani exhaled. "I'm sorry..." His head lolled to the side.

Madalina stood as Sujani turned to dust. Taking three steps, she knelt in front of Adina. "NOW IT IS YOUR TURN TO DO AS WE REQUESTED."

Adina blinked. Wait, what? She thought she was going to be stabbing Sophie, Maja, Ahion or whoever they were. Not her friend. "Now? But what will happen to Madalina?"

Madalina pointed upward. "SHE WILL ASCEND BACK TO HER RIGHTFUL PLACE AMONG THE STARS."

"What? No!" Sigfried heaved himself to his feet and lunged toward them.

Adina held up her hand. "No, I agree with Sigfried. If I'm going to end Madalina, I'd like to talk to *her* before I do so." Not that she didn't trust the gods, but...she didn't trust the gods.

Madalina blinked, her eyes going back to normal. She smiled at Adina and glanced at the sky. "It's all right, Adina. The stars are calling me home. My time has just begun."

Adina shook her head. "No. I can't kill you, not after all of this." She'd pseudo-agreed to kill Maja and Ahion. No way had she signed up for killing someone she cared about. She may be an assassin, but even she had limits.

Madalina smiled. "It's alright. Of anyone, I'm glad it's you—my best friend—who gets to send me home."

Adina's hands went numb. Her vision went watery and she blinked to keep the betraying tears at bay. She couldn't do it. A sudden under-standing of why Sujani had turned his blade on himself rather than on the goddess he loved flashed through her muscles with a jolt.

"No way! Absolutely not, I forbid it!" René stepped between them, gracelessly shoving Adina aside. "Maddy, what are you doing? I told you channeling oracles and gods was going to scramble your brain."

Sigfried stood shoulder-to-shoulder with René, practically blocking Adina's view. He crossed his arms and glowered. "No."

Madalina shook her head. "Don't be so dramatic, Frere René. When Maja and Ahion pass beyond the gate, someone needs to stay behind to look after everything." She gave them a wide smile that reminded Adina of the first time they'd met, in the courtyard in Brachia. "That person will be me."

René scoffed. "Don't be ridiculous."

"You'll always have a friend among the stars. I'll be able to watch over you and make sure you're alright. Who knows? I may even come down and say hi once in a while." She stared at René for several heartbeats before turning her attention to Adina.

The tension drained from Adina's muscles with a sigh as her heartbeat calmed. Erik's hand settled on her shoulder, a reassuring weight.

Adina's throat thickened, and she swallowed past the sudden lump there. "Are you certain?"

Madalina nodded and turned toward Sigfried, who stood frozen like a statue. Holding out her hand, she asked, "Will you come with me?"

He studied her hand and glanced at the sky. "Into the stars?" His voice wobbled uncharacteristically.

"Into our next big adventure."

"Hmm." He paused. "There is a lot of space up there, but it's very high up."

She nodded. "You'll never have to be indoors again. We can run with the stars. Together."

Stepping forward, he took her hand. "Together." He glanced at Adina. A strange peace stole over his face. His shoulders relaxed as he exhaled, pulling Madalina into an embrace.

Madalina hugged him back.

She turned to Adina, her eyes again fully black. "WE CANNOT UNDO THE DAMAGE OUR PRIEST HAS DONE, BUT WE CAN MAKE YOU AS YOU USED TO BE FOR A FULL DAY, AS A THANK YOU."

As I used to be? Her thoughts froze for a moment before her heart lurched. "You mean, mortal?"

Madalina nodded. "HUMAN. FOR ONE SUN-CYCLE."

Adina locked gazes with Erik. His lips were parted and his breathing shallow, the longing on his face twisted her gut. She turned back to Madalina. "All of us?"

Madalina nodded. "EVERYONE HERE."

She glanced at Erik and nodded. "Do it."

Stepping away from Sigfried, Madalina breathed on her, and the entire area lit up as though it were midday.

Adina resisted the urge to lunge for shade, lest the sun burn her to a crisp. The burning hunger at the back of her throat disappeared, along with the parched feeling to her veins.

Adina bit back the laugh bubbling up in her throat. Her blood warmed. Holding her hands in front of her, she gaped as they flushed like living tissue.

"AND NOW, KEEP YOUR HALF OF THE BARGAIN." Madalina smiled and winked. "MORTAL."

Right.

Adina bit her lower lip. She needed the last Bone Shard Blade. She'd used hers on Sujani, and Sujani had stabbed Damon with his.

Shoving herself to her feet, she strode to where Damon had lain. His blood still splattered across the stone. Off to the side, as though it had fallen carelessly from his belt, lay the final dragon bone dagger.

She grabbed it, bracing herself as the power that emanated from the divine weapon reverberated up her arm. It felt warm, wrapping her in a fuzzy blanket of sunlight.

"This feels different than it did before," she said as she trudged back to Madalina and Sigfried.

"OF COURSE. YOU ARE MORTAL NOW."

Adina licked her lips as her throat thickened. She swallowed. Things were going to be very different after this.

Madalina pointed to an empty spot in the sky. "LOOK FOR US THERE AND KNOW THAT WE ARE WATCHING OVER YOU." With a deep breath, she took both of Sigfried's hands in hers. "ARE YOU READY?"

He nodded, seemingly lost for words.

Madalina glanced at Adina. "DO IT."

Adina's heart raced, pounding a staccato rhythm against her ribs. Air rushed in and out of her nose too quickly—she couldn't breathe! A trickle of sweat crawled its way down her temple as she fought to pull more oxygen into her lungs.

The dagger shook in her trembling hands as her peripheral vision faded away until the only thing she could see was the tip of the blade and Madalina.

A heavy weight settled on her shoulder.

"It's okay," Erik said, his mouth close to her ear as his hand wrapped around her shoulder and pulled him to her. "The gods never ask for more than we can give."

His soothing voice unclenched something inside her, and the uncomfortable burning in her lungs faded.

Sophie and Ahion stared at her through Madalina's eyes.

Clenching her jaw, Adina raised the Bone Shard Blade and plunged it through Madalina's chest and into her heart, making sure she struck true. The dagger crumbled into bits, disappearing between one heartbeat and the next.

Her blood roared past her ears, pounding between her temples as if the entire world was one giant heartbeat. The air pressure pulsed as thunder rumbled.

Bits of marble and mortar crumbled from the temple, rolling into the courtyard.

God's teeth! She leaped to the side, throwing her arms over her head. They needed to get out of here. Blinking, she glanced from side to side, but the dust was too thick to see through.

"Erik?"

"Adina!" Hands grabbed her, jerking her back, away from Madalina and Sigfried.

Then, Erik was holding her, backing them away into the exact center of the courtyard, where they would be less likely to be crushed by debris. The air was clearer, too.

The earth beneath their feet rocked and buckled. She grabbed his shoulders for support as her legs gave out from under her.

"The earthquake! I can't control it!" Hana called from above.

"Get down here before that balcony collapses!" René yelled, the whites of his bulging eyes stood out against his dirty skin. "If you die now, I'll kill you!" A drop of sweat rolled down his temple.

Adina's stomach hardened as each crack and explosion grated against her ears. Erik's arms tightened around her. Maja had turned them mortal for a day, but she'd never guaranteed they'd survive long enough to enjoy it.

Madalina and Sigfried disappeared into a ball of light so bright, Adina couldn't bear to look.

Instead, she scanned the clearing through the dust and crumbling rocks. Septimus and Holt were nowhere to be seen.

The temple pillars split with a *crack* that felt like a snapping bone as the roof collapsed.

Her breath caught in her throat.

Hopefully Hana had gotten to safety.

The blinding light abated, leaving no sign of Madalina or Sigfried.

As if they'd ceased to exist.

The two eroded altars crumbled to dust.

An invisible knife twisted in Adina's gut. She'd miss Madalina's eternal cheerfulness and companionship.

René ran by, tugging Hana along behind him. "Come on, you guys! We need to get out of here before this entire place collapses!"

Adina blinked.

"He's right," Erik said, grabbing her hand and hauling her toward one of the fallen temple walls and the cliffs beyond.

"Sophie wouldn't trap us down here," Adina said, sprinting hard to keep up. Would she?

René called over his shoulder. "She's dead! I don't think she has any say in what happens going forward."

No, but Madalina and Sigfried did.

It would be the height of irony to regain her fragile humanity, only to lose it within the first hour of rebirth.

"But what about Septimus and Holt?"

"They can look after themselves," Erik said.

Just like they always had.

Before Adina knew it, they were at the base of the stairs. Her lungs and muscles burned as they climbed each step, two at a time. She reached for her Talent, only to find that particular well dry.

A side benefit of being mortal.

Halfway up, Hana bent over, her hands on her knees. "Hang on, everyone. I need a breather. I think I'm too old for this."

Adina leaned against the cliff face, secretly grateful for the break to ease the burning in her lungs and leg muscles, as well.

The ambient light in the area was growing brighter. Sunrise must be almost upon them somewhere above, though she still had no idea how, being this far below ground, the cavern was lit.

Between gasping breaths, she shook her head.

Dead gods and their magic…

Erik ran his fingers through his hair, pulling the sweat-drenched strands away from his face as his chest heaved. "I'm not used to feeling this weak…it's like I have no energy to draw on."

Below them, the final section of the temple collapsed in a cloud of dust and debris. Something twisted in Adina's gut at the loss of all the knowledge buried inside.

The memory of Sujani threatening her with a spelled ring flashed through her mind.

But perhaps some things were best forgotten.

The bottom section of the stairs crumbled.

René stared behind them, his eyes wide. The vein at his temple pulsed. "Come on." He grabbed Hana's hand, tugging her up the stairs. "We need to keep going before we fall to our deaths."

Two more steps crumbled away below them.

By the gods.

Adina's lungs still heaved air past her burning throat, and her legs trembled, but she couldn't argue with her own eyes. If they stayed here, they'd fall to their deaths in minutes. "Alright," she said more to herself than anyone else as she took the next step.

The world reduced to the burning in her thighs, the ache in her lungs, and the endless steps. The trail zigged and zagged up the cliff, as the rock crumbling behind them chased them ever higher.

"Thank the ancestors," Hana said as she threw herself to the ground outside the entrance to the Catacombs. "If I never have to walk up another stair, it'll be too soon." She threw an arm over her eyes.

Adina collapsed, sitting against the cliff wall, letting her legs dangle over the edge. "Agreed." She massaged her thighs, attempting to work out some of the knots.

Erik leaned against the rock face above her, staring down at the valley. "I think we'll be the last ones to ever see this place."

"At least, as it was," Adina said, nodding. "I guess its time is past, too."

"I found it!" René popped out of the Catacombs, brandishing a torch.

Adina hadn't even noticed him disappear.

"Now at least we won't have to stumble around in the dark as we try to find our way back up to the surface."

Blinking, Adina shook her head, gathering her thoughts. She hadn't even considered that. "Good job, René."

The cliffs shook as the last of the stairs crumbled.

Erik pulled her back from the ledge. "Let's not tempt fate, shall we?"

"No," Adina said, staring into the abyss. "We should probably go. Who knows? We may get up top soon enough to watch the sunrise."

Erik blinked, his face going blank with longing. "I haven't seen a sunrise in over a century."

New motivation giving speed to their feet, they followed René into the Catacombs.

Chapter 27
Adina

Adina blinked as Erik pushed the manhole cover open and fresh air spilled in from the outside. She reached for her Talent to blow the stench of the sewers away, but again, nothing responded.

She smiled, reveling in her mortality.

Erik turned and offered her a hand, pulling her the rest of the way onto the street.

Mortal or not, he was still incredibly strong.

Hana and René followed.

Brushing her hands off on her pants, Hana glanced around at the rapidly brightening ultramarine sky. "Well, would you both like to refresh yourselves at *my* estate?" she asked, a sparkle of mischief in her eyes. "Though I suppose now that Sujani and Damon are dead, you're going to be wanting it back?"

Adina opened her mouth and closed it, at a loss. Yes, she loved living here. The Drowned City could be her permanent home. But in Arthur's estate...

Erik wove his fingers between Adina's. "Perhaps in a little bit." He stared into her eyes as he kissed her knuckles. "Care to step outside the city and watch a sunrise with me?"

Heat rose in her core as she bathed in the intensity of his gaze. "I'd love that."

Erik winked at René and Hana. "We'll meet you for a regular, human breakfast after?"

René pulled Hana close, heat smoldering in his eyes. "Agreed. A long while after."

Adina climbed to the tallest dune outside the city as the sky shifted from purple to pink.

Erik sat in the sand, heedless of the grit getting in his armor.

She threaded her fingers through his and rested her head on his shoulder. "I can't believe I get to watch a sunrise with you."

"It hardly seems real, does it?" He brushed his rough knuckles down her jaw line, leaving tingles that stirred heat in her core in their wake. His thumb lingered, circling her lower lip.

All thoughts evaporated and there was nothing except the caress of his finger over her mouth.

Wordless, she shook her head. An ache inside her spread, burning through every limb, fanned by the stroking of his thumb.

Leaning toward her ear, he whispered, "I love you." His hand slipped from her face and brushed an errant strand of hair behind her ear. Instead of releasing her hair, though, he clenched it, as though he wanted to let her go but couldn't.

By the gods. This is what it felt like to want someone so badly it hurt. "I love you, too, Erik. Forever." She turned her head, tilting back until she caught his lips with hers.

He wrapped his arms around her and pulled her close with a groan that set every nerve ending in her skin ablaze. The spark between them exploded, hotter and deadlier than any magic the gods could conjure.

The sun burst over an orange sky as they fell backward onto the sand.

This is the end of *Goddess of Blood and Shadows* but the series continues. Watch for Book 4: *Streets of Blood and Dreams* (a prequel), available Q1 2025!

Enjoying the series? I'd love for you to leave a review for *Goddess of Blood and Shadows*. Reviews really help me get the word out to new readers.

To stay up-to-date on the newest releases, and to download a free novella available only to newsletter subscribers about how René became a vampire, join my monthly newsletter at https://author.michelle-darnell.com/subscribe/. I will never sell or rent your information, and you can unsubscribe at any time.

You can also visit my website at https://author.michelle-darnell.com or follow me on social media for the latest updates without the pressure of signing up for the newsletter.

Acknowledgements

This novel, in particular, could not have evolved into the story it did without the help of a multitude of people. Special thanks to my alpha reader, Livia Daniela, without whose input the characters would still be sitting in the rain-soaked Gorlinian inn from Chapter 1 trying to figure out what they do next. Also, my wonderful beta readers: John Gunningham, E. Marie Robertson, J. Logan C. Rice, Marc B. DeGeorge and Jade Mills. Thank you for your endless patience, encouragement, and the honest feedback.

And to my parents, Mike Bloomdahl and Julie Bloomdahl, whose relentless support and willingness to read a paranormal vampire fantasy (even when it's nothing like what they typically enjoy reading, and René annoys the heck out of them) just because I wrote it.

I would like to also thank my wonderful and ever-patient editor, Hannah VanVels Ausbury. If you ever find yourself in need of a good editor who will build you up and help you grow, I highly recommend her.

No book is ever complete without a good proofread. My sincere thanks to Rachel Murphy for taking time out of her extremely crazy schedule to catch all my typos and grammatical errors. I also salute all the stealthy typos that managed to make it through my countless rewrites, six alpha/beta readers, an editor and proofreader. For their diligence and fortitude, they deserve to remain and so they shall.

And thank you to Ravven (http://ravven.com/) for the amazing cover art. I am blown away at your talent and am so fortunate to be able to work with such a gifted artist.

And huge thank you to my readers. Writing stories would not be nearly as rewarding if there was no one to enjoy them.

About the Author

 Michelle A. Darnell started writing as a way to decompress after a long day at work. Working with the public in a science heavy field, sometimes it's a nice change of pace when she can solve problems by throwing a fireball at them. When it turned out people enjoyed reading her stories, she decided to publish her novels so others would have the chance to enjoy them.

She grew up in Western Montana before moving to the Spokane, WA area in 1999 for college. Michelle now lives in Eastern Washington with her husband and one incredibly spoiled cat. She enjoys hiking, especially when she can take her sisters and her camera with her. She also enjoys reading, painting and biking.

Also by

If you enjoyed **Goddess of Blood and Secrets**, I hope you will also love

the other Vampire Assassin Chronicles:

Streets of Blood and Dreams – A Prequel

Coming early 2025

And announcing a new series: The Shifter Queen

To Kill a King – Book 1

Coming August 29th, 2024

To Save a Kingdom – Book 2

Coming in 2025